Finding Jane

by

S N Pearse

Published in 2015 by FeedARead.com Publishing

First Edition

A CIP catalogue record for this title is available from the British
Library.

Acknowledgements

My thanks, of course to my wife, Gilly, for her patience and understanding during my long periods on the keyboard and for her encouragement, belief and support, not forgetting the invaluable assistance in keeping my glass topped up.

Thanks also to Suzanne, Jane and Susan for their proof reading and feedback without which the end result may well have been different.

Thanks are due to Jofi for her humour, coffee and sly digs whilst keeping me corrected on the Goth scene.

The Goth community have been attending Whitby in large numbers for many years now, they bring colour and vibrancy to the town as well as much needed trade. My experiences of them and with them have been almost entirely positive in nature and I thank them as a whole for their time and help during my research.

The book is a work of fiction and whilst there is reference to a number of actual locations this is purely and simply intended to help in creating the atmosphere of the beautiful town that is Whitby.

The characters within the book are entirely fictional and any similarity or likeness to a person living or dead is purely coincidental and not intended.

For Jazz, Jofi & Gilly

Finding Jane

One.

"To the rear of Aelfleda Terrace, towards the Donkey Path," repeated the controller from the comfort of an air-conditioned control room at Newby Wiske. She was letting her frustration show now, but to her the on screen map looked very clear and she couldn't understand why the officer was having difficulty finding it. "I mean, how many dead bodies can there be in Whitby today, and wasn't its finder still there?" Maybe she didn't know, or gave little thought to, the fact that the area had been subject to a massive landslip recently and that as a result walking in that area could be damn nigh perilous. Tom Parsons, a 20 year old newcomer to the police service was still in his first posting. Freshly confirmed as a constable after serving his two year probationary period he had previously led a sheltered and somewhat cosy existence; he felt far from comfortable now as he braced himself against the biting cold winds at the end of another long night shift.

Surveying the scene in front of him he had little inclination to go paddling in the dark, slippery mud below Whitby's famous Abbey and why had his colleague been allowed to finish early, leaving him single crewed for the final two hours of the shift?

"Over here!" Tom heard the call and on looking across to where the end four houses had slipped down the cliff side, he could see a torch light waving across to him. The torch was only about fifty yards or so away but it was not possible to reach it across the mud-slicked terrain in front of him, why hadn't the controller said to him that the caller was waiting there? It was another five minutes before the two finally did meet. Joe Starr, a wizened, weather-beaten man, dressed in dark waterproof clothing and wellington boots turned over at their tops to show three inches of thick woollen socks, and whom Tom placed in his late sixties, pointed with his torch to what he had seen only a short while before. "What the hell are you doing out here, amongst all this?" was the slightly less than professional greeting from Tom. Starr was shivering, either from cold or as a result of what he had seen, Tom was unsure. "Freezing my bollocks off waiting for you," was the tongue in cheek reply." I was looking around at how much further it's all slipped since yesterday, I know I shouldn't be here but all my stuff is still in there," he continued pointing towards a nearby cottage beneath the slippage. Starr had been reluctant at first to speak with anyone as the houses had all been evacuated only days earlier when the council declared them unfit and dangerous due to the falling debris from above and the potential for the houses to collapse due to the foundations being washed away but now felt he had no choice. He had hidden in his home having returned in darkness to collect further belongings. Being the only permanent resident of Aelfleda Terrace, the other small terraced houses having succumbed to the booming tourist industry or second homes for the well off, he lived alone when on shore but spent many of his days at sea on one of the few trawlers still working out of the port.

Through the shadows, it was difficult to be certain, but it certainly looked like a corpse, partly covered in mud and underneath the overhanging remains of the damaged houses above, was apparently the upper half of a body.

"It'll be one of them from t' graveyard at' top." said Joe, "-weren't there yesterdi any road"

Tom knew he should call his supervisor but wanted to be clear in his mind just what he was reporting. He had gone "state 6" when he saw Joe and knew that both his sergeant and the control room would be expecting an update as soon as possible.

"236 from 877." Tom spoke into his encrypted radio, which was only the size of a mobile phone but provided confidential communication with his colleagues. "Can you please contact me on my mobile?" This was never really the right way to do things but sure to keep a conversation confidential between just two people rather than have a whole talk group listening.

"Stand by" replied Police Sergeant 236 Leigh James a tall, well built man, ex-forces and with almost twenty three years Police service, the last eight of which were in his current rank. He was known throughout the force area as being hesitant if not reluctant to make decisions. Policies and procedures were there for a reason and should be followed at all times, preferably supervised by someone in at least the rank of Inspector.

Tom Parsons was joined by the only other two constables working the Whitby area that night. Knowing that he was on his own and yet not knowing just what he had found they had attended in order to check that he was all right, not in any danger; but also they had heard the initial call and were curious as to what he may have found? Such was the ethos of policing this relatively remote area, that whenever a single crewed officer was directed to a job, if possible colleagues would provide support, the fact being that they all had to look after each other as best they could.

PC's John McFarlane and Howard Small were both seasoned cops, each happy with their lot and neither apparently in any rush to gain promotion or seek a move away from the picturesque town of Whitby.

Armed with strong torches or 'dragon lights' they made their way across to Aelfleda Terrace, Tom being more visible now that that the sun had begun to rise over the Abbey and casting its first rays through the rain and across the harbour and the River Esk below.

"He's coming up now" Tom said as he replaced his phone in his bright high viz coat pocket, referring to Sergeant James, but John McFarlane was already shining his light across to the body and making decisions in his head before the supervisor arrived. He always felt it best to provide Leigh James with a course of action rather than ask for one, done in such a way as to make him think the directions would be of his own choosing and with which he could brief the CID, who would have to be called out later.

"Tom, get a first account from Starr now, before he disappears or chooses to forget," directed John, "Howie, will you make sure that we seal off any access, as soon as it's daylight proper the place will be crawling wi' folk noseying." his CID training as an aide earlier in his career was going to be useful and, he thought, "I might even have a chance of being co-opted onto the enquiry if it's got any legs?"

"1642 to control," called John McFarlane, "it appears we have a body uncovered, under a building, part decomposed but not accessible at present" he went on to explain the terrain and the fact that it was in the area deemed unsafe by the council so he required the presence of a safety officer. Having also found that Starr had returned to his empty property without authority it was going to be necessary to check the others too and put something in place to prevent further access. "CSI and CID will also be needed on site," he continued, making the decision before Leigh James arrived and started stuttering and debating.

Howard Small, working on a similar thought process had begun 'a crime scene log', a paper record of what was at the scene, what actions had been taken, by whom and who had subsequently attended. Leigh James arrived shortly afterwards and on seeing what had been done knew that his officers believed the incident to be at least suspicious. In the increasing daylight as the end of the shift approached, it was now possible to see that the body was part hidden by a small brick wall and a number of flagstones covering the waist down, it appeared to be the body of adult size but with no discernible features due to decomposition and natures creatures feeding from it. It was most certainly not from the graveyard above as Starr had suggested, St. Mary's Church was indeed at the cliff top and did have a sizeable graveyard around it but the slippage could now be seen to be quite some distance away from the church, directly above the houses; a steep bank with rows of terraced houses and flats providing accommodation for locals but also increasingly for holiday lets and second homes for incomers, often from the south. Leigh James concurred with the actions put in place by John McFarlane and informed control room of this; "just for the record," before seeking out Tom Parsons who had taken the necessary details from Starr and told him that he would be in touch again later.

"You'd better get back to the nick and write up a handover Tom, I'll see you back there shortly," said Leigh James, seeing the reality that after already working a nine hour night shift from 10.00pm last night, he was going nowhere soon. The early turn would be on in the next half hour or so and would all need briefing before they could relieve his crew. CID and CSI, still regarded as SOCO by anyone with over five years service and who didn't watch American TV, would have to travel across from Scarborough so wouldn't be here for at least another hour, the Borough Council might be even later, at least the rain was letting up a bit.

Two

It was 8.50am when Detective Inspector Neil Maughan arrived on scene with Detective Sergeant Suzanne Collins, they had both updated themselves on the force computer system before Collins had set off from Scarborough's Northway Police station to drive the twenty or so miles north on the A171 coast road taking the back road, known as Whitby Laithes, along the cliff top from Hawsker, past the camping and caravan sites and turning left onto Green Lane, the steeply inclined road that was the main route from Whitby Town centre to the Abbey, where she met up with her locally based boss.

Reviewing the scene both were disappointed that the council had not yet sent anyone to verify the safe access. Had someone been actually been in danger at that time then the decision would have been a no brainer, make the rescue and deal with the Health and Safety consequences later, but this wasn't the same hurry, though none of the four houses could be guaranteed to be upright for much longer. Huge areas of land had given way above the houses due to the incessant rain over the recent weeks and the land slips had crushed against the rear elevations of the terraced houses, which in turn had put pressure on the entire buildings and set in place a potential domino effect on the properties immediately below. Access had now been limited to the area with only authorised persons allowed anywhere near the rendezvous point created at the rear of Green Lane Play centre.

Maughan wanted to erect the crime scene tent over the site of the body as there was already press interest due to the houses falling and it was a certainty that any camera with a half decent lens would be able to view and record the corpse. Using his mobile phone he made contact with colleagues and directed them to the Borough Council Offices to express the urgency of the situation and, in an attempt to keep the press away from the scene, he contacted the force press office to set up an initial media release and to arrange a meeting at Whitby Police Station later that morning. It felt somewhat ironic that looking directly across the river the police station on Spring Hill could be seen clearly yet he hoped that by asking the press to be there they wouldn't attend the scene until later; he knew they would not keep away for long.

Within the hour, and sooner than was expected on a weekend, Paul Woodbridge a senior surveyor from Scarborough Council was on site and in attendance with him were a team of four who were directed to erect a windbreak around the area and create an access route in. He was reticent in the extreme as he was essentially having to give access to what was in his opinion an unsafe site, one to which he had already said was to be a demolition site, with the flattening to take place by using cranes and heavy plant to take down the houses from top down rather than chance further damage and risk to life by working at ground level. It was two further hours before Maughan was able to get to the body, but only seconds later that he could confirm his suspicions. The body had, at first sight, apparently previously been buried under a garden patio area; it was now to be confirmed as a murder enquiry. A home office pathologist would be needed to attend and CSI would immediately need further support.

Three

"Yes, I can confirm that the body of an unknown female has been found on East Cliff this morning." Maughan answered the press contingent, swollen in size due to the local interest in the weather damage and re-directed to pick up what they could to start reporting this development. Squeezed together in a first floor room at Whitby's Spring Hill, Police Station, a three storey 1960's building on the West side of town and looking all its fifty years of age now from the outside. The large room to the front of the building was once the rest room for officers, and also once the site of a full size snooker table, making it a popular with visiting officers, and doubling up as a secure incident room when required with Holmes computers and dedicated staff drafted in from around the division or even force wide as necessary. For now it was the only room big enough at the town's police station to accommodate the swollen ranks of journalists being shown upstairs by Jean; a forthright but very capable, if not formidable, middle aged lady, who had only been there for a few short years but whose character was such that the station appeared to revolve around her.

"And yes, we will be treating it as suspicious at this time. I would make a specific request for members of the press and of the public to refrain from attending the scene as it is potentially dangerous due to the ongoing weather problems and all that goes with that. The previous Council safety warnings remain in place."

It was now just after 10.00am and Neil Maughan was not intending to keep the press briefing open too much longer, he had no intention of taking further questions at this time and informed those gathered in the room, "we hope to be able to give you an update at 2.00 o'clock this afternoon, when the press officer will take your questions but please ladies and gents accept that we are still very much in the early stages of this investigation, the usual appeal for anyone who believes they may be a witness or have anything that may help, to contact us on 101 is a given, and now if you'll excuse me I have some important work to do."

As he arose from his chair several of the journalists, including the inexperienced but enthusiastic Eleanor, "call me Elli," Stanford of the local paper The Whitby Gazette, shouted questions, notebooks and digital recorders in hand, but Maughan swept past them directing a uniformed PC to show everyone from the building.

Waiting for him in his office at the opposite end of the building was Sergeant Ian Jackson, just a few months short of retirement at 54 years old, possibly looking even older and noted for his dour approach, he was the uniformed supervisor for the morning shift and was seeking a briefing update, his shift members having, all bar one, been deployed to scene security and site safety; leaving a single other unfortunate officer having to pick up the remainder of the calls for the whole area. Whilst in no way dynamic, there was little Ian didn't know about his job or indeed about Whitby having been stationed at the small coastal town for the previous fifteen years, but having also been brought up there as a child prior to his postings elsewhere across the county during his long career. He considered it to be something akin to an honour to represent the face of law and order in his home town.

"Sorry Ian, you know the score, we'll need them for the whole shift, any help from Scarborough or Malton available or is that a daft question?" Maughan knew that the shift pattern tended towards putting uniforms on the streets at evening time to be visible when most of the public perceived anti social behaviour was at its worst and this often meant lower numbers on daytime shifts. This was the same across the Eastern District and there was little chance of any support being available.

"We can free up a couple from the scene if you're happy to use PCSO's instead to man the tapes, leave Keith with the log and I'll keep in touch throughout the day." Ian countered, "you know most of the houses up there are holiday cottages now and haven't had locals in for at least five or six years except of course, Joe Starr, stubborn old sod could've made a real killing if he'd sold up, now his place'll be worthless and he won't have any insurance."

"Do what you can Ian, I need to call Sue for an update, have you got anyone checking the missing persons lists? I don't know how long the body's been there but if we start over the last twelve months and see where that takes us first."

"It's already in hand sir, there's very few outstanding of our own so I've asked for the force area as well as the surrounding forces, Durham, Cleveland, West and South Yorkshire and Humberside to be checked as well."

A bit of initiative, unusual but welcome help from an unexpected source, the first bit of good news of the morning.

Maughan settled behind his desk, the remainder of the day stretched ahead of him and it was likely to be a long one, not that he minded; he had a reputation of working all the hours he could; even though overtime was now a thing of the distant past for Inspecting ranks and above.

A knock on the door was followed by Sue Collins walking in looking somewhat windswept, red in face but composed; "We've got The Fire Brigade lifting the body out to the undertaker's car, the council say they don't want anyone else in until they can assure safety of site but can't give a time scale. Doc Kavanagh will do the PM first thing tomorrow and uniforms are getting restless 'cos its bloody freezing up there," she said before sitting opposite him in one of the two chairs left, "I've tried to keep SOCO in for another couple of hours though before they get proper barriers in place"

"I've got some relief cover arranged for this aft but they'll just have to moan until then, makes up for the day's when nowt happens," Maughan replied, "what are Des and Mark doing then?" he asked of his two Detective Constable's who he had not yet seen during the day. "I've got them looking into the ownership of the cottages and I'm bringing two up from Scarborough to do some local door to door and statement taking." Maughan was pleased that his colleague had taken control of the first basics and knew that she was a more than capable officer, destined for a good career if she kept her nose clean and continued to make the impression she had started with. With a law degree from Durham University and an inquisitive mind, not to mention her very obvious good looks; twenty nine years old, tall at five foot eleven inches with silky dark hair, high cheek bones and an infectious smile she was just what he would like in his team and she knew that he regarded her highly, but then again she knew she was never short of admirers wherever she went; in fact with a few elocution lessons to polish off the rough edges she had it all.

The Inspector made coffee for them both, using the percolator sited on top of the filing cabinet at the back of the room and for which he had been many times thankful when needing a caffeine injection during the long night shifts; then the tactics meeting got under way.

It was early afternoon before the initial pathology report came in, very brief due to the limited access at the site and the difficulty in working around the body but suggesting a female, possibly aged between fifteen and twenty four years of age and having been dead, best guess, between twelve and eighteen months, but which maybe could be narrowed down after further examination. No cause of death immediately apparent due to the almost totally skeletal remains, but a full post mortem examination would be conducted tomorrow morning after which the body may then require to be subject to further forensic tests.

Maughan had arranged for the Eastern area Police Search Advisor, POLSA, to attend and also for the on duty Support Unit; consisting of a uniformed Sergeant and six specially trained constables to attend the scene before he updated his Superintendent and asked that an investigation team be put together, initially for collating the information already to hand and to make immediate enquiries, then, dependent on the outcome of the autopsy, for a Holmes Team to be put in place.

13

Operation Caedmon had begun.

Four

Whitby Goth Weekend, held twice a year since 1994, usually in April and October, had been something secretly engaging the thoughts of Jane Hammond for years since she had caught the bug of the alternative scene. Loving the elaborate clothing, the music and atmosphere generated across the town for those long weekends she was hooked, and though she had not yet attended due to the influence of her parents; Graham, a lay preacher and architect of some local repute in the Leeds area and Penelope or Penny, as she preferred to be known, an economics and finance manager with the local council, was planning her outfits and contacts for when she could be. Her plans had always included sharing accommodation with friends, some of whom she may see only during the events themselves, but whom she remained in touch with via social media, X-Box and other online gaming and through the WGW blog; increasingly so as the dates drew nearer. Having reluctantly adhered to the strict parental policy of not attending whilst studying for her A levels, and being subjected to much ridicule from her friends as a result, she had entered into the scene with gusto, but still without her parents knowledge, in the two years since passing her A levels with flying colours and moving to Liverpool where she was studying zoology at John Moore's University. Jane had taken the decision to avoid confrontation whilst at home by keeping her parents in the dark about her ongoing passion, leading them to believe that she was, in the words of her father, "growing up and becoming a responsible adult." It wasn't too difficult to do this as she saw very little of them during term time and was quite content to behave as expected when visiting them, that way she retained their very generous financial support without the usual grief that went with it.

At 21 Jane was full of life, very slim, fit with ample breasts and what she lacked in looks, bearing slightly prominent teeth under a Roman nose, spectacles and a freckled face, she made up for in brains, humour and sharpness of thought. Her arrangements this year included staying over for the full weekend, Friday to Tuesday, sharing Bed and Breakfast accommodation with three other facebook friends on Royal Crescent, almost overlooking The Spa Pavilion where many events were held and with views over the North Sea beyond.

Siobhan Prentice or Shiv, a facebook friend of Jane and a Goth who actually lived in Whitby, was known as someone who would always help to find accommodation for her like minded friends when she could, putting some up in her own flat and viewing The Whitby Gazette, for other options as well as using her local contacts. Of a similar age and inclination to Jane she was equally looking forward to the weekend, which was only a fortnight away now.

Shiv however was not like Jane in any other way, she had left school at sixteen and apart from a few jobs as a seasonal waitress and bar staff she had never held a full time job, getting by on benefits and undeclared earnings from part time, cash in hand jobs where she could. She had no long term plans in her life beyond the next gig or event and was happy to take life as she found it, except she was reliant on those state hand outs. She had however found the vacancies at The Harbour Guest House in Royal Crescent and through her facebook contacts booked it for Jane, Geoff and Linda, a young couple from Newcastle and Gail, a single mum from Middlesbrough whom she had met at a previous Goth weekend. All had agreed to share the two bed roomed flat, knowing that rooms would be in short supply nearer the time and were happy to forward funds to Shiv in order to ensure the booking was made. The event regularly brought several thousand visitors to the town and could well challenge the twice annual folk weeks as the town's biggest tourist draw.

Jane had passed her driving test at the age of 17 and had been bought a car by her father for doing so, just a standard, blue, Renault Clio, one of the lesser powered one's available at that, but new and economical; his thinking being in line with his conservative, almost strait laced approach to life that it was fit for purpose without the need for all the gimmick's fitted to most cars these days. It also looked the part on the driveway of their large five bed roomed detached house on the highly regarded Scotland Lane area of Horsforth, a suburb of Leeds but on the fringes of Bradford and on the flight path from Leeds Bradford airport. Her upbringing had led to Jane being sheltered from many of life's realities for her first 18 years; she had been the perfect child according to her mother who would regularly sing her praises at the monthly meetings of the Towns Women's Guild. Jane was happy for her parents to continue having that opinion, but in reality things had changed quickly when she moved out to university, she had made friends easily but they were friends that would not necessarily be of her parents choosing, being pierced, tattooed and dressed to shock more often than not. Jane trod a careful line, as she was reliant upon the healthy financial support given by her parents, retaining clothes that would meet with approval in Horsforth but wearing garish if good quality clothing in Liverpool and elsewhere on the alternative scene. Her own piercings were out of sight in the most part and her one single tattoo was most definitely so.

16

FIVE

It was 8.30 the following morning and Maughan was stood in his office, overlooking the harbour and the River Esk, contemplating the many different facets of the town, once a great whaling port landing over 270 whales and many thousand seals for subsequent rendering into leather from the skin, cartilage for glue, oils for soap paints and lubricants; recognised worldwide as the home of Captain Cook, despite him being born some 25 miles away in Great Ayton. A statue of Cook stood at the top of Khyber Pass adjacent to a set of whalebones overlooking the harbour from another angle, taking in the piers on either side of the river stretching out due north to the surprise of many and splitting the town into its eastern and western sides. Historically the East side was the home of the fishermen, with its cobbled streets and small cottages under the cliffs behind. The 199 steps up to the abbey would have been counted by many thousands of visitors over the years and now served to give access to the town from a large purpose built car park hidden away behind the abbey and the visitor centre. The West Cliff housed the wealthy ship owners in days gone by but now was the home of the tourist industry in the form of hotels and guest houses, eating places and hostelries as well as the single night club on Wellington Road.

Home now to approximately 13,500 residents and, in peak season, maybe twice as many visitors, Whitby was a small enough town for Maughan to remain up to speed with the local criminals and their activities but he hadn't had an inkling of this serious crime having been committed on his manor. Born locally himself, but having trained as a uniformed officer in The Metropolitan Police he had moved back to North Yorkshire as a Detective Constable twelve years earlier and rising to his current rank had settled in Whitby to provide a perfect upbringing for his children, now aged six and nine years. The safest place to live in England as the new Police and Crime Commissioner had recently reminded him and one of the most beautiful too he considered as he looked out at what must be one of the best views available from an office window anywhere in the country?

"Penny for them boss?" enquired Des Mason on entering the office through the already half opened door, "you look miles away."

"Just pondering, just pondering. Aelfleda Terrace is almost directly across the river from my office and yet we've got a body buried there and you know, without the landslip we might never have known."

"Scary i'nt it?" Replied the DC, "and we think we've got our finger on the pulse?"

"Anything of any worth from yesterday Des?"

17

"Not really, but then it's been weekend so t'council aren't any help with who owns the cottages and house to house is hopeless as they're nearly all holiday lets or second homes for the rich."

"Keep on it today though Des and get Mark on to it as well. Check where we are with mispers, uniforms have made a start already."

"Okay boss, will do, but Sue had asked me to go across to the PM with her today?"

"Yeah, well scrub around that, I'm gonna have to go to this one as SIO, I'll see her there, something's bugging me with this?"

"Okies, I'll let her know."

Maughan set off from Whitby in the old Peugeot 405 diesel he had run for years, sounded more like a tractor than a car these days but seemed to keep going and as far as Maughan was concerned, he had no interest in cars and it did its job in getting him from A to B at work.

The post mortem examination was to be conducted at Scarborough Hospital by Home Office Pathologist Dr James Middleditch, known to both Maughan and Collins all too well and held in somewhat high regard by both. At only 5 foot 7 inches tall and of slight frame he was a diminutive man in stature but with a wicked sense of humour and a keen eye for detail he seemed ideally suited to his role as one of only thirty Home Office accredited pathologists in the country. Frequently using his humour to deflect the attention from his actual work he would often help younger Police Officers, new to this part of their role, through their first autopsies by engaging them in good humoured banter, though that shouldn't be necessary today.

"Good morning Inspector, Sergeant," Middleditch greeted the officers, "make yourselves comfortable, and we shall begin, though don't expect miracles from this one, there's not much to go on."

"Good morning Jim," responded Maughan, "we're not likely to get much from the scene so we're hoping you can find something for us or we're going to struggle."

"I'll do my best Neil, as always, I'll do my best."

The cadaver was already laid out on the stainless steel table below, in the operating room; Sue Collins and Neil Maughan seated themselves behind the glass screen, watching over proceedings and listening via the intercom system to comments made by Jim Middleditch, who in turn was speaking into a microphone in order to record his work.

"Let's get this show on the road then." Continued Middleditch, followed by a run through commentary of the circumstances under which the body was found. His assistant, Kevan, a large, muscular man with crew cut hair and square cut jaw line sporting cultured stubble was already taking photographs of the deceased from every possible angle before clothing; or what was left of it, could be cut free and removed.

"No obvious signs of major trauma to the skull, no fractures to arms or legs," Jim Middleditch spoke into his mouthpiece as Kevan cut the cloth remnants from the body, though most of what little was left fell away under the pressure of the sharp scissors and needed no actual cutting. Earth stained leggings and some sort of shirt collar from around the neck were taken and carefully bagged, sealed and labelled before being placed on a nearby table.

"Minor damage in the form of greenstick fractures to two ribs, upper right and also a bow fracture to the humerus again on the right, but at this time I am not able to say if this happened pre or post mortem," the doctor continued his commentary, "initial signs of damage to the right cheek bone but an apparent full set of teeth, which may help identify our body, which, I would concur with yesterdays findings, is that of a young female of late teenage years to mid twenties."

"Jim, is there anything, that could actually confirm foul play or not?" asked Neil Maughan from his seat on the balcony, "Am I dealing with a murder?" He felt a little awkward asking this as from the position in which the body was found it had to be treated as such anyway.

"I am going to be at least another couple of hours, if not more here Neil, there is nothing immediately obvious but as I have said there are fractures which need to be investigated, samples to be taken for DNA analysis and even then I will need to run tests on the skeletal frame to determine how long it has been buried; why don't you get back to the nick and I'll call you if I find anything significant?"

Maughan knew he had an obligation to remain at the PM but felt that he could delegate on this occasion to his deputy SIO, Sue Collins.

SIX

"Wow, that's fantastic!" exclaimed Phoebe, a friend of Jane's from the university and an envious, if shy critic of the lifestyle she had chosen. They were housemates this semester and Jane was trying on her new corset, ordered online from Vollers, who Jane considered to be the best manufacturer, made to measure in a soft leather with steel bones; it had just arrived in the post and Jane was so excited that she wanted to try it immediately even though she knew it would make her late for her next lecture.

Phoebe would love to have had Jane's confidence to even consider wearing something so daring; "I mean it barely covers anything and it displays a cleavage men would never tire of ogling," she thought but would never say for fear of appearing to be square or prudish, whilst secretly wishing she had the nerve to wear something similar. She knew that she was the better looking of the two and was never short of admirers but it was Jane's personality, panache and devil may care attitude that lifted her above her peers, something Phoebe didn't possess and most probably never would, indeed Jane considered that her parents would have loved her to be just the same as Phoebe and it suited her to be seen in such company by them, which on the rare occasion of a visit to see her, they invariably would.

"I'll try it with the rest of my gear tonight," said Jane, mindful of how little time she had before she needed to rush off, "you alright for later to help me back into it?"

"Yeah, 'course, 'can't wait to see ya in it properly."

Despite the rush Jane neatly folded the corset back into its box and placed it carefully back in her wardrobe near to her Victorian dress, laced boots and silk gloves; there was never such a rush as would cause her not to look after her Goth clothes.

With Whitby Goth weekend now fast approaching, two weeks and counting, Jane was even more eager to keep in touch with old acquaintances and was very active on facebook, letting everyone know how her own arrangements were going and confirming plans to meet up, checking which bands were playing and also searching websites for more up to date news or gossip from like minded souls.

Despite being a very social person at uni she retreated almost imperceptibly and unknowingly into her shell at this time as more and more of her attention and time was given up to the event; she was all but obsessive with it but her close friends knew what to expect and knew that she would be back to her university self in a few short weeks, only full of stories brought back from Whitby.

Under the user name, ScouseVixn, Jane subscribed to the Whitby Goth Weekend website and was a regular contributor across the different forums, with her photograph included several times; showing her attention to detail on her costumes and make up. She was so confident of her appearance that she didn't have any worries about her parents seeing the site, not that she genuinely expected they would even look; or even recognising her if they did; her hair was coloured purple and blue, her white foundation and black eye shadow and lipstick gave her a completely different look. She would wear contact lenses whilst at the event, coloured, giving the impression of bloodshot eyes and often wore a mask too. Corsets were her favourite item of clothing, worn as an outer garment and enhancing her cleavage and cinching her waist, her appearance was as far removed from the prissy little Horsforth girl as one could imagine.

She liked this, she liked the secrecy of the double life she led, knowing that she could return to her parents and fit in to the suburban set, be looked upon as the model daughter, destined for great things and without a blemish to be found anywhere in her character; yet, whilst still wanting to achieve and indeed very likely to do so, she was living a quite promiscuous life, no steady relationship but several different partners, both students and Goths but not necessarily equally so and none of whom had met her parents. In many ways this was nothing different from many of her student friends and colleagues she considered, the only difference being that her parents were not as accepting of modern ways as many others were and hence she felt almost pushed into the duplicitous life she led.

That night came and with a bottle of wine and a pizza each for company, Phoebe and Jane tried on different combinations of clothing, some for day wear others more formal for particular events across the Goth weekend, teaming up accessories with each outfit and with Jane getting more excited with each one she felt her plans were coming together just nicely thank you very much. Phoebe, for her part, had helped with the squeezing into waist cinches, fastening the hooks and eyes, of which there seemed to be hundreds, on the dresses and generally adding to the evening by heaping praise on her highly excited friend.

SEVEN

Detective Superintendent Simon Pithers was a huge man, at six foot five inches tall and arguably the same across his shoulders, short cropped dark hair just beginning to recede at the sides, designer stubble that maybe looked just too neat and dressed as always, impeccably in his Austin Reed, made to measure suit of charcoal grey with a thin shadow stripe, and all finished off with a red patterned silk tie and Loake brogues; he was the epitome, at least in police circles, of being dressed to impress and he knew it. He also knew that he was well liked across the force for his hard but fair approach and his tenacity in the field of crime detection, an opinion shared by Neil Maughan.

Pithers was at Whitby to sit in on the formal briefing of Operation Caedmon being chaired by his Inspector and to be followed by the first full press briefing that afternoon. He had been in touch over the weekend and was up to speed with the progress made so far, he had authorised the necessary additional staffing required for a formal murder investigation, for that is what it now was and he had come to add his own not inconsiderable weight to the briefing.

"The time is 8.35am on the morning of Tuesday 15th January 2013 and this is the fourth day of Operation Caedmon," Neil Maughan opened the briefing, "welcome to the new officers, I believe most of you know each other so I am not going to make any formal introductions so listen in." Behind Maughan were a row of three whiteboards with details of the enquiry on each, the victim, as yet unidentified but confirmed as female, was the header on one, the location on the second and suspects on the third. This third board was almost clear and as such stood out from the others which contained sub headings and sections that were in turn linked by lines of differing colours. HOLMES 2 had been set up in the office next door and a full team put in place on twelve hour shifts to ensure that everything was maintained and entered correctly and that tasks were allocated accordingly.

"Sue, can you please bring us all up to date with the PM results?"

"Yes sir, in addition to what we already knew there isn't a great deal that can be said with absolute certainty," she began, "the fractures are likely to have been caused prior to death and may be a contributory factor but very unlikely to be the cause. There was nothing in terms of blood or body tissue, or vital organs. The clothing such as it was has been bagged and is ready for forensics. Samples have been taken for DNA analysis and that will obviously help if not actually identify the body, it depends if the deceased is on the National database?"

"One thing that was found was what appears to be a small item of jewellery which was loose in the clothing when it was cut from the body." Sue Collins looked around the room wondering if there would be any comments on what she had said so far but as she had already alluded to, there was very little of any real substance.

"Thanks Sue," said Neil Maughan, taking back the reins, "what about the search of the cottage, have we managed to get in there properly?"

"We're in sir and still working through the rooms," said Sergeant 1123 Graham Dawson, the POLSA lead in charge of the search. "We've been limited to four people at any one time on the premises due to the council risk assessment and whilst it goes against the grain, I have to agree with their views on this occasion, it could go at any time. So far CSI have lifted no end of fingerprints, but there is nothing to suggest any struggle or any commission of crime. I have given direction to the team on scene and I'll be overseeing it here on in."

"How long do you reckon you'll need Graham?"

"How long is that piece of string sir, a room at a time, but we'll be working as quickly as we can as it might all collapse before we get anywhere?"

"Point taken, be careful." Maughan responded before continuing, "Have we found the owner of the cottage yet? Is it rented out on short term lets or is it just a second home?"

Des Mason interjected, "the cottage, Esk View, is registered to a Harriet Wilcock from Bradford, I've asked the local CID to make some enquiries for us as soon as. It is let out for holiday stays, advertised mainly in the West Yorkshire area as far as I can tell so far."

"Good work Des, if its holiday let's then there's no telling who's been in but it's something positive, a first step forward."

The briefing continued with actions being given to each officer, inside teams for phone enquiries, research and inputting, outside teams for visits and house to house enquiries being set up and the policy book being updated with the decisions made and reasons why, before Simon Pithers thanked everyone for their time and effort and asked them all to remain fully focused and give of their best.

EIGHT

There on the mat just behind the new uPVC door lay the brown envelope addressed to Miss Jane Hammond, Scholars House, Russell Street, Liverpool, L3 5LJ.

At least the landlord must have a sense of humour Jane again thought, seeing the house name instead of the number. A small mews type house in modern parlance, in reality a small but nice two bed-roomed mid terrace that afforded comfortable accommodation for her and Phoebe and which had obviously been bought by its current owner with student lets in mind. Near to the campus yet far enough away from the town it even had residents parking in addition to a fitted kitchen, two small reception rooms and a newly refurbished bathroom with separate power shower from which Jane had just emerged and was now making her way down the stairs.

Her face beamed as she made her way down the final steps two at a time and picking up the envelope she saw the stamped logo of WGW, Whitby Goth Weekend, at last the tickets that in turn would be exchanged for wristbands that would then give her access to the Spa Pavilion for the bands, bizarre and other events had arrived and Jane considered herself ready for her next adventure to begin. She would spend the remainder of the day carefully packing her Carlton Airtec wheeled suitcase, updating facebook and making a telephone call to her mother confirming that she would be visiting friends over the holiday and so would not be home. She did promise however to stay in touch and let her know that she was back safely. At twenty one years of age she was still reporting in to her parents but she felt it a small price to pay to keep them from prying too deep into her life.

Her alarm went off at 8.00am on Thursday morning, the first day of WGW, but Jane had been awake for at least an hour, laying in her bed and going through her anticipated itinerary, she reached over to her phone and shut down the alarm before getting out of bed and making her way across to the shower, she could hear that Phoebe was already up and about and shouted, "Hya," to her as she crossed the landing to the bathroom, "be down soon."

An hour later Phoebe helped Jane put her things into the Clio, gave her a hug and waved her off as she began the journey from the West coast to the East, a journey she expected to take around three to four hours dependent on traffic conditions." Keep in touch, I want to know all about it," she shouted as the car drove off. Phoebe herself was returning to her parents' home in Nottingham for the holidays and was a little envious but knew she couldn't live Jane's kind of life.

NINE

"Body unearthed in Whitby Land slip." Shouted the headline in the Scarborough Evening News and was to Maughan's mind a whole lot better than, "Murder uncovered on East Cliff." As was emblazoned across the front Page of The Whitby Gazette, he had open on his desk; followed by an opening paragraph of further sensationalism, misquoting him as confirming the death as a murder and asking the question, "will there be any more?"

"What the fuck do they think they are doing?" he shouted to no one in particular, "We'll have a serial killer on our hands at this rate." Throwing the paper down again he walked down the corridor to the incident room, which was a hive of activity. He studied the white boards which had been updated with what little information had so far come to light, but which did not include the identity of the deceased. "Who was she?" he pondered, "Where was she from and why hasn't she been reported missing?"

The DNA profile taken from the body had been checked against the National database but had not come up with anything at all, the missing person checks across the neighbouring force areas had likewise come up with nothing, but this was somebody's daughter. Turning to the duty Detective Sergeant, in charge of the incident room, he asked, "What's the latest on the house search?"

"All but complete sir," replied Detective Sergeant Andy Goodall, "just bedroom two to finish and then the outside if they can with all that's around it."

"Anything useful so far?" queried Maughan, knowing in his heart that he would already have been told if there had been, but more in hope than expectation.

"There are signs of it being used, but we know that it has been let out on a fairly regular basis over our time frame. We've drawn up a list of all tenants and have sent out requests to all the force areas involved to make the necessary enquiries; West Yorks' are really chuffed as most of them seem to come from their area."

"Thanks Andy, keep up the good work, something always turns up." Next he returned to his office where Jean had left him a coffee and bacon sandwich, taking it upon herself to ensure that he maintained his food intake, as she knew of old that he simply forgot himself once he was immersed in his job. "I must remember to pay her back sometime," he thought yet again knowing that the cost was to her and he simply never remembered to do so. Finishing the sandwich, bought on the morning butty run to the butchers in nearby Ruswarp village, he picked up the phone and spoke to the press office, trying to come up with something to suppress the damage that may have been caused by the Gazette headline, which in turn had promoted further interest from the Nationals'.

"Whitby Police are continuing their enquiries into the identity of and circumstances behind, the discovery of a body found on the East Cliff on the morning of Sunday 11th January 2013. The body of a young female was found in what Police are describing as suspicious circumstances following a land slip and an incident room has been established in the Town's Police Station under the direction of Detective Inspector Neil Maughan. The investigation into what is described by Detective Inspector Maughan as "an isolated and thankfully very rare occurrence in North Yorkshire," is focusing initially on the identity of the deceased who it is believed had been buried many months previously.

Anyone who believes they may have any information that may assist is asked to contact the incident room on the number below or ring Crime stoppers on 0800 555 111. The information can be left anonymously. There is nothing to suggest that this investigation is linked to any other at this time and nor is it anticipated that any further such discoveries will be made here or elsewhere in the Whitby area, which remains one of the safest areas in England in which to live, work or visit."

"Always have to focus on the positives." said Maughan to Mark Taylor, who in turn smiled at the inference of political correctness and hint of deference to the corporate approach in his bosses' comments. He hit the send button on his computer and emailed his offering to the press office at Force HQ who now had to authorise it and pass it on to their contacts in the media. They would field any questions in return, though the local reporters would always try to circumvent the system and ring Maughan direct through the office direct line.

TEN

Arriving shortly after 2.15pm, having travelled eastwards on the M62 before joining the A64 and stopping at Thomson's fish and chip shop just outside York for a tasty lunch; and finding nowhere local to park, Jane looked up at The Harbour Guest House, an imposing building of the Georgian era set in an arc of other similar houses that formed the crescent set just a little way back from the North Promenade and in turn the Spa Pavilion or focus of Jane's planned weekend. She counted the eight steps up to the front door and saw the clearly displayed, No Vacancies, sign in the bay window. Taking out her new Samsung mobile phone she dialled the number displayed on the signboard swinging freely outside the Guest House immediately above the large wooden door.

After just three rings she heard, "Good afternoon, Harbour Guest House, how can I help you?"

"Is nowhere free from the claws of so called corporate gob shite and strap lines?" She thought, "Not even an independent local seaside guest house?" though she didn't say that, she replied, "Yes hello, I'm booked in for the weekend, I'm outside now but can't find any parking, do you have any?"

"Yes we do, it's around the back, but it will be busy as we are booked solid for the weekend." the voice had softened a bit and sounded normal now, not convoluted and patronizing, "If you drive to the end of the road there is an archway, drive through there and back towards us there is a sign up outside the gate. I'll see you shortly."

Jane thanked the as yet unnamed voice and drove to the rear of Royal Crescent where there were quite surprisingly several spaces to park, not marked out in any way but a large cindered area seemingly free to use. Having parked the Clio she set off back around the front, pulling her suitcase behind her and taking in the fresh air blowing in from the sea she began to smile, her weekend started here.

ELEVEN

Detective Superintendent Simon Pithers sat quietly in his office at Newby Wiske Hall; an old stately home only a short distance from the county town of Northallerton and that now formed the Force Headquarters of North Yorkshire Police. He was not pleased that five days after the body had been found in Whitby there appeared to be no progress into how it had got there, why, by whom or even when, let alone who it was. He was due to speak with the Chief Constable and other members of the Senior Management Team at the weekly meeting of the SMT and was uncomfortable at not being able to provide any answers. His latest contact with the incident room a few minutes earlier confirmed what he already knew, that everything possible was being done.

The newly appointed Police and Crime Commissioner was to be interviewed later that day on local television and there was no doubt that questions would be asked about this enquiry, after all it was currently the only active murder enquiry ongoing in North Yorkshire, therefore very much necessary to find a positive angle where none were apparent.

Simon Pithers assured his colleagues around the table that everything was in place to further the investigation and that whilst additional staff to assist with enquiries would always be welcomed that the team in place were working hard and he hoped for a breakthrough shortly. He intended to return to Whitby himself later that day and liaise directly with the staff on site; he was a firm believer that the presence of senior officers on the ground raised morale and indicated a willingness to become involved; he was well aware of colleagues, past and present, that hid behind their desks in distant offices compiling statistics in different guises for personal gain, he had no time for them.

It was agreed that two Detectives would be sent to work with their West Yorkshire colleagues in order to progress the investigation with previous occupants of Esk View and that the Operational Support Unit, OPSU for short, would remain until further notice or stood down by the SIO.

It was just over three hours later that Simon Pithers stood on The Ropery, a small street with a mixture of council houses and ex council houses, where almost everyone knew their neighbours and many knew the families of their neighbours from generations ago; above Aelfleda Terrace and as near as he could reasonably be expected to get in a vehicle to the crime scene. He pondered the logistics of taking an unwilling party to this location, difficult at best and damn near impossible if the reluctant person was putting up anything of a struggle, well not without someone knowing anyway. Below him were steps that, in turn, would take him past other houses set into the steep banking over Church Street, to a footpath above Eskside Cottages and the old Seaman's Hospital Cottages, above him were further semi-detached houses that formed the only residential premises between him and the Abbey at the cliff top; a narrow and not very well kept path, known locally as The Donkey Path ran across the open field area to the large car park built quite recently to provide for the thousands of tourists Whitby now attracted each year. "Was that the route someone could have used?" he pondered.

Walking the route to the scene, still marked off by the blue and white plastic tape that always characterised a police incident, he took in the feel of the place, a mixture of beautiful views out to sea, onto the harbour and further inland to The New ridge and beyond and yet a feeling of, well, if not poverty then certainly a reduced standard of living that belied the image of other parts of the town. Showing his warrant card and signing himself in, he spoke with the Police Community Support Officer and thanked him for his work, "only what he was paid to do but a word of thanks goes a long way and costs nothing but a moment in time," he thought. He saw the OPSU Team working in what was, in all likelihood, the garden or patio area of Esk View; painstakingly lifting everything they could under the guidance of Graham Dawson, SOCO staff were present too, working alongside their colleagues and such was their level of concentration that none appeared to notice his presence, until Graham Dawson spoke up; "Hello sir, come to see how the other half live?" he said, knowing that this particular senior officer wouldn't take offence where others may have done.

"Glad of the chance Graham, glad of the chance. How's it going?"

"Just about wrapped up inside, Crime Scene Manager is just reviewing where she is with her team and mine's busy going through the mess that used to be upright at the rear and under the patio at the front."

"What's the score with access inside now? Are the council still here?"

"Yeah, it's Paul Woodbridge, to be honest he's played a blinder for us, I'm not sure anyone else would have let so many of us inside or turned a blind eye when needed."

"Duly noted, I'll make sure I see him and thank him personally." He replied before poking his head through the gap where the front door used to be and seeing for himself the unstable nature of the building and the white suited CSM, Alison Reed, sealing up a doorway and marking it as completed.

Treading carefully on her way out, she saw Pithers and gave him a smile; they had worked many times together previously and shared a mutual trust of each others' skills and expertise.

"That's my team finished here, now we just have to sort it all out back at the nick and see what we can use." She began, "Been shitting myself in case it all came down on top of us." she added as she eased past him and out into the open again.

"What are your thoughts Al?"

"Not sure, we've taken a lot but that's because we won't get a second chance and maybe if we had more time I could have been a bit more selective?"

"Do you have a gut feeling?"

"I really don't, it's obvious that the place has been lived in and even regularly cleaned I would say. If you're relying on me this time I fear you might be disappointed, but as I said we'll have to see what we have bagged up."

"I know you'll do your best. Are you headed back to HQ or calling in at Whitby?"

"Thought I'd call in on Neil before I left, update him and the incident room."

"See you back there shortly then."

Simon Pithers stayed just long enough to speak with some of the other staff still working at the scene and also to thank Paul Woodbridge for his help before retracing his steps back to his car and heading back to the Spring Hill Office and the incident room.

Jane let herself into the Harbour View reception area and rang the bell
that was placed on top of a small wooden bureau just to the right of the
hallway alongside a whole host of leaflets for the attractions in and
around Whitby. A visitor book that she saw was full of complimentary
comments left by previous guests was open to view alongside a heavy,
well thumbed diary that she took to be the lettings book.

The deep red carpet was what might be expected, dark and patterned in
order not to show the wear and tear or stains from continual use, it
continued up the stairs as far as she could see, bordered by very deep
skirting boards that matched the cornice that topped the walls, which in
turn were painted in a matt finish colour that complemented the period
of the house.

"First impressions very good," she thought, "Shiv's done us proud this
time."

"Hello, you found somewhere to park ok then?" said a tall thin man
dressed older than his forty three years in a yellowish V neck sweater
over a checked shirt and brown trousers.

"Yes thank you."

"I'm Gerry," the man said, by way of introduction, "can I ask you to fill in
your details in this book?" as he opened the diary and pointed to today's
date. "You're in room three on the first floor; it's our biggest room which
we use for families normally, a double bed and two singles with an en-
suite shower room. Breakfast is served between 8.00am and 9.30am in
the dining room at the end of the hall. Can I take your case for you?"

"That's great thanks," she said completing her details and following him
upstairs to her room.

On opening the door to her room she was shown the usual
complimentary tea and coffee making equipment, flat screen TV and
DVD player and then left to it. The room, which was actually two rooms
plus the bathroom, was above average standard with nice clean bedding,
matched to the decor of the room, ample storage for her clothing and
that of her friends, yet to arrive. She chose one of the single beds near to
the large bay window and threw herself down on it, glad of the rest after
her drive but also happy to just to be there.

Over the next couple of hours Jane sorted all her clothing out, hung it up
in the wardrobes neatly and met, for the first time, Geoff and Linda
Boyes, both in their thirties and who had travelled the short distance
down from Middlesbrough via train to nearby Saltburn and then bus to
Whitby dressed in their Goth clothing and also Gail, who was a little
older at maybe forty, who had driven down and seemed to have very

little in the way of baggage. Though many would think such an arrangement unusual many Goths were willing to share accommodation for these two weekends each year and besides they were all mates of Shiv so there was every chance they would gel as a group.

They all exchanged pleasantries for a while and chatted over coffee, each knowing that they had at least a shared interest in all things Goth, if seemingly from very different backgrounds after which they arranged to go their separate ways before meeting up later in the evening. Jane, keen to have everything in place; said she was going to the Spa to get her wristband and then for a wander around town.

"Don't you mean a promenade?" said Linda, as she did a twirl to show off her resplendent outfit, "We Goths don't just wander we promenade, we let everyone see how we look."

"O.K. a promenade it is then." Jane corrected herself, smiling broadly; she felt a common bond already.

THIRTEEN

Sat around the briefing table again, Neil Maughan addressed the team and, after the usual opening, he asked for updates from each of the sub groups, making notes in the policy book as he listened. It was approaching 6.00pm and most hoped they would be getting off soon, many knew it would be unlikely; having family commitments and appointments counted for very little in this job when there was a murder to solve.

"We've now traced the owners of Esk View sir." offered DC Mark Taylor, mindful that the Superintendent was in attendance and thus not using the usual first name terms, "The Wilcock's, it's registered in the wife's name for tax purposes apparently, but they are an elderly couple from Bradford, they have owned the property for over thirty years but haven't used it themselves for at least the last ten. They consider it part of their pension plan and take the profits from its lettings to supplement their income. They leave the running of the place to an agency. Des is talking to them now."

"Good, thanks Mark, we'll need a list of anyone who stayed there over the last two years, names addresses, contact numbers; you know the drill."

Alison Reed spoke next, updating the team with the same information as she had given to Simon Pithers earlier that day before adding, " We'll need a presence throughout the period of demolition and Paul Woodbridge tells me that could take up to four weeks as they have to do it top down, for safety's sake."

"We've got the scene secure Al, what else do you need?" asked Neil Maughan

"At least one, if not two, of my team around the clock until it's completely down. We've completed all we can in the house and in the garden but considering that the body was buried we need to be sure that nothing else has been, either in the garden or anywhere else. I'm sorry but it will cost and my overtime budget is bust already.

"One of your team and a uniform from the duty shift Al." interrupted Simon Pithers, "If something crops up we'll look at again then."

"Thanks Boss."

It was another half hour before everybody had given their take on their own progress and was dismissed by Simon Pithers with a thank you and a request to keep up their good work again in the morning.

It was a further hour and a half before he and Neil Maughan would leave after discussing everything over again in Neil's office, coffees in hand, brains engaged. Both were married, both had families and yet neither felt in any rush to leave. They hadn't visited the scene together yet and decided that now was as good a time as any. Despite the darkness of the evening each knew that sometimes it was just a moment's inspiration or hunch that could provide a breakthrough.

Simon Pithers made the decision not to travel in Neil Maughan's Peugeot but gave the excuse that if he travelled in his own car he could set off for home and not return to the station; whilst this was no doubt true it was more a case of not wanting either to ruin his street cred by being seen in the Peugeot but neither did he want to be an accessory to any of the construction and use offences any half decent traffic cop would find on it. He would never live it down.

The generators that had been set up to provide the energy for the portable lighting could be heard from The Ropery as the two detectives parked their cars and began the walk back to Aelfleda Terrace.

"I'm surprised the locals haven't kicked off with this racket going on 24/7?" uttered Simon Pithers above the monotonous drone of the small diesel engines; putting on his Berghaus coat with the cold evening ever more evident.

"They're a very tolerant bunch, well those that aren't pissed or stoned any way, most of them are enjoying being in the limelight of the media."

"Are we missing anything Neil?" asked the thoughtful Superintendent.

"I don't think we are boss, but the more I look, the more I think she was murdered here and not elsewhere."

"Me too, it would be one hell of a job to move a body here unseen, but we can't rule it out. Yet."

The two men in charge of the investigation signed back into the site and now stood, gazing over the condemned house and beyond, towards the Donkey Path, as if each were trying to see an alternative route that would allow the transportation of a dead weight body from the car park down. There was a silence between the two, that lasted only seconds but which seemed much longer, before Neil Maughan began to walk further into the site, past the safety barriers carrying the No Entry signs and onto the patio, from beneath which, only a week ago, the remains were found. Pithers, in turn, walked around to the rear, stepping over the piled up heaps of mud and stone that had slipped down the cliff and lay against the wall of Esk View. "The landscape above had changed forever," he thought as he looked upwards, "and no doubt would do so again, but how soon?"

"I can't see the picture here, most murder victims know their killers as we know, if it was a domestic then surely we'd have heard something about it; there's no record of any calls to this terrace for anything of that nature in the past three years, in fact apart from a couple of cycle thefts and a burglary dwelling with a tele going missing then it's a crime free zone." Neil Maughan was talking to himself really but was overheard by his senior officer.

"No hunch then Neil? No light bulb moment?"

"No boss, it's going to be down to good old fashioned bobbying on this one."

The colleagues began their walk back to The Ropery, both probably thinking for the first time about what explanation they would give their loved ones this time for being so late home; not that either of their wives would think any more of it, both being more than used to this scenario.

"How's Helen and the family?" enquired Simon Pithers.

"I think they're fine, don't seem to have seen them for a week at least."

"Well get straight off home now then and don't stop off at the Red Lion on the way, give Helen my regards and apologies for keeping you back so late."

"Will do, see you tomorrow?"

"No doubt, now get off."

Two thoughtful cops began their respective drives home, one a short journey of just four or so miles, to the village of Sleights, the other a fifty mile plus journey to York beginning with a drive up Blue Bank and over the North York Moors.

FOURTEEN

Having collected her wristband, Jane had remained at The Spa Pavilion for longer than she had first considered doing; she had taken the opportunity to meet other so called Whitby Virgins, the name given by the organisers to those who hadn't been to the event previously, not necessarily, or even likely, those who were sexually naive. A small number of the organisers were present and on hand to give out advice, maps of the town with the various locations of trade stands, music events and suchlike highlighted thereon together with an opportunity to mingle and ask questions as needed. There was also an information stall with a huge banner over it and around which were gathered a group of about a dozen Goths exchanging questions and answers.

Jane listened at first, on the edge of a small cluster, before joining in one of the conversations, suggesting to the group, that in her opinion, "The Res' is a good place to start, it's free downstairs and there's always some music on." She was, in fact, repeating what she had been told only a short while earlier by Geoff and Linda, veterans of the Goth Weekend and very knowledgeable with it.

She referred to The Resolution Public House, a three storey building, recently renovated as a hotel, on a naval theme, and on the corner of Flowergate and Skinner Street on the town's west side. Very popular with the locals as well as The Goth community; she had been on there on a previous visit and thought the atmosphere came near to that of the organised events and as such she enjoyed going to both.

"The Elsinore was always full last time I came," she continued, referring to a much smaller pub, also on Flowergate and thought by some to be the spiritual home of The Goths. Jane wasn't sure but she did know that such was its popularity that dozens of Goths strayed out of the pub, drinks in hand, onto the footpaths and road outside causing pedestrians and vehicles to slow down and occasionally even to stop. This was one of the few minuses that The Goths brought to the town, but to Jane, she considered, "they should just shut the road down for a few days, there are plenty of other routes to use."

She talked with the group a short while longer before they all decided to "promenade," as she now considered the appropriate term, along the aptly named North Promenade to North Terrace, followed by a right turn at the Whale Bones, a prominent local landmark adjacent to the statue of Captain Cook, which in turn stood proud looking out to the sea. Continuing on East Terrace to Cliff Street and then slightly back uphill to The Resolution. They were surprised at just how many of their contemporaries were already there. The Elsinore could be seen already

36

to be full and inside, the first floor of The Res' was filling up quickly to the sound of 80's music and the promise of live bands later.

Jane decided that before it got too busy she would send texts to her parents and also to Phoebe, as she had promised to do. To her parents, she sent;

"Hi, M & D just arrived at Pheebs. All cool. Goin out 2nite so will ring u 2moz. LU XX"

It wasn't total text speak, as her mum and dad just wouldn't cope with that, in fact her dad would cringe at not using proper English language complete with all the correct punctuation. "Chill out dad, live with it." she thought.

To Phoebe, she sent;

"Hi Babes, its gr8 2b@WGW, AFT, BIO ☺, CMAP, thx. LU XX

Phoebe would instantly read this and understand but it was unlikely that her parents would if they should pick up her mobile,

"Hi Babes, it's great to be at Whitby Goth Week, about fucking time, Bring it on, Cover my arse pal, thank you. Love you. Xx"

Phoebe would also delete the message after answering as she wouldn't want to incriminate herself in any wrongdoing, she was "so under the thumb of her parents." thought Jane.

After receiving a brief response from each, Jane set about drinking, dancing and getting to know her new friends.

FIFTEEN

"Good morning everyone, the time is 8.40am on Friday 18th January 2013 and this is the seventh day of Operation Caedmon, the investigation into the death of an as yet un-named female, the body of whom was found on Aelfleda Terrace last Saturday morning." The tone of the introduction, though only a week old was now less than inspirational and some might argue it as monotonous, but Neil Maughan wasn't just going through the motions he was getting the formalities out of the way before turning to the whiteboards and asking the team for more intelligence to add to them.

"We need to pick up guys, what have we got to go forward into week two?"

"Boss we've now got statements from over thirty holiday tenants of Esk View across the period from August 2011 to April 2012, the details are all being entered into the system but nothing yet stands out as helpful. We've gone through all the misper's within a hundred mile radius and have now asked to look Nationwide, we've still got two of ours in West Yorks' taking further statements and chasing up their oppo's from Bradford and we've got accounts from every household on The Ropery, St. Mary's Crescent, Green Lane and Church Street around the old chapel area." said an upbeat Sue Collins, picking up on Maughan's drive to enthuse his colleagues.

"Good, thanks Sue, now let's get the same from each of the cottages near to Esk View; let me know numbers and we'll see what we need in terms of additional staff." There was urgency in Maughan's voice as, whilst it was in some ways an old crime, it was very much a current case and it was somebody's daughter, deserving of the best investigation he could provide. Besides it was something he could get his teeth into instead of the usual number crunching that befell everyone of his rank these days, since the introduction of league tables and so called accountability; oh how he hated the bean counters.

"Al anything else from the scene?" he asked, more in hope than expectation.

"Not exactly, but we do have something. Do you remember the small piece of jewellery found in the clothing? Well it is 22 carat gold and has a small ruby set in it. Most unusually though and probably most important for us is that it's what's called a captive ring and is used in genital piercing." She paused a while to let the information settle in the minds of those around the table before continuing; "Firstly it is not cheap, in fact I would suggest 22 carat gold is very rare these days and secondly I would think it's not something every woman would want done."

She paused again knowing that there would be some glances around the room and some comments between, the mostly male, colleagues sat in the room.

"Bloody 'ell it's making my eyes water thinking about it," cringed Mark Taylor.

"They say it's great for clitoral stimulation," responded Andy Brown, one of the analysts, maybe just too quickly?

"Let's keep on track gents," interrupted Maughan," if that's right Al, then it might be our first breakthrough, I mean how many places are there that carry out that sort of piercing?

"Quite a lot these days boss," chirped up Des Mason, "I mean she could literally be from anywhere as we know and not everywhere is as backward as us woolly backs up here in Yorkshire."

"Get on to it then Sue, task someone with just that. We need to know what sort of numbers we are dealing with, and we are not talking back streets here with 22 carat gold and rubies as well so start high." He looked around the table again before adding, "I want this kept private so absolute discretion please folks."

"Boss, maybe we should be looking at some of our folkies, Goths or other alternative types then. I mean we have two Goth weekends, a folk festival and who knows who else comes here." proffered Mark, looking quizzically at Andy Brown as he did so.

"You're right Mark, but at the moment we haven't traced a misper yet never mind narrowing our search for an alternative one. We do need to get some of this intelligence out to other forces now though and a suitably worded press update, nationally.

"Sue, do we know if any of the holiday lets been to any of these groups of people? Can you cross check the dates and make sure everyone from each of the properties is visited personally again?"

"Will do"

Maughan rounded up the briefing feeling somewhat more upbeat than when it started; he had a clue, something to work on, to focus the minds of the team to look forward; a small but significant step in the right direction. He was actually smiling by the time he reached his office to update Simon Pithers.

SIXTEEN

As the evening wore on Jane was easing into the scene, still in The Res' she was five ciders down the line to breaking her first rule and becoming drunk on the first night. She had read somewhere that many first time visitors threw themselves into the event so wholeheartedly on day one that they missed day two and sometimes, more.

As a student she had no issues herself with the drunkenness but she was disappointed in her lack of resolve, but not enough to stop drinking. Geoff and Linda had arrived but were mingling with other friends and showing off their stunning outfits outside on Flowergate, drinks in hand and seemingly ignored by the passing police vans; drinking in the streets not being allowed in this part of the town. Gail had joined Jane at her table and was now sharing a round with Jane and three others, but was three drinks behind and therefore quite sober by comparison.

The first floor was now filling up, mostly with Goths but also with the locals who were either happy to share the event or those who just wanted to ogle the freaks or weirdo's who descended on their town twice a year. Music from the 80's blasted out from large speakers suspended from the ceiling around the room, Duran Duran's Hungry like a wolf now replacing Bon Jovi and Livin' on a prayer; the mood was that of enjoyment and participation and the DJ was doing his best to keep it that way with great links and a good rapport with his audience.

Jane was not alone in singing along to the words of the song despite it being from a completely different generation, she was "just having a great time," she said, to anyone who was listening, but mostly to an all male group on a nearby table overlooking the small dance floor. Though dressed in dark clothing it was clear that none were Goths and they appeared to be taking it in turns to point out to each other different Goths around the room before laughing in unison at some unheard comment. The group began laughing at Jane, as she was the only one who responded to their behaviour, others choosing to ignore them; after all it was they who were in the minority tonight. Gail took Jane by the arm and they returned to their table where to Gail's dismay Jane finished her next drink in one swift go.

"Jane, slow down." It was almost an order from Gail, but stopped just short of what she wanted to say as she felt that it was only a new friendship and afterwards they had to share a room for the rest of the weekend.

"I'm not pissed." Shouted Jane, in such a manner that suggested it was at odds with the very words coming out of her mouth.

"No but you will be if you don't slow down." Still trying the route of soft persuasion, Gail put an arm around Jane and smiled the smile of companionship and support.

It seemed to work and they sat at their table, almost oblivious to the goodbyes from others leaving en-route to The Spa Pavilion or elsewhere. "Have you had anything to eat since you arrived?" asked Gail, guessing she knew the answer before it came.

"No, let's get some Whitby Fish and Chips." the voice didn't seem quite so loud or drink affected now.

"O.K. there's a chip shop just down the road, The Royal or some'rt like that I think, shall we go now?"

As they left the pub arm in arm they heard one of the males shouting something about them "probably being lezzers," Gail managed however to keep Jane walking to the door, ignoring the jibe and letting the two bouncers, or Door Supervisors, as they now preferred to be called, speak with them.

Walking down Flowergate the short distance to the hill that was Brunswick Street and left onto Baxtergate they arrived at Royal Fisheries only minutes later. Pleased to see it open but not to see the queue of maybe fifteen people waiting to be served they entered the fish shop and perused the menu board, despite knowing that all they really wanted was cod and chips, or one of each as it was known locally. By the time they were served, it seemed a while but in reality it was only a few minutes, Jane was feeling much better, more relaxed, and less intense; they left the shop and sat on a low wall that formed the boundary around The Church of Saint John the Evangelist.

"Thanks Gail, I've just been looking forward to it so much that I didn't stop to think."

"It's only about 9.00 o'clock, there's plenty of time yet. Don't spoil it for yourself."

They ate their fish supper in relative silence after that, joining in with others watching all manner of weird and wonderful costumes walk past them, from the theatrical to the risqué that belied the cool chill in the air; and Jane remembered what had drawn her to the Goth scene in the first place, it was not the drink but the dress, the alternative lifestyle and the fun of being who you are and not being who others want you to be.

Putting their wrappers in the nearby bin the two new friends walked along Baxtergate towards the swing bridge, turning left onto St. Anne's Staithe, Marine Parade and onto Pier Road, where the Pier Inn was full to bursting and the amusement arcades were lighting up the whole street and from which the splendour of the harbour could be seen at sea level.

41

The atmosphere was just as Jane had hoped for; she had been to Whitby many times before but not seen it in this light, the true Goths or Traditionalist' were now out in force and making their way between venues by the longest possible route to show off their costumes to as many people as they could, or promenading as Jane would now forever call it; mingling with the posers who didn't share the Goth beliefs but were happy to dress up, The Cyber Goths with their black costumes and neon hints almost glowing in the luminescence from the arcades, the Steam Punks in almost industrial garb and the Victorian Goths who were, perhaps the best dressed, in Jane's humble opinion. "How had she been stupid enough to almost miss this on the first evening?"
The thought didn't last too long before she replaced it with a new found optimism for the rest of the weekend, beginning right now with her return to The Spa Pavilion.

SEVENTEEN

Sat in the quiet best room, as it had been described on their arrival; at the front of the small but well appointed bungalow Neil Maughan and Sue Collins looked out over well manicured gardens as they waited for Harriet Wilcock to return with tea and biscuits. Opposite, across the room and in a new looking riser chair, sat Henry Wilcock, looking all his 82 years, with obvious signs of hip problems he sat very much to the front of his chair with one leg noticeably shorter than the other and crutches propped against the wall at his side; his appearance however belied his still very active and astute state of mind. He spoke well, had a good vocabulary and a memory that many half his age would wish for. The detectives were visiting the owners of Esk View to personally interview them having previously read the statements obtained by their West Yorkshire colleagues. Henry Wilcock had been born and brought up in Bradford but had lost the Yorkshire twang and his accent was difficult to place now, he had also been brought up to respect the police and other figures of authority, as had, he thought, most of his generation, therefore to have a Detective Inspector and Sergeant sat opposite him was something of an occasion; if for all the wrong reasons.

Harriet walked unsteadily back into the room, pushing a tea trolley, which to Sue Collins way of thinking was more for her own balance than to carry the tea and neatly arranged biscuits all on the best china tea service.

Reviewing the intelligence he already possessed about Esk View Neil Maughan asked, "What arrangements do you have with the letting agency, with respect to who rents it?"

"We pretty much leave it to the agency to carry out all the advertising and bookings, they use their own web site and also have our details in a brochure that they still send out; not everyone, it seems books holidays on computers yet."

"But do you have any restrictions on who can rent it?"

"Well it's only a small cottage and we don't like it to be used by all male or all female groups as we've had trouble before, with them."

"Trouble? What sort of trouble?"

"Just the usual sort of things I suppose, broken crockery, glasses and even furniture on one occasion, but that was a long time ago and we learnt our lesson. Since we've let to couples or families we haven't had any problems at all, have we Harriet?"

"No dear." she confirmed, almost automatically in support of anything her husband said.

"Who repairs the damage, do you have a contract with anyone for that?"

"Again it's left to the agency, they must have contracts with local tradesmen," Henry continued, "We do get copies of bills if we ask but we just pass all the paperwork on to the accountant and she sorts it all out. As long as we get seventy per cent of our lettings each year we were comfortable and it's was much more than that now; it seems the seasons don't stop in Whitby."

"We're not rich though Dear," piped up Harriet, for fear of seeming aloof or above their station.

Sue Collins noted Harriet's comment but politely ignored it, asking, "When did you last visit the cottage?"

"Ooh, it's over ten years Sergeant, I think, isn't it Henry?"

"September 2002," he responded, leafing through a diary he had taken from a wooden bureau at his side. It appeared he kept a diary of most things, a custom he had developed whilst in business as a Market Gardener some years earlier; "we stayed for three nights, Friday, Saturday and Sunday 6th, 7th and 8th. It was your Audrey's 70th birthday bash. We lost a week's rental for that weekend." His Yorkshire upbringing returning to the surface now.

"And did you have the patio laid at that time?"

"There's been a patio for a long time, flag stones. They've been re-laid a couple of times because they tend to move a little and you're liable if anyone trips now."

"Can you tell us when?" Neil Maughan hoped for a glimmer of something useful in return.

"I can go through my diaries if you're prepared to wait or I can send something from my accounts"

"We're happy to wait Mr Wilcock." Maughan wasn't necessarily happy but was prepared to wait for something positive, another move forward perhaps.

"Would you like a top up, while you wait?" ever the hostess, Harriet stood up to pour more tea.

A cup of tea and two more biscuits later, Henry Wilcock said, "Here it is, March 2nd 1989, Atkins builders and then again November 8th 2011, at least they're the dates on the bills. The last one is just from the agency though."

"That's great, thank you, could I have a copy of those bills please Mr Wilcock?"

"Yes, of course, anything to help."

Neil Maughan was happy to close the visit at that time before Harriet Wilcock, spoke, "What will happen now?" she asked, "Our insurance company have written to us and they won't pay anything out until they find the cause of the landslip and now there's this terrible thing."

44

"We won't be there much longer Mrs Wilcock." Neil Maughan answered, "But I can't advise you about your insurance, I'm sorry."

"It's bloody obvious what caused the landslip," argued Henry, "they just look for any way out of paying out money. They're quick enough to take the premiums though."

Neil Maughan let the comment ride over him, looking to wind up the visit, as it wasn't going to provide a great deal more than they already knew. "I'll make sure we get in touch with the agency as soon as we are completed and of course we'll let you know too."

"Just before we leave you to the rest of your day, can I ask if you knew any of the neighbours on Aelfleda Terrace, any of the owners of the other cottages?"

"Used to know them all," Henry shrugged, "But it seems that the locals have all gone and they're all second homes now. I don't know any of them."

Sue Collins noted the irony in what he said and stood up to hasten their departure.

Thanking Mrs Wilcock for the tea and biscuits and shaking the hand of Henry Wilcock the two detectives left the pristine bungalow and walked the sort distance to their car, parked further down the Cul- De- Sac.

"What do you think?" Sue Collins asked as they walked.

"Glad we came but not sure that we're any further forward. I would've hoped that our enquiries with the agencies had picked up those dates, but at least we can follow up on them."

As they reached Sue Collins' car, a red BMW M3 convertible, they pondered the drive back.

"Let's take the scenic route back, via HQ. It's not every day I get the chance to be driven around in such luxury; a bit ostentatious though Sue?" Maughan had not aired his views about the car on the drive across as his focus was very much on the Wilcock's' and what he needed or hoped to achieve.

"If you've got it, flaunt it," she smiled, "If you had it, I would be seeing it as a penis extension, but when I have it I can get away with it." she tossed her hair back and said, "Roof up or down boss?"

"Up, it's fucking freezing!"

EIGHTEEN

Nearly five hours after returning to The Spa Pavilion, as the clock showed 2.30am, Jane had survived her first night at Whitby Goth Weekend and was physically knackered, emotionally drawn and yet very much still wired into the whole experience. Having drunk several energy drinks, some as a mixer with another shot of vodka, she had resisted the offers of amphetamine that had been made as the evening wore into the night and then the morning but her mind still buzzed as she made her way back the short distance to The Harbour View Guest House. Still in the company of Gail, who she considered had really saved the night for her; they linked arms as they crossed North Terrace towards Royal Crescent.

"That was fantastic." Jane enthused, watching other Goths leaving the venue, walking past the very visible Battenberg liveried police transit van parked nearby, a driver in her stab proof vest and bright yellow fluorescent jacket opened at the neck leaning forward onto the steering wheel whilst her similarly dressed, front seat male passenger appeared to be sleeping, head back, mouth open.

"Night shifts in Whitby," thought Gail "Weren't too bad then?"

Behind the police van and en-route to their temporary digs was a seating area amongst the walled gardens and lawns that provided day time respite for Whitby's tourist throng; "Let's sit here for a while, watch everyone go past again." suggested Gail, sitting on one of the bench seats and patting the wooden slats next to her, inferring Jane to sit there.

Jane chose to sit on the back edge of the seat with her feet on the wooden slats, an edge of defiance against the authorities and accepted rules of normality.

"Is there any talent out there Gail?"

"You've had offers all night long, you tart." Gail joked, but she was right; whilst not the best looking girl present she was full of energy and verve and had drawn many admiring glances with her costume and energetic, almost non-stop dancing.

"I know but I wasn't interested then, I am now."

"You'll have to wait for tomorrow now."

"Nah, let's go for a walk an' see who's about."

"I'm not sure Jane, it's late." Gail was most certainly the more conservative of the two, but this was the first hint of disagreement between the two new friends.

"Come on, just for a while, let's just go to the whale bones and see who's there then, it's only 'round the corner."

"OK." Gail tried to appear enthusiastic again but mentally had begun to feel that it was time to turn in for the night.

Returning to North Terrace they walked, arm in arm, Jane linking up for the fun and Gail, noticing the depth of cold at that time of morning, to keep warm. There were a number of others sat on benches, including one that had been dedicated to Sophie Lancaster; others sat on the steps and grassed area surrounding the famous landmark, most wearing heavy coats of the Victorian style and all taking in the view of small fishing boats leaving the harbour on that nights tide.

Taking their places amongst the small group seemed to have a calming effect on Jane, or was it that she too started to feel the cold. It did appear that of those in the group all were in couples and none appeared too inclined to be boisterous, there was an air of post event relaxation, a sense of energy conservation; ready for the next instalment. They chatted with individuals around them, making idle conversation for the best part of half an hour before seeing that there was an almost common consensus that the time had arrived to retire for the night.

Walking back again Jane felt the need to give Gail a small hug, hoping to quash those initial misgivings that had surfaced only a short time earlier; after all she had to spend another four nights sharing a room with her. Gail returned the hug and as they reached Harbour View all seemed well with the world again.

NINETEEN

It was late afternoon when, after a drive along the A658 through to Harrogate and then the A61 to Ripon, before skirting the edge of Thirsk, the BMW turned left into the long driveway that led up to Newby Wiske Hall and Neil Maughan was pleased to see there were spaces in the front car park; he could not believe that so many people worked at Head Quarters; it wasn't unusual to spend the first fifteen minutes searching for somewhere to park your car before you got in.

Walking the hundred metres or so to the front door of the imposing building Neil and Sue Collins joked about how the ACPO ranked Officers all had their cars parked immediately outside the offices; they had previously all had Range Rovers or Land Rover Discoveries but that had all changed when questions were asked about how much they were costing when officer numbers were being cut. Nobody seemed to know just how much pressure was applied from whom but Chief Officers now had more modest Ford Focus cars and seemed less possessive of them as a result.

The reception area was busy with a number of people apparently waiting to be seen and others gathering to use one of the conference rooms leading from the foyer. Sue Collins swiped her warrant card to open the glass door and allow the two of them access into the main corridor, halfway along which was Simon Pithers office.

Simon Pithers had a well known and accepted, but very simple protocol for access to his office; if the door was ajar then knock and enter, if it was shut, there was a reason for it; he did not wish to be disturbed. They were in luck, it was open;

"Sue, Neil, come on in," he did not rise from his seat but waved his arms across his desk gesturing towards two seats opposite, either side of a small table. Having finished typing up the latest updates and hitting the send button to email them to his support assistant for inclusion in the myriad of tables and reports for the seemingly endless meetings he acknowledged their presence and joined them at the table.

"Curry for lunch then was it?" knowing they had been across to Bradford, "I'd better sit back a bit then?"

Raising a smile, more out of politeness than in recognition of the attempt at humour, Neil Maughan gave the boss a résumé of what had and had not been achieved before agreeing that it had been a worthwhile exercise.

"Are Atkins builders still in existence then Neil?"

"I believe so sir, but it's unlikely that there's anyone left there that worked as long ago as 1989, but if they also did the work in 2011 then we may be onto something."

"You never know Neil, some of these people work 'til they drop, check with the agency as soon as we can and get a list of anyone and everyone who may have worked at the cottage anytime."

"It's already in hand sir, Sue rang it in from the car on the way over here."

"Hands free." Sue Collins quickly chipped in with a smile.

"I'm intrigued about this item of jewellery as well; how is it that only that piece was found?"

"Well, we don't know just what the deceased would have worn sir, but when I discussed it with Alison Reed; she suggested that it was because it was trapped within clothing when other items, earrings etcetera would likely have been displaced with any earth movement over the time she'd been buried."

"The search has been very thorough sir and nothing else has been located at or near the scene but there's literally hundreds of tons of earth there as you've seen" added Neil

"I know; I just want to be clear that everything we can do has been done. What have we found out about the ring?"

"We've ruled out a lot of places but again there are literally tens of thousands of jewellers across the country; we need to be able to narrow the search to a locality if we can and then concentrate in that area." Sue Collins added as positively as she could, knowing that it was currently a thankless task.

"We now have a list of over sixteen thousand names of mispers who have been missing for over a year and our body means there are over a thousand un-named dead as well." Neil Maughan had been doing his research, "We could naturally half those number as we know we have a dead female, we could likely bring it down by another sixty or so per cent with checks on age, but we're still looking at over three thousand missing people."

"That's naming the dead Neil, how many suspects, living suspects do we have?"

"No clear suspect, no motive, no cause yet sir."

"It'll all drop into place Neil, just keep plugging away; keep the intelligence updated and stay positive. How's everyone coping with the longer hours, anyone flagging yet?"

"We do have one issue boss; I've not really had a proper chance to discuss it with Neil yet but I suppose now is as good a time as any, if you've got time that is?"

"Do I need to know Sue, or is it best looked at locally first?"

"We can discuss it on the way back across to Whitby sir, I'll update you next time we talk." Neil Maughan, caught by the surprise of Sue Collins comment tried to buy some time; he was upset that she had brought this up without any comment to him; after all they had spent most of the day together.

Closing the meeting at that point Simon Pithers stood up, thanked his colleagues for their hard work and promised his support before asking them to close the door on the way out.

The mood as they walked back to the car park was not the happy, jovial one that it was on the way in.

TWENTY

Sat in her bed, Jane looked at the time on her mobile phone and saw the display; 04:16, she was now coming down from the high of the previous night; she had chatted with Gail when they got back to the room, Geoff and Linda were assumed to be asleep as there was no noise from their room and when Gail nodded off to sleep Jane mentally reviewed her first night. Overall it had been a huge success but there had certainly been blips along the way. She was happy to have made a friend in Gail and thought that she would get to know Geoff and Linda as the weekend wore on. She saw that there were unread messages from Phoebe on her phone and considered, albeit very briefly, if she should reply so late at night; then she began typing;

"Hi Babe RU da? "

After waiting only a few seconds and receiving no reply to the question, "are you there?" Jane continued;

"TISC. Hope UR KPC T2UL. XX" or "This is so cool. Hope you are keeping parents clueless. Talk to you later. Kisses"

She decided it wasn't the time to send anything to her parents but made a mental note to do so later in the morning. It was sometime before the tiredness took its grip and she fell asleep, only to be woken in what felt like a few minutes, but in reality was nearly six hours. It was late morning and Gail had brought her a glass of orange juice and a slice of toast.

"I didn't wake you for breakfast; you wouldn't have thanked me after so little sleep."

Rubbing the sleep from her eyes, Jane looked up at Gail who was now sat on the edge of her own bed; "Thanks." was about all that Jane could manage at this time.

"I'm going to get changed and go down to the bazaar with Linda. Geoff's gone out for a walk already."

Jane put down the glass after taking a sip from it and picked up the toast, "I'll catch up soon Gail, I need a shower first. See you down there?"

"No probs. See you later then."

Linda stepped into the room, "You ready Doll?"

"Coming"

Jane saw that Linda looked fantastic, dressed to the nines in Victorian splendour from hat to toe and was a little envious, she seemed to carry the style so well and with such confidence. She wondered if she would ever truly have that same confidence and not just that which she portrayed to others that masked the little doubt she had about her looks.

Finishing her toast she said goodbye to them both and arranged to meet up with them later, her excitement starting to kick in again. She used speed dial to call Phoebe, who answered straight away;

"Hya, tell me all about it then."

"It's great you should be here, the place is buzzing." she went on to talk in great detail about the previous night, with Phoebe listening intently. The conversation lasted a good half hour before Jane ended the call saying, "gotta go Babe, round two's under way. I said I'd meet them all at The Spa."

After hanging up she made another shorter call, to her parents, more a check in than anything else and confirmation that she was fit and well; enjoying her time at Phoebes?

It was another hour before Jane, coming to terms with the bright sunshine, walked the short distance back to The Spa, to the aptly named, Bizarre Bazaar. Held in the main hall of The Spa the bazaar was a mass of stalls catering for everything Goth, from small trinkets and badges to costumes costing many hundreds of pounds; it was also a place to see others and to be seen, to mingle and, in modern parlance, to network or create contacts and initiate friendships and swap ideas.

Jane caught up with Linda and Gail and enjoyed their company whilst looking around the stalls, happy to take advice from Linda in particular, who was being seen as a Goth Guru by both girls. It came at a cost however as Linda had expensive taste and Jane was keen to take her advice, spending a fortune on a new dress and boots and making a big dent in her budget for the rest of the weekend.

Packing the bags under her arms Jane walked with Gail and Linda, down to the coffee bar that stood adjacent to the main hall and yet had superb views directly out to sea; in fact the view suggested that the waves were rolling under the building and crashing into the walls beneath. Taking a large Moccachino with an extra shot of espresso to give her the lift she still felt she needed together with a Danish pastry, Jane spent the next hour, people watching and listening to Linda as she espoused stories of previous Goth weekends and of what to expect as this weekend wore on. She was at peace with the world and with herself, and when the caffeine kicked in she knew that she would be ready to commit to another round of promenading and dancing. Bring it on.

TWENTY ONE

"What issue do we have then Sue that you couldn't have told me about earlier?" Neil Maughan had stopped short of slamming the car door when he got in but he felt he could easily have done so.

"I'm sorry Neil, I meant to tell you but the time never seemed right."

"Well what is it?"

"It's Des. Well more specifically it's his daughter Gemma."

"Gemma, what is it? She's not had an accident or anything has she?"

"No. Maybe that would be better in some ways. She's causing all sorts of problems and Des is at his wits end. It's come to a point this week after him working all the twelve hour plus shifts we've had to work."

"She's at uni' isn't she?"

"She should have been; she's just walked away, packed it all in."

During the next hour's drive from Newby Wiske back to Whitby Sue Collins explained in as much detail as she could about Des Mason and his family problems. She apologised again for keeping it from her boss, explaining that she felt initially that she could keep it under wraps and deal with it herself.

"I can't believe it. " Sounding somewhat aghast at what he had heard, Neil Maughan got out of the car, now safely parked in the rear yard of Spring Hill Police Station and peered over the concrete wall panels across to the harbour and then to Aelfleda Terrace, almost on the horizon from his vantage point.

"I've asked him to come in to see me again tomorrow morning; will you be free to sit in as well if he turns up?"

"I'll make sure I'm free, what time?"

"I said to come in after the morning briefing, about half nine?"

"Good, put it in the diary. Who's picking up his tasks?"

"I've split them with Mark and myself, trying to cover without making an issue of it just for now."

"Right, that's got to stop. I need you fresh to work in your role as a Sergeant, not spending your time doing a DC's job. Get another D from the pool; if Des comes back he can cover division in lieu of whoever you get, that way he shouldn't have permanent long shifts."

"Will do sir," Sue Collins wanted to say more, to explain why she didn't think that the solution was quite so straight forward, but, in the rear yard of the police station, with other staff passing all too frequently she decided against it; "I'll go update the incident room then." She said as she turned on her heels and walked to the rear entrance door, leaving Neil Maughan staring out over the town.

Taking out his mobile phone he checked for messages and missed calls before making a call of his own, "Mark, are you free to speak?"

It is possibly only policemen that start a conversation in that way, but there was a pause at the other end before Mark Taylor said, "Go ahead now Boss." He had closed the office door, having seen Neil Maughan in the yard from his office window he had correctly assumed that it must be something he didn't want broadcasting to all.

"If what you're doing isn't urgent, desperate, pause it for now and meet me at Bothams in five minutes will you?"

"No problem, see you down there, no sugar in mine." Mark tried to inject some levity into the conversation but knew that something was bothering his Inspector to want to meet him away from the office.

Making his excuses Mark left the office and walked down Bobbies Bank from the Police Station, across to Wellington Road and into Baxtergate, reaching Bothams Cafe just as two coffees were being delivered to a table at the back of the premises, away from the busier street front seats.

Gesturing for Mark to sit down, Neil Maughan asked, "You ok Mark?"

"Yeah, fine, why?" knowing this wasn't just the usual greeting at the end of a days' work

"Well Sue's just brought me up to speed about Des and I wanted to see that you were ok."

"I'm fine boss thanks, but then I ain't got Des's problems to cope with have I?"

"Tell me about them"

"You said Sue had brought you up to speed, what can I say?"

"You don't need to be defensive Mark, that's why I've asked you to come here to talk. You work with Des every day, Sue supervises him but you know him better than almost anyone else in the job."

"Well if it's off the record Boss, I think he's struggling badly. Sue'll have told you about Gemma dropping out of uni I suppose?"

"Yeah"

"Well she's spent a fortune as well, all the funds that Des had put aside for her lodgings and stuff have gone; Thousands, she's addicted to some computer game or other, costs a fortune and draws you in, she's on it fifteen sixteen hours a day, only seems t stop for sleep."

"Bloody Hell, how can you do that? She was at Cambridge wasn't she?"

"Yeah, gifted kid, gone off the rails. If I hadn't seen it myself and listened to Des, I wouldn't have believed it."

"Where is she now?"

"I think at some friend's home in Egton. Des was going round there today but I haven't spoken to him since. If she has internet access there she'll be running up more debt if she can. Des has stopped all her bank cards and also the direct debit that paid for the internet but he's struggling to keep up as is Jill, his wife. As I said she's a smart kid."

The two continued to debate their colleague and Neil Maughan thanked Mark for his honesty and frankness before they walked back up to the station, each glad that their own domestic situations were on a better footing than those of a highly regarded co-worker and friend.

TWENTY TWO

"Spent up yet?" Geoff shouted across to the three girls as they walked along Marine Parade clutching at carrier bags and exchanging smiles. "There's always another outfit to be bought, you know that." Linda responded, seeing Geoff sat at a table outside a wine bar, watching the world go by.

Joining him at the table Linda sat down, placing her bags under her chair. Jane and Gail remained standing, realising that the couple probably wanted some time together. Gail broke the silence saying; "I fancy having a proper look at the shops, you coming?" she took Jane's arm and began walking away before even waiting for a response. "See you later."

The two new friends walked on, along the picturesque harbour side and towards the swing bridge, turning right onto Baxtergate, considered by many to be Whitby's main shopping street. The place was alive with Goths, not for them, dressing up just on a night time but seriously into the promenade; into showing off not just their costumes but their personalities, their diversity and yet somehow their individualism. Jane stopped to look in a shop window at a display full of Victorian splendour and was genuinely surprised to see that it was actually a charity shop. The whole of Whitby, it seemed, joined in this celebration of non conformity. She had to go inside.

In conversation with one of the shop staff Jane learnt that any items of clothing given as a donation and deemed suitable for selling at Goth weekend was put aside for just that reason and that most, if not all, charity shops in the town did the same; she went on to explain that other shops also traded what she called, pre-loved clothing, for a commission.

Gail had seen a lovely coat and was trying it on when Jane finished her conversation with the shop assistant; "that's fabulous Babe." She exclaimed, causing several other shoppers to turn towards them, one of whom shouted her agreement, "I tried it on, but it was too small, but it looks great on you."

Looking at the price tag of only £15 Gail saw that there was a sleeve button missing but otherwise the coat looked and felt perfect. "I'm having that." She said aloud, placing it on the counter and taking out cash to pay for it.

It was becoming a great day already as they continued their look around Whitby; crossing over the Swing Bridge onto the East side of town they turned left onto Sandgate, a very narrow street, with cafes, shops, a bakery and a photographers.

"Let's have our photo taken Jane?" Gail was visibly excited at the prospect of recording her day.

"OK. I'm up for it." Jane momentarily considered if the photo may get into her parents hands but decided that it was highly unlikely as she could keep it at Uni.

Making their way into the shop they were greeted by a tall, slim man, in maybe his early thirties, well dressed in what may have been described as formal attire, but was in fact his take on Victorian finery for the occasion.

"Good afternoon, how can I help you gorgeous ladies?" his voice bordered on condescending, twee and altogether a bit too sickly for Jane's liking, but Gail was not to be deterred.

"If we have a photo taken now when would it be ready?"

The man, who identified himself as Phillip, went on to give a whole range of options for the photographs; different sizes, different prices, with and without frames, colour, sepia or black and white variations. He was trying just too hard.

"We just want a nice photo of the two of us together." Jane's voice had a slight edge of impatience; this man was beginning to spoil what was so far a great day.

"That's no problem," Phillip picked up on the tone and immediately changed tack, suggesting a colour photo, 12" x 8" with a presentation folder. "They are £19.99 each or if you both wanted a copy I will do two for £35. They'll be ready in an hour."

"That's great." Gail made the decision for both of them and Jane relaxed a little.

Ten minutes afterwards they had paid for two photographs and were back on Sandgate, having agreed to return later in the day to collect them.

"Good afternoon, you gorgeous ladies" Jane mocked Phillips voice as they walked towards the Market Place, where a busker stood on the raised platform, between two of the four imposing pillars that acted as support for the building above and the clock tower above that. The busker was good, singing several different songs and playing his guitar well; a crowd of people gathered around, some stood, others sat on the steps beneath the platform. Gail and Jane watched and listened for a while, tossing some loose change into the flat cap placed on the ground in front before deciding to carry on their walk.

Walking carefully on cobbled Church Street and gazing into the windows of several jewellers, looking at the displays of Jet jewellery, much of which was described as being made on the premises the two found themselves outside of The Duke of York pub at the junction with Henrietta Street and within sight of the famous Abbey steps. Whether it was the smell of the food from inside or the sight of the menu at the door

Jane didn't know, but she did know that she now felt hungry and she suggested to Gail that they went in for something to eat.

Inside the place was about three quarters full, Jane estimated; nobody she recognised, but then again she didn't expect to and the clientele appeared to be a mixture of locals, tourists and Goths. As they made their way towards the bar Gail saw a table being vacated near to a window overlooking the River Esk and made a bee line for it, "Will you get me a pint of cider Jane; I'll grab these seats while I can?"

Gail was looking out at the view down towards the river mouth when Jane arrived with the drinks and two menus tucked under her arm.

"This place is great, I could live here." Gail said almost lost in the moment.

"First impressions are great but I've not seen too much talent yet, so I'll reserve my judgement."

Jane took a drink from her pint glass and let her eyes roam around the room, taking in everything and everyone whilst waiting for Gail to make her choice from the menu.

It would be quite some time before they were served she thought, best get comfy.

TWENTY THREE

Neil Maughan was in early the following morning, clearing up the backlog of emails and the day to day clerical that was all too easy to forget when a major investigation took place. He completed these tasks before anyone else from the team arrived and then made his way to the incident room and made sure all the updates were completed, the white boards refreshed and that there were no outstanding tasks.

He satisfied himself that everything was as it should be before setting up a new white board and using a new red marker pen splitting it into four different sections, which he gave titles to; the first, absolute facts, followed by, facts (to be confirmed), possibilities and finally comments \ remarks. He then cleared another board and beginning in the centre he started writing, his own brainstorming session, no holds barred, nothing too trivial, nothing taken for granted, just emptying his mind onto the board in what anyone watching would describe as total random scribbling. The usual location, victim, motive, suspects etcetera were all included as were the known facts about the jewellery, age and sex of the victim, timescale and method of disposal of the body. Over the next half hour or so he continued in this vein until the board was almost completely covered with words and then lines drawn in different colours linking different aspects to each other. Yes, it would all be stored on The HOLMES 2 system but this way he could look at it and ponder, make the links first hand and review what was left; it was his own approach, but one which had stood him in good stead for many years and one which he did not wish to let go.

"Bloody Hell Neil, did you shit the bed?" Ian Jackson had entered the incident room expecting to find it empty at this time of day and was surprised to see Neil Maughan staring at the boards, looking as though he had done a days' work already.

"Morning Ian, no, I haven't shit the bed, but I find if I can get in early, before the day staff I can often get more done in a couple of hours than I can the rest of the day."

"You can, but you don't get any medals for all the extra time you're putting in." Ian Jackson was displaying his usual indifferent self, albeit one that did not show his true colours of always wanting to do the right thing, but only up to the end of the shift, not before or after, at least without overtime pay.

"What brings you up here Ian?"

"I try to look at the boards if I'm on early turn then if I get a low baller from the press I can manoeuvre out of the way without saying anything I shouldn't, and anyway it's the only way us uniforms get to know what's going on."

"You know the score Ian, we can't have everyone knowing everything now can we? That way there'd be no mystery about us detectives."

The two chatted for a while, Neil Maughan asking Ian to make sure that uniform crews were thanked for their efforts so far and advising him in broad terms what position the investigation was now at, before settling down to prepare for the formal briefing that was to follow shortly.

"Good Morning everyone, it is 8.35am on Wednesday 23rd January 2013 and this is the twelfth day of Operation Caedmon. I want to keep this briefing short if I can as there are some issues I have to attend to outside the meeting. At present we still do not have an identity of the missing person, who can tell me anything about where we are with that?"

"We now have every known and reported female misper from the country on the system but the intelligence is changing daily, we have obviously narrowed down from the thousands initially listed to a few hundred that have been long term missing and that fit our profile." Mark Taylor sounded exhausted at the sheer magnitude of just this part of the task." We are now looking at those for which we can make a DNA search against our controlled sample from the deceased."

"Good, thank you Mark, but keep up with it, the sooner we have ID the better. Anything from the builders or Letting Agents yet?"

"I've been given the follow up for that Boss." An unfamiliar voice from the side of the room piped up, "DC Alderson sir, Geoff Alderson, I'm new to the Division and have been told to report here this morning."

"Welcome to the team Geoff, we'll catch up later for a proper introduction. I'm keen to get this information from the Wilcock's checked and followed up so we can open up that side of the investigation. I want personal visits not phone calls and I don't want any fob offs about old paperwork, I want answers today please."

Neil Maughan saw Geoff's' introduction as an opportunity to explain Des Masons' absence, "You will all have noticed that DC Des Mason is missing this morning, he is coming in to see me shortly but all you need to know is that for personal reasons he is returning to Eastern Area duties; I wish to thank him for his work so far on Operation Caedmon and also to confirm that this return to core duties in no way reflects detrimentally on his commitment to the role. I know that he would wish to remain"

Several of those around the table began talking quietly amongst themselves, obviously questioning the reasons behind this turn of events causing Neil Maughan to call order again,

"Ladies and Gents, I want no further discussion about this, we have enough work on our hands with this case and I require your total attention. Now let's get on with the briefing."

Further tasks were again allocated and it was Ian Jackson who reminded Neil that a further press release may be worthwhile, "Elli Stanford is pestering again and whilst she's been repeatedly told to ring the press office it's easier for her to come here. Yorkshire Coast Radio have also asked for an update." he added

"I'll sort something out Ian, thank you. I appreciate that it may seem to be a nuisance but we actually need to keep them onside, they can be a valuable source of communication."

It was 9.30am on the dot when Sue Collins knocked on the door of Neil Maughan's office and was invited in; she was accompanied by Des Mason who, in turn, looked tired and the jovial, bouncy personality that usually defined him was noticeable by its absence. Neil Maughan shook his hand and closed the door behind him, moving his seat around the desk in order to sit nearer to Des and without a physical barrier between them, Neil opened up the conversation,

"I'm sorry Des, I didn't know until yesterday."

"You've a lot on your plate Boss; I didn't want to add my troubles to your workload. I don't want to let you down."

"Des, people, family, always come first. How is Jill?"

"Her Mum's come round today, Gemma's at her friends, Amy Walton at Egton. I'm going around there when I leave here."

"As you know, I've spoken to Sue and to Mark, as far as I know there is nobody else aware of any of this and obviously it won't go any further, but I need to know what I can do to help you. Have you signed off sick officially?"

"No." there was a degree of panic in his voice; "I don't want to go off sick." he looked at both Neil Maughan and Sue Collins trying to judge their respective responses.

"Des, I need focused cops on my team, I know that you would never let me down but you need time to get around this, get some help if need be and Jill will need your support too."

"Can't I just take some leave? I haven't had a day's sick in the last three years and I don't want it on my record."

"I'm not a fan of staff using annual leave to cover for sickness Des, it's got to be your decision as to whether you feel you are ill or not but you certainly need some time." turning his attention to Sue he continued, "What leave does Des have left?"

"I've checked after our chat yesterday and he still has 32 hours left, plus 4 rest days in lieu so we can say at least a week."

61

"Des take the week and see how you go. Have you been in touch with welfare?"

"No. What can they do, it's my problem?"

"They are there to support us all; you probably don't even know the ways that they can help. Will you let me speak to them on your behalf?" There was a longer pause than anyone expected and it only finished when Des broke down, he began sobbing, rubbing his eyes with his hands before reaching into his trouser pocket for the handkerchief he knew he had.

"I'm sorry," he said, "I just don't know what to do. She won't talk to me, that's why she's gone to Amy's. Her parents have spoken to me and said she can stay as long as necessary but what does that make me look like?" Both Neil and Sue provided words of comfort and support to their colleague who continued to fall apart in front of them. He had been, from the outside at least the model parent to a gifted child and yet here he was in tatters with his daughter staying at someone else's home. Over the next thirty to forty minutes Des related the whole story again, including details of the debt that had been run up, the terrible toll that the addiction to an online computer game had caused; the betrayal felt by Des and Jill and the lack of trust they felt they now had in their eldest child and the knock effect it was having on their younger son, who was getting left out amidst the domestic turmoil.

"If you're not coping Des, there is help available. Please go see your Doctor, please speak with the welfare team and please take as much time as you need. I will help in any way I can and Sue likewise will keep in touch. I think you need to go to Egton now, but promise me that you will keep me up to date."

A few minutes later Des Mason left the Police Station and drove to Egton, tears dried on his face as he made the short journey, heart in mouth, not knowing what sort of reception he was going to get; his daughter seeing him as the ogre, the one who had done everything to cut off her main raison d'être.

Having closed his office door behind him Neil Maughan looked across to Sue Collins and sighed, "Families eh, give me a murder to solve any day."

TWENTY FOUR

After a longer stop at the Duke of York than either Gail or Jane had planned, realised or expected, the time had reached 6.17pm and they stood again on Sandgate, outside the photographers and looked at the sign on the door saying, Closed, a further sign adjacent to that, indicated that the shop would open again at 10.30am the following morning until 5.30pm.

"Fuck it!" Jane exclaimed.

"Don't worry; we can always come back tomorrow."

"Yeah, s'pose so."

It was two slightly dejected Goths that headed back towards the swing bridge only to hear a bell sounding and the barriers being closed by a man dressed in the fluorescent yellow uniform of Scarborough Borough Council. Having closed the East Side to both pedestrian and vehicular traffic the man from the council made his way back across the bridge and repeated the process with the West Side barrier before retreating into his small shed-like building that abutted the bridge. Hidden from public view the man operated whatever mechanism was contained therein and the bridge began its swinging motion, thereby opening to allow waterborne traffic access to the harbour mouth and vice versa.

Within a matter of minutes there were huge numbers of pedestrians either side of the river, some with large shopping bags, others, probably tourists with carrier bags and rucksacks. Jane looked around and suggested that they have another drink at The Dolphin pub which was immediately next to the bridge and had a small tabled area outside the front door. Gail took little persuading, although she did want to watch the trawler set out on its journey to sea, a throw back almost to the days when this sight would have been much more frequently seen.

Jane stood at the bar and ordered two drinks, looking across to Gail who was stood near to a window and watching as the bridge began to close again.

"Hi there." a voice Jane didn't recognise but which was obviously aimed towards her sounded to her left. She turned in that direction and saw a very well built man, possibly in his late twenties, six foot tall she estimated and, she thought, gorgeous. Dressed in black trousers and a black polo t-shirt he asked,

"Are you enjoying your weekend?"

Unsure who he was, but all too willing to engage in conversation she smiled and replied, "Yeah, great time thanks," before adding, "do I know you?"

"No, sorry, I'm Mike. I was at The Res' last night when that idiot started giving you some grief."

Jane had forgotten the incident but remembered the brief incident when one of the youths shouted at her group.

"Oh I'd not even thought about it. There's always some Dick Head about who can't hold his beer."

Mike smiled at the comment and Jane thought that this made him even more attractive, his big, somewhat weathered face, positively beamed with his bright white teeth to the fore, his dark, close cropped hair and designer stubble framing his features and emphasising his broad grin.

"I work at The Res' on the door, so maybe see you up there again eh?"

"Sure will, are you going now?"

"Got to, late already but I'll blame it on the bridge, just caught sight of you and thought I'd say hello."

"Glad you did. See you later then." Jane was in seventh heaven; after all he had chosen to approach her hadn't he?

"Hey smiler, remember me?" Gail had been stood watching Jane and Mike and didn't want to spoil the moment, but now wanted to ask all about it.

"Who's that then? He's lush."

"His name's Mike, he works at The Res, yer know, where we went last night."

"And no doubt where we'll be heading back to, sometime tonight?"

"Oh Yes. Now here, get that down yer neck." she passed Gail her drink and they giggled as they sat looking out at the river again. A roller coaster of emotions for Jane continued, but she was certainly looking up at the moment and already making plans about what she would be wearing later that night for her second Goth night out in Whitby.

TWENTY FIVE

"Sir, I've got the statements from Atkins Builders, the Boss there is a man called, Len Thompson now, he's been at the firm for about twelve years, mostly as a foreman then he bought the business when old man Atkins retired but kept the name as it is a well regarded business locally. Len says he has no records of any work at Esk View in the last twenty years, which is when they started the computer records. He did confirm that they had done some work previously, including the patio in 1989 that Mr Wilcock mentioned."

DC Geoff Alderson passed the written statement and a copy invoice to Neil Maughan for him to read before continuing; "Apparently Mr Wilcock was a good payer but always wanted the best possible job at the cheapest possible price and was unhappy with a couple of bills he got so stopped using Atkins and asked the agents to sort out another cheaper option."

"Thanks Geoff and welcome to the team." Neil Maughan recognised the intuitive nature of a good detective when he looked at the fresh faced cop in front of him, "And you've seen the Agent?"

"Yes sir," he replied handing over a second statement.

Reading through the second statement Neil Maughan saw that the work had been done by a handyman service under the trading name of Abbey Property Services, before seeing that they were no longer trading as far as the agent was aware.

"A proper bodge it and scarper outfit, just shows you get what you pay for."

"I've started to ask around already sir, it's only a couple of years since the work was done so I'm sure someone will know who it is."

"I've been here a long time Geoff and I can't place the name but I know the font of all knowledge that is Jean, will know. Let's go ask her."

Walking down the stairs to the ground floor Neil updated his new DC, filling in the gaps in his knowledge, both of the investigation and his new place of work. On entering the front office, Neil saw Jean typing whilst talking to someone on the phone and seemingly passing instructions to one of the uniformed cops sat on a table near to her. It was a very relaxed office most of the time, but everyone knew how far they could go with both the bosses and Jean and that if either made it clear that it was time to leave then there was no arguing.

Waiting for the phone call to finish Neil stood behind Jean, took in the view across the harbour, visible from every window on the East side of the building and pointed across to Aelfleda Terrace, or what was left of it anyway. In a hushed voice he pointed out the key locations, access points and landmarks pertinent to the investigation and introduced Geoff to the other staff present. Jean, for her part, knew he was there and having not met the new boy was keen to end her call and meet him.

"Thank you, we'll let you know if anything turns up. Bye" with a loud sigh Jean ended the call and turned to her visitors saying, "Bloody tourists, how can you be so stupid?"

Neil knew not to ask for any further information and gestured with a raised eyebrow to Geoff before introducing the two to each other.

"Jean, we need some local info." Geoff, after the formalities were concluded carried on, "I'm told there is nothing that you don't know or can't find out."

"I know, but they don't pay me any extra."

"Have you heard of Abbey Property Services?"

"He's keen," Jean directed her comment to Neil but gestured to Geoff with a flick of her head, "first one not to ask if the kettle's on, then ask about the job."

"He'll go far Jean, by the way, is the kettle on?"

Walking into the small adjacent room, followed by the two detectives, Jean switched the kettle on and put two teabags into the teapot. "Abbey Property Services were a real fly by night affair, it was an odd job team run by Willie Raynor, gave work to anyone for a backhander, no questions asked."

"Willie Raynor? Give me a clue Jean."

"He's on the rigs now, but his wife Ann, used to be Ann Clifford from Stakesby Vale; she still takes on work for him, why?"

"Need to know basis Jean, where do they live now?"

"On the new Persimmon estate somewhere I'll look it up for you, they do a small ad in the Gazette sometimes, not that they need the money now, he's raking it in from the rigs."

Jean returned to her desk and took out an old copy of the Whitby Gazette from one of the drawers, scanning the pages she soon found the small box advert and copied it on the nearby Xerox.

"Thanks Jean. Much appreciated." Geoff Alderson was very impressed, both with the knowledge and the tea. Making their way back upstairs to the incident room Neil Maughan directed his colleague to make enquiries into Willie Raynor a priority.

"I want to know more about him and his company than his mother knows."

"I'll try to get more than even Jean knows" Geoff Alderson quipped, already feeling that he had made some progress towards integration into the team.

Smiling, Neil Maughan replied, "Just remember Geoff you're in Whitby now, kick one person today and you'll find twenty limping tomorrow; word soon spreads. Tread carefully."

"Will do Boss, I'll just update the incident room and I'll make a start."

It was a slightly more upbeat Neil Maughan that returned to his office, could this be the breakthrough that he had been waiting for?

TWENTY SIX

Sat crossed leg on her bed Jane was updating Phoebe, in truth she couldn't wait to tell her about Mike and had rung immediately on returning to Harbour View.

"He's absolutely fit as."

"Are you meeting him then?"

"Well he's working again tonight but I'll make sure I see him, if yer know what I mean?"

"You're an absolute tart, Jane Hammond." Phoebe laughed as she spoke, knowing that Jane would be looking for any opportunity to bed this man if he was even half as fit as she said he was.

"I'll be the real Scouse Vixen tonight, given half the chance."

They chatted a while longer before Jane ended the call as she planned to contact her parents and then had to get changed, but only after confirming that she would text later.

Jane showered and then dressed in a new costume, bought for the occasion and one which emphasised her womanly curves to best effect. The new Vollers corset required assistance from Gail to fasten at the back, a short leather skirt over hold up stockings and Victorian style ankle boots with a suitably high heel. Jane felt on top of the world and when Gail complimented her on how she looked after helping with her makeup, she gave her a hug and thanked her profusely.

Geoff and Linda had already gone out as they planned to eat at Trenchers, the fish restaurant on Newquay Road before joining the others at The Resolution later in the evening. Jane and Gail drank a large vodka and orange each before leaving The Harbour View and walking down Skinner Street to The Res. The place was absolutely buzzing and there were large groups of Goths just stood in the road on Flowergate, drinking, smoking and generally just enjoying being there. A look up towards the Old Church House opposite indicated that the groups were being monitored by the CCTV operator, now based in Scarborough with radio and telephone links to the police control room; it being somewhat convolutedly based in York.

"There's Mike," Gail had to shout to be heard above the noise of everyone around her, "On the bottom door."

"Let's see if we can get in there then?" Jane responded, walking down the hill to the bottom door.

Mike was stood in the entrance to the pub alongside a colleague, each dressed in the standard black uniform all door staff seem to wear these days, a polo shirt with the single word, STAFF, printed in yellow across it's back and left breast and a laminated badge worn on their upper arms being the only distinguishing features to single them out from the customers of whom over ninety per cent were also dressed in black.

"Wow, look at you then." Mike recognised Jane but only after she had walked directly up to him,

"You like?" she teased,

"Sure do, pity I'm working."

"Not all night, you're not?" Jane presumed that Mike would finish when the pub closed at 1.00am.

"You never know in this job. Here, come on in. The bottom bar isn't as busy as the others; it'll save you some waiting time."

"Thanks." Jane and Gail squeezed past the two doormen and into the pub, making a beeline for the bar. Buying two pints of cider Jane looked back towards the door and saw that Mike and his colleague, whose name they didn't get, were busy refusing entry to someone all too obviously drunk. The woman, who wouldn't seem to take no for an answer began shouting the usual obscenities associated with drunken females when directed at male door staff, but to no avail. Her friends or so Jane assumed, took her by the arms and began ushering her away from the door.

"He's going to be busy tonight," Gail pointed at Mike before continuing, "let's party and you can catch up with him later."

"Let's go upstairs then where the music's on."

They carried their drinks up the carpeted stair way to the middle bar which was packed; there was no seating to be seen and very little standing room, the dance floor was full and the queues for drinks were four deep at least all along the length of the bar.

They inched their way into the throng, part dancing, part walking looking to find Geoff and Linda but without any luck.

The industrial music of Throbbing Gristle played loudly to the mass and further encouraged the different sections of Goths to separate into their sub groups, the Trads seemingly as one vacated the dance floor, taking their opportunity to return to their tables or outside for a cigarette or just to mingle. Jane and Gail waited a while, people watching and just savouring the atmosphere before exiting onto the street. The road outside now resembled a music festival and there were cars at the top of the street unable to get through; all the way down to The Elsinore, which some believed to be the original and favourite Goth pub, and the triangle formed by that, The Little Angel opposite and up to the more recently popular Resolution, Goths gathered, stopped to chat and to show off their finest garb.

Jane saw that Mike was still busy, indeed he didn't even appear to make eye contact at that time such was the crush at the doors.

69

Two Police Officers attended in a marked van from the direction of the Pannett Park above, drove past the waiting traffic, slowly, but with blue lights flashing as they needed to pass. This caused everyone to look towards them, some cheered, and other's jeered as the two cops, both male, exited the van in their bright yellow coats with stab proof vests very much evident. Drivers of waiting cars shouted at the cops, "This happens every year; it's a bloody joke," was one shout, others were less polite but conveyed a similar message, while some of The Goths saw the presence of the officers as provocative in itself and jeered them even more as they asked the masses to clear the road. It was a thankless task as it appeared each time some made way by stepping back onto the footpaths that others had to step out into the road to make way. There simply wasn't sufficient room as Jane estimated a crowd of up to three thousand plus were grouped together in such a small space. Thankfully, at least so far, everyone appeared to be in good spirits, including the cops who seemed to accept that their task of clearing the road was a thankless one and returned to their van, from which they took out a number of once bright, yellow cones and placed them across the road together a blue, road closed sign.

There was a loud cheer from The Goth groups in the triangle who saw this as a small victory and one which meant that the road had now become a pedestrian walkway on which they could continue to promenade and drink, despite the nearby signs suggesting that it was an offence to do so. No doubt the locals would have something to say the following week when their town returned to normal, but for now at least, it appeared that a decision based on common sense had been taken rather than one which could have turned the evening nasty.

Jane and Gail took full advantage of the situation by using the whole road to mingle with their new found friends and were soon chatting with others in the middle of what was normally a main thoroughfare for vehicles. Jane saw Gail operating at her cool best in chatting up a fellow Goth; a tall dark haired, but then weren't they all, slim man, dressed in black from head to toe and a smile that lit up the street. Jane watched as Gail tilted her head slightly to one side as she listened to a joke told by the man, laughing slightly longer than most others in the group and brushing her hair to one side subtly but elegantly. Gail looked across to Jane, almost as if asking for permission to continue, to leave Jane if she got lucky? Jane thought only that she would just get on with it and hope for the best; the best being getting laid by a very good looking bloke; she smiled at Gail and nodded her approval. Gail smiled back and edged closer to the man, engaging him in conversation and making her play for his attention. Jane knew that her play would be successful as she had seen the man returning her smiles with his own; and without speaking wished her well. She in turn edged away, thereby not distracting her friend from her mission.

TWENTY SEVEN

"William Edward Raynor, born eleven, eight, seventy two at Scarborough, currently resident at 72 Resolution Way, Whitby with his wife Ann Marie Raynor, nee Clifford, born twenty two, six, seventy four at Whitby. He runs a handyman stroke Repair Company, Abbey Property Services, on an ad-hoc basis and may be our first real suspect in this investigation." Neil Maughan was speaking at the latest briefing of Operation Caedmon and was drumming up enthusiasm, giving news of what he considered to be positive progress.

"The paperwork in front of you gives details of all those people who we believe at this time to have worked for him over the past three years. I want visits to each and everyone to be a priority; I want to know what work they did, where and with whom. It is my belief that the patio at Esk View was laid by someone working for Raynor, if not by Raynor himself; obviously that places someone at the scene of our crime. I want to know who that was."

Maughan was aware of everyone now scanning the list of workers on the printed sheets on the table but continued;

"Our enquiries suggest that Raynor is working on the rigs at the moment and is due back home, which is one of the new Persimmon homes, at the end of next week. Checks on the Intel system show he has previous for assault, public order and driving offences, nothing significant but a record all the same. There is also a lot of information that suggests most of his work is done on cash in hand basis which may just be useful to us later on. DC Geoff Alderson has been tasked to build up that Intel and to ensure it is all fed into this enquiry, Sue I want you to allocate a D to each of the names on that list and I want some answers soonest."

There was a buzz around the room and Neil Maughan didn't want it to falter so he ended the briefing sooner than planned and indicated that a de-brief of the day would take place at 5.30pm that night.

Returning to his office Neil Maughan had to decide whether to go to Raynor, on the rigs, or to wait for him to return home? On the one hand, the option to go to the rig may have the element of surprise, on the other, Raynor could reasonably just refuse to talk to him without his solicitor present and that was a non starter in Maughan's opinion. The alternative would be to speak to him at Spring Hill and if that meant an arrest, with subsequent conditional bail then so be it. There was always the tax evasion element that could be introduced to create an opportunity to exert some control. Shame really, a trip to Aberdeen wouldn't be all bad.

Ringing Simon Pithers was the next step, an update and at last a positive one, the step in the right direction that they had all been looking for from the outset.

"Good work Neil, make sure everyone on the team knows my position on this, that I am pleased so far." Simon Pithers stopped just short of real congratulations; he would save that for the time when a suspect was convicted. "I'll work something up for the press as they haven't had anything for a while, nothing worth the print any way, though Elli Stanford doesn't give up I get a call at least twice a day from her."

"Thanks sir, I get the same calls too, trying to get in through any avenue she can."

"No problem. How has Geoff Alderson fit in?"

"Very well sir, I've been impressed so far."

"He's a good lad Neil, don't spoil him. Not everyone grew up in the old school of John Regan and The Sweeney; we're not all Diamond Geezers"

"Mores' the pity some would say."

Moving the conversation back to the matter in hand, Simon Pithers continued,

"Neil, I'd like you and Sue to visit this Ann Raynor, put some pressure on to get some answers about that patio; I dare say she'll deny all knowledge but she'll know who laid it and possibly then, who our killer is or at least a first real suspect?"

"Will do sir, I'll speak after the de-brief this evening."

Placing the phone back in its place on the desk, Neil Maughan, sighed aloud as he leant back in his chair, hands intertwined behind his head. He was still in that position when Mark Taylor, knocked and entered his room;

"Sorry Boss but I thought you'd want to see this," holding out a copy of the latest Whitby Gazette, folded in half to show only the headline;

NO PROGRESS SO FAR IN WHITBY MURDER ENQUIRY.

Followed by an article that started;

"Despite it being nearly three weeks since the body of a young female was found on Whitby's historic East Cliff, in what Police at the time referred to as suspicious circumstances, no progress seems to have been made in naming a suspect or finding the person responsible.

Chief reporter Elli Stanford has made numerous enquiries with North Yorkshire Police, including almost daily contact with the Senior Investigating Officer in the case, Detective Inspector Neil Maughan and has so far been unable to put a name to the deceased or obtain any statement from The Police as to the cause of death or the state of the enquiry so far. We believe it is in the best interest of the Whitby residents to ask, "Have we a killer in our midst?"

The remainder of the article was padded out by repeating quotes made by either D/Supt Pithers or D/Inspector Maughan given in earlier press releases. Neil Maughan saw it for what it was; deliberately inflammatory and designed to elicit a response and sell more copy. He was however, still very much pissed off; he had always tried to keep the press onside and wasn't it only a few minutes ago that he had actually asked the Superintendent for a new press release?

"Fuckin' Hell Mark, her timing's brilliant."

"I know Boss, she's been on the blower again today and I said we'd have something later. Obviously she thought I was just palming her off again but she must have known what was on the front page when she rang?"

"Well bollocks to 'em. Let's get this Willie Raynor in and see what we can squeeze out of him."

Neil Maughan picked up the phone again, a hint to Mark that he was pushing on with his work and that he should do the same.

TWENTY EIGHT

It was just before midnight when Jane entered The Spa pavilion, she was with Gail and her new man, or Ashley as she now knew him to be and a group of about eight others that had made their way from the triangle. Jane had spoken to Mike who had been busy all night and looked likely to be for some time yet. He had told her that he would come up to The Spa when he finished at about half past one, "Barring disasters." He added cautiously as he gave her a peck on the cheek and a squeeze on the arse.

Jane was very upbeat for the next hour or so and was going mental on the dance floor to the beat of electro body music from Faderhead, XR-X, Eisenfunk, and Nachtmah. Glow sticks in hand she was high, not on drink or chemical substances, but on the expectation of passion with Mike. She accepted that she was being almost childish in her actions and thoughts but was even happier for being so, she was being Jane, finding the person she truly believed herself to be, not the one her parents had groomed her to be.

After what seemed to be only a matter of minutes the DJ announced that it was time for the last of the music and that the lights would be turned on after the beats stopped. The dance floor was full and Jane was close to exhausted but excited and wired. When the lights did go on Jane sat down and finished her drink before it was collected by the bar staff who quite obviously wanted to get home. Gail came over to her and said;

"Will you be OK Doll? I'm going back to Ashley's."

"You dirty bitch." Jane quipped, jealous but pleased at the same time. Hoping that she too would be absent from a Harbour View breakfast. They hugged briefly before Gail saw Ashley stood near to the door and let Jane go, saying her goodbyes as she made her way towards him.

Jane waved and watched them walk out together before emptying her glass, placing it on the table and following them out. As she reached the end of the long driveway up from the Spa towards the car park Jane saw just what she had hoped for; Mark was sat on the low wall, watching for her leaving and, standing up as he saw her, he smiled and waved to make sure she could see him. Jane ran the short distance to him and threw her arms around him. A short distance away Gail saw this and smiled to herself; result.

TWENTY NINE

It was only about half a mile away but Sue Collins and Neil Maughan took a car anyway. As they drove down Resolution Way, first built, he thought, in the 1960's but extended over the last few years by Persimmon Homes, Neil Maughan reflected on the fact that he knew at least two uniformed officers lived on the estate and that when he was first posted to Whitby, he too had considered doing the same. It was once considered an up and coming postcode to some of the incomers but his wife, Helen, had wanted somewhere free of cops, somewhere where the family could forget policing when Neil wasn't at work.

Number 72 was a large detached house on a corner plot, with lawned gardens to the front, a driveway up to a double garage and a large wooden gate to the side which in turn afforded access to an even larger rear garden with views across fields and down towards Ruswarp and the iconic railway viaduct.

Arriving at 8.50am, following the early morning briefing, the detectives were very much aware that there would be curtains twitching along the street as they walked the short distance from the car to the driveway; not much got past the inquisitive housewives of this neighbourhood. Dressed smartly in their respective suits they would be easily identifiable as cops or else mistaken for Jehovah's witnesses; Sue Collins wasn't sure which was worse?

Before they had chance to ring the door bell the front door opened and a slightly dishevelled woman, dressed in jogging bottoms and tee shirt, stood before them.

"Hello?" questioned the woman, seemingly surprised at the two visitors' presence.

"Mrs Raynor?" Sue Collins returned the question with one of her own.

"Yes."

"I'm Detective Sergeant Suzanne Collins and this is Detective Inspector Neil Maughan, we'd like to have a word with you please." Sue Collins was already inching forward to confirm the suggestion that they should be invited inside.

"Has something happened? Is Willie OK?"

It was obvious that Ann Raynor was not aware of the reason for the visit and had taken it as bad news from the oil rig; a reasonable assumption considered Sue Collins as it's not every day you get a surprise visit from two police officers.

"We're not here to give you that sort news." She reassured, "But we would like to speak with you if we may?"

Ann Raynor held open the uPVC door and indicated for the officers to enter, closing the door behind her, but not before looking out to see whom she could catch sight of watching her.

Directing them through to a room to the left of the small hallway Ann Raynor started tidying up as they entered, why is it she thought, that you only get visitors when the place is untidy? In truth it was apparent that, like in so many households at this time in a morning, the kids have just left for school and they have left the usual bombsite behind them, clothes thrown over chair arms, laptops left on the floor, shoes under tables etc. Plumping up cushions she gestured for them to sit down on a large cream sofa, opposite the cinema sized screen television on the wall. Ann Raynor sat down in a chair to one side and nervously asked,

"What's up then if it's not about Willie?"

Taking the lead now, Neil Maughan responded,

"Well it's not about Willie's health and well being but we do have some questions about his property repair company."

"Oh, he hardly bothers with it now. He only keeps a few older customers on that have regular custom; ya know like holiday cottages an' that; when they can't get over to do it themselves"

Great, thought Neil Maughan, a good starter for ten. It always seems to work that if you allow people the time to talk they will give you more information than they intended to.

"Do you get involved in the business?"

"Well while he's away he can't take the phone calls can he?" She was feeling aggrieved now, as though she knew she shouldn't have said anything at all.

"So do you take all the calls and book the work in?"

"I have to when he's not here. Look what's this all about? We've done nowt wrong."

"I haven't suggested otherwise Mrs. Raynor, but we are investigating the suspicious death on The East Cliff and we believe that your husband's firm may have done some work there in the past."

"Well he ain't murdered anyone if that's what you're thinking."

"Mrs. Raynor we haven't said anything of the sort, we merely need to confirm whether your husband's firm have done any work at the cottages on Aelfleda Terrace in the past three years."

"I dun no, can't it wait 'til he comes home next week?"

"I'm afraid it can't. As I said this is an investigation into a suspicious death and we would ask for your co-operation."

"Look can we start again? Can I get you a drink, a cup of tea or coffee?"

Ann Raynor was now starting to think on her feet and was playing for time. There was a doubt in her mind as to what could be hidden in the information that they were asking for. She didn't consider, nor had she ever considered that Willie was involved in anything like hiding a body; she knew of course that he took backhanders and avoided paying any taxes where they could be avoided, i.e. cash in hand work was never declared but what did the cops want?

"No thank you, not for me." Neil Maughan was the first to respond. Taking the lead from her superior, Sue Collins responded in kind, "Thank you but it's not long since I had one."

"What records do you have at home Mrs. Raynor?" Neil Maughan continued.

"Well I've got my diaries and workbooks but they've got all my contact details in them, I'll need them if any work does come in."

"Can we have a look please?"

This was said in such a way as to leave Ann Raynor in no uncertainty that they would be looked at with or without her permission and that with may be the best option.

"I'll go and get them."

Neil Maughan didn't feel it necessary to accompany her to an adjacent room that had been set up as an office or study, after all Willie Raynor was literally at sea and couldn't return if he wanted to.

Returning a short while later, Ann Raynor handed three A4 size diaries to Neil Maughan, having made the decision to leave her filofax and laptop where they were on the desk and not to bring anything else from the office other than what was directly asked for.

"These are what I book the jobs into, but it's all in my handwriting and you may not understand it all."

"I'm sure we'll manage Mrs Raynor; and if not we can always come back." Neil Maughan left that thought to hang in the air before asking;

"Who allocates the work and who do you have on your books?"

"Like I said, there's not much now, just the regulars."

"Do you have a regular workforce too?"

"Not as such, we just get people in as we need them."

Sue Collins recognised this as the lie that it was but let it go; she knew that one lie often led to another and that you need to have a very good memory to be a good liar; she wasn't sure that Ann Raynor was.

"Who does your accounts Mrs Raynor?" continued Maughan

"I do, but they go to an accountant for tax returns and stuff like that." she was now starting to feel uncomfortable.

"Which one?"

"Birtles and Durant on Victoria Square"

"We may need to see the books at some time, but we can wait for that until we've gone through the diaries first."

"What are you looking for? We haven't done owt wrong. I've even told him to pack it in cos we don't need the money now."

"When does Willie get home?" asked Sue Collins

"Thursday, but it depends on the weather up there, if they can get the chopper out to the rig."

"We will need to speak with him too."

"What's this about, you said it was the East Cliff thing but you're asking about our books not anything to do with the body."

"Do you know anything about the body?"

"No, course not. I was just saying." Ann Raynor was showing her nerves now and reacting just as the detectives thought she would under even just a little pressure.

"Well we'll leave you to the rest of your day now Mrs. Raynor. Thank you for your help."

"What about the diaries, when can I have them back?"

"We'll be in touch, but it won't be anytime soon."

"But I need them."

"So do we, I'll write you a receipt." again Neil Maughan was not asking but telling.

"You'll hear from my solicitor about this, I can't run my business without them."

"Mrs Raynor, I will leave you with my business card. Your solicitor will be able to contact me at Spring Hill Police Station, the numbers on there." He handed the card to her and headed for the hallway and back towards the front door.

"You wanna stop going after us hard working folk and sort out them bloody druggies and burglars in town if you ask me." Ann Raynor half shouted as they left. There was no reply necessary.

THIRTY

Walking along the beach from The Spa towards the slipway Jane was almost in seventh heaven, in fact it was only the biting cold offshore wind that dampened her spirits; that was until Mike removed his jacket and wrapped it around her shoulders. She snuggled into him, wrapping her arms around his waist and staring upwards into his dark eyes she leant in for the first kiss that would lead, hopefully, to many more.

Much as it was very enjoyable to both, the cold wind dictated that they wouldn't remain on the beach for long; they made their way up the slipway and along St. Anne's Staith towards the swing bridge. There were other small gatherings of people, Goths and locals, some in couples and others in groups of both males and females; some quite obviously drunk, others not quite. Much the same as in most urban areas at this time of night but with the exception that more than half were dressed in the black clothing that was so prevalent this weekend.

Having made their way over the bridge, Mike tapped on the window of The Dolphin pub and almost immediately it was opened by another man dressed similarly to Mike but, in the opinion of Jane without the looks. Inside were a group of four men and three women all in their late twenties or early thirties, sat around a table at the side of the bar and out of the view of the windows. Mike introduced Jane to the group who were staff at The Dolphin and friends of his with whom he regularly spent time whilst coming down from the oft adrenaline fuelled shifts as a doorman. Jane was at first disappointed, she had wanted to be with Mike, to have him to herself and not to share. She had already been drinking but of course they had not, they had all been working until only a short time ago. Introductions made however she sat down and joined in with the jocularity and banter.

Drinks flowed, inhibitions lowered and time passed. Jane really was enjoying herself and she felt that Mike was too, he had introduced her to his close friends without any conditions or preconceived ideas of how she would adapt to them and them to her. It was, she thought, everything she could have asked for at this stage, and that was the only note of caution; at this stage?

As the clock ticked around to 4.00am Mike took the hint from Jane that she wanted to be with him and they made their move to leave, saying their goodbyes to all they left by the front door and Jane asked;

"Where are we going?"

"It's not far. I'm doing some work on a couple of cottages up there." he said, pointing in the general direction of the East Cliff. "I'm staying there whilst the works done cos I have to have them finished for Christmas bookings and it saves time and money if I stay on site. Means I can have my tools there too without having to put them away every day."

They linked arms again, Jane still wearing Mikes Jacket, and they walked along Church Street and then turned left walking behind some of the street front houses and flats and onto a small footpath that took them gently up the cliff side. As they reached the end of Aelfleda Terrace Jane looked back at the scene below her, the lights reflecting in the river, the pubs and houses on the west side lit up with occasional silhouettes seen in windows; an idyllic scene she thought, one which she would treasure as she grew older, one which would link her to her first night with Mike forever.

She was brought back to earth somewhat sharply when Mike whispered; "Come on, you might be warm with that nice jacket on but some of us are fucking freezing."

Smiling back at him she said, "OK Master, your word is my command."

"Really?" he teased, "You might regret that?"

"Might I?" Jane loved the smile that Mike gave her as she immediately set off walking again towards the row of four cottages that were Aelfleda Terrace.

All four cottages were in darkness and Jane didn't know which one to look to, but Mike quickly placed his arms on her shoulders and guided her towards Cliff Cottage the third of the four, next to Esk Cottage on the far side, Rose Cottage and Hilda's Cottage making up the Terrace.

Unlocking the door using only a Yale type key, Mike gestured for Jane to enter, straight into the small but very modern kitchen with a greater assortment of appliances that would at first seem possible given the size of the room.

Once inside Jane wasted no time in turning around and throwing her arms around Mike's broad shoulders and kissing him full and passionately on the lips. Their tongues explored each other's mouths and skipping any tour of the rest of the cottage they made their way upstairs to a bedroom. Old fashioned in style but not in fixtures and fittings the room had a large double bed, two oak wardrobes and a small chair in front of an oak dressing table under the window looking out to the harbour. Jane hardly noticed any of this however; she did see the clothing strewn across the floor and on the bed but only as she sat on it and pulled Mike down to her side. She then proceeded to envelop him in kisses, starting on his lips, his neck, running her hands over his chest as she did so and following down with her mouth. She was just where she wanted to be and, for now at least, with just the person she wanted to be with.

81

"It's 8.42am on Wednesday 6th February 2013 and this is the 26th day briefing of Operation Caedmon, investigating the death of the un-named female found on The East Cliff at Whitby. I am leading this briefing as I wish to know from the horse's mouths where we are with our enquiries." It was unusual for the Superintendent to lead on the daily briefings but Simon Pithers wasn't the usual person to hold that rank and he probably felt more comfortable in this role than his regular role of distance supervision.

"Right let's get started, who's first?"

Sue Collins was quickest to respond and opened with;

"Sir, we've compiled a full list of workers used by Abbey Property Services run by William Raynor and his wife Ann. Most of them were on our original list but we've since analysed the three diaries taken from Ann Raynor and added to that list as a result. There are further enquiries to clarify some of the names where initials or nicknames have been used but James Gilchrist; one of the analysts is working on that as we speak. The diaries are obviously the first notes made by Ann Raynor and the way they are written up suggests most of the detail is stored elsewhere, probably on the laptop she had on her desk or even on a separate computer used by Willie Raynor and kept on the rig. We have had officers visit almost everyone on the list and statements have been obtained as to what work they carried out, when and where; on each occasion they were sketchy about how much they were paid."

"Surprise, Surprise eh?" Simon Pithers reacted the way the others were also thinking.

Sue Collins continued;

"Of those outstanding, two, John Sigston and Andrew Ward are working on the rigs with Raynor and two others, Mike Davies and Paul Coles are living and working out of county and we have colleagues attending their home addresses to obtain similar statements from them. It's obvious that with Raynor working away most of the time now that work has dropped off, as Ann Raynor said when we visited. At least she was honest about something."

"Thanks Sue. There's still plenty of follow up work to do on that so keep at it and if push comes to shove we'll go to the North Sea to speak with Messrs. Raynor, Sigston and Ward. Where are the other two?"

"Davies is working in Wales, Pembrokeshire and Coles a bit closer in Northampton. I've spoken with both forces and expressed to them the urgency of the enquiries sir."

"If there's no response by Friday, I want to know."

"Neil, let's have a warrant and get back to Resolution Way for the computers, mobile phones and any other records of work, payments to staff, invoices etc. I'm sure the lovely Ann will have been chatting to hubby and trying to bin evidence of tax evasion but she's not too bright from what I hear, there'll be plenty left for us, after all I don't give a shit about her tax affairs unless it gives us a way in. I also want Raynor, Sigston and Ward seen as soon as they set foot home."

"Will do sir."

"Where are we with the girl's identity?"

"Not a lot of progress I'm afraid sir. We have no matches on DNA or dental records yet but we are still looking." A rather timid DC Sara Thornton said from the back of the room.

"Not good enough. We need to identify this girl, she's missing from somewhere, she's somebody's daughter, sister, maybe even mother. Neil, I want another D to support Sara on that line of enquiry, it's a priority."

"Sir." Neil Maughan recognised the injection of urgency his boss was giving to the investigation and was happy to maintain the flow of the briefing.

"What about this jewellery then? How unique is it and where was it from?"

"Des Mason had been tasked with that boss but Geoff's picked it up now." Sue Collins interjected.

"It's a needle in haystack job sir. We've had over twelve thousand responses of similar items so far and all the info's been fed into the system." Geoff Alderson updated, "We'll find it, but it won't be overnight unless we get lucky."

"Let's hope we do get lucky then."

"What's the official line with the press now sir, you'll have seen the latest headline?" Neil Maughan posed the rhetorical question as he knew the answer but wanted Simon Pithers to reiterate the release to the troops.

"I've seen the headlines and I've made my views very much known to the editor. They have to sell papers and we have to respect that they are in business; they have to learn to respect that we are in a different business and that we will not divulge everything but will work with them where we can. The official line, going out from the press office today is copied here."

Passing out photocopies of a pre-prepared statement he continued;

"You will see that we are pushing the positives and re-affirming our appeal for any information from readers who may have witnessed something, anything. The name of the deceased is of paramount importance in order that we can build up our victim profile. The same press release is being published on the force website and on a link from crime stoppers. On a local level I am going to give an interview to Elli Stanford after this briefing to appease her and let her think she has something others haven't. She will only get the same information but in the spoken form, not written down or typed up. We are entering a very important stage of this investigation Ladies and Gents and I want you all to remain fully focused. Thank you all for your efforts so far, we are going to solve this."

With that Simon Pithers dismissed the team but asked Neil Maughan, "A word in your office please Neil?"

THIRTY TWO

It was only just 8.00am; barely an hour after she had finally gone to sleep; but Jane was woken when she felt a hand on her thigh, tracing the shape of a burnt orange coloured snake tattoo around to her shaven pubic mound where the snake's tongue reached out to her piercing, set with a single ruby and placed to give maximum pleasure when stimulated. Mike had been fascinated with the design and he had not been the first.

"Sorry to wake you Babe, but I've gotta do some work this morning."

"Mmmm, must you?"

"Sorry; yeah I must, but not for another hour or so. You wanna eat?"

"I could eat you darling."

"Again?"

Jane laughed aloud, remembering the night they had just spent together; "I could eat you for breakfast any day of the week. Every day of the week."

"Well you'll have to come back for more then." There was an element of tease in Mike's voice but each knew the offer was genuine and each knew it would be taken up.

Had they been in a play or television show the next scene, thought Jane, would be Mike making passionate love to her again before leaving for work, or if before the 9.00pm watershed making a breakfast of Eggs Benedict served with healthy fruit juice and Earl Grey Tea. The reality was that she was offered a dressing gown that absolutely buried her, a small bowl of cornflakes and a mug of what she would call Builders Tea. She couldn't be happier.

"I've got to get some plastering finished and I'm back at The Res at eight tonight to deal with all these unruly Goths again?" Mike continued to balance giving Jane information with a trace of playful torment.

"I need some sleep; I'll go back to the guest house."

"OK. I can get you a cab if you like?"

"Well I'm not fucking walking through town in last night's clothing."

"Well there'll be plenty of lookers if you go without them."

Jane turned around, picked up a pillow and, turning back, threw it across the room at him.

Having caught the pillow, Mike took out his mobile phone and called a local taxi firm, arranging for a cab to pick up Jane from The Ropery. Jane showered and dressed and walked the short distance to the pickup point arm in arm with Mike. Kissing him before he left she got into the Skoda Octavia and was driven back to Royal Crescent, only now wondering whether Gail would be there and what sort of night she had had with

Ashley? She ran up the steps to Harbour View two at a time and by the time she opened the door to her room was a little out of breath. Closing the door behind her she was disappointed that no-one was in; Gail's bed hadn't been slept in and a note left on a bedside cabinet explained that Geoff and Linda would catch up with them both later.

Jane was still buzzing with excitement and wanting to tell someone about her night; in the absence of Gail, who else but Phoebe would she turn to?

Texting Phoebe again she typed;

"Hi Babe RU da? "

There was no reply; after all it was barely 9.30am on a Sunday Morning. Tiredness was now catching up with her and she decided against trying again but did text her parents, knowing that they would be going to church she didn't bother making a call but sent the message; sending a copy to Phoebe in case she received a call from her mum and dad;

"Hi M&D going out for walk with Pheebs. Call you this afternoon. LU both. XX"

No sooner had she sent the text than her phone rang, the display showed the caller to be her mother, she couldn't not answer having just used the phone so she took the call;

"Hi Mum."

"Hi, I thought I'd ring you instead of this texting. You know I struggle with that."

"Oh Mum its just practice. How's Dad?"

"I'm not pleased. He's gone off to the golf club again. He knows I disapprove of him playing on a Sunday morning."

"But he's the Vice Captain Mum." there was more than a trace of sarcasm in Jane's voice. She had even less time for golf than her mother did, in fact she pretty much regarded all sports in the same way. A waste of time.

"Yes I know dear and he works very hard so I shouldn't resent him his own time."

"He'll be Captain next year and you'll be expected to attend all the functions too Mum. You'll be like local Royalty." Jane pictured her mother with a blue rinse, ball gown and tiara and struggled to hide her laughter.

"I'll always support him and do all I can, you know that but it doesn't mean I have to like him going out on a Sunday morning. Any way I rang to see how you were not your Dad, I see him every day."

"I'm fine, we're going out for a walk soon, there's a park nearby and Phoebe's a great laugh."

"That's lovely, are you keeping up with your studies though."

"Yes Mum." This is where it gets to be all too much thought Jane. This is just why I can't ever tell you what I really do, who I really am, "I've got to go now, Phoebe's shouting me."
"OK Darling. Keep in touch."
"Will do Mum, love to Dad too."
"Love you, Bye."
Putting the phone onto charge, Jane undressed and went to bed; this time to sleep.

THIRTY THREE

Closing the door behind them Simon Pithers took a seat in Neil Maughan's office and asked;

"What's this issue with Des? The sick note says stress but Des has always seemed to be very upbeat, a happy family man?"

"Don't we all seem that way to our colleagues' boss? We all try to leave our home lives at home and pretend all is ok even when it isn't?" He continued, "From what I can gather, his eldest, Gemma has become hooked on an online computer game, one that you have to pay to play and of course the more you get into the greater the costs and like any addiction it's taken a hold of her."

"Wasn't Gemma studying at Cambridge?"

"Yeah, one of life's great achievers, or so we all thought. I've not spoken to her myself but Des tells me that she's like a druggy now, she sleeps through most of the day, stays up late because her online opponents are awake then, mostly in the States I think and has effectively stolen all her uni' funds to use to buy time on the game."

"And Sue is managing his sick leave?"

"Yeah, obviously I'll oversee it but Sue is well capable."

"She's a very capable detective Neil, but she is a young in service manager. Everybody wants to help Des, but it can sometimes become too emotional if we get too involved. Has she spoken with Karen White at Welfare Department?"

"I believe so, but its early days yet."

"In some ways I agree but on the other hand, especially with stress related stuff it can be good to get an early intervention. These things can become habitual and whilst I want to support Des as much as we can whilst ever he's off someone else has to pick up his work."

"I know sir; I'll speak with Sue today. Des is signed off for a fortnight so far, I know that Gemma is back at home just now so at least there is improvement or at least I hope that's what it means. He'll be due a welfare visit soon anyway, I'll bring it forward, see what we can do"

"Thanks Neil, keep me posted and make sure that Karen is brought up to speed. Now where's that coffee machine of yours, I'll take my caffeine intake before seeing just what young Ellie Stanford has to say for herself?"

"That's one strong coffee coming up then?"

"I'm hopeful that we are going to be in a position soon to be giving a press conference about important arrests being made."

"We will Boss, we will." Passing the coffee across the desk, Neil Maughan asked, "Do you want to see Elli in here or are you going to use the usual room."

"If you can spare it for a while Neil it might just help to put her off balance for a while, make her just that bit uncomfortable. I want her to leave here knowing who's running the show and what her role is in it."

"I'll see her up then I've plenty to be getting on with. The office is all yours."

"Thanks Neil, the team are working well, make sure they know it and keep it up."

Maughan acknowledged the comments as he left the office to go to escort Elli Stanford back up to the room, true enough she did seem surprised at being invited upstairs instead of being ushered into the customary ground floor office. Maughan did like Elli, she was young, enthusiastic and this was, to his knowledge at least, her first real scoop. He felt that her editor had let her down by printing the headline which was always going to be provocative and he hoped that Simon Pithers didn't totally destroy her confidence.

THIRTY FOUR

It was after lunch when Jane was awoken by the noises from outside, the seagulls were in full voice and the cars, motorcycles and coaches making use of the nearby West Cliff Car Park each made their own noises as they drove by. The rooms were still empty, Gail, as far as could be seen had not returned and Geoff and Linda would be out until it was time to change into their evening outfits.

Jane showered and dressed in dark warm daytime clothing, not the costume she would wear later in the day for what was known as Sexy Sunday. Sexy Sunday was the main event of the day, or night as would be more appropriate; a time when all the Goths dressed provocatively and, as the name suggests, as sexy as they can. For now though, brunch was needed and then a trip to The Turnbull Ground, home of Whitby Town Football Club and venue of the annual fund raising game between teams from The Whitby Gazette and one from The Goths.

Real Gothic versus Athletico Gazette was how the posters advertised the game, a parody on the great derby games between the Spanish football teams of Madrid, though little to do with the quality of the football usually played on the day.

Jane rang Gail and arranged to meet up with her at The Spa for something to eat; she then put on her heavy overcoat, which she hoped would keep out the wind whilst she attended the football match, and set off across Royal Crescent to walk the short distance to The Spa Pavilion.

"Well? Spill the beans." Gail had seen Jane as she entered the building and almost ran across the foyer to greet her.

"You first, you dirty bitch?" Said in jest but still wishing for an answer.

"Bit of a letdown really, usual talking the talk but not up to much where it matters. You?"

"Mike can certainly walk the walk as well and he most certainly did." Jane paused, and then added "more than once."

"Come on then, I wanna know all there is to tell."

"Fuck off. Perv."

"Well not all the gory details, I can probably work those out myself."

"You think?" Jane was teasing again as they headed to the cafe area and after choosing a Panini and latte with an extra shot and a Burrito with espresso for Gail they chose a table near to the windows again, with the view out to sea.

"We didn't get to his place until late, we went to another pub first but then when we got to this place where he's working he was just fabulous."

"What do you mean, where he's working?"

"It's some cottage on The East Side; he's staying there while he does it up a bit. He's there now."

"And?"

"And?"

"And are you seeing him again?"

"We didn't make plans but yeah, too good not to."

"You'll need more than a Panini then; you'll have to keep your strength up."

"It's Mike who'll need to keep his strength up or at least keep something up." Jane burst into laughter and Gail followed her lead.

The two girls ate their meals and stayed chatting for a while before setting off to walk to the football; cutting through the West Cliff car park and onto Upgang Lane, they made their way to the turnstiles and happily paid the entrance fee, knowing that all takings were going to charity. Inside the ground, which was in need of money being spent on it, but money the Evo-Stik premier league club didn't have, they decided to go to the bar and stay inside until the match started. Neither had any particular interest in football but it was an event rather than a match as far as they were concerned and a place to mingle again.

Ordering a pint of cider each they remained stood in the bar and began chatting again and people watching. It was a cold day and this was reflected in the attire that people were wearing, covering most of the costumes with heavy trench coats or full length leather coats in some cases, heavy looking New Rock boots added inches to the height of their many wearers and an array of hats which would have put Ascot Ladies Day to shame had they not all been black.

As 2.00 o'clock approached and the teams ran out onto the pitch Gail and Jane made their way out and up to some of the seats in the main grandstand area, sheltered to a great extent from the offshore winds that would certainly affect the game.

THIRTY FIVE

Simon Pithers sat upright in his seat as he looked across the desk to the slight figure of the nervous Eleanor Stanford; she was used to asking questions and was normally very self confident but this somehow felt different, almost as though she had been summoned to the Head Masters office. The Superintendent had met her with the usual formalities and shown her to her seat without ever making her feel comfortable'

"Now Ms Stanford or can I call you Elli?"

"Elli's fine."

"You will be aware that I have spoken to your editor and I would hope that my disappointment at the last headline has been passed on to you?" Pithers paused to allow an answer but none was forthcoming so he continued;

"No-one knows better than me how important the local press can be as an investigative resource and I am quite aware of your job and the need to create a sensational headline to sell your newspaper; I will not however allow your needs to undermine my investigation. In order for us to successfully conduct an investigation we have to have the support of our local community and that includes The Whitby Gazette. We have made every attempt to keep the media informed in this enquiry and you will appreciate that we cannot tell you everything as this may jeopardise or destabilise the process. I am quite willing to be interviewed as is Detective Inspector Maughan, with whom I am sure you are familiar?"

"I, we, have always tried to support the police and we will continue to do so Mr Pithers, but, as I am sure my editor explained, we have a duty to represent the views of the whole community."

"Representing views and being provocative or sensationalist are two very different things Elli. The headline I refer to is deliberately aimed at sensationalism and does nothing to assist me even if it does sell you another dozen or so copies."

"Mr Pithers I am trying to keep the case alive and to the forefront of the community's thinking, I have had very little in terms of positive update since the first accounts went out."

"North Yorkshire Police have a press office that is updated daily and they in turn update the media releases on the same basis. I am aware that The Whitby Gazette has made daily contact with the press office and you therefore are as up to date as anyone."

"As the only local paper Superintendent, we had hoped that we may be favoured with something extra?" Elli was pitching this request somewhere between expectant and merely hopeful whilst in truth knowing it was probably just wishful thinking.

"Elli, I love a Trier and you are most certainly that. Look at it from my side though, how can I be seen to be giving you more information than I give to others without it being considered favouritism or even worse, unlawful? We're a million miles removed from The News of the World and The Leveson enquiry at the moment, but please forgive me if I wish to keep it that way."

"Is there nothing that you can give me?"

"I can say that we are making some progress and that with further help from the community then we are hopeful of making arrests at the earliest possible stage. We do need to make a positive identification of the body and to this end a nationwide search is underway for information that will assist us in this endeavour."

"Do you have a cause of death?"

"I am not prepared to answer that Elli as to do so may muddy the waters for our team."

"Do you think the offender is local then?"

"I can't say and wouldn't say if I could."

"Well this is the point of our previous headline Superintendent. Is Whitby a safe place to live if we have a killer on the loose?"

"Whitby is one of the safest places to live in the entire country; it is an area of historically low crime rates and its crime levels continue to fall year on year. Most unfortunately a body has been discovered that has been buried for over a year and possibly even longer, whilst we are treating this death as a murder enquiry, no further crimes of a similar nature have been committed in the time since and more importantly none are expected to be."

"But you can't be sure can you?"

"I can give you an assurance that we are doing everything possible to bring this enquiry to an early conclusion and to bring any offenders to justice."

"How many officers are working on the case?"

"We have a dedicated team of detectives under the local supervision of Detective Inspector Neil Maughan permanently attached to this investigation. We also have the valuable assistance of our uniformed staff and dedicated specialist support staff. More officers will be drafted in if deemed necessary and appropriate."

"What advice would you give to the people of Whitby?"

"To continue to support us in any way you can, to come forward and give us any information you may have, even if you consider it to be minimal; let us decide, as your information may just be the missing piece of the jigsaw."

"Thank you Superintendent. I appreciate your time and hope you have early success with your enquiries." There was a hint of a sardonic smile on Elli's face as she spoke that didn't go unnoticed by Simon Pithers. "We will catch the offender Elli; we will not stop until we do." He was paying particular attention to the word offender and not using the emotive alternative option of Killer, thereby not giving Elli Stanford the headline she was pitching for.

THIRTY SIX

"Hi Babes, can you believe it, me, watching a footy match?" Jane had grown a bit bored with the game itself and decided to ring Phoebe for a catch up.

"You can't stand football?"

"I know but there's loads' of Goths here and I can chill out a bit."

"So what's he like then?"

"Who?"

"Waddya mean who, your fella?"

"Oh him?" Jane did her best to hide the smile that had appeared on her face and had transmitted as giggles on the phone, "He's great."

"And?"

"He's an absolute dish and even better shag."

"So, you seeing him again then?" Phoebe was being equally facetious with Jane now, "I mean he doesn't sound much does he?"

"Pheebs, he is absolutely gorgeous, out of my league."

"Well obviously he doesn't think so and you look a million dollars in your costumes."

"And out of them he says."

There was laughter at each end of the conversation and they continued to chat for a while before Gail interrupted.

"Half time Jane, do you wanna drink?"

"Yeah, I'll come with you, I'm freezing out here."

Saying her goodbyes to Phoebe Jane joined Gail on her way back to the bar;

"I'm not sure about staying until the end Gail, what about going for the photos at that shop and getting something to eat?"

"OK Babe, you wouldn't want to go to The Res again would you?"

"Well maybe, but not necessarily. Mike won't be there 'til later and I quite liked The Duke of York."

"The Duke it is then, but let's have another drink here first."

Having bought two more drinks they took seats inside and spent the next half hour chatting in the warmth of the bar and just enjoying each other's company.

They were about to leave when they were approached by a young woman who they had earlier seen talking to others outside near the turnstiles and also at the players changing rooms.

"Hello, my name is Elli Stanford, I'm a reporter for the Whitby Gazette and I'm putting something together for Tuesday's paper, have you got a few minutes to chat?"

"Sure." Both Gail and Jane spoke in unison, both excited at possibly being in the paper.

"Where have you travelled from?"

"Just from Boro' " Gail pitched in first.

"Leeds" Jane was honest but at the same time vague, could the article reach The Yorkshire Post and be read by her mother or father?

"So did you meet here then?"

"Sort of. Social networks, facebook, yer know?" Gail took the lead

"And your highlights so far?"

Jane resisted the giggles that she felt returning, she knew what her highlight had been so far but had no intention of sharing that with the rest of Whitby or even Yorkshire.

"The whole atmosphere of the weekend is fantastic. The people the venues, the hospitality, everything" was the best she could come up with.

"Is everyone as welcoming as you hoped for or have you come across anyone who is opposed to Goths?"

"So far everyone's been great."

"How long have you been here?"

"All weekend." replied Gail,

"Since Thursday," added Jane

"Do you mind if we take your photo' for the paper?"

"No, that's fine." Gail responded immediately not giving Jane the opportunity to even consider saying no.

Grabbing Jane by the arm and putting on her best smile, Gail looked around for the photographer, who in turn was ushered across by Elli.

"Just in case it's your photo's the editor chooses for the article can I take your names to print alongside?"

"Sure, I'm Gail Thompson" was an instant, even excited reply but Jane appeared more hesitant and this was picked up upon by Gail who added "and this is Jane, in fact I don't know what your last name is?"

"Sorry, it's Lamont, Jane Lamont." Jane hoped her reservations didn't show but this was the best she could think of spontaneously and she thought it sounded like Hammond if anyone questioned it. She was however, momentarily at least, very unsure of herself; she knew that one lie often led to another and she didn't like it.

Photos taken, Elli thanked the two girls and moved on to the next table, no doubt to ask very similar questions. Gail and Jane fastened their coats and left the Turnbull Ground, heading along Upgang Lane, down Flowergate, Brunswick Street and Newquay Road to the Swing Bridge and left onto Sandgate again. They collected their photographs and a CD copy of them for an extra £3.95 from the shop and continued their walk along Church Street towards The Duke of York.

THIRTY SEVEN

It was barely 7.30am on Thursday 7th February when the long wheel based and liveried Ford Transit van pulled up outside 72 Resolution Way. Front seat passenger Sergeant Graham Dawson had already briefed his team of five specially trained constables and they were in possession of the obligatory search warrant which gave them authorisation to force entry if needs be but which hopefully wouldn't be necessary. Sue Collins and Mark Taylor parked behind the van and would join their colleagues once entry had been gained.

From the side doors of the transit van alighted six Police Officers all dressed in dark blue overalls and gloves, one carried what was affectionately known as the big red key, but in fact was a heavy steel battering ram used to force entry when it wasn't permitted by the residents.

The noise caused by the opening and closing of the van doors and the very fact that many local residents were ready to start their morning commute to work caused curtains to twitch along the road and there were not many who did not watch as Graham Dawson with his team behind him knocked on the door of the Raynor household.

"Who the fu-?'" the words strangled in her mouth as Ann Raynor saw the uniformed officers in front of her and heard Graham Dawson say;

"Mrs Raynor, I am Sergeant Dawson of North Yorkshire Police and I have here a warrant which entitles me to search these premises. May I come inside in order that we can continue the conversation in some privacy?" Without really waiting he took a step forward into the hall, followed by his colleagues and then the two detectives.

"What warrant? Why? Who?" the questions flowed without any real coherence from the mouth of Ann Raynor, her hair not yet brushed, devoid of any make-up and dressed in cream coloured leggings and a darker, un-ironed beige tee shirt she was certainly not expecting visitors and that boded well for the search team.

"Mrs Raynor, the warrant has been granted by Whitby Magistrates Court and allows us to search the whole house, garages, sheds and any outbuildings. We are looking for anything relating to Abbey Property Services as well as any computers and digitals storage devices. A copy of the warrant will be left with you and will include all the officer's names and collar numbers." Pausing to let the information sink in he gestured for his team to start searching.

"My kids are getting ready for school; you can't go in their rooms." The sense that she wasn't in control was evident in her voice and more so when she heard;

Who is it mum, what's going on?" Natalie, the eldest of the three Raynor offspring shouted from the upstairs landing. Dressed in only a soft pink towelling dressing gown and slippers and en route to the bathroom she had seen men in overalls, carrying a variety of large brown paper and polythene bags climbing the stairs, not registering the word POLICE printed boldly across their backs.

"Get dressed now and tell the others to as well."

"Mrs Raynor, we will try not to disrupt you any more than is absolutely necessary." Graham Dawson was very calm and professional, after all this was one of the easier jobs for him, no forced entry needed, no physical resistance from the occupants or weapons to contend with, just a rather lame wife and mother caught unaware of the possibility of a search even being considered. "Can you please show me to the office or study, the place you keep any computer?"

"You can't take that, I need it."

"I'm sorry Mrs Raynor but as I explained we will be seizing any computer we find together with any storage system we believe may have been used in your husband's business or financial affairs."

"You can't. You can't. I'm calling my solicitor."

"That's your prerogative Mrs Raynor, but in the meantime we will continue our work."

Three dressed but dishevelled looking youngsters came down the stairs and into the kitchen, all wearing something that could be taken as school uniform but unlikely to be seen on the front page of any brochure of their respective schools.

"What's going on Mum? Why have we got the pigs in our house?" Natalie, aged fourteen, but thinking herself to be more worldly wise than her years questioned her mother knowing that her comments would be heard by the officers nearby. Knowing what Natalie was doing, her siblings, Nicola twelve and Dominic a further two years younger both struggled to contain their smiles, and took seats at the breakfast table.

"They've got a warrant to search the house. They're looking for computers and stuff."

"Well they're not fucking having mine. I need it for school"

"I know Nat; I wish your dad was here."

Hearing the exchange Sue Collins stepped forward and spoke to Ann Raynor and her children;

"We will need to take all the computers, I'm sorry I know this will make it difficult at school but we will aim to return them as soon as we have finished analysing them." She knew that she was stretching the truth a little in that it wasn't likely to be anytime soon and if anything was found then they would be retained as evidence.

"You can't, all my works on there and my facebook 'n stuff."

"We can and we will, we are investigating a serious crime and will do all we need to, now I suggest that you hand over your laptop to save us rooting in your bag." Sue Collins stared directly at Natalie to reinforce her comment and to put down the challenge; if a young and, in her opinion insignificant, girl wanted to try it on then she was in no mood to back down.

Natalie recognised she was beaten and got up from her seat to get her bag from a nearby work-surface; taking out her laptop she meekly handed it over, saying;

"It's all password protected anyhow."

"No problem." Sue Collins took hold of the computer and placed it in a clear plastic bag before handing it to the exhibits officer, Steve Parker, to record its seizure.

Ann Raynor had been trying to contact her solicitor only to be fobbed off with an out of hours recorded message, she returned the phone to its docking point and watched as the officers bagged items from the office cum study, leaving silhouettes in the dust on the desk from where they had been removed. She sat at the table and took a sip from a coffee that Natalie had made for her. She looked a very dejected figure and could only sit and wait until she was told the search was completed.

It was, in fact, over an hour before Graham Dawson spoke with Sue Collins;

"We've got what we came for, 2 desktops, 4 laptops including the kid's and a couple of external hard drives that they are probably using as back up discs. Interestingly there were a few older mobile phones in the desk drawers, could just be old but there were some loose sim cards as well."

"What about accounts books, bills, invoices and such?"

"All done, quite organised in some ways, made it easy for us."

"Loft space, garage, and sheds done?"

"Checking the loft now, others done, we'll be wrapped up in half hour or so unless there's anything else, then we'll go and book it all in?"

"Great, thanks Graham, are you going to update Neil or do you want me to?"

"I'll see him when we get back, no problem. Steve'll give you a copy of what we've taken and I'll leave you to wrap up the signatures etcetera with the delightful Mrs Raynor." The sarcasm wasn't lost on Sue Collins as she looked across at Ann Raynor, someone who liked to be looked up to at all times and who wasn't averse to showing off her husband's wealth, well she would have to face the neighbours in a different way after this morning.

THIRTY EIGHT

"Let's have another look at that Photo Jane." Gail had liked the picture when she had seen it at the gallery and had had no hesitation in paying for the CD as an extra copy; she wanted to look again at the two of them smiling on their first day together in Whitby, a day she thought she would treasure forever.

Jane reached down to the carrier bag at her feet, leant up against the table leg and took out one of the two identical prints mounted in a black and silver card designed especially with this weekend in mind. Opening it up on the table Jane held it at arm's length to take in the whole picture she was very pleased with the outcome. What would her parents say if they knew of this side of her life? One for University not for the home collection.

Passing it across to Gail, she said, "Like fucking models me and you. First this then the papers."

"If only, I've gotta go back to Boro' tomorra. Parmo's not exactly caviar yer know?"

"What's Parmo when it's at home?"

"Parmo. It's fantastic, you'll have to come to Boro' and have one, it's a delicacy where I'm from. It's like fried chicken, breadcrumbs and a sauce with that parmesan cheese all over it."

"Sound disgusting."

"They're great you gotta try it to know."

"Well maybe another time, I'm starving now, what we gonna have?"

Picking up the menu again Jane browsed the options before deciding on Gammon;

"Don't want any garlic stuff; don't want to scare Mike off later."

"Hey is this serious?"

"I've only known him a couple of days but I'm gonna ask him if I can stay for a couple of days after this weekend's over."

"Wow, you sure? I mean you don't know him very well do you?"

"Nothing ventured as they say?"

"Well, keep your phone on just in case."

"Ooh you sound like my mother. What do you want to eat; I'm off to the bar."

"Steak pie then please."

Jane placed the orders and got two more drinks before returning to the table.

"Gail, will you do me a massive favour please?"

"Yeah if I can."

"My mum and dad don't know I'm here, I know this sounds daft at my age but they're real squares, Gay. Will you just pretend you're called Phoebe for me and I'll give 'em a call to let 'em know I'm ok?"

Gail burst out laughing, "You've just told me you're gonna stay with Mike a couple more nights at least and then you tell me that your mum won't let you out to play?"

"I know, it's stupid really but I don't want to hurt them. They think I'm still their sweet little twelve year old virgin daughter."

"You're certainly not that."

"Please"

"Go on then, give 'em a call."

Using the speed dial settings again Jane rang home,

It was her dad that answered, obviously after using the caller display,

"Hello Dear"

"Hi Dad, how's you two?"

"We're fine dear, how are you? When will we see you?"

"Well that's why I'm ringing Dad; I'm going to stay with Phoebe a bit longer so I won't see you for a while. I'm sorry"

"Oh that's a shame we were looking forward to seeing you."

"Sorry Dad, I'll miss you too but I'm having a really cool time and Phoebe asked me to stay a bit longer."

"It's your choice dear. What are you up to then that keeps you away from us?"

"Don't be like that Dad; we're just out for a meal now, enjoying each other's company, listening to music that sort of thing."

"I was only joking, of course we will miss you but as long as you're happy then that's fine."

"How's Mum?"

"She's fine dear, doing her TWG things just now, around at Dorothy's. She'll be sorry to have missed you."

"Well give her my love won't you?"

"I will."

"Jane, the meals are here." Gail thought that by shouting out that it would cut short what seemed to be a stilted conversation.

"OK." Looking slightly puzzled Jane glanced at Gail, "Dad I have to go, my dinners arrived."

"Alright, short but sweet. Keep in touch."

Ending the call, Jane looked again at Gail, "What was all that about?"

"I thought you were going to put our foot in it telling him all about life at Phoebe's whilst thinking about Mike."

Jane laughed aloud, "And you thought I might put you on to chat?"

"Well there was that."

The two girls ate their meals and enjoyed each other's company even more, each feeling that they had made a good friend.

THIRTY NINE

"Good job Graham, I'll get the Techy's onto it straight away." Neil Maughan was pleased with the mornings search and wanted it progressing as quickly as possible.

"You'll be lucky Neil, there's a three month waiting list for priority stuff. Karl's been off for ages with his broken leg so the team's short."

"I want it in three days not three fucking months."

"You and everyone else in the force, that's why they don't even prioritise priorities now cos everyone thinks theirs is a bigger priority than the others."

"It's a fucking murder investigation for God's sake, leave it with me Graham and pass on my thanks to your team we can always rely on them to do their bit for us."

"Cheers Neil. Good Luck."

"Sounds like I'll need it. See you soon."

Picking up the phone Neil Maughan rang the Headquarters IT Department;

"HQ F.I.T, Duncan speaking."

"Duncan It's Detective Inspector Neil Maughan from Whitby. I'm heading up Op. Caedmon, the murder enquiry. I've got half a dozen computers, some hard drives and a selection of mobiles and sim cards that I need analysing and fast, what's the score with you guys now?"

"Hya Sir, I'm sorry but we're snowed under we've got a ten to twelve week waiting list for our priority stuff and more than twice that for the rest. Everything is IT linked these days and until NYP invests in The Department properly we're always lagging behind the gain line."

"How soon could you do it if I could get everything to you today?"

"There's no point sir, I simply can't fit it in."

"Duncan, if I can pull some strings to make this your top priority what time scale can you put on it?"

"How long is a piece of string, without looking at the hard drives I don't know what we're up against or how long it could take to see whatever you're looking for."

"I'm looking for financials, for names, diaries, work rotas. I'm trying to see who has done what and when?"

"It might all be on one file which shouldn't take long at all but then again it might not be. I wish I could be more helpful."

"Leave it with me I'll get it all over to you with the paperwork and I'll see about jumping the queue. Thanks Duncan."

Neil Maughan was very frustrated but needed to make another call to jump that queue. Dialling Simon Pithers number he heard the phone ringing at the other end;

"Pithers"

"Sir, its Neil Maughan."

"Neil, is it urgent I'm up to my neck in it?"

"Yes Boss I think it is. Have you got just a couple of minutes?"

"Go on, what's up?"

Neil Maughan explained the circumstances surrounding the potential delay in analysing Data from the seized computers and the discussion he had just had with Duncan.

"Right, leave it with me, get the stuff over here this afternoon and make sure the paperwork is done properly."

"Will do Boss. Thanks."

Short but hopefully productive, Maughan shouted through to Graham Dawson in the next office;

"Graham, I need another favour."

"Can you free up one of your team to get the computers from this morning's job through to HQ? I need someone who can make sure the jobs done right first time, the Boss is pulling some strings and I don't want any cock ups."

"Leave it with me, we're still booking it all in and writing statements but I'll get Beth to sort it out. Is there anything in particular you want to push to the front?"

"The two desk tops and hard drives please Graham; I'm thinking that the laptops and tablets are more for personal use than what we're looking for."

"Consider it done."

"That's yet another favour I owe you. Cheers."

Graham Dawson was in the enviable position of being able to chop and change the makeup of his team as necessary and knew that in Beth Granger he had an administrative angel; someone for whom all the processes of admin just seemed to come naturally and who was a great team player, happy to take on roles others shied away from.

Maughan reflected on how the investigation had moved forward, Raynor would be arrested on his return and together with the diaries and computers what he said should give a proper insight into who had the opportunity to spend time at Esk View, to bury a body, build a patio and hide the remains of a young female life. Job done; If only it was that simple, it was in books and on TV wasn't it?

FORTY

It was just by coincidence but both Gail and Jane had bought very tight fitting PVC dresses for Sexy Sunday, viewed by some as the best night of Whitby Goth Weekend and certainly the most bizarre. Gail had chosen a knee length strapless violet dress worn with complimentary high stiletto heeled shoes; Jane meanwhile was wearing a short mini skirt length dress with corset top and visible suspenders holding up black fishnet stockings. The dress was short enough to show the lower part of Jane's tattoo above the stocking tops and this naturally drew the eyes higher along the snakes body until it disappeared under her hemline and the hinted at delights beyond. Black high heeled ankle boots, a bold black fascinator and over the top makeup completed her look and they took it in turns to take photographs on their respective mobiles for their facebook pages.

"I want a photo just for Mike, Gail."

"Something that won't go on facebook I take it?"

"Nor in the family album."

Jane began striking poses, using the settee and bed as props while Gail used Jane's phone to take some quite provocative photos.

"Here, you choose what to send him. He'll like them all I'm sure."

"I'll only send one though, leave him wanting more."

"You tease."

"You bet."

Jane looked through the photographs in the view display on her phone and selected one that she thought showed her smiling and had her tattoo showing to best effect, leaving just enough to keep a hint of mystery about what may lay ahead. She was very proud of the tattoo and felt that it showed her true self, but was careful not to reveal the extra charm of the gem in its pleasing but ultimately hidden position.

Jane sent Mike the chosen picture with the text message, "Ready to play snakes and ladders lover?" before she picked up her bag, took Gail by the arm and headed for the door and onto The Spa Pavilion for the finale of the Whitby Goth Weekend.

Across town Mike received the MMS as he sat at a table at The Resolution with his doormen colleagues, a group of doormen that had worked together previously but not often, Craig, Johnno, Sandy, Rob, Dave and the only female in the team, Bev.

Seeing the smile appear on Mikes face, Craig snatched the phone from him and looked at what had caused his reaction;

"Wow, are you on a promise tonight or what? You lucky git."

The phone was passed around the table and each of the doormen made a comment about Jane, how she looked and in some cases what they would like to do to her given the opportunity. Mike appeared to take the comments in good humour but in reality he was a little upset about some of the latter, which although he realised were said in jest he thought were a bit too graphic whilst he was present.

The phone worked its way back to Mike who sent a reply to Jane, "See you after work. XX"

His colleagues, to a man, taunted him with comments and gestures, blew kisses and generally mocked him;

"Mmwahh Mmwahh. Love you Babe." laughed Dave.

"See you later Honey. Love you" was Craig's offering.

"Fuck off you jealous bastards." was not his most eloquent quote ever but was all Mike could come up with to quell the rowdy comments of his mates, but it seemed only to add fuel to their fire and they all continued to mock until they had to separate and begin work at their respective doors. Mike was allocated to work the top door with Sandy for the first part of the shift.

"Hey, your bird looks to be a right goer Mike?"

"I've only met her this weekend Sandy, give us a break eh?"

"I wouldn't mind being that snake though?"

"Well you've got no chance mate, but I think she'll be charming my snake again later."

Smirking together, Mike and Sandy began to work the doors on what looked like being the beginning of another busy night. The atmosphere was palpably one of excitement as Mike stood at the junction of Skinner Street and Flowergate, watching The Goths in some quite revealing, and occasionally, absurd costumes parading down the streets into town.

"Sexy Sunday, just an excuse to get your tits out and show yer arse." Sandy remarked, "And that's just the fellas" he added in jest.

"It could be worse, Sandy. Just enjoy 'cos looking is about as far as you'll get tonight." responded Mike, seeing the opportunity to have a dig back at one of his tormentors.

"You never know, 'as your bird got a mate then?"

"She never said, but even if she had she wouldn't want you, you old git." Mike made reference to Sandy being the oldest member of the team. At 43 years old he was even older than the company boss, Ged Turner, who tended to just take a back seat now, allocating other staff to do the work after years on the doors himself.

"I might be old but I'm still fitter than you."

Sandy was known to everyone as a bit of a body builder and regular visitor to the gym where he put himself through some serious workouts.

He had previously taken part in body building competitions but that was several years ago and whilst he still had an impressive physique it was not now competition standard. It still looked the part for his current role however.

"As if, old timer." Mike teased.

It was shortly after 10.00pm when the banter was interrupted with a group of women, well on the way to being drunk and trying to get into the pub. They were already drawing attention to themselves when one of them appeared to trip on a step and crashed to the ground, hitting the side of her face hard on another step as she did so. As the blood began to flow from the deep cut others in the group reacted; some started screaming, others crying and as always seemed to be the case, some shouted abuse at the doormen.

"You fucking pushed her. I saw you." screamed one.

"I'm calling the cops." shouted another.

The women separated into two distinct groups, one trying to help their friend whilst the others contented themselves by making phone calls, including a 999 call to the police and generally creating more of a nuisance.

Mike tried to take control of the situation by tending to the injured woman, a short slim woman, he guessed to be in her late twenties with bleached blonde hair, too much makeup, wearing only a crop top and short skirt over her miniscule underwear. He saw that one of her shoes had a broken heel and realised that this must have caused her to miss the step, together with the no doubt half bottle of vodka before coming out.

"Keep off her." shouted one of the woman's friends, "You did that. You pushed her."

"I'm trying to help her." Mike responded, "Get an ambulance Sandy, she's bleeding."

Sandy was already using his radio to ask for help from his colleagues, a radio message that was monitored by the CCTV controllers in the control room in Scarborough, who, in turn, promptly began to monitor the melee from their remote location. Sandy asked for an ambulance and stated it was a head injury to ensure that the call was treated urgently,

"You'd better send the cops as well." he added, fearing or sensing allegations from the women and thinking that could be a prelude to disorder.

It was only a matter of a couple of minutes later when Flowergate was lit up by flashing blue lights as the police van arrived, if there was going to be a problem this was one street that figured high on the briefings and the call had come as no surprise.

FORTY ONE

"Look at him, he looks mental." Gail pointed to a man across the hall at The Spa dressed only in a neon green mankini and New Rock knee high boots.

"I bet that's a sock in there? We're over dressed, can you believe it?"

"No way." exclaimed Gail, "let's have a walk round, see what else we can see?"

"Look there," Jane pointed to another sparsely clad Goth, this time a curvaceous female dressed in a very tight corset, black stockings, high stiletto heeled boots and a smile, "She looks fabulous."

"Stop pointing Jane." Gail took hold of Jane's hand and held it down by her side, "It is Sexy Sunday after all."

"Well let's get sexy then." Gail made her way out onto the dance floor, dragging Jane with her and they started dancing to the sound of Gary Numan and Rosetta stone, unwittingly creating the same impression on others as the mankini man had made on them; they looked stunning as a pair and were soon joined by other revellers, both male and female.

It was over half an hour before Gail started to flag a little and sidled across to a nearby table and sat down, Jane kept going a short while longer before she too started to wilt a little and joined Gail at the table. Within minutes they were joined by Geoff and Linda who they hadn't seen since the early afternoon.

"Saw the dancing girls, great but no stamina eh?" Geoff taunted

"Hey old timer, we're just warming up." Jane responded with a smile, "pacing ourselves."

"There's some great outfits here aren't there?" Gail gestured

"Fantastic, just wait until later though, a lot of what is being worn now will be discarded by the end of the night." Geoff replied,

"Really?" Gail looked genuinely curious.

"Really, only the hard core, and some of those that do, shouldn't. They should realise that they no longer have the looks or the figures that they once had."

"Well I won't be revealing any more than this." Gail said, pushing up her cleavage with both hands and drawing admiring glances from all.

"Who's for a drink then?" Geoff asked.

The girls gave their orders and Geoff left them at the table whilst he made his way to the bar.

"You girls alright then?" Linda asked as she took a seat.

"Yeah great, what you been doing today then?" Jane replied.

"Well he wanted to go to the football match but I can't stand it at the best of times so I wasn't gonna sit in the freezing cold to watch that."

"We stayed for half of it but that's all."

"Well I needed some supplies as well."

"Supplies?" Gail looked vaguely at Linda until she saw her take her hand from her clutch bag and show a handful of small plastic bags, some with powder and others with coloured tablets in.

"I've gotta find something to help me keep up with you youngsters."

"What have you got then?"

"A few E's, some Speed and some Grass for Geoff."

"You're like a walking chemist shop." Jane interrupted.

"Sshhhh, not so loud, there's plenty around but no point shouting about it." Linda chastened Jane.

"Well is the chemist open for business if I need any."

"This chemist is always open for business."

Jane hadn't used drugs before; she had never felt the need to, always being able to keep up with her peers but didn't want to appear naive in front of her new friends.

"I'll have a couple of E's then Linda"

"You sure you want two?"

"Yeah, I might not see you later."

"OK."

After the deal was done, Jane put the pills in her pocket and the group continued chatting for a while. Geoff had brought the drinks back to the table but then moved on to chat with another group he knew.

FORTY TWO

"Inspector Neil Maughan please." It was shortly after 9.30am on Monday 11th February when Willie Raynor stood at the front desk of Whitby Police Station alongside his solicitor, Paul Waterman, a highly respected solicitor from Whitby's oldest practice, but one whose expertise was in the commercial sector; business law not criminal law.

"Is he expecting you?" Jean knew full well the answer to her own question but enjoyed playing the game.

"He's been pestering my wife and kids while I've been away so he better be."

Paul Waterman placed his hand on Willie Raynor's arm and spoke quietly to him, "Steady Willie, she's only doing her job."

"They're all in it together."

"Willie, when you came to see me you told me you wouldn't lose your temper if I came here with you so I'm asking you not to."

"I'm sorry Paul, it's just Ann and the kids are upset and that makes me get upset."

Jean returned to the bank style window that separated Willie Raynor and Paul Waterman from her and spoke to them both, "Detective Inspector Maughan will be with you shortly, please take a seat." with that she gestured to the bench style seat that was fastened to the wall behind them and which was monitored via CCTV images in Jeans office. The two men took their respective places on the seat, each as uncomfortable as the other on the slatted wooden bench. Neil Maughan stood with Sue Collins behind Jean as she took her seat in the front office; all three were watching the TV screens in front of them.

"Well it hasn't taken him long to pay us a visit." Sue Collins spoke quietly as she knew just how thin the walls were between this office and the reception foyer.

"Well they can wait a bit longer Sue, just enough to get unsettled, impatient; that way if he loses any composure he might have had he may just say a bit more than he first wanted to." Neil Maughan, turned to walk back up to his own office; "Give them ten minutes Jean and then we can show them down to the interview room; see what they have to say."

"OK Neil; will do."

"I don't want to push him far this first time Sue, let's see what he has to say, let him know that we are looking closely at everything he does and then let him stew for a while."

"Are we looking to arrest him so we can bail him out and keep some control or just interview at this stage?"

"We haven't enough to arrest him in connection with the body, and I don't want to take the piss by arresting him for the financial stuff just to keep him on bail; he'll be happy to come back if he thinks we're giving the delightful Mrs Raynor grief."

"No probs, I'll just get my file."

Neil Maughan opened the door to the reception area a short while later to see Willie Raynor stood up, back to the camera, looking across the foyer to his solicitor.

"I'm sorry to have kept you, would you like to step inside?"

Shaking Paul Waterman's hand, Neil Maughan introduced himself and Sue Collins and gestured the pair to walk down the corridor to the stairs at the far end and down to the old custody suite where the soundproofed interview room was still located.

"What's all this about then?" Willie Raynor did not like the fact that he was now in a formal interview room and was beginning to feel uncomfortable about his decision to come to the Police Station at all.

"All in good time Mr Raynor. There are just a few formalities I have to go through first then I'll explain all." Neil Maughan was enjoying the unease which Raynor displayed but stopped just short of showing it.

Sue Collins went through the process of recording the time of arrival and reason for the visit of Raynor and Waterman before they all took a seat in the small interview room which contained only a table, four chairs, digital recording equipment and a prominent red push button on one wall and a kick strip around all four walls which, if activated, sounded an alarm around the station to which any officer present would guarantee to respond; a scenario that Sue Collins thought could see the end of Paul Waterman, a well dressed but portly figure of a man in his early sixties she guessed and used to the good things in life.

Sue Collins gestured for everyone to take a seat, ensuring that she and Neil Maughan had the seats nearest the door and thus placing Raynor in a corner that would best display his reactions to the video camera fitted on the wall opposite.

"You do not have to say anything. But it may harm your defence if you do not mention when questioned something which you later rely on in court. Anything you do say may be given in evidence." Sue Collins gave the formal caution and explained the use of recording equipment and the fact that Raynor was not under arrest and was therefore free to leave at any time. All four persons present then introduced themselves before Neil Maughan took up the interview.

"Thank you for coming into the station Mr Raynor, as you know we have been making enquiries into the discovery of a body on the West Cliff on Saturday 12th February this year."

"What's that got to do wi' me?"

"Well if you would let me explain Mr Raynor, the body was found after a landslip occurred at Esk View, Aelfleda Terrace and I understand that Abbey Property Services carried out work there?"

"So?" The question seemed to go straight over Raynor's head

"So, Mr Raynor, I understand that you are the owner and Manager of Abbey Property Services?"

"Yes, that's no secret in this town. So what?"

"So we have been looking into what work has been carried out and when and by whom?" Maughan had no interest in the almost petulant, childlike response given by Raynor;

"And is that why you've taken every computer there was from my house?"

"It's one reason, yes."

"Well it's fucking ridiculous, my kids can't do their homework or anything."

"Was it really necessary to take the children's computers Inspector?" Waterman asked politely.

"This is an enquiry into a suspicious death, a murder enquiry. I, we, will take any and every opportunity to obtain all the available evidence from any source. As we have not yet had a chance to analyse the computers yet we need to retain them for that purpose. You will appreciate that in my position I have to look at every prospect, every possible avenue to progress the investigation and I can assure you Mr Waterman and you Mr Raynor that our actions are wholly in line with those expected in this type of enquiry."

"And what about my kids education?"

"I'm afraid Mr Raynor that I cannot advise you on that but I am sure that their school teachers can, the computers will be returned once our enquiries have been completed."

Glances were exchanged between Raynor and Waterman, after which each gave a shrug, seemingly accepting the situation for what it was.

"Can you please tell me, Mr Raynor who you employed to work at Esk View and what work was undertaken by them?"

"I thought you had all the information from my diaries?"

"I would like you to tell me please."

"I can't remember exactly who did what without looking at my books, but do you really think that I'm involved in this body thing?"

"We have to look at every line of enquiry as I said and, obviously this line is of great interest to us. I would ask you to let us decide what is important and what isn't"

"I have a group of mates who do work for me, Johnny Sigston or Siggy as we call him, Paul Coles, Andy Ward and Mike Davies are the regulars then Gavin Tate and Ben McLeod or Macca do bits for me."

"I will need contact details for all of them please. Did any of them work on Esk View?"

"I know Mike and Ben did for certain, I think Siggy did a bit of plumbing but I'll need to check to be sure."

"That's great; do you have any invoices or bills to show when the work was carried out and who would have done it?"

"Yeah, there'll be notes in the diaries you have and Ann does the printed invoices."

"They should show up in the computer analysis then. Will we find any entries on any computer used by your children, any other than the desk top from the study?"

Raynor looked ill at ease and shuffled in his chair, breathing shallower than normal and looking upwards towards the ceiling on his left.

"Like I said, my wife usually keeps all the computer stuff updated, for invoices, tax returns etcetera."

"Mr Raynor, just to put you at ease for the moment can I just make it clear that I am not investigating tax irregularities so please tell me now if there is anything on the computers that will help me with my enquiries."

"What like?"

"Anything at all, I'll judge as to whether it's of value."

"Can I please have a moment with my client Inspector?" Paul Waterman was beginning to feel the interview moving even further away from his comfort zone and wanted to buy some time. Willie Raynor had not mentioned anything to him about computers other than the police had taken them all and he was uncertain about what he might say.

"Mr Waterman, we have only just begun the interview and I would like to continue a little longer if you would please bear with me?"

"Detective Inspector, your colleague made it clear that my client was free to leave at any time, I would ask that we suspend the interview for me to give advice or end it now for my client to leave?"

Neil Maughan was disappointed with this turn of events as he had not even asked a challenging question at this time but in the circumstances felt he had little choice;

"The time by my watch is 10.17am and at the request of solicitor Mr Paul Waterman the interview is suspended."

Sue Collins stopped the recorder and tidied up the notes before Neil Maughan spoke to Paul Waterman again;

"Mr Waterman we are merely trying to ascertain, in the quickest time possible, whether there is anything in terms of helpful intelligence on any of the computers we have seized from Mr Raynor and his family. We will be analysing the computers in the fullness of time but surely your client would wish to help us progress our investigation?"

Leaving Raynor and Waterman in the interview office the two detectives left and closed the door behind them.

"Well that didn't last long boss."

"You know as I do Sue that we haven't started yet."

FORTY THREE

"What's the score lads?" PC1101 Howard Small asked of the ambulance crew as they tended to the injured girl.

"It's never good news when there's a discharge or blood from the ears, but it's too early to tell. We'll take her to Scarborough and get her checked over. Have you got any details yet?"

"Not yet, just trying to calm things down first."

"Well, it could just be a bit of concussion but it could be very serious."

"I'll get the details to you as soon as I can." Looking up Howard Small could see his colleagues were separating the group of girls from the doormen, the blue lights of the ambulance were still flashing and this added to the tension of the moment with friends of the injured girl screaming, crying and shouting at the doormen, Mike in particular.

"That bastard there pushed her down the steps." shouted one of the group again to PC Small, pointing to Mike.

Howard Small took the young woman to one side and listened to her as she assured him that she had seen Mike use his right hand to push her backwards causing her to fall. Taking out his notebook he wrote down her name, Emma Sadler, her date of birth, address and brief details of what she said she had seen. Taking charge of the scene he requested further assistance from his colleagues and asked for the top doors to The Resolution to be closed.

"You've no chance of that, look at the queues." Sandy responded

"I'm not asking you, I'm telling you that no-one else is going in or out of these doors until I know what has happened and that it's not a crime scene."

"What are you on about?" Sandy was puzzled at the use of the term crime scene, he had certainly not seen anything untoward, the girl had been pissed and fallen on the steps, usual weekend stuff.

"Look I realise it's busy but I just need to check some stuff out and then we'll see where we're at. Just get everyone to go in at the side door for now."

Hearing what their colleague had said the other officers took it into their hands to do the door staff's job and redirected the waiting crowd around to the side door. Colleagues arrived in support and one, PC Dave Morgan was directed to obtain details of all door staff present together with anyone who witnessed the incident.

Howard Small gathered Emma Sadler and her friends together and took all their details including those of the injured girl, who he now knew as, Fleur Brennan, a 19 year old girl from Stakesby Vale in Whitby. He then began speaking to each one in private in the nearby Police van.

The general consensus was that it was very busy, there was boisterous behaviour and everyone appeared to be in high spirits when Fleur fell to the ground and hit her head. Significantly, two others as well, in addition to Emma Sadler stated they had seen the doorman push Fleur to the ground and that they thought it was deliberate. If what they said was true it was a serious allegation given the possible level of injury sustained. Knowing that his Sergeant, Leigh James would be there shortly he made his own decision to treat the allegation as genuine and not just one made by half drunken friends of the injured party.

"1101 to control." he called the control to provide an update and ask for some further information; "I can confirm one injured female en-route to SDH with head injuries, allegation of assault made against door staff. So far?" the last words checking that the message had been received up to that point.

"Received, 236 did you monitor?" Control staff were checking that Sergeant Leigh James was aware of the incident.

"236 monitored en route. Has CCTV been requested?"

"Affirmative"

Arriving shortly afterwards Leigh James was updated by Howard Small. An inspection of the scene indicated blood on the third step up at the entrance to the pub and Leigh James, playing safely, instructed photographs to be taken as it wasn't feasible to call out CIS for what may only be a minor injury assault.

"The witnesses say the doorman pushed her backwards causing her to fall Sarge, but do you want me to make an arrest tonight when it's this busy?"

"Damned if we do, damned if we don't Howie. Do they identify which one?"

"They've pointed him out so yes."

"Bring him in then, I'll get someone to get details of any other witnesses."

"It's already in place Sarge but I'll go get my man."

"236 to control any update on the injured girl, Fleur Brennan?"

"Affirmative, are you state 12?" the status code used nationally now by Police Forces allowed concise and succinct questions to be asked, usually without the general public understanding. State 12 asked if the recipient was in a position to receive a confidential message.

"Yes go ahead."

"Fleur Brennan is said to be unconscious and undergoing a scan to identify the severity of injury, she is said to be very poorly but stable. The DI has been informed and asks for the scene to be secured and has authorised CIS call out."

"All received." he said before turning again to Howard Small and passing on the details, "Fuck; that's all we need tonight." he added.

Howard Small approached Mike, being the doorman that had been pointed out to him by witnesses and asked to speak to him in his van, as they walked back to the van Mike asked,

"How's the girl, any news?"

"She's not good I'm afraid, would you just sit in here for me?" he pointed to seats in the rear of the van behind a caged door leaving no-one in any doubt as to why they were there.

"What, in the cage?"

"There's been an allegation and I have to inform you that I'm arresting you on suspicion of assault. You don't have to say anything but,"

Mike interrupted him mid flow and pleaded, "I didn't touch her, she fell on the steps. Fucking hell I tried to help her."

"Well you'll get a chance to tell me all about it in interview, now please sit down and I'll be with you in a minute."

Howard got a colleague to assist him in an initial search, looking for Mike's phone and anything that might be sharp and which would allow him to harm himself or others. Placing those items in a bag a more thorough search would take place in the custody suite.

"I'm working; you know how busy it is out there. This is mad."

Closing and locking the door on him Howard Small walked away from the van and informed Leigh James that the suspect had been arrested.

"Are you happy to take him on your own Howie, we're gonna need everyone we can here if we need to preserve this scene?"

"No problem Sarge, he seems to be compliant." he replied and got into the driver's seat to begin the journey to Scarborough's custody suite.

FORTY FOUR

Just as Geoff had suggested the evening at The Spa became raunchier or even vulgar with people turning up later having drunk a little more and others becoming ever more audacious with their outfits, revealing more flesh than either Jane or Gail could have imagined. The music too became louder and more boisterous with the sounds of London after Midnight, Lacuna Coil and Sex Gang Children providing the motivation to participate.

Jane took one of the pills from her bag and popped it onto her tongue before swallowing it down with some of her vodka and red bull. Linda saw this and was immediately worried, she was happy to use ecstasy but she stayed off the alcohol whilst she did, not feeling the need for both and concerned about the mix and not knowing Jane very well, even whether she had used E's before?

"Go steady on the booze babe." Linda reached across the table and placed her hand over the glass in front of Jane, "That E will kick in soon, give it a chance."

"OK. Babe, wanna dance?"

"Yeah why not, what about you Gail, coming?"

The three girls went onto the dance floor and picked up the fast paced beat of the music, throwing themselves into it with enthusiasm and no little flamboyance.

After about half an hour it was noticeable that Jane's energy levels appeared to have increased and she remained on the dance floor throughout, taking no breaks and throwing herself into anything. It wasn't long before she was joined by others outside her normal circle of friends who were equally exuberant and egging each other on to greater efforts. Jane appeared to Gail to be enjoying the attention but the pace was too much for her and she sat back down with Linda and Geoff; watching as Jane threw her arms around one of the other dancers and began to embrace him, he in turn placed his arms around her and they danced to The Doors and David Bowie.

"She was besotted with Mike a couple of hours ago." Gail voiced to Linda above the sound of the music.

"She's young, she's enjoying herself and you should be too."

"She's a tart." Gail laughed as she spoke to emphasise she was joking.

"There's a lot of it about." replied Linda gesturing to the dance floor which was now reaching the point of overflow and most of those on it were wearing much less than seemed right to anyone with any scruples.

"Come on let's get back out there." Linda's pill was obviously kicking as well and she dragged Gail back out to the floor and joined the group to which Jane seemed to be the central figure.

As the night progressed Jane grew ever more in tune with the extreme Goths in terms of both dress and dance, the PVC dress was hitched even higher, the corset, suspenders and stockings revealed more flesh as well as the tattoo and this in turn created massive interest from those around her. The ecstasy had well and truly taken effect and Jane had few if any inhibitions left, she was there to enjoy herself, an ambition realised to the full. Gail had tried to intervene, but had met with discouragement from Jane and many others equally in tune with the finale to Sexy Sunday. Realising the futility of trying again Gail decided the best course of action was to join in, even though she decided to stay dressed.

"There's a party on the beach afterwards" Jane heard the words but didn't know where they had come from.

"Where? Whose?" she was excited and happy to go but didn't know any more than that.

"Just stick with me."

Darren was just one from the group who Jane had spent the last couple of hours with and the invite was an open one, to as many as wished to carry on with the night's entertainment on the beach immediately below The Spa Pavilion.

"I'm up for that, what about you Gail? Geoff, Linda?"

"You betcha Babe." Linda drank up her Red Bull and picked up her bag before heading for the door, Geoff followed as she knew he would, Gail was less certain but tagged along anyway.

FORTY FIVE

"It is now 10.42am on Monday 11th February 2013, the same people are present and we are continuing the interview of Mr William Raynor. Mr Raynor I must remind you that you are still under caution, do you understand?" Sue Collins had put new discs into the recorder and was going through the introductions before resuming the interview.

"Mr Raynor, you have now had an opportunity to receive private advice from your solicitor, have you anything you wish to say before I resume?" Neil Maughan wanted to give Raynor the opportunity to offer something of his own volition before resuming his questions.

"I don't want my wife involving in any of this; she only did what I asked her to do. I've given you all the names and all the addresses and phone numbers that are on the APS file on the desk top. I did pay cash in hand for some jobs because I can get away without charging VAT if I do that and what the lads do with tax is up to them."

"Thank you. You said Mike, Ben and Siggy did some work up at Esk View, can you remember who did what?"

"Not off the top of my head, it was ages ago. I know Mike does most of the bricklaying and plastering for me, Macca does the sparks but is happy to earn a few quid labouring as well and Siggy's a plumber."

"What's your trade, your skill set?"

"I'm an engineer but I took to being a builder years ago when the work dried up and the plastics factory shut down. I got some redundancy money and set up on my own."

"And that's when Abbey Property Services started?"

"Yeah, I've managed to keep my head above water, got some mates to help me when I needed it."

"You mean Mike, Ben and the others?"

"Yeah"

"How long have you known each of them?"

"I've known Mike and Siggy since schooldays but Andy, Paul and Gav I've met since setting up the business and Macca works the doors with Mike and he got him to help us out once and he stayed with us."

"And who would agree the work with them?"

"I would, I know what's needed and I can leave them to it; pay the going rate and know I'm gonna get a decent job done."

"Do you use an agency?"

"You know I do. I get work from the letting agent, that's where a lot of my work comes from."

"And how does that work?"

"The agent has to check the properties after each let or when a problem's raised. They decide what wants doing and then ring us to sort it. They know they can ring any time and that's why we keep the contracts."

"And who checks the work?"

"I do if I'm home or the owner or the agent."

"What about bigger jobs, walls, patios etcetera?"

"If it's a big job I'll agree a price and timescale with the owner or agent. You've gotta understand that we can only do the work when the properties are empty and if they're empty then they're losing money."

"So what bigger jobs have you done on Aelfleda Terrace?"

"Well none that are still standing now that's for sure."

Neil Maughan understood what Raynor was saying but didn't see the statement as being funny and remained silent; as is often the case when there is a pause in the interview the suspect tries to fill it;

"I didn't mean that to sound as it did, I mean we have built the garden walls and laid patios, we've also totally rewired one of the houses and put a damp course in another before doing all the plastering."

"And all these jobs will be in your books and on the laptop or desktop?"

"Yeah."

"Of the above what jobs did you do at Esk View?"

"I can remember we rewired 'cos the owner argued about the costs and we did half the patio cos the mean old git wouldn't pay for the whole thing to be re-laid."

"And when was that?"

"About 18 months ago I would think, he'd seen that next door had had theirs done but wouldn't pay for the proper job, he wanted a two grand job done for two hundred."

"And who did that work for you?"

"Macca and Mike as far as I can remember."

"And what about you, did you do any of the work or go to the house?"

"I priced up earlier in the year when the owners were there and then I checked the job after it was finished, but not straight away cos I was on the rigs."

"And was everything as you expected?"

"Yeah, always is. Good job."

The interview continued over the next hour or so covering the work carried out by Abbey Property Services, both on the East Cliff and elsewhere in the town; Willie Raynor was as helpful as could be expected and Neil Maughan felt he had made some ground in his investigation. Thanking Raynor and Paul Waterman as he showed them out he reminded them that it was an ongoing enquiry and not to discuss the interview with his work mates. He always felt that this needed to be done but felt it was a very naive person who thought that mates wouldn't discuss a police interview and if they did happen to be involved in criminal activity they would merely regard the request as a joke.

"Waddya think Sue?"

Sue Collins had remained almost entirely silent through the interview but had made copious notes.

"I think he's more bothered about his taxes than anything else. I wouldn't bet your mortgage let alone my own of him being involved."

"No me neither but we can go and look at the others. Let's get the team together this afternoon and get moving again."

FORTY SIX

"I'm authorising your detention to secure and preserve evidence and to do so by means of questioning. Do you understand?"

The custody officer at Scarborough Police station, Sergeant Brian Denness, looked down at Mike from his seat behind the purpose built dais in the centre of the custody suite.

"No I fucking don't. All I did was try to help her and you lot fucking lock me up. So much for helping each other eh?" Mike's frustration and anxiety was now coming to the fore.

"An allegation has been made and we have to investigate it fully. The officer here will search you and then I'll go through a procedure to ensure you understand your rights and to be certain that the correct care is in place."

"Care? What do you fucking care? You've brought me here when I've done nowt wrong."

Howard Small stepped in and tried to calm Mike down before he made matters worse for himself.

"Mike, the Sergeant is only doing his job, he's not going to change his mind. We'll take some statements, check the CCTV and then interview you later. You'll get your chance to tell us your side then."

"How long will all that take then?"

"I can't tell you cos I don't know yet but as quick as I can." Howard Small was in time honoured mode of not giving anything away yet trying to placate an angry man before he became really angry and needed restraint.

"What time is it now?"

"There's a clock there. It's nearly twelve."

"Busiest time of night and I'm here. Great."

The custody officer continued with the booking in procedure, giving Mike his rights and asking about his well being, whether he wanted anyone informing of his arrest, did he require a solicitor and all in a matter of fact manner that became a man of twenty years service and too many of those in the custody environment.

By the time Howard Small directed Mike to the cells, he was resigned to the fact that he was staying, he was minus his boots, his belt, mobile phone and all personal belongings; these had been taken from him logged on the custody record and placed in a large plastic bag before being deposited in a locker.

"Are you in a position to interview Howard, first account?"

"No chance Sarge, I don't even know how the victim is yet, I've got a list of at least three witnesses who have said they saw him push her but it was right outside the pub so there are potentially dozens of others to see as well as CCTV from the pub and the Council."

"Well I can update you on the injury, she's being kept in overnight after her scan, and she's described as very poorly. Did you know that the DI was involved?"

"I heard something on the radio. Well if that's the case then he won't be getting interviewed tonight, it'll probably be CID in the morning."

"Well he can sleep it out then."

"He seemed a decent sort of bloke, for a doorman anyway. I'll go round to the council offices and get a copy of the tapes now and then head back. It's a busy night."

"For Whitby maybe."

The sarcasm wasn't lost on Howard as he left the custody office, at times, he thought, you wouldn't believe we were all working together.

FORTY SEVEN

Jane woke with a start, looking around she saw Gail was still asleep in her bed; the sun was shining through the thin patterned curtains and the gap between forming shadows on the wall behind her. She looked across at the bedside clock and through the foggy haze of her semi focused eyes she saw that it showed 11:54 in a bright red LCD display. Reaching out to the small table at the side of the bed she began to realise the depth of her hangover which kicked in as she leant over and picked up her phone. There were four unread messages and opening them up she saw that they were all from Phoebe asking about Sexy Sunday; this in turn focused her mind back on the last ten hours or so. Where did she get to? What did she do and with who? She started piecing together the early hours again as she sat on her bed with the duvet still wrapped around her shoulders and yet still wearing the PVC dress from last night. Her head began pounding but, thankfully, she didn't have the feeling of sickness that often accompanied the nausea; she remembered leaving the Spa with Geoff and Linda with Gail a short distance behind and Darren running after them after chatting to his mates; all of them walking down past the line of beach chalets and onto the beach. Someone had managed to start a fire; she thought with driftwood but didn't know for sure, others were sat on the sands and rocks around it smoking and drinking and generally just extending the night albeit a now rather cold one.

Her mouth felt dry and she also felt hungry, Gail was restless but still sleeping, there was no noise from any other room that she could hear and she decided that she first needed to take a couple of paracetamols before anything else. Walking through to the other room she got a glass of water and then took a battered box of pills from her handbag. Taking two pills from the blister pack she remembered the two tablets that she had bought from Linda, she could only remember having taken one yet couldn't think what she may have done with the other. Making her way back to her bed she took off the dress and corset, replacing them with a tee shirt. Her flimsy pants were torn, she noticed, without remembering how they had become so.

"Hey you." Gail murmured from her bed, "how you feeling?"

"Pretty shit really. You?"

"I'm feeling better than you look. Fucking hell babe, you looked in the mirror this morning?"

"Thanks for that. Some mate you are." said in a frivolous manner and accompanied by a pillow thrown across the room in Gail's' direction Jane laughed, until her headache reminded her that she shouldn't.

"I thought you were going to meet Mike again last night, so what changed?"

"Oh shit, I haven't even thought of that this morning."

"So you haven't rung him then?"

"No, but he hasn't rung me either. There's no message on my phone."

"Really?"

"No."

"Maybe he's pissed off at you not showing up?"

"I don't think I even noticed if he was there or not?"

"Well if he was he would have seen Darren chasing you down the footpath and trying to touch you up."

"I thought he'd have said some'rt though if he was there and why hasn't he rung?"

"Maybe he got held up at work, try ringing him, that is, if you still want to?"

Jane rang Mike's mobile number but it went straight to answer phone so she tried a text instead but got no reply.

"Maybe he's still asleep if he had a shit shift last night?" Gail didn't really believe this but was trying to look for a positive in the situation.

"He could still have phoned or texted."

"Well maybe he didn't get a chance, try him again in a few minutes, he might be somewhere where there's no signal, its crap in places around here?"

"I will, and then I'll go to the cottage, see if he's there?"

"You need something to eat and drink first and a shower, you still look like shit."

"And so do you." a second pillow made its way across the room in the direction of Gail but was swatted away by Gail who was quite obviously more alert than Jane.

Gail made two strong coffees and picked up a couple of the foil wrapped biscuits from the complimentary tray and they chatted about the previous night as they drank. Gail explained that Darren had been very attentive but ultimately unsuccessful in his endeavours, partly because it was a very cold night and also because of the drink and presence of so many others. She went on to say that Jane appeared to be "well out of it" as the cold air got to her but that they had all stayed until well after four o'clock when everyone seemed to make a collective decision that they had run out of firewood and it was too cold to stay any longer without a fire. Everyone had said their respective goodbyes, more meaningful to some as they would be going home later that day, in fact only a few diehards or those without jobs to return to seemed to be staying.

Gail explained that Darren had been persistent in asking for Jane's mobile phone number and that eventually she had given it just to shut him up and that shortly afterwards he had helped to walk her home but was given the brush off at the door. When they had reached their room they had literally just crashed onto their beds and let exhaustion take its course.

Jane checked her phone again, there were no other missed calls or texts that she had missed so either Darren had given up on her or else he too was still flat out in his, or someone else's bed? She then checked her photo gallery and saw a number of photos that she didn't immediately recognise together with a couple of videos she had taken earlier in the evening of Gail, Geoff and Linda messing about at The Spa. Working through the photos she saw several of her with Darren, just in stupid poses really and quite obviously both pissed; she was unrecognisable from the little Horsforth girl that would visit her parents at the weekend, scantily clad and with Darren having his head buried in her cleavage whilst others looked on, she was sure she would be seen as a tart, "a woman of ill repute and very few morals," as her mother would no doubt say.

Darren did still look good though she thought, so her man radar was still working ok and if things didn't work out with Mike she would give him a second chance. This thought dragged her back to reality though and to Mike, why hadn't he rung, she was certain he would? Finishing her drink she made her way into the bathroom and once in the shower let the water rain down on her head and over her back whilst she pondered what to do next? She held onto the chrome rail that was placed conveniently for that purpose and let the affects of her indulgence wash away.

"Oy, how long are you gonna be in there? Some of us 'ave got homes to go to yer know?"

Jane had forgotten that Gail was returning home today, she would miss her company and support but it brought a decision to mind; she would pack her things too and go to the cottage and stay with Mike until she set off home. She was certain that wouldn't be a problem as long as she hadn't done anything stupid with Darren.

Decision made she came out of the bathroom wrapped only in a towel; it was supposed to be a bath sheet but was about half the size it should have been to match that description. Gail was dressed and had her clothing packed in a sports holdall which was open on her bed.

"What time you off?"

"Trains not 'til after 2.00 o'clock so if you want a breakfast somewhere I'll walk down town with you."

"Nah, I'm gonna pack first and I'm off too."

"What, home?"

"No, Mike's." she explained her thoughts about driving up there to The Ropery, parking her car and just taking enough stuff for the night. "A chill night in if he's not working again, he must get some time off."

"Yeah for good behaviour eh?"

"Not if I can help it, I missed out on his bad behaviour last night remember?"

"Well, if you're not going out yet I'm gonna say ta'ra now 'cos I'm hungry and I won't get owt on the train."

The two hugged, promised to stay in touch and then Jane watched from the large bay window as Gail walked away from Harbour View towards Skinner Street, looking backwards Gail waved back and then strode on. Jane had welcomed Gail as a friend but already felt that it was a friendship born of circumstance rather than shared ideals; she wouldn't shun her but felt that it was unlikely to be the start of a long term acquaintance closeness, the sort she knew she had with Phoebe.

FORTY EIGHT

The whiteboards that had once been clean were now covered in names, actions and all manner of lines drawn across linking names with each other and with times and dates. Printed photographs were pinned on boards nearby and blue tacked onto walls with names, dates of birth, CRO numbers, where applicable, and addresses typed underneath. There were eight desk top computers arranged around a group of four tables at one end of the room with a further desk behind these which itself had a lap top on it, the other end of the room had two tables pushed together to one side of the whiteboards and a number of chairs facing towards them, a projector was set up, suspended from the ceiling between the rows and aimed towards the smart board for the purpose of briefing those present; many were, including Simon Pithers and Neil Maughan. "Ladies and Gentlemen," Simon Pithers, in a slightly raised voice focused the attention of all those present; "Let's get this briefing underway please."

He sat down at the head of the table and continued, "Good afternoon everyone and welcome to the latest briefing of Operation Caedmon, it is now 4.10pm on Monday 11th February 2013 and I'd like to think that this briefing represents an important watershed in this investigation. As many of you are aware Detectives, Inspector Maughan and Sergeant Collins interviewed William Raynor earlier today and as a result we can now confirm that Abbey Property Services did carry out work at our crime scene; including the laying of a patio." He emphasised this last point and then paused knowing that everyone would want a second or two to register this point and decide on their own response.

As he expected, there was a general nattering around the room and glances exchanged across the tables. Carrying on Simon Pithers added; "Obviously what we do not have is a signed confession from Mr Raynor that declares anyone buried our body under that patio; but what we do have is a starter for ten Ladies and Gents and I want the bloody bonus points to add to that. Sue will be allocating some tasks shortly and included in those will be the locating, arresting and interviewing everyone who has worked for Abbey Property Services at that address." Pithers was engaging in his tone and inspiring in his demeanour, it was an opportunity to put fresh impetus into the investigation. "As yet we do not know the identity of our deceased victim which leads me to think more than ever that she is not one of ours, not from Whitby, not from North Yorkshire: somewhere someone is missing a daughter, maybe a sister or even a mother? Sadly not every force can be said to be meticulous in their enquiries when they involve girls or young women who may choose to leave home against the wishes of their parents or even their partners. Please indulge me here, but let's assume for a minute that we may be dealing with a promiscuous teenager, old enough to live a life of her own but a life that sits outside of the parental parameters; might that not fit with our item of jewellery? Sue let's have a couple of D's solely looking at Mispers with a -," pausing to ensure he spoke correctly, "shall we say less than pure background, look at the social media sites see who's talking about mispers, friends, enemies, associates, anyone who may be missing someone? What about partners, spouses, have we anyone grieving the loss of their loved one but who has no idea where they are or maybe a partner who has left of their own free will but against a husbands wish? "

Simon Pithers looked around the table before standing up; his stature drew attention just by its presence and there was quiet attention around the room. Pithers pointed to the whiteboards, to which now were added the names of all the workers from Abbey Property Services, under the not too imaginative heading of APS, together with all relevant details known of them. "Sue, please go through what is known about each of these employees, one of these people must know something about the burial of our victim, if not indeed be our killer?"

Standing up from her seat at the table, Sue Collins made her way over to the whiteboards; pointing to the boards she began by outlining that day's interview with Raynor;

"My gut feeling is that he is not our man," realising that Simon Pithers was stood next to her and not wanting to appear to have made up her mind yet, she carried on, "but may well know more than he has currently said and we shouldn't rule him out. He is still taking on work for APS and still paying for the work in backhanders so that might be a lever we can use in other interviews. He has one of our club numbers but nothing for the last ten years or so. He has been working on the rigs on and off for the last four years and as such is away from home for long periods at a time."

Using a black bic biro she pointed at the next name on the list,

"John Paul Sigston, born eighth August nineteen seventy three in Whitby, lives on Fountains Close when he's at home but is currently with Raynor on the rigs; known to us only for historical stuff including, possession, low level theft, shoplifting and the expected public order in his teens. Employed as a plumber by APS and a friend of Raynor's from schooldays, he has been visited once and given an account that he worked for two days at Esk View. He should be in Whitby now as he works the same rota as Raynor, so Mark I want you and Geoff to bring him in please."

Pausing to allow everyone to catch up making their notes she then carried on with the others on the list;

"Andrew Mark Ward, born fourteenth January nineteen seventy four, home address on Auckland Way, Whitby, is the third of the group who work together in the North Sea and therefore should also be at home. Another local, born and bred in Whitby, CRO for public order and a cannabis warning; again all historical," she realised she was becoming staccato in her delivery but the task in hand lent itself to this approach. "Fi, can you and Dan bring Mr Ward in?" two of the numerous detectives drafted in just for this case, Fiona Prentice and Dan McArdle were sat directly across from Sue making notes.

Moving on down the list she continued;

"Paul Coles, no middle name, born second March nineteen seventy six in Chester, presently working with a builders gang in Northampton; again we've had a statement from him earlier and I'll get Northampton to bring him in again so we can talk to him ourselves up here. Pre-cons for ABH in a pub brawl a couple of years ago. Not known if he's done any work at our scene but nothing in his statement, we'll see?"

Carrying on quickly in order not to lose the enthusiasm of her audience she turned again to the boards;

"Michael Raymond Davies, born fourth December nineteen eighty four at Scarborough. Seems to be a bit of a Nomad, believed to be currently working in St David's in Pembroke, and has previously worked in Hull, Carlisle and the North East. Interestingly for us he was arrested for assault on a female whilst working as a doorman about eighteen months ago. I'll do some more background checks on him after this briefing. Again I've arranged for his arrest and we'll bring him back up here to interview him."

"I hope he hasn't developed on them bloody Welsh accents." Mark Taylor interjected, "I can't stand that accent, all Boyo and Bollocks if you ask me?"

"No-one is asking you DC Taylor." Neil Maughan couldn't be seen to be condoning such comments in front of the Superintendent, even though he was very much in agreement with his colleague. For his part, Simon Pithers appeared impassive and for his part; Mark Taylor looked suitably chastised.

"Well, that's probably a good point for me to hand over to you sir." Sue Collins didn't want to become party to a political correctness debate, not that Simon Pithers would tolerate debate, he was black and white on this one, as he had been instructed, from on high, to be.

Neil Maughan stood up to continue the briefing, or more correctly to foreclose it;

"Thanks Sue, Ladies and Gents we have created an opportunity to make some serious progress in this investigation, well done to everyone; now let's get on with our tasks and start pulling it all together. We'll meet up again tomorrow now get off and prepare for a busy time."

FORTY NINE

"When is someone going to talk to me?" Mike asked the SDO as he had come to know as the acronym for Security Detention Officer.

"Not my decision mate, I only do the meals and checks. I'd guess that CID will want to interview you though, so probably after nine, they don't rush."

"CID, why would they want to talk to me?"

"Sorry mate I've said too much already."

"You can't do that, you can't say CID want me then not tell me why. Can I talk to someone please; I'd better have a solicitor."

"I'll get the Custody Officer to come and see you."

"OK. What time is it?"

"Half past four or thereabouts."

The SDO closed the cell door hatch and went back to the main desk where it was still busy despite it being well into Monday morning.

"Sarge, cell 6, Davies; says he wants a solicitor now."

"OK. Get these two in first then bring him back out." The Custody Officer gestured towards the latest prisoners to be brought in that night, two teenage men, both dressed in loose fitting jeans, torn tee shirts and each sporting cuts and bruises and reeking of stale alcohol and spilt kebab; a true representation of the stereotypical binge drinking culture.

It was after five o'clock when Mike was brought from the cell and given the option of speaking to the duty solicitor or indicating a personal choice. He elected to go for the duty solicitor believing, wrongly, that this option would elicit the quickest response. Having signed the electronic pad to record his request, he asked,

"What do CID want to see me for? The SDO said CID will want to see me?"

"That's not my decision and certainly not his. Somebody will decide in the morning, it's too late to start interviews now and they're still taking statements."

"But I haven't done anything. This is just fucking ridiculous."

"I'll put the call in for your solicitor and you can tell them all about it but for now you'll have to go back to the cell."

Mike walked sullenly back to cell 6 and sat on the hard mattress, he began to retrace everything he had done that night in his head and the more he thought the more he knew that he had done nothing wrong; but then why was he sat in a cell waiting for a solicitor?

A further twenty minutes or so passed before the key turned in the lock again and he was asked to go back to the main desk for a telephone consultation with the duty solicitor. The reception was quiet now, disturbed only by the shouting between some of the cells and the faint voices heard on the officer's airwave radios.

Taking the telephone from the Custody Officer he spoke into the mouthpiece, "Hello."

"Hello, Mr Davies, I'm Paul Jeffries, the duty solicitor for tonight."

"Good, can you get me out of here, I've done nowt wrong."

"I'll need to confirm some details with you first then we can discuss the situation."

Mike spent the next few minutes answering basic questions to confirm his name, address, date of birth and some other personal details before even getting to mention his arrest.

"I've been in here for hours already and nowt's happening. I don't even know why I'm here."

"The Custody Officer has advised me that you have been arrested on suspicion of a serious assault and that officers are currently taking statements and obtaining CCTV evidence. He has indicated that you will not be interviewed until the morning."

"Can they do that?"

"Unfortunately for you, yes they can. Your detention will be reviewed by an Inspector shortly, but given what I have already been told I am certain that you will be kept in for questioning later. I will ask for some representations to be made about your arrest but on the face of it all that has been done so far seems to be in accordance with the legal framework. I can be available to attend for the interview if you wish?"

"So I've just got to sit and wait?"

"Until morning yes. I'm sorry but there really is no other alternative."

"They said it'll be CID. Why?"

"It would appear that the extent of injuries is such that CID have taken on the investigation, that's often the case for GBH."

"GBH, What the fuck are you talking about, I never touched her." Mike was genuinely shocked at the use of that phrase, "What injuries? I haven't fucking done anything."

As Mike's voice reached higher levels the Custody Officer decided that enough was enough and asked, in no uncertain way for the phone back before ordering Mike back to his cell again. Despite his anger Mike was not stupid enough to take his anger out on those present and reluctantly made his way back to his room for the night.

Still on the phone, Paul Jeffries wrote down details of the alleged offence, including the most up to date report on the victim's injuries; those were that Fleur Brennan was in the Intensive Care Unit and would need surgery that night on a fractured skull. She was, in the usual hospital parlance, very poorly but stable.

It was to be a long night for Mike.

FIFTY

Jane had finished packing her belongings into her suitcase, had written a note for Geoff and Linda, which she left on the coffee table where it would be clearly visible on their return. She was in fact keeping herself busy as she was still unable to contact Mike; she had tried again several times and had not received replies to any texts she had sent. She was becoming fearful, not that Mike was unwell or anything of that nature, but more that he didn't want to see her again. She felt insecure for the first time since she had arrived in Whitby and had just watched her closest available friend walk away to her train.

What did she always do in these circumstances? She rang Phoebe.

"Hi Pheebs," no other words came out after that as Jane began sobbing, tears rolled down her cheeks and onto her tee shirt. She had bottled up her feelings whilst with Gail, even tried the jokey route but now she was talking to her soul mate she couldn't hold back the tears.

"What's up Babe?"

There were only sobs in reply for what seemed like ages but was probably less than a minute in truth before Jane managed;

"It's Mike, I don't know what's happened and he won't answer my calls or texts or anything."

"Babe, he's probably just forgotten to charge his phone, don't get upset like this when you don't know."

"I just know there's something wrong Pheebs."

"Well, you don't know really do you, you're just thinking the worst and making yourself feel bad."

"I do know. He would always reply."

"Jane, you've only known him a couple of days. He might just have had a real bad night and be at home asleep."

"I know you're right but I just needed to hear it from someone else."

"Well you have now so come on tell me about Sexy Sunday."

Jane perked up a bit and it wasn't long before a smile came across her face as her friend proved just what a good listener she was, prompting at the right moments and eliciting possibly more information than was intended. Before she had realised what she was saying Jane had mentioned Darren, Mankini Man, ecstasy tablets and beach parties. Whilst she was happy to share most of this she hadn't wanted to mention the drugs as she knew Phoebe was against their use. Thankfully it seemed that Phoebe was more interested in Darren than the drug and began teasing her about her loose morals, imitating her mother's voice in a reprimand. The tone of the call had lifted considerably and Jane again felt the warmth of her friendship with Phoebe raising her from the doldrums to a happy place.

 Before ending the call Jane agreed to send some photos across and to visit Phoebe as soon as she could, but she was ever more certain that she could now drive to Mikes and see just what the problem was.

Placing her Samsung in her jeans pocket Jane put on her jacket and raised the handle of her suitcase to pull it down the stairs and out of the front door. She stopped at the small reception desk and scribbled a short entry in the guest book advising future guests and her hosts that she had enjoyed her stay in Whitby and would definitely consider returning to The Harbour View. Placing the pen back down, she took her case and opened the main door, leaving for the last time.

FIFTY ONE

"Sigston's problem is that he can't stop talking" Sue Collins was being updated over the phone by DC Mark Taylor, "Trouble is, he's just spouting shite and we're not really getting anywhere yet."

"Well, give him enough rope and the right questions Mark and I'm sure we'll get something out of him?"

"He's gone over his statement again and he agrees that he was there for two days a couple of years ago, he says he fitted a new shower cubicle and changed the taps on the bath and basin. He works on his own and said that Raynor paid him three hundred quid for two days work, plus the parts at cost."

"Seems like we're in the wrong job Mark; anyone else working at the same time on any other job?"

"He say's not and he said that there was no patio laid at the time he was there, only a few paving flags that had been put down by, as he described it; someone with no idea, no real inclination nor any fucking patience."

"Sounds a real professional job then?"

"Yeah, but if it was a crap job, does that mean that it was because it was done in a rush, maybe to bury a body before it was missed?"

"Well it could do, but surely the owners must have noticed something if that was the case, or even the agents or holiday guests?"

"Just a thought really; do we know when the proper patio was laid then?"

"About eighteen months ago, according to the Wilcock's, the owners"

"Right, well we've got it all on disc and he's just being kept in for a while until we get Andy Ward into interview, then he can be bailed out to come back whenever."

"OK Mark, please ask Fi and Dan to call in on me and let me know how they've got on."

"Will do Sue," Mark Taylor replaced the phone in its cradle and made his way out of the office and through to the custody suite where DC's Prentice and McArdle were ready to start their interview with Andy Ward.

"Do you understand the caution Mr Ward?" Fi Prentice opened the interview as usual by clarifying the formalities, everyone had introduced themselves and she was keen that Ward was aware of his rights;

"Yeah, what I don't understand is what I'm doing here?"

"Well, as you were told at the time of your arrest we are investigating a murder and we believe that you may be able to help with that." Fi Prentice continued to be very formal and correct in her methods, after all any interview record could be called to be used in evidence.

"Are you joking? Is it an April Fools or is Jeremy Beadle gonna come in the room in a minute?"

"I can assure you that it is no joke and it is important that you realise this too. Can I confirm that you are happy to be interviewed without a solicitor present?"

"Yeah, I've nowt to hide an' I just wanna get off home again."

"Right; then we'll crack on."

The opening questions all related to Wards name, address and background; easing him into the mode of answering simple questions and hopefully creating a rapport that would help to elicit information later. In response Ward had explained that he was a general builder and had worked in the trade on and off since he left school and until recently when he had taken a role on the rigs meaning he had no need to take on casual work anymore.

"Have you ever worked for Abbey Property Services?" DC Prentice asked one of the few closed questions she would ask that day.

"Yeah, who hasn't? Will'd take anyone on if the price was right."

"Can you tell me what work you have done in the last two years then?"

"Can we stop pissing about? You just mean on that cottage on the East Side don't you?"

"Which cottage do you mean?"

"The one where you found that girl, right?"

"Well what can you tell me about that then?"

"Not much, I helped Mike with some internal walls, bit of filling' and plastering', bit of coving to replace but I didn't do much at all really; Mike had most of it sorted."

"Mike?"

"Mike Davies. Isn't he on your list?"

"Did you work with Mike?"

"Sometimes, like I said, he did most of the work on that cottage but I did a bit to help him finish off. He was behind schedule and it was due to be let I think."

"What work did you do outside?"

"None, like I said, I did some filling and plastering on the walls and a bit of coving. I hate that coving, too fucking finicky for my liking."

"Did anyone do any work outside whilst you were there?"

"No. None to do as far as I could see."

"Who else worked there with you and Mike?"

"That time, no-one, just me an' him."

"Any other time?"

"Well I've worked with Siggy, plastering up when he's done his plumbing and bits on my own, but nowt recently like I said"

"Do you keep any records of your building work?"

"Nah, not really. I might put it in my diary on my phone so's I don't forget it but I don't keep books or owt, it's not worth my while."

"So do you know when you worked at Esk View?"

"Not really, well not exactly like; 'bout two years ago I would think was the last time."

"Which door did you use to go into the cottage?"

"Back door, above t'arbour."

"And did you see any signs of recently completed work or even work in progress on the outside?"

"No but then I didn't look either."

"The patio for instance?"

"Is that what you call it, a few flagstones, all over the shop they were?"

"Can you explain what you mean by that?"

"Well to me it looked like someone without a clue had laid them, not done any prep work and not levelled them up, certainly not put a mix in, so when it rains and someone walks on them they go all over the place."

"That could be important to us Mr Ward; can I ask you please to think very carefully when this would have been?"

"Willie will probably have it down somewhere, Willie Raynor. I can't remember exactly."

Dan McArdle asked some further questions and they both clarified certain points but there was not much more to gain at this time; each left the interview room knowing that it was a job that had to be done but that it was highly unlikely that Ward was their man.

FIFTY TWO

"Mr Davies, my name is Detective Sergeant Brian Jameson and I am now in charge of this investigation. I understand that you have asked for your solicitor to be present for the interview, is that correct?"

"Yes; he's not my solicitor as such but one that we called last night, this morning; earlier."

The two men were stood at the entrance to cell number six, Brian Jameson, an experienced Detective of nearly thirty years service with a gnarled, pock marked face below a grey comb over, had read through the file left by the night shift and was officially introducing himself to the prisoner; in reality he was getting a feel for him, measuring him up mentally and physically to adapt his approach to the interview accordingly. Dressed in a somewhat dishevelled dark grey suit that must have been in fashion at some time or other, but not in living memory, and which covered a pale blue creased shirt that didn't look as though it had seen a washer for many a month, Brian, or Columbo to his mates in the station; was a mystery to his colleagues; most Detectives took something of a pride in the way they dressed; Brian's dress sense was seen as an abomination by most and pitied by others, yet he was a well respected cop, meticulous in his work and known to submit the most complex files with great attention to detail and accuracy; he was often sought out for advice by his colleagues of both lower and higher ranks. Why oh why didn't he pay that much attention to himself?

"Well Mr Davies, I have some bad news for you; I have to inform you that I am now arresting you on suspicion of the manslaughter of Fleur Brennan last night, I must also remind you that you do not have to say anything but that it may harm your defence if you do not mention when questioned something upon which you later rely on in court. Anything you do say may be given in evidence. Do you understand?"

"What? Who's Fleur Brennan? Manslaughter, what do you mean?" Mike Davies didn't know whether to shout, cry and scream or what to do. He could feel the walls closing in on him as he looked around the cell; he could see the partial face of his accuser through the small hatch in the metal door, the graffiti scratched onto it. He felt his knees go weak and thought that he might collapse; he genuinely didn't know what was going on or what to do about it.

Brian Jameson recognised what he was watching and spoke again, "Fleur Brennan is the girl who you were alleged to have assaulted last night; she died a short while ago in hospital."

"I didn't do anything, I didn't assault anybody." The words came out in a low, almost whispered voice just short of crying. For all he was a very physical, well built man he felt very inadequate at this moment in time, out of his depth in a world he knew little of.

"I'll update the Custody Officer and I would advise that you speak again with your solicitor." Brian shut the hatch by lifting it up and sliding the small bolt across before making his way back to Custody Reception. He updated the SDO who in turn added another entry to the computer generated custody record.

"I need to look again at the CCTV in the CPM's office and get a copy, but I should be ready in about an hour if the solicitor can get here."

"No probs, I'll give him a call." The SDO was actually happy for something to do, most of the overnight drunks had been either given a fixed penalty notice or released without charge he thought; the usual domestic violence cases had seen retractions made by the injured party, usually the wife or girlfriend who just wanted their other half out of the way for a night and sought police assistance to achieve their aims. Only four cells remained occupied for the morning shift and the Case Progression Manager had arranged for three of those to be dealt with as low level crimes by his team of civilian support staff.

As agreed, it was just over an hour later when Brian returned in the company of DC Des Mason from Whitby. They saw through the glass walls that Mike Davies was in a side room talking to his solicitor, Paul Jeffries, known to both detectives as someone who would advise his clients to say "No comment." to each and every question unless it was absolutely without fail obvious to everyone what had gone on and who was responsible.

"How long's he been in with him?" Des Mason asked the custody officer.

"Twenty minutes or more, he's shitting himself that she's died"

"Good, he ought to be."

"Still says he done nowt mind."

"And we've never heard that before have we?"

The officers all began laughing together which didn't go unnoticed by both Mike Davies and his legal advisor.

There was an air of mistrust in interview room number two as Des Mason placed the discs in the recorder and went through the introductory process. Mike Davies had always tried to work with the police he felt when working the doors, in fact he considered himself to be on friendship terms with some. Now, as he sat adjacent to Paul Jeffries, facing those he saw to be his accusers and who he believed were laughing at him he was angry; gone was the sadness and disbelief of earlier, replaced with a determination to stop what he saw as the cops laughing at him.

142

"My client wishes to emphasise that he completely denies the accusation and I have advised him not to make any comment during this interview or until such time as we have had full access to any available information or evidence."

There was no need for Paul Jeffries to have made his introductory speech except to try to impress his client, thought Brian Jameson; he knew that the questions would still be asked and that his client was more than likely, at some time, to answer one of those questions; either through impatience, anger or frustration.

"Thank you Mr Jeffries your comments are noted but as you will understand we shall still be asking your client questions and we will give him every chance to answer if he so wishes. I would be grateful if you gave him the same opportunity."

Des Mason, watched by all those present, placed a disc in the TV/DVD player ready for use later in the interview before taking his seat alongside his colleague and opposite Mike Davies and going through the usual introductory process, including handing over a printed copy of the disclosure, the information on which the police were basing their decision making but without the minutia on which they would question their detainee later. Brian Jameson then began to talk;

"Mr Davies you have been arrested on suspicion of manslaughter, which relates to an incident at The Resolution Public House in Whitby last night; do you understand?"

"No comment"

"Can you please confirm that you are employed to work as a doorman at The Resolution?"

"No comment"

"Mr Davies, I can see, as can the video camera, that you are wearing a black shirt with the logo of a security company on the breast pocket. Is that the shirt you wear when working as a doorman?"

"No comment."

"Do you know anyone by the name of Fleur Brennan?"

The officers saw the exchange of glances between solicitor and client with the latter wearing a worried face, a bead of sweat already appearing on his brow; a slight shake of the head from Paul Jeffries indicating the advised response.

"No comment."

Des Mason then read out a witness statement taken from one Emma Sadler, it was a detailed account and included the fact that she saw Davies pushing Fleur Brennan back and resulting in her falling to the ground and striking her head on a step. Davies listened intently as each word was spoken, his hands rubbing together, his teeth grinding in order to prevent him speaking out. He managed and looked again at his solicitor for guidance, a slight nod of approval being given in return.

"Mr Davies, my colleague has just read out a statement given by a witness who was present last night, do you have any comment to make?"

"No comment."

"Do you have any reason to believe that the witness account is flawed?"

"No comment."

"I have two further witness accounts that I can read to you and they tend to corroborate that first account. Do you wish me to read them out?"

"No comment."

"That is a total of three witnesses so far who all tell me that you pushed Fleur Brennan deliberately and that as a result she fell causing her to injure herself and which subsequently resulted in her death?"

"No comment."

This time Brian Jameson let the reply hang in the air and did not ask a further question.

"I said no comment. It's all a fit up; you're trying to set me up."

Paul Jeffries was visibly disappointed at this reaction and interjected;

"My client wishes to make no further comment Sergeant."

"On the contrary Mr Jeffries, I believe that he does."

"My advice to him is to make no further comment."

"Your client obviously has his own mind Mr Jeffries, can I remind you that it is your place to advise and not to answer on behalf of your client. I will continue to ask questions whilst I believe there are outstanding matters to clear up." Brian Jameson leant across the table slightly as if to emphasise who was in charge.

"I'm sorry." Mike Davies looked at the solicitor as he spoke, feeling a little like the schoolboy who had misbehaved in class.

"Mr Davies you don't need to apologise, it is your prerogative to answer any of my questions as you see fit; we are just trying to obtain all the available evidence."

Brian Jameson made the comment to ensure that Davies knew he was responsive to the reply before asking Des to read out the two further statements, asking the same questions at the end of each one. Mike Davies had however recovered his composure and returned to his stock reply each time. Des Mason then turned on the small TV in the corner of the room and using the remote control pressed play to set the DVD going to show the recording of the incident outside The Resolution.

Mike Davies watched the screen intently; he saw himself and Sandy at the door, his colleagues at the other doors and the mixed crowds of Goths and the regular Townies flocking down from Skinner Street and Flowergate, down the sloping roads towards the town centre. He saw

144

how too many people were gathering on the narrow steps outside the pub and how a group of girls were playfully goading each other, looking worse for drink and all trying to get in at the same time. He watched as Sandy and he held out their hands out wide in a gesture aimed at preventing everyone pushing through in one mass, and he saw his arm move from a position at his side to one in front of him at the same time as the girl, Fleur Brennan as he now knew her, fell to the ground. He looked at the others in the room and saw that everyone was actually looking at each other, realising that what they had just seen was the pivotal moment on the recording.

FIFTY THREE

Without the benefit of satnav and not even knowing the address, it was some considerable time before Jane drove her Renault onto The Ropery; she had known that she had to cross the river and knew that her destination lay behind the rows of houses and flats on Church Street on the bank somewhere in front of the abbey; but she didn't know how to get there in a car.

The Ropery was no more than an access road to the houses in and around that area and the few streets that ran off it, such as St Mary's Crescent, Boulby Bank and also to the new premises on the purpose built small business park.

Parallel parking was not one of her strengths and the limited space available Jane felt challenged as she put the car into reverse and began the manoeuvre, looking over her shoulder as the car inched backwards into the space barely big enough; thankfully her father had bought her a car with parking sensors and Jane heard the sharp electronic bleeps as she neared the front of the Ford Focus directly behind her. Her concentration was broken however when she heard a loud thumping noise on her bonnet and an even louder voice from outside;

"Oy, you, yer can't park there. Its residents only parking here."

Jane was visibly shaken and stalled the car as a result, thankfully not hitting the Focus. She turned her attention back to the front and saw a young woman, a similar age to herself she thought, but dressed in torn black leggings that made her legs look skeletally thin and an ill fitting tee shirt, again much too big, with the once yellow colour fading to a drab beige shade. She saw that the woman had piercings in her lower lip and her left eyebrow that seemed only to enhance the shallowness of her expression, and that she wore tattoos that appeared to be self inflicted, 'Mum and Dad' on her right upper arm and 'Made in Whitby' around her belly button, which was also pierced. Jane liked her own tattoo and had just spent the weekend with friends who had tattoos and piercings but none looked as poorly done as these indigo scrawls; and the marks on the woman's inner forearm just above the wrist and almost up to her elbow were a dead giveaway that she was a regular drug user.

The woman banged on the window of the driver's door next;

"I said yer can't park 'ere, it's for us residents."

Jane was reluctant to lower the window and felt under threat having stalled the car.

"OK I'll move." she shouted through the still closed window. Turning the key in the ignition the car sprang back into life and Jane hastily put it into first gear and began to move forward, inching past the irate low life who in turn aimed a kick at the car as she did so, missing and half falling against the rear door as she fell. Jane drove on up The Ropery to discover it was a dead end with only a turning circle and no exit route; she immediately reversed into the far reaches of the available space and in a further three manoeuvres turned her car around and faced back along the route from whence she came. The woman, she saw, was back on her feet and thankfully making her way up towards St Mary's Crescent; Jane waited a short while giving her plenty of time to leave before driving carefully back along the road, past the original parking space and further back up the road; she found an alternative spot and safely parked her car and took time out to get her thoughts back together. What a contrast from the people she had met over the weekend, all of whom had been so kind and welcoming; she had heard tell that The East Side differed greatly from The West but thought nothing of it other than a historical allegory based on the fact that it was the fisherman that lived here and the ship owners, and therefore the wealthier folk, who were resident across the river. Maybe they were right after all?

Jane got out of the car, made sure that everything was in the boot and that the cover was on and nothing was visible in the car, she then secured it and walked back again along the same road. She knew that she had to find a path to her left but wasn't certain where it was so hoped she would recognise it when she came across it. She took in the views of The River Esk and across to the large houses on The West side, those that would have been owned by the wealthy ship owners and the respective gentry of olden day Whitby. It really was a beautiful place. As she walked on she recognised the footpath she had been looking for and turning onto it she began the short descent to Aelfleda Terrace. Walking on she saw the builder's materials in the yard of a cottage, together with a wheelbarrow pushed up against the house wall and covered partially with a tarpaulin. She saw that it contained a plethora of tools, spade, shovel, several trowels as well as other items she didn't know the purpose of. Where else, she thought, could you leave things out in a yard like this and not fear for it being stolen? She recognised it as being the place Mike had brought her only a couple of nights ago, her heart jumped to her mouth as she approached; would he be there? What would he say or do if he was and what would she do? She opened the gate and thought she saw movement in the ground floor room, but couldn't be sure. The back door was slightly ajar and there were noises from inside, Mike must be there; pushing the door gently she shouted,

"Mike. Mike, it's me, Jane."

There was no reply, which was strange as she was certain she had heard someone moving around, so she shouted again; but with greater concern;

"Mike, Mike is that you? Mike its Jane."

She heard movement again and then the kitchen door opened,

"Who are you, where's Mike?" Jane was both scared for herself and worried about Mike.

"So you're the girl with the snake tattoo? The Goth with the secret between her legs?"

That was more information than anyone should know she thought, anyone but Mike that was, in this town anyway.

"Who are you, do you know Mike?"

"Oh yes I know Mike, he's asked me to get some things together for him. Not coming back for a while he says."

"Why, what do you mean he's not coming back?"

"Just what I say, he's not coming back. He didn't say that I should expect you though."

"Well where is he then?" Jane was becoming just a little frantic; it was as if crossing the river had turned everything upside down, from nervous but happy to anxious and scared.

"Now I can't tell you that young lady 'cos he swore me to secrecy. He didn't want folk knowing where he's been or where he is now. That's what he said."

"But I'm his, erm. " What was she? She was going to say girlfriend but when she stopped and considered this she couldn't really bring herself to say it; she had known him a couple of days, slept with him and now he had disappeared and she didn't know where, nor would this ape of a man tell her where.

"You're his what? His slut, his bit of stuff. You're his current shag and nothing else."

Jane was shaken at the words she heard from this man she had never met before and was wishing she hadn't made her decision to come here after all. It was supposed to have been a happy reunion with Mike leading to a day in bed consummating their renewed relationship; it was anything but.

"Maybe you've come to show me that fine tattoo he's told us all about, maybe you want me to find that little gem of yours?" The man was becoming very frightening now and Jane was feeling very vulnerable, she was in someone else's house, someone she thought she knew but now had serious misgivings about; someone who had passed on secrets about her that her had no right to do. She stuttered a response as she tried to back up towards the door back into the rear room but the man had blocked her way.

"Let me go then please. I'm sorry I disturbed you. I just came to see Mike." The words were spoken in a very staccato manner with the threat of tears to follow.

"Now why would I want you to go, I hardly know you, but Mike; well Mike said you were very accommodating in a loose sort of way; if you know what I mean?"

"No!" Jane shouted at him, she wanted to scream but couldn't, she reached for the door but he got there first and took hold of her arm. She shouted again, "Let me go; let me go." But the man's grip was secure and he just smiled at her and lifted her arm away from the door handle.

"It's no use shouting and bawling my little Miss Jane, there's no-one to hear you down here, all holiday lets and all empty. We've got the place to ourselves."

FIFTY FOUR

Neil Maughan and Sue Collins travelled together to the relatively recently built Cardigan Police Station where Michael Raymond Davies was being held on their behalf. Having notified Dyed Powys of the need to arrest Davies and obtained intelligence that he was settled in an address at nearby Newport, they had asked that he be arrested on the morning of their travel in order that they would have decent travelling conditions and still be left with a good part of the day for interviews; something that The Police and Criminal Evidence Act or PACE placed great limitations on. The interviews, so far, with the other employees of APS had all suggested that Mike Davies was the one who had carried out most of the work at Esk Cottage and had also been resident whilst working there.

"If this was a TV show then it would all be done and dusted in an hour." Sue Collins laughed as she made the comment to her partner, "None of this travelling half way round the country taking up two days of our time and not knowing what we're going to get out of it?"

"Yeah, you're right and I'd be six foot two tall, dark haired, suited, booted and even more handsome and you'd be; well I suppose you'd just be the same as you are now."

Was he flirting with her she pondered, he did have a reputation but not usually within the work environment? He was married but then that didn't appear to stop many men in her profession and rumour had it that he had strayed previously; she put the thought to one side but made a mental note of it, smiling at the hinted compliment however.

"Yes and we'd both have IQ's of one forty or more, that is I'd still be the same but you'd be a bit cleverer."

"We'll see." Neil Maughan had seen the smile on her face, sometimes it was good to get away from the station, from the norm, to do something even just a bit different; it relieved some of the underlying tedium that even a murder enquiry could have; especially what was in effect a cold case anyway.

"Chester services are just up the road do you fancy a leg stretch?"

"Why not? I could do with a snack as well. Drive on James"

"Observation's clearly not your strong point then?" Sue teased him by sitting up straight, pulling her shoulders back and sticking out her breasts, "James indeed."

Six miles further on the car pulled off the M56 at junction 14 and into the service station; Sue found a space not too far away from the front of the building and after parking up they cleared their notes and laptops from the car, placing them out of site in the boot and made their way in.

Finding the usual branch of Costa they chatted away at the bar as they placed their order and Neil Maughan paid, keeping his receipt for his expenses claim. They then took comfortable seats near the window. Placing his cup back on the saucer and replacing it in his hand with the cheese and bacon Panini, Neil Maughan began thinking out loud;

"I can't say that I'm over confident about this guy you know?"

"Why? I did that research you asked for and he was locked up by Howard Small about eighteen months ago for an assault on a female; maybe that's his bag, how he gets off?" There was a touch of anger in her voice as she spoke the words; did this man have an issue with women?

"Yeah, but from what I gather it didn't get anywhere did it?"

"CPS wouldn't run it in the end; usual thing, it wasn't two hundred per cent certain of a conviction."

"What's your thought then?"

"You know that I've worked in the PVP unit and anyone who can hit a woman once can do it again in my opinion, it doesn't matter whether it's domestic or not."

"I know and I agree but are we certain that he even did it?"

"Well the custody officer must have been certain and Columbo clearly was; he never asks for a charge unless it's all belted and braced."

"But his background was checked at the time and as far as I can remember there was nothing in his past. Isn't it odd that someone with no previous should suddenly be a suspect in two separate deaths?"

"Well what do they say on tele, keep an open mind?"

"That's one thing that they do get right and we must. How much further is it from here?"

"About a hundred and fifty I'd say, best part of three hours depends on traffic?"

Looking at his wrist watch Neil Maughan, sighed;

"It'll be about twelve then when we get there. Seems late when we had a six o'clock start."

"Yeah well, we'd have been off earlier if you hadn't stopped to check in on the cells before we started. Still we can chill later; the local plods have booked us into a decent hotel, or so they say anyway."

Having refuelled, the BMW made its way back onto the motorway to start the remainder of the journey. It wasn't long before Neil Maughan had his head back against the seat and was nodding off, sometimes it was nice to have a driver and he would or should be more refreshed for the interview of Mike Davies; his only remaining suspect.

FIFTY FIVE

"Detective, I would like to ask for a break in the interview now, we have been going for nearly two hours and I consider it will be an act of oppression to continue without a break."

Paul Jeffries needed to buy some time for both himself and his client, he knew that there was to be CCTV evidence but hadn't been certain what was in the short clip. He knew now and although it was unclear exactly what happened there were obvious consistencies with the witness statements but did he push her or not?

"Mr Jeffries, I will allow a short break though challenge your assertion at the interview being oppressive. I'll arrange for a drink to be brought for you both and we will resume in ten minutes." Brian Jameson was still just reasserting his authority; younger officers may be eased off when a challenge such as this was issued but for Columbo it added spice to the process and was often an indication of panic or confusion from the accused.

"What do you think Bri?" asked Des Mason

"I don't know to be honest Des, Was it a push or not, it's not that clear is it?"

"No, but it fits with the witness accounts."

"I know it's just that I have a hunch that this guy is a genuine bloke, he looked scared when he saw the CCTV; as though he couldn't believe it."

"Couldn't believe it was on camera you mean?"

"Yeah well maybe you're right. Anyway it's not our decision to make is it, CPS will love this one."

"Let's get a brew any way and get back in."

The break turned out to be over 15 minutes and on recommencing the interview Paul Jeffries was first to speak'

"Detectives, my client wishes to make a statement after which he has been instructed not to answer any further questions."

"Well I must first remind you Mr Davies that you are still under caution and that, again, it may harm your defence if you fail to mention when questioned anything which you later rely upon in court. Do you understand this?"

"Yes I do."

"Then go ahead."

Mike Davies read from a sheet of A4 paper that he had been handed by his solicitor, his face was pale and the paper served to emphasise the shaking of his hands as he held at table level;

"I, Michael Raymond Davies wish to make a statement about the incident that occurred at The Resolution Public House and for which I have been placed under arrest. I wish to state that I was at work, as a doorman that night and that I was accompanied by a colleague, Alex Saunderson or Alex as I know him. There were large numbers of people present at the time of the alleged incident and I undertook my duties with all due care and in line with my training to ensure the safety of everyone present. I saw that a young female had fallen and I offered first aid and asked for colleagues to contact the emergency services. Colleagues arrived to assist me and then the Police and Ambulance crews came a short while afterwards.

I have done nothing wrong and I deny any allegations that have been made against me."

Mike Davies handed the sheet of paper back to his solicitor; despite it being he who had pleaded to say something he wasn't convinced that the statement was very good in the circumstances and put it down to the limited time available, but instead of being more comfortable he felt more uneasy.

Brian Jameson allowed the silence in the room to hang a little as he looked across the table at Mike Davies; he was trying to see something of a reaction in his face, trying to determine if the man sat in front of him was a man guilty of pushing this woman down the steps or was he in fact an innocent man guilty only being present when someone fell in a tragic accident?

It was Paul Jeffries who broke the silence;

"Mr Jameson, I did explain that my client would refrain from answering any further questions after giving his statement."

It was enough to draw Columbo back on track; he really didn't like solicitors assuming that they were in control when in fact they were there to advise and ensure that PACE was being adhered to. It was.

"Thank you Mr Jeffries, I remember very well what you said and I trust that you remember my earlier response to a similar comment of yours?" A steely look across the table indicated to Jeffries that an answer wasn't required nor expected.

"Now Mike, thank you for your statement, but you will understand that I still have some unanswered questions and I would ask you to consider the wording of the caution very carefully before you make any decision on your response."

Mike Davies nodded, he felt as though the little exchange between detective and solicitor had not been in his favour, the intensity in the room appeared to have increased.

"Mike you have now seen the CCTV footage of the incident, have you anything you wish to say after that?"

153

"No comment." it was a softly spoken reply full of nerves and anxiety. He wanted to say that he had only held out his arm to stop the crush of the crowd, to stop anyone getting hurt not to hurt somebody.

"The camera footage appears to show you reaching out and pushing at Fleur Brennan just before she fell?"

"No comment"

"And immediately after you push her she falls to the ground and her head hits the steps."

"No comment"

"Fleur Brennan has died as a result of this incident Mike, are you certain that you don't want to answer any questions, to give your account?"

"I've given my account; I've just given you my statement."

There was anger in his voice now as the confusion of this situation and the lack of control he had over the outcome took their toll.

"Yes Mike and I just want to clarify a few points, is that ok?"

Paul Jeffries leant across and put his hand onto Mikes arm; shaking his head he made it clear that he didn't want his client to say any more at this time.

"Mike, in your statement you said you saw a woman falling, where was she, in relation to you when she fell?"

"No comment."

"Is the woman that you saw falling, the same woman on the CCTV footage, Fleur Brennan?"

"No comment?"

"You also said that you undertook your duties in line with your training, what training is that?"

"No comment?"

"You referred in your statement to using due care, what do you understand or mean by that?"

"No comment"

"When I viewed the CCTV images it looked to me as though you moved your arms from your side to the front, to push Fleur Brennan back; back down the steps. Is that using due care Mike?"

"I didn't--. I mean No comment" Columbo had definitely touched a nerve now.

"You're a big fella Mike, what are you, maybe six two, well built? If you were to push a female backwards down some steps it would really be difficult for her to withstand your push wouldn't it?"

"Mr Jameson, that's a leading question." Paul Jeffries could see where this was going and tried to head it off with an interruption.

"I'm sorry Mr Jeffries, but your client can challenge me if he wishes to, or he can tell me what he thinks happened, I'm merely suggesting that someone of Mr Davies' size would have a significant impact if he were to push someone smaller in stature."

"I have advised my client not to make any comment and you know that." The interview continued for another thirty minutes or so with Mike offering no further comment to any question and Paul Jeffries making copious notes and ensuring he obtained copies of the disclosure papers offered by Des Mason.

When the interview was over the detectives stood up and asked Mike to return with them to the cell whilst they spoke with the custody officer.

"Why? Isn't it over now? I thought I could go after the interview?"

It was explained to him that a decision had to be made as to how to proceed and that he would be spoken to soon. That didn't sound too good as the steel door slammed shut again.

FIFTY SIX

Jane lashed out with her free arm, catching the man on the side of his face with the phone she held tightly in her hand and drawing blood from a cut it created.

He strengthened his grip on her left arm and knocked the phone out of her grasp with his big hand, hurting her as he did so. He hadn't intended to hurt her but likewise he hadn't expected this sort of reaction, but now he was angry, he wanted to make her pay in some way. He was still thinking this when he felt the full force of her boot as his scrotum was crushed under the force of her kick which caused him to release his grip on her arm and allowed her to reach for the door again. She pulled at the door handle and just as the door opened she felt her head smash into it as he had launched himself at her, knocking the wind out of her and causing her to see stars as her world became no more than a daze. In her daze she turned to face her attacker and was met with a slap to the side of the head that felt like a sledge hammer, she felt nothing more as she lost consciousness and slid down the door and onto the floor.

When she woke and was able to focus again she saw that the door was closed and though she couldn't be certain, she felt sure that it was now locked, that she now had a real problem. She saw the man, wiping the side of his face with a tea towel held in his huge hand; she could see the small cut on his right cheek, and saw that it had stopped bleeding but that a bruise was already forming. He was stood by the kitchen sink, he had taken his shirt off and she saw it, with a spattering of blood on the collar thrown over the back of a nearby chair. She didn't think that he had noticed her yet and she was looking around the room, trying to decide what she should do next; she didn't think she could now reason with him, she knew that there was no other way out and she knew also that there was no way that if the door was locked that she could escape. She quickly checked herself over; her head was throbbing from the blow, her ear felt swollen and her lips were split open. How could someone do so much damage so quickly and with seemingly so little effort?

Jane watched the brute as he threw the towel down on the work surface and turned to face her.

"Get up Bitch." he growled

Jane didn't answer, she couldn't, fear gripped her and she felt as though all her senses were in limbo. What did he want? What could she do? What should she do? She placed her hands palm down on the wooden floor to push herself up.

"I said, get up Bitch." the voice was louder this time, angrier, threatening.

He didn't really know why he wanted her to get up, it was anger driving him, the sense that he had to take control and that he should not trust this woman, the woman who had hit him; in his mind for no good reason. Jane used the door to help her to get to her feet, pushing against it to take her weight; it wasn't until she had almost stood up that she thought that he might see this as another attempt to open the door.

"It's no fucking use, trying that. It's locked."

"I wasn't, I was just-"

"Shut the fuck up and get over there" he pointed to the small sofa in the adjacent room.

"W w what do you want?" her fear rising to the surface now

There was no response, just another angry glance. In truth he didn't know what he wanted, this was now heading out of control. He had, at first, wanted to tease, taunt her, then when he saw her and she had spoken to him in that manner he had reverted to type; used the only means at his disposal to grasp control and that was his strength. He now couldn't think what he was going to do next. Jane meanwhile inched across the room towards the sofa, keeping as much space between herself and her tormentor as she could; she reached the couch and as she sat she heard a noise, the unmistakeable ringtone of her phone; Opheliac, a track from Emilie Autumn's album of the same name, she had almost forgotten it was there.

The noise broke the tension in the room for a moment but then replaced it with another as she looked around to where the noise was coming from. The phone was by the sink unit and he was letting it ring out. A few seconds later another ringtone came through, a text message. He picked up the phone and pressed the yellow envelope icon to read the text, 'Voicemail has 1 new message. Please dial 121. He did.

"Hi Babe, just to let you know I'm back in good old 'Boro. Boring. Oops sorry I shouldn't have called should I cos you're no doubt shagging that gorgeous bloke of yours again? Missing you. Call me."

"Fuck." he exclaimed, "That's all I need. Who else knows you're here?"

"I dunno. No-one."

"Yeah right."

What was he going to do now? He certainly hadn't thought he could end up in this position, he had thought he was going to be alone through the day and yet here he was having hit a young woman, cuts on his own face and a problem; how to keep it quiet?

FIFTY SEVEN

"Here we are then, Cardigan Police Station. Wales' answer to ecological policing."

Sue Collins was being facetious about the nearly new building in front of them. Opened in 2010 it was at the time said to be state of the art and very ecologically friendly with solar panels on the roof, natural ventilation, day-lighting sensors and even rainwater harvesting features for washing the vehicles.

"Apparently they've even landscaped everywhere," she added and then smirked, "to increase the bio-diversity they've used native trees and a wild flower meadow."

"What are you on about? Bio what?" Neil Maughan wasn't known for his green credentials and he bit, just as she knew he would.

"Bio-diversity, it's the degree of variation of life forms within a given species. The-"

"Alright little Miss Clever clogs. It's still just a fucking cop shop when all's said and done."

"I know I've just been reading up about it when I knew we were coming here. The bonus for us though is there's a new custody suite though so I'm hoping it's air conditioned, with all mod cons."

"And I'm hoping the kettle's on and the prisoners' here."

Having parked up they went back around to the main reception and after showing their warrant cards were shown up to the local CID office.

Cardigans' duty Detective Sergeant was Cerys Jones who met them with a smile and the offer of tea or coffee much to the relief of Neil Maughan and the amusement of Sue Collins.

"He's quite agitated," DS Jones said as they took seats in the office, "Says you Yorkies have tried to stitch him up before."

"He's been a suspect before," Sue Collins replied, "In fact he's been charged before but the case didn't run."

"Yeah, I saw on PNC that he'd been charged, with manslaughter? Is this one the same MO then?"

"We don't really know; it's a bit of a cold case in a way. Body found after a landslip, we've not identified her yet and can't be sure of cause of death because we didn't have a body to work with really."

"Right, well he was brought in at about ten past seven this morning so he'll be due his first review shortly. I'll let the Inspector know you've arrived. Are you ready to go straight in or do you want something to eat first?"

"Let him have his meal, and then we won't need to break the interview. Is his solicitor here?"

"He's local and waiting for a call so can be here in ten minutes or so."

"Can we see him then?"

Cerys Jones stood up and led them down to the custody suite, which met with all Sue Collins' expectations. It was less than an hour before the two Yorkshire Detectives were sat opposite Mike Davies and his duty solicitor, youngish, early twenties, Neil Maughan thought; a tall, slim, dark haired woman with a slightly olive coloured skin that suggested that she may be of Mediterranean origins and dressed very well in a smart tailored suit.

"Good afternoon Inspector, I'm Charlotte Sheppard, duty solicitor for Mr Davies. Do you have any disclosure prepared?"

Very proficient start, considered Maughan, good first impression, especially for her client to see. In order to make his own statement he replied,

"Yes, indeed Ms Sheppard," noting the absence of any ring on her wedding finger, but not wanting to be presumptuous; "Can we discuss this outside for a moment?"

The two of them got up from their respective chairs and left the interview room for a discussion in an empty adjacent office where Neil Maughan presented a written disclosure and answered the two or three questions from his sparring partner before returning to join their colleague and client respectively.

"Do you need any further time with your client before we begin Ms Sheppard?"

"No thank you; there is nothing in the disclosure that wasn't to be expected; indeed I believe that this interview is little more than a fishing trip and that the only evidence you have against my client is that he was employed to carry out some work at or near the scene of the crime? I don't even believe that you know the date of the crime and therefore have nothing to link him with the crime at all."

Sue Collins and Neil Maughan listened before exchanging glances; the summing up by the solicitor wasn't far away from the truth. Yes they had evidence that placed him at the scene, even staying over at the cottage but very little else. Still let's see what he has to say for himself.

Sue placed the discs in the recorder and went through the initial introductory process and caution. Mike Davies sat impassively on the opposite side of the small fixed table, hands held together in front of him, knowing full well what was about to take place.

FIFTY EIGHT

"Let's go back to the office and see exactly what we do have Des. I don't like to let someone out just because they've no commented all the way through, but I think we're a bit light on solid evidence."

Back in their own office they met with the DCI, Jill Stewart, a dynamic, driven cop with a reputation for achievement, getting results and demanding the same of her team. At only 36 she was well on her way to holding a very senior position and had only been in this post for a matter of a few months. Dressed in smart black, well pressed trousers a pink and blue striped shirt and well polished Gabor shoes she cut an imposing figure at nearly 5foot 11inches tall, a smart chopped hair cut and little make up, but carefully applied, she would not have been out of place on a catwalk; except that she was cop through and through.

Despite her well manicured appearance though, her willingness to work with her team, to get involved with them at the scene or just be able to make the all important decisions endeared her to all her colleagues and she was keen to get an update from the interview.

"Bri, Des, come through please."

The two cops, papers still in hand walked through to her office and were gestured to sit at the small round table in the opposite corner of the room to her very busy looking desk.

"How did it go then?"

There was a brief exchange of glances before Columbo took it upon himself to make the reply;

"I can't quite make my mind up yet Jill, he did the no comment routine for much of the time, but then we expected that from a Paul Jeffries' client. He's certainly there; he's certainly moved his hands towards the victim but he's denied the allegation in a statement he read out."

Jill Stewart read the notes Des Mason had made and asked to see the CCTV again; she had already known what was contained in the witness statements.

Des Mason set up the TV in Jill Stewarts' office and set the footage going again, as the scene progressed towards Fleur Brennan and her friends turning up she asked Des to pause the playback.

"Can you just confirm Des who the witnesses are here, what was their line of vision to Fleur she fell or when she was pushed?"

Des Mason used his bic biro to point out each witness in turn, naming them and reading the pertinent sections of their respective statements aloud, before Jill asked for the film to be moved on at slow speed in order to see clearly the actions taken and movements made by each party, not least the suspect, Mike Davies.

"It's not clear that he pushed her is it?" Jill Stewart was taking the required objective view as she reviewed the moment that Mike Davies laid hands on Fleur Brennan

"It's not clear at all, that's the issue we have Jill, but all the witnesses describe it as a push." Brian Jameson was watching intently, rewinding the film and playing it over and over in the vain hope that it would be clearer the next time.

"What's the medical report say?" Jill Stewart asked.

"We're still waiting for the full autopsy report but there is no doubt that the fall was the cause of death, just from the hospital report."

"Are there any statements that say anything other than a push; that is from those that saw anything?"

"None at all, they either weren't watching or say that it was definitely a push."

"Put it all together Des, quickly; Bri, I want you and me to speak with CPS now, get some clarity on their position."

Des Mason left the room and after a quick phone call to check their availability, Jill Stewart and Brian Jameson walked down the corridor and into the office of senior CPS lawyer, John Glover.

It was over an hour later that they left and were actually very surprised at the decision to charge Mike Davies.

FIFTY NINE

He was still deep in thought when Jane looked across the room at him, a lumbering brute of a man, not tall but well built with short cropped hair but which was still visibly receding, a well worn tee shirt with small tears at the seams under the arms and which barely covered his torso nor reached his cargo type shorts. His short muscular legs looked even shorter than they probably were because he was wearing rigger boots. He was rubbing his chin in his gorilla sized hand and to all intents and purposes appeared to be in a trance so deep were his thoughts; Jane scoured the room with her eyes as she sat motionless on the sofa, it was a small room and the process took no time at all. The brute was blocking the exit back to the kitchen, he was also too near to the small hallway which led to the stairs up to the first floor, a small window which she saw was surprisingly uPVC and which seemed out of place in such a traditional seaman's cottage was hinged open. She saw that a chair stood between her and the window but that there was ample room to the side for her to get round it if need be; glancing back to the thug-like monster she saw that he still appeared to be in a state of daydream; she made up her mind and despite the intense throbbing still pounding in her head she jumped up from the sofa and raced across the room, behind the chair and to the window. It was to be her final decision as the noise of her movement brought the brute back from his stupor and his street wise upbringing came to the fore as panic set in. He launched himself across the room, crashing into the chair and pushing it back with the full force of his not inconsiderable weight allied to the momentum he had generated in his movement. The chair in turn struck Jane and the impact crushed her against the wall, sending a searing pain up her spine and across to her shoulders dazing her again. It was probably just as well that her consciousness was limited as a fist struck her at the side of the head and she slid down the wall as far as the chair would allow, her head falling to one side and resting on her shoulder, limp, lifeless.

Pulling the chair away from her and almost throwing it behind him he shouted;

"Get up, Get up now bitch."

There was no reply, no movement as Jane slumped to the floor and remained motionless.

"Get up!" he shouted again but with less anger and more panic in his voice. It was dawning on him what had happened, what he had caused. He tried to jostle her with his foot, rolling her over onto her back but it was obvious that she was not breathing; there was no heaving of her chest, no noise of breath being taken in or exhaled but he knew he was wasting his time; he didn't even bend down to make any proper checks, just turned his back rolled his massive hands up into fists and brought them down on the wall in total exasperation.

He remained leaning against the wall for a few seconds only before the reality of the situation kicked in, setting in motion his instincts for self preservation.

He had no emotional link to this person and probably, more importantly, nor did anyone link her with him.

He sat down on the sofa and gathered his thoughts. He had just killed a girl he didn't know. Other than what he had heard of her on the rumour mill he knew nothing of her, yet there she lay, in front of him on the floor. He remembered her mobile phone which was now sat on the draining board; taking only the three steps he needed to cross the room, he picked up the phone and listened again to the voicemail message he had heard earlier then left the phone to play through earlier messages. Apart from confirming the victims name it was also obvious that someone called 'Pheebs' and Jane's parents were the most frequent callers and this suggested immediately that she had no permanent boyfriend. He saw that as a good thing as he considered a boyfriend likely to be possessive and therefore likely to miss her quickly. One thing he knew that he did need was time.

Having listened, he then began to explore the phone further; it was almost surreal; there he was looking at photos, reading personal emails, text messages, facebook content and the like and the content all related to a person who lay dead not six feet away.

He relaxed a little, it was as though having some knowledge of the victim had empowered him, given him options. It was obvious that come what may he had to dispose of the body first and then cover his tracks.

It would be several hours before nightfall and he couldn't risk being seen moving the body so he decided quickly that she would find her final resting place only yards away from where she had expected to be laying in the arms of her lover. Work was already being carried out by Mike at the cottage so there was an immediate cover to any disturbance or noise that he may cause. Decision made he started to clear up the cottage, removing the limp lifeless body of Jane into the small hallway he replaced the sofa and chair to their former positions, straightened the rug and tidied the rooms and the kitchen work surfaces, paying attention to place things back as near to what he could remember of them from only an hour or two earlier and not to be too precise as to draw attention. He wiped his own finger marks from any surface he considered may be useful to the police if ever they did check for anything; though in his mind he knew he could give a reasonable explanation for his presence there should the need ever arise.

He then went outside where he stood and looked at his options; he reviewed everything in his head, was everything here that he would need, did he have enough time to finish the job today or did he need to risk coming back? There was one thing in his favour; he had never been shy of hard work, so he began.

He lifted several loose flagstones from the somewhat amateur patio construction; the stones had just been laid on a bed of sand it seemed and were therefore easy to lift without causing damage, and he placed them neatly against the cottage wall. He then said a small thank you to the absent Mike for leaving him all the tools he would need and a wheelbarrow to assist. Scraping the sand from the top of the earth he made a small mound from it for future use and then he began digging.

SIXTY

Having completed the round of introductions Neil Maughan opened the interview;

"Mr Davies, I'm sure that you will understand your arrest is linked to the investigation into the death of a female in Whitby, North Yorkshire and whose body was found on Saturday 12th January this year. I would be grateful if you would tell me anything you know of and which may help our investigation."

Maughan was deliberately being as vague as possible whilst leaving the question as open as he could.

"My client does not wish to answer any questions Inspector but a wish to distance him from the matter, which he states clearly has nothing whatsoever to do with him."

Charlotte Sheppard was sat up straight on her chair and had an air of confidence beyond that normally expected of someone of her age. Maughan thought that this came from having the knowledge of the disclosure which despite his best efforts still fell short of implicating Davies.

"Ms Sheppard, you know that I will continue to ask the questions and also that your client can choose whether or not to answer so I note your comment but would ask you now to refrain from interfering and stick to advising your client." Not too subtle but nothing that could be construed as rude or officious, Maughan thought.

There followed the oft run interview process of question and answer, with the answer being "No comment" throughout. Davies had been through this before and had vowed to himself to say absolutely nothing else at all other than to confirm his identity. Charlotte Sheppard sat quietly but wore a confident smile throughout, as if challenging Maughan to produce his best.

It was a frustrated and resigned Maughan who closed the interview nearly two hours later having covered everything he could in several different ways without eliciting anything at all. Sue Collins who had been almost a spectator throughout removed the discs from the recorder with a sigh and placed them in their sleeves and signed the seals.

After watching this process Davies unexpectedly spoke out;

"You bastards have tried to stitch me up once, don't think I'm gonna help you do it again."

"Not now Mr Davies." Charlotte Sheppard spoke gently trying to diffuse the situation quickly.

"Well what happens now then. I didn't do anything last time and they charged me, do they do the same again?"

"There is no evidence to charge you and I will make that very clear in my representations to the custody officer."

Turning to the detectives she asked;

"Have you anything further to put to my client or is he going to be released now?"

"I will be asking for him to be remanded on bail Ms Sheppard pending further enquiries."

"And I shall ask for his release if there is no further evidence that you can produce."

"Then we shall see what decision the custody officer reaches, shan't we?"

Davies was returned to his cell whilst the officers and solicitor made representations to a custody officer that, unusually, was known to the solicitor more than the detective.

In truth it was always likely to result in a remand of the prisoner on unconditional bail, but to answer that bail in Scarborough in a month's time. The situation was relayed to Mike Davies by the custody officer in the presence of all concerned.

"What the fuck do I have to go to Scarborough for? You're fucking joking aren't you?"

Not rising to the swearing or raised voice, the custody officer, who had seen and heard it all before replied;

"The investigation is being conducted by North Yorkshire Police and it is their prerogative to ask for that. Your solicitor will obviously explain anything further. In the meantime if you will sign the pad in front of you I will return your property and you may leave."

Having looked at Charlotte Sheppard for guidance and received the nod he signed his name as requested and agreed thereby to answer bail in Yorkshire. He could not however resist one last comment.

"You're all fucking bent."

He was shown the exit by a custody support officer, leaving behind two frustrated detectives.

Making their way back up to the CID offices Sue Collins and Neil Maughan reflected on what was to all intents and purposes a waste of two days.

"He's either a very good actor or he's not involved in my opinion." Sue Collins surprised her colleague with the statement.

"Then who is involved Sue? As far as we know and I suppose to be fair we still know nothing for certain, he is the only person who would have had that sort of free access to the cottage at the time of the death."

"You know that before this interview I thought he was nailed on as a prime suspect, especially with Columbo's job in the background. Surely he can't be that good as to be suspect in two deaths and still appear to play the innocent so well?"

"I know Simon Pithers isn't going to be too pleased when I update him."

"He's a realist Neil, he knew we didn't have much, that it's a process not a given but where do we go from here?"

"The fucking hotel if it's up to me, you're driving's knackered me." Injecting some levity at the end of a hard day Neil Maughan picked up the phone to call his boss.

SIXTY ONE

Jill Stewart left it to Columbo to charge his man; it was often seen as the culmination of a job well done to be able to charge the prisoner with the offence for which he had been arrested but on this occasion all concerned were left feeling a little doubtful and that didn't auger well. True they were pleased and after Mike Davies had been charged and told he would remain in custody until he appeared before the magistrates on Tuesday morning they had retreated to Jill's office for a debrief. Mike Davies for his part was weeping in a cell, unable to come to terms with what was unfolding in his life.

"I'm really not sure about this one Jill. Normally we have to bust a gut to get anything past Jessy, this time she was arguing for the charge and we were the doubters."

Jessica Aldridge was the senior CPS solicitor covering the region and it was she who had sanctioned the charge much to the astonishment of all the detectives. They had presented their case well and were happy that they had collected independent evidence as well as that of victim's friends and suspect's colleagues. The CCTV they had thought to be inconclusive was seen by Jessica as a definite act undertaken by a man, who by his own admission had received training in that aspect of his job. In her view it was an act of gross negligence and as such should be viewed in the context of the Adomako Test. That test, Jessica had explained, required four elements to be present in order to prove the case; those being;

a) the existence of a duty of care to the deceased;

b) a breach of that duty of care which;

c) causes (or significantly contributes) to the death of the victim; and

d) the breach should be characterised as gross negligence, and therefore a crime.

Between the CPS staff and the police officers present they had reviewed everything and concluded that the facts were there to be seen and it was clear that there was sufficient evidence to have a realistic chance of obtaining a conviction.

The decision was accepted and legislation required the serious consideration of a remand in custody, which from the police perspective meant that he would be detained at Scarborough Police Station until he could be taken to the nearby court on Tuesday morning.

To Mike Davies his world appeared to be at an end; he was adamant that he had done nothing wrong, that he was merely doing his job, a job that had helped the police on any number of occasions previously when things became out of hand or unruly in the pubs and clubs of Whitby. He felt betrayed by the system, by the police and by his colleagues who had apparently said little to defend him, mostly claiming not to have seen anything of the incident.

Paul Jeffries had informed him on the telephone that he would be there at court on Tuesday but that there was nothing now that he could do to help.

"Well thanks a fucking lot for that." was the exasperated final comment from Mike as he handed the phone back to the custody officer before being led to his cell, a place he would now be spending at least another night.

Jill Stewart quickly drafted a press release and emailed it to the press office for review and circulation. There were guidelines to press releases that had to be followed and as such Jill knew that the review would not change anything, in fact if changes were made she would want to know why and by whom in double quick time.

"Following the tragic incident on Skinner Street on Sunday 30th October which resulted in the death of Whitby resident Fleur Brennan, 23yrs, a local man has been charged with an offence of manslaughter and will appear at Scarborough Magistrates Court on Tuesday.

Whitby Police are still appealing for witnesses and anyone believes they may have any information relating to the incident, which occurred outside The Resolution Hotel at approx 10.15 pm is asked to contact the CID office using the telephone number 101 and asking for extension 8546.

Detective Chief Inspector Jill Stewart wishes to emphasise that the investigation is still ongoing and that all calls will be treated in the strictest confidence and dealt with by suitably trained officers.

This incident is one of an unfortunate nature which has far reaching consequences for the Brennan family and the local community.

Thankfully incidents such as this are very much a rare occurrence in Whitby which is and remains to be a very safe place to live, work and visit."

She always felt at times like this that she should express her feelings for the bereaved family but it was felt that to do so would detract from the impartiality that she not only had to have but which she had to be seen to have.

SIXTY TWO

It wasn't long before he had dug a hole more than large enough for the small body of Jane, not pretty, not dignified but to be her final resting place within the shadows of Whitby's iconic abbey.

Making his way back inside he looked at Jane, the colour now gone from her face, a pallid almost fluorescent transparency about her skin, laid out in the hall. A terrible waste of a life he thought, but then he hadn't planned it this way; he had to look after himself now, make sure he couldn't be linked to this unfortunate, in his mind at least, chain of events. Reaching down to pick her up he lifted her up quite easily, but then felt something in her jeans pocket and put her back down almost immediately. Reaching into her pockets he felt the Renault keys, some loose change and a couple of business cards containing details of Gothic clothing suppliers that she had picked up at the bazaar. He removed them all, put them in his own pocket for now and carried her out. Laying her gently in the shallow grave he took one last look before picking up the spade again and began the process of filling in the space above her with the recently dug soil. The excess soil was scattered onto the small untended flower beds at the end of the garden and within an hour it was difficult to tell that any digging had taken place. The sand was then mixed with the remains from an open bag of cement and spread back over the soil and the flagstones were positioned back in place. Finishing the job properly he swept the cement mix between the flags and looked down on his afternoon's work with a sense of pride. Mike couldn't have done a better job had he been there, but at least he, unwittingly, had supplied the necessary materials.

Placing everything back where he had found it, wheelbarrow covered with tarpaulin and back up against the wall, he swept the yard clean, finished tidying the cottage and walked away, not looking back.

Once on The Ropery he felt in his pockets for the car keys, saw the Renault key fob and tried the remote opening feature of the fob as he walked along the street. He was pleased to see that the car they belonged to was almost new, clean and most importantly, now available.

Adjusting the driver's seat and rear view mirror he started the car engine and manoeuvred out of the tight parking space and along the road to its junction with Green Lane, turning left up the hill towards Whitby Laithes and right at the top towards Hawsker. Driving along the quiet Laithes he crossed over the A171 Whitby to Scarborough Road and into the small village of Sneatonthorpe, and then onto minor roads that brought him to a local beauty spot known as Falling Foss. It would have been busy in spring and summer but was deserted today apart from a single 4x4 vehicle with a dog cage in the back. He parked away from the 4x4 and took Jane's phone from his pocket. He read some more of the texts she had saved that gave an account of her weekend thus far and checking some photos again he thought she looked every bit as good as Mike had said. She was gone now though and he had to cover that loss up somehow, buy himself some time.

He then got out of the car and opened the boot, saw that it was full of cases containing clothing, a couple of carrier bags, one with a pair of walking boots and one with some Whitby souvenirs in and then he found the laptop in its case. He looked at the content of the laptop in the same way as he had done with the phone, thinking that he had never used a password and whilst he thought others generally did, Jane thankfully hadn't. Within twenty minutes or so he had built up a functional knowledge of Jane's life, her friends, her parents, their address and what they looked like, Liverpool University and her mates there, her address at student digs; in fact had he been cleverer than he was on a computer he had Jane's life available to him, but then that thought brought him back; she didn't have a life anymore.

Putting the laptop back in its case and the phone in his pocket he started the car up again and drove back into Whitby Town, parking on Normanby Terrace on the west side of town, a residential street with a number of Bed and Breakfast houses showing vacancies again after the Goth weekend. Placing the laptop back in the boot he left the car and walked into the town. He needed a drink.

SIXTY THREE

Sitting in the hotel lounge with a pint of lager in his hand Neil Maughan looked across the table at Sue Collins. He liked what he saw, always had, she seemed to have everything, looks, brains, presence and that twinkle in her eye that meant, at least in his mind, that she could have what she wanted. They had changed after leaving Cardigan Police Station and were waiting to have a meal; he in his conservative pair of chinos and polo shirt looked as though he had stepped out of Marks and Spencer's menswear whilst she, a lesser earner but with no dependants dressed in a similar casual style but a total class above, a thin pale cream sleeveless blouse over a pair of tailored navy blue trousers and mid heeled shoes of a similar colour. She possessed a flawless complexion and had done something to her hair that left it shiny and smooth even to the male observer.

"Penny for them?" Sue had seen Neil's expression glazing over.

"Ugh, sorry Sue, I was miles away."

"I could see that, anywhere nice?"

"Not really," he lied; his thoughts had taken him into places he would love to be sharing with her that night.

"Shame." her reply was partnered with a smile that lit the whole place up.

"It is" he replied before taking another drink. "You ready to go through?" he pointed to the restaurant.

"Lead on" she said, standing up to her full height and towering over him as he sat in his seat.

Over dinner the discussion initially returned to the case in hand, the real reason that they were there.

"I'm struggling with it Sue, Davies is sitting pretty just now. As it stands all he has to do is keep shtum and we've got nothing but a hunch."

"We knew that though before we came down here. It's no different to normal; we just have to prove it."

"Can we though? Are we any further forward at all?"

"Neil, we've both worked cases which have taken ages to get the breakthrough, in reality we haven't been on this very long at all and it's not the usual where we have evidence from the scene to work with."

"I know but it doesn't make it any easier does it?"

"What will? A team hug?" A tease she thought being quite obviously the only team member present, but quite willing to oblige; with a hug and more.

Neil didn't answer other than to look at his companion and smile. It seemed as though his spirits were rising and he picked up the menu.

The conversation was lighter as they ate and the mood lifted too. Neil Maughan knew that he would have to make contact with Simon Pithers back in North Yorkshire for the expected end of day update following the local debrief but he was more at ease now, more accepting of the situation and yet somehow disappointed that his colleague had had to bring him back on line. He wasn't however sure where they were going next with the investigation.

They had finished their meals and decided to make use of the small guest lounge adjacent to the dining room. Equipped with a couple of leather sofas and an assortment of easy chairs, it was comfortable and functional without being anything else. Neil Maughan made his call to Simon Pithers using his mobile but, as was to be expected, there had been little to add to their earlier conversation and so he ordered another bottle of wine, a nice Cote du Rhone that wouldn't be part of their permitted expenses and decided his best move would be to relax and enjoy what was left of the evening.

SIXTY FOUR

"Is there to be an application for bail Mr Jeffries?" Christopher Harland the Chair of the sitting Magistrates asked after hearing the charge against Mike Davies and accepting a plea of not guilty from the accused. "There is Your Worship." Paul Jeffries stood up to answer the question and looked across to his counterpart, Jenny Hassall, who was acting as prosecutor in the case.

"And are there any objections to bail being granted Ms Helliwell?" Christopher Harland asked.

"There are Your Worship," again standing to answer and remaining stood to continue her address to the bench, "The offence is a serious offence, one which will need to be heard at Crown Court and which carries a maximum sentence of life imprisonment;"

She paused as the seated public and press reporters collectively gathered their thoughts; "Though one which we accept is highly unlikely to be such in this case."

She continued, "The case is also one which has created high levels of emotion within the community and as such we wish to ensure that there are no reprisals or communications with witnesses or potential witnesses from the accused."

"Mr Jeffries." Christopher Harland nodded to Paul Jeffries who stood up and looked at his client in the dock, with security officers stood either side of him.

"Your Worships, my client is a man of previous good character, who denies any wrong doing and who has assisted the police," pausing for effect, before continuing; "and therefore the justice system many times in the past. There is nothing in his antecedent history to suggest that he may try to obstruct the course of justice, nor to try to interfere with any prosecution witnesses. He has an alternative address that he can use if you see fit to grant conditional bail; that would see him reside in Wales. This, together with other restrictions you may consider, such as reporting to a local Police Station and limiting contact with others would seem more than adequate to ensure his attendance at court."

"Thank you Mr Jeffries, we shall retire now and consider."

Mike Davies sat in the dock as the three magistrates, all local people who gave their time freely, retired into a back room to discuss what they had heard.

Paul Jeffries approached him and saw him visibly shaking at the thought of being potentially remanded in custody, potentially being placed in the same prison as some of those he had helped to arrest previously; overall well out of his comfort zone.

"I think we might be ok Mike."

"We; there is no fucking we. It's me they're considering sending down, not you."

"Well I don't think that Jenny is too concerned about RIC, but she has to show willing."

"RIC, what's that?"

"Sorry, remand in custody. We tend to accept that people understand acronyms, I apologise."

"How would I know acronyms for this stuff, I've never been arrested before, I told you, I've never been in bother before now."

"Well let's see then, they'll be back soon."

With that Paul Jeffries turned away and walked across to Jenny Hassall who had remained seated throughout as no prosecution witnesses were needed at this hearing.

He sat down next to her and began a conversation in whispered tones. Mike Davies looked on and saw that she was waving the court clerk across. He observed the clerk bowing down to accept a small piece of paper from Jenny Helliwell and then leave with a swish of his gown, through a door to the rear of the court room.

The longest twelve minutes of Mike Davies' life ended when that same door opened and the magistrates reappeared and took their respective seats.

Mike Davies was asked to stand as Christopher Harland spoke;

"Mr Davies, you will be remanded on bail to appear at York Crown Court in 28 days time; you will reside......"

The remainder of the speech was not heard by Mike Davies who had heard all he needed to hear, that he had been granted bail; he didn't care at all what the conditions were, he would at least be at liberty to walk the streets. His worst fear had been avoided.

SIXTY FIVE

He had stayed a little longer than he had originally planned, drunk a little more than he had intended to, but then he often did do just that so nothing would appear out of sorts to anyone. The Granby, a smallish pub at the top of Skinner Street was one used less by tourists, despite its proximity to the many nearby guest houses, and more by a small group of locals and regulars and on that night a team of ladies darts players from the local league.

He had stayed until after 11.00pm, chatted with some of the regulars and surprisingly seemed at ease with himself considering what had happened only hours earlier. He had however reached a decision and, after sufficient sleep to see off any affects of alcohol, a shower, a shave and a change to more casual clothing of jeans, a rugby shirt and navy blue crew neck sweater, he had made his way to the local supermarket where he bought a snack, some mints and some screen wipes. With a clear head and clarity of purpose he then returned to the car. He knew that he would have at least a day or two before the car was missed, indeed he was hoping he would have at least that time before Jane was missed.

It was now nearing lunch time as he sat again in the driver's seat, checked that the car had sufficient fuel, he was pleased to see a more than half full tank; and drove out of Whitby onto the A171 Guisborough road, turning left onto the A169 Pickering and Malton road and then, after about 45 minutes, the A64 west bound carriageway towards York. So far so good.

It was another half hour before he pulled into the large lay-by just outside York that boasted the Highwayman Cafe, a regular haunt for hauliers and tourists alike, offering in his opinion, plain food, reasonably priced and somewhere to stretch your legs if on a long journey. He ordered and ate his all day breakfast before taking out Jane's phone from his trouser pocket. He read some of the text messages from both Phoebe and Jane's parents and decided to send each one a message now. He wasn't however as mobile savvy as he would have liked and therefore didn't quite know all the text shorthand he could see Jane had used previously. He read Phoebe's texts again and again, using the messages to and from her to build up sufficient knowledge, and happy to plagiarise as necessary, he sent a short message;

"Hi Babes, its bn gr8 @WGW but OMW BCNU soon. LU XX"

Which he hoped and believed translated to, "Hi Babes, it's been great at Whitby Goth Weekend but on my way be seeing you soon. Love You. Xx

A second message to her parents read;

"Hi, M & D, hope ur both ok. Will ring soon. LU. XX

This, he believed was more straight forward and anyway he was confident that they wouldn't have any better understanding of text messaging than he did.

Finishing his large mug of tea and making use of the facilities he returned to the Renault and set off again westwards before joining the M1 southbound and the M62 west, sign posted at junction 42, Manchester.

He knew this route well as he had travelled many times to the airport for holidays and he was relaxing into the journey, the radio playing some middle of the road easy listening he had to remind himself not to relax too much, not to be seen speeding or switching lanes too often; the last thing he needed was to be checked in a car he didn't own and whose owner was now buried under newly laid flagstones.

Approaching Manchester airport from the M56 he followed the signs for terminal 1 and then past The Hilton and Bewleys hotels before entering the car park. If all went well there would be spaces left available for those customers who chose to just turn up rather than book in advance. He took his token from the machine and drove into the park where there were numerous spaces available. Choosing a space in the middle of the park he stopped and put on the handbrake. He sat for a moment or two, observing that there was no-one nearby and he then took the wipes he had purchased earlier and wiped each surface he had come into contact with, the dashboard, steering wheel, radio and CD switches and even the seat controls. Checking again that no-one had any interest in him, or was looking his way, why should they, all holiday makers with kids and suitcases to look after, plenty to keep them occupied he thought, he did the same in the boot of the car before taking the laptop out and walking away; locking the car remotely as he did so.

Making his way to the bus terminal he saw that the 105 to Manchester city centre was due to leave within the next ten minutes. He waited at the bus stop rather than on the bus, knowing that buses all had CCTV these days he wanted to limit the opportunities that he may be seen, should anyone ever even decide to look here? He took the opportunity to drop the Renault keys into a waste bin whilst waiting and then selecting a window seat, he boarded the bus that would take him via Wythenshawe, Benchill, Sharston, Northenden and Moss Side to his next destination.

SIXTY SIX

Breakfast the following morning was going to be a little awkward. Had they really slept together? Stupid question, of course they had; it had been on the cards from the moment they had ordered the second additional bottle of wine and decided to take it to his room. There were chairs in the room but they were not that comfortable and Sue had decided that she would be more relaxed sat on the bed, relaxation had led to flirtation and despite their professional relationship being current they had succumbed to temptation and now had to face each other the morning after.

Sue had returned to her own room earlier to shower and change and was later down to breakfast; she had fewer concerns, after all she was a free agent but knew that Neil was married with a family; she did not want to be a scarlet woman and home breaker but maybe it was too late for that? No, Neil had been very much a willing participant in their night together and he knew what he had at home; it was his choice as much as hers.

"Good morning." she said as she walked serenely into the dining room, looking every inch the confident professional, dressed in a tailored shirt and sharp navy skirt that just reached her knees and yet another change of shoes to match the outfit.

"Hi Sue," was a slightly less confident response from the seated Maughan, dressed more casually in expectation of spending most of the day sat in a car again.

"You ok? With last night?"

"Yeah, you?"

"Neil, I'm fine with it." Sitting down opposite him, she held out her hand to touch his, "No regrets?" It was part statement and part question to him.

"No regrets." he replied, looking across the table at her, he managed a smile and relaxed a little. The first words were always going to be the hardest and they had navigated safely through those waters now.

Ordering their breakfasts, he, typically, full English and she salmon; they chatted about their return journey and the next stage of the investigation.

"What next then Neil? We still haven't any absolute certainties in this one?"

"Well, we'll have to review everything when we get back, I spoke to the boss earlier and he wants us to get our heads together before the weeks out."

"What more can we do to identify the body? I think that's our best chance and it seems odd that we aren't really any closer; nobody's banging on our door saying is it my daughter, my sister?"

"You're right, of course but we have part of the team dedicated to just that, trawling the misper databases, in touch with every force."

"Yes I know, but you know as well as I do that unless the DCI or whoever heads the department is on the ball these things get pushed on to the back burner. There's always something more urgent, something that ticks more immediate boxes for the bean counters."

"We need to be sure we're perfect before we make accusations about others Sue."

"I know, I'm just thinking out loud I suppose."

"Taking a completely different tack, what about looking at the events in Whitby, The Regatta, The Folk Weeks, Goth Weekends, Soul Weekends etcetera; is it worth trying to focus on any or all of these for our victim. A visitor that never returned home?"

"I thought that was what we were doing really, I mean surely if she was local we would have heard directly and not been checking other forces?"

"Maybe it's me thinking out loud now then? Come on eat up and let's get on our way back. I think better on my own ground."

Within the hour they had finished breakfast, second cups of tea and coffee had been taken and now they were in the car again. Neil Maughan looked across at his driver and his eyes drifted down to her knees, now visible as the skirt rose above them, just, not enough to be obvious but with his new found knowledge of what lay above, enough to be of much interest to him.

Sue caught him looking but said nothing just smiled inwardly. She had enjoyed their trip to Wales and wouldn't be shy of repeating it if the opportunity arose. She let the smile reach her face and turned the music up a little, tapping her hands on the steering wheel in time with the beat of Van Morrison's Brown Eyed Girl. The motorway stretched out in front of them but she thought it was going to be a nice ride.

179

SIXTY SEVEN

- To reside at 177 Grove Park Lane, Cardigan, SA43 1AX
- To report every Monday and Thursday to Cardigan Police Station between 1700hrs and 1900hrs
- Not to enter North Yorkshire unless for a pre-arranged visit to see a solicitor or for court appearances.
- Not to make any contact by any means whatsoever with.... there followed a list of names supplied by the police and included all witnesses involved in the case.

These conditions were imposed by the magistrates at Scarborough Law Courts and were readily accepted by Mike Davies as a far more attractive alternative to the remand in custody initially requested by the prosecution. Mike had made contact with an old work colleague who was more than happy to provide accommodation for a friend and especially one who could help with his workload. Mike in turn was happy to be able to see the outside world again after spending far too long in a cell or in the dock. He left the court in the company of Paul Jeffries and returned initially to the neighbouring Police station to collect his property, the items that had been taken from him on his arrival, what seemed so long ago.

"When do I have to leave for Wales?"

"Straight away I'm afraid, the conditions are imposed immediately and last until your next court appearance when they may or may not be renewed."

"What about my gear, some clothing, work tools; that sort of thing?"

"We'll have to arrange family or friends to sort something out for you. Do you have any cash or a card to get some?"

"Yeah, I'll sort it. Thanks, I'm sorry for swearing earlier."

"Don't worry, I've heard all there is to hear. Stay in touch and keep your mobile on. Don't forget to sign in at Cardigan Nick."

"I won't."

A shake of the hand and Mike was on his way down Northway to Scarborough's railway station to try to work out how to get down to Wales. For now he felt good but he still could not believe how he had been charged with such a serious offence when he genuinely believed that he had done no wrong at all?

He called his father and explained as best he could what had happened over the last couple of days and after going through the stages of shock and disbelief, he obviously knew about the incident at The Resolution, the grapevine worked very efficiently in the small town of Whitby, but did not know Mike was involved. He told Mike to stay at the station and he would pick him up and take him down to Cardigan. He had a key to Mikes flat, albeit he had never had cause to use it before; he agreed to pick up as much clothing as he could but said he wouldn't be able to collect his work tools as he couldn't carry them that far, from Aelfleda Terrace to The Ropery. Mike said he would get someone else to collect them later and keep them until he could make alternative arrangements. It was nearly two hours before Mikes father arrived at Scarborough Railway station to collect him, time for Mike to reflect on what had happened? He hadn't given much thought to Jane; he had been too wrapped up in his own issues to think of her, what did that say about him? He looked at some of the photos on his mobile and read some of the texts sent between the two of them and he was surprised that his mood lifted, a smile briefly flickered onto his face until he wondered where she was, what was she doing now? He saw that there were no further texts from her and feared that she had just moved on, left him without knowing what had happened to him. He rang her number but got no reply, he left a message, "Hi Jane, its Mike, I'm sorry I missed you on Sunday night; give me a chance to explain. Please call me. Please." He nearly said, "Love you" at the end of that sentence but stopped just short. He did think the world of her, he hadn't expected to think the way he was now, he should have rung earlier, whilst he was in his cell he should have been thinking about her but he had been in shock, angry, upset and selfish he thought.

"Come on Mike, I'm parked on double yellows." Mikes father shouted from the doorway to the station.

Mike made his way across and then hugged his dad, probably the first time he had done that in twenty years, then he cried. Tears filled his eyes and his whole body went weak.

"I'm scared dad"

"I know son, I know. Come on, we'll chat in the car."

SIXTY EIGHT

He didn't feel comfortable carrying the lap top around in a case, not for the fear of being mugged, no, he was big enough to cope with that eventuality and anyway it wasn't his to lose so why be bothered; he just felt that the bags were a bit poncey, made him feel a bit of what he still called, a pooftah, in his non enlightened world, with the case hung from his shoulder.

Entering Manchester's Piccadilly railway station, he saw a Costa coffee outlet and having bought a large mocha found a seat where he could make use of the laptop and his own mobile phone to browse the internet. He saw that he could get a train to Liverpool for as little as £11.50 but he wanted to pay cash at the ticket office not book online, that would leave a trace; glancing at his mobile he saw it was approaching 5.00pm and that accounted for just how busy the place was becoming, he saw that there was train due out at 1701hours on the screen but also another at 1737hrs, that gave him nearly three quarters of an hour to have a leisurely coffee and a snack.

What to do in Liverpool was the only thing he hadn't considered, he knew that he wanted to drop the mobile phone there, thinking that would leave a trace for anyone looking not for him but for Jane. Similarly he thought, he could dispose of the laptop there but needed to do that in such a way that it wouldn't be found as the hard drive would show it had been used up to this date.

Finishing his coffee he put the laptop back in his case, his mobile in his jeans pocket and made his way in the ever growing throng to the ticket office where he bought his one way ticket to Liverpool Lime Street and found there was standing room only on the train which pulled out of Manchester bang on time.

Shortly after 6.30pm the train entered Liverpool Lime Street Station and he was glad as he had remained standing for the entire journey. Most of the other travellers appeared to be either shoppers or business men and women in the same boring suits and ties as they seem to wear right across the country, a uniform in all but name he thought. He mingled in with the crowds as they left the station thinking again that the best disguise was to be as naturally in view as he could be, just another commuter, except that on leaving the station and standing at the top of the many steps leading down from the huge arched frontage he stopped, turned around and walked straight back in. He found a seat in the main concourse directly across from two statues, one he thought he recognised immediately as being of Ken Dodd, the other, of Bessie Braddock he didn't recognise and, if he were honest with himself, nor did he care that she was the woman who allegedly challenged Winston Churchill for being drunk with the following exchange in 1946;

Bessie Braddock MP: "Winston, you are drunk, and what's more you are disgustingly drunk."

Churchill: "Bessie my dear, you are ugly, and what's more you are disgustingly ugly. But tomorrow I shall be sober and you will still be disgustingly ugly."

The statues, had he been the slightest bit interested, were the work of sculptor, Tom Murphy and together made up a piece entitled 'chance meeting' and had stood proudly in the concourse for nearly four years since being unveiled by Ken Dodd himself in June 2009.

Using Jane's mobile phone he sent two more text messages, one each again to Phoebe and Jane's parents;

"Hi Babes, back in town, chat l8r. LU XX"

He was less certain with the text speak this time but had to hope that as a one off he would be ok, and that Phoebe would just accept it as it was; after all he was going to dispose of the phone shortly.

"Hi M & D back in Liverpool, will ring 2moro. XX"

He had never been to university but thought that anyone who did wouldn't be in touch with their parents too often and this would again allow him to get back home before anyone even missed her; he hoped?

He surprised himself by how calm and organised he felt he was, he began to ask himself if he was missing something obvious, not seeing the wood for the trees? After pausing to think this through he smiled again, no, he thought, I'm ok.

Lifted by this thought he made his way back to the ticket office, something he hadn't done for years before today yet now seemed to be habit forming. A train to York was due to leave shortly after 7.20pm and with a journey time less than three hours he would be back in York just after 10.00pm; from there he was within a phone call to a mate and shouting distance of home and all in a day. Would anyone even know that he'd been away? He doubted it very much and smiled again as he again made for the ever visible Costa Coffee and sat with a large espresso this time.

With over half an hour to kill he cleaned the mobile phone with his handkerchief before placing it on the table in front of him. He drank his coffee and then got up, deliberately leaving the phone on the table as he did so and made his way to the gents, laptop and case over shoulder. He closed the cubicle door behind him and, once seated, he cleaned the laptop thoroughly before putting it back in the case and placing that on the floor at his side. He then left the cubicle, washed his hand and left, walking straight through the cafe and out of the door onto the concourse where he quickly became part of the still busy throng. Within a further five minutes he had bought a newspaper and was sat on the train waiting for its departure.

PART TWO

"Hello Phoebe, it's Graham Hammond; Jane's father. I just wondered if Jane was still with you. She was going to call but has probably just forgotten and I can't get a reply from her mobile?"

"Erm, Hi Mr Hammond, no I'm sorry she's had to nip back to her digs in Liverpool for some bits and pieces. I think she stayed a bit longer than expected and didn't bring everything she needed."

Having to think on her feet she wasn't sure what to say to Graham Hammond, she didn't really want to lie, but she didn't want to drop her best mate in it either. She didn't think she had been that convincing in what she had said but she was surprised at the call and puzzled that Jane hadn't called; Jane was usually very reliable where her parents were concerned, but then, she thought, she has just spent the weekend shagging her new bloke, she will have plenty of other things to occupy her mind.

"Oh, right, maybe if she's driving she won't have got our calls."

"I'm sure she'll call when she gets your message Mr Hammond."

"Yes, thank you Phoebe. How are you anyway?"

"Very well, thank you. Just catching up with everyone over the break, you know how it is."

"Yes, well we were hoping to catch up with Jane too before you all get back to your studies."

"I'm sure she'll call you Mr Hammond, or maybe she might even come straight over. A surprise visit."

"I would much sooner she just rang when she said she would, but thank you Phoebe."

"That's ok. Bye then."

Phoebe wanted to end the conversation as quickly as she could now, quit whilst she was at least still holding her own.

"Bye Phoebe, if Jane does call please would you tell her I rang, and thanks again."

Graham Hammond was undoubtedly worried about Jane, she had always been so reliable, but then he had always tried to ensure that she was; he had instilled into her the ethos of being polite, honest, dependable and trustworthy. He and his wife, Penny, a God-fearing, well respected and highly intelligent woman had brought Jane up to respect others, to be diligent in all she did and to be studious in order to make the best of her undoubted intelligence and quick wittedness. There had been times, he reflected, when others thought that Jane had been overly protected, even stifled by the constant attention of her parents. For Graham's part he dealt with this accusation by telling himself that he was doing his utmost to make sure Jane had every opportunity to excel at anything she did. So far, she had indeed excelled.

Phoebe, looked at her latest messages from Jane, "Back in town" did she mean Liverpool? She can't have meant Horsforth, not after the call from her dad. Using her speed dial option she tried ringing Jane but she too got a recorded voicemail message;

"Hi, you've reached Jane's phone, sorry I can't take your call just now 'cos I'm doing something that's either fun or necessary. Leave your message and I'll get back to you as soon as I can. Byeeeee"

"Jane, its Pheebs, call me."

She decided to send a text message too, not because she thought anything was wrong, just to give Jane a heads up, a warning that her dad was checking up on her.

"Hi Babes, WAYN? WAYD? CM LU XX"

"Hi Babes, where are you now? What are you doing? Call me Love you. XX"

There was no reply, Phoebe hadn't been sure that she expected one really. She knew that Jane would get back to her when she could, probably when she had stopped driving. She pictured her being stuck somewhere on the M62 in nose to tail traffic through the miles of road works that seemed to have been there forever. She knew that Jane wouldn't use her mobile in the car as she had been caught doing so once and had to sit through a thirty minute road safety lecture in order to avoid points on her licence. She had viewed scenes of carnage that the Police Officer giving the lecture attributed to use of mobile phones in cars. It did the trick; Jane had been scared shitless by what she had seen. Putting her phone down Phoebe went back to her music and thought no more of it.

TWO

"Good Morning everyone, it is now 8.45am on Monday 18th March 2013 and this is the sixty fifth day briefing of Operation Caedmon." There was an air of resignation in the tone that Simon Pithers delivered his greeting from his seat at the head of the table, but only recognisable under the determined expression in his voice and the look on his face as he studied the ever changing white boards that still dominated the briefing room.

"We're well into this case now Ladies and Gents and I would like to know from everyone if you think we are still working in the right direction? Are we missing something obvious or not looking far enough? I am very much mindful that Detective Inspector Maughan and myself have taken the lead so far and that is only right, however I am also aware that we are all working hard and that there may be thoughts from around the table that haven't been aired yet. I intend to go through what is known at this stage before asking for all your thoughts; do not think that I have all the answers or that I will dismiss your suggestions, this is very much a team effort."

With that he stood up and began to review the boards; the most obvious omission from them was the name of the victim; it had been over two months since the remains of this female had been found, up to two years maybe since she had been killed and yet still they had no name to put to her.

"Why, Ladies and Gents haven't we got a name yet? Has no-one missed their daughter, sister even, dare I say, mother? I don't think so, someone knows our victim, someone is missing her, why haven't we picked her out yet? Who is looking at mispers?"

Simon Pithers had moved straight from his open stance perspective to a figurehead again in a very short time.

"DC Alderson sir and Admin Support Officer Lynn Groves." Sue Collins was quick off the mark,

"Geoff, where are we then with this line of enquiry?" Simon Pithers asked.

"I've got a shortlist of thirty odd sir, based on an age group of eighteen to twenty two, but the bigger the age range the bigger the target group. I'm collating the DNA data we have from these but so far nearly half haven't had samples taken by the investigating force, including, sadly ours for one of them."

"Thanks Geoff, I want to know which one of ours hasn't been taken and a request out to each force today to get out and take samples from theirs, this is basics for missing person enquiries for fucks sake. Let me have the list after this briefing."

"Will do sir."

Despite his opening comments being well received Simon Pithers was quickly becoming frustrated that basic policing principles were being ignored and that meant that someone wasn't doing their job properly. "Sue what about our builders? Where are we with them?"

"All arrested, interviewed and bailed sir. All have given accounts that distance themselves from our scene; in fact we are going to have to cancel their bail unless we get something else soon."

"Right well I want you and Neil to meet with me straight after this and we'll go over each one and make our decisions then. We can always arrest again if we get any further evidence, but I want to make sure that we've gone as far as we can with each one first."

"No problem sir."

"Have we got anyone dedicated to social networks, can we check who has stopped using them in our time frame? Is it even feasible to do that?"

"No-one yet sir," Sue Collins answered again, "I don't know if it is feasible, but we could certainly look at that with Geoff's list."

"Let's start there then and see where it takes us. I want someone allocated to that straight away then."

"Consider it done."

"Clothing, jewellery? Anything from that?"

"Nothing at all sir. The clothing could be from anywhere, we've insufficient detail to narrow down the options and we've had no luck tracing the jewellery either even though we've released photographs to the press and had D's allocated to just that line of enquiry." Sue Collins spoke with an air of authority matching that of her superior officer; though she always referred to them as senior officers not superior; she didn't see anyone as superior.

"What about foreign Nationals sir?" an uncertain voice piped up from the back of the room. Sally Palmer only 19 and relatively new to the job of civilian admin support staff and who had been drafted in to help with the data input was very self conscious, especially following a very certain and positive Sue Collins.

"Go on."

"Well I was thinking that Whitby has folk festivals and Goth weekends that I know attract foreign visitors, my sister goes to some of the events; it's just a thought sir."

"And a good one. Neil, have we looked at that?"

"We've looked at it as far as including a search of foreign nationals being reported as missing here but not any further afield."

"Well get onto it," turning to the duty sergeant he continued; "Make sure we check with The Border Agency and International Forces. Sally, thank you and well done. That's what I want from you all; everyone should be thinking of options, I want to ensure that we miss nothing. Now has anyone anything else at this time?"

There were murmurs around the table but nothing coming forward.

"Right then, check with the task allocations and let's get onto this again. Neil, Sue, can we talk in my office in ten minutes please?"

The team were left clearly understanding that the investigation was still very much to be driven forward despite an apparent inertia in terms of results.

Mike Davies was grateful to his friend, Adam, not just for putting him up in the spare room but for finding him some work whilst he was there. It had been over three weeks now since he had sat in Scarborough Magistrates Court, three weeks of reporting to Cardigan Police Station and, at least in his eyes, being treated like a criminal. He had talked extensively with his dad on the way down; he had cried at the injustice of it all and asked his dad to believe in him. He had made numerous calls also to Paul Jeffries to keep in touch with any developments

He had spoken to Sandy on the phone and had asked him to get some of his tools from the Cottage and to drop them off at his dads before his next court appearance so he could take them back down with him. He had been assured that all his door staff work colleagues were supportive of him but that the cops had taken statements from everyone and were still asking questions. He had also taken to reading The Whitby Gazette online to try to gauge local opinion; it was there, as he sat at the breakfast table with his laptop open, that he had read his name under the headline,

"WHITBY DEATH. LOCAL MAN CHARGED"

The article, as always seemed to be the case, had been written by Elli Stanford and had named him in the first paragraph, following his initial court appearance; after which she had put together; in his opinion, a very one sided story of how he had pushed Fleur Brennan to her death. "Tragic misfortune of a fun loving local girl who died whilst celebrating with friends at Whitby nightspot. Family mourns for lost daughter and sister and Tributes pour out to lost friend." were all lines in the article which accompanied a photograph that must have been supplied by the family and showed a happy smiling, butter wouldn't melt teenager; not the drunken, foul mouthed woman who had tried to get in the pub that night; who, he maintained, fell on the steps."

"Bitch!" he spoke aloud his thoughts; "She's got me tried and convicted before I even get my chance to give my side of things. Well fuck 'em all"

He shut the lid on the computer and finished his cup of tea before standing up and making his way to the door. He had been found some labouring work and had the chance to add some building and plastering work when he got his kit together; he was already considering making the move permanent to get away from what he now saw as an insular, inbred community that was judging him in his absence and without all the facts.

His enquiries so far had confirmed to him what he had thought, that property prices and rental accommodation was a lot cheaper here than in Whitby; if he could keep in work he would probably be better off here, make a new start. For now he had to get down to the site, a small development of half a dozen houses on the edge of town, it was an overcast day with the drizzle being just about strong enough to wet his jeans, if not work its way through his coat and with the forecast of more rain to come later he wasn't in the best frame of mind; Adam had left earlier to open up the site and allocate work as needed, he would meet him again down there.

By the time he had reached the site, a twenty minute walk, the rain had picked up sufficiently to suspend any outside work and Mike had sat down with the others in the small Portakabin that served as a kitchen cum canteen for the crew. If this weather kept up he wouldn't earn anything today as some of the others would with their interior work.

He was still feeling a bit sorry for himself when his mobile rang; looking at the screen he saw it was Paul Jeffries. He swiped the green display to answer and listened to the voice;

"Mike, Good morning it's Paul Jeffries."

Mike frowned a bit; he often wondered why people did this when they knew their name would be displayed on the screen.

"Morning Paul."

"Have you had your mail delivered yet today?"

"What? No. Why?"

"Well, it's good news. The CPS have dropped the case; your bail has been cancelled and you're free to get on with your life."

Mike was taken aback, not initially believing what he was hearing. His silence prompted Paul Jeffries to ask;

"Mike, are you still there? Mike?"

"Yes, sorry, I, I don't know what to say. What's happened?"

"They've reviewed all the evidence again, crucially they've included some new, independent witness evidence and it appears that they have now accepted your account that it was a tragic accident, that you were only doing your job. Apparently a witness has come forward with some video evidence, taken using her mobile phone from a different angle and it clearly shows that you were just stopping the victim moving forward, not actually pushing her back."

"Well what happens now?"

"There are i's to dot and some t's to cross but, as I said, you're a free man again. I would like to see you again, just to tie up some loose ends, that sort of thing if you can get back up here anytime?"

"Yeah, 'course, I'll let you know. I can't believe it."

"Well do believe it and enjoy it. Call me when you know when you can get back."

Mike's delight at the news was obviously evident to his colleagues who were all looking at him as he punched the air and shouted;

"YES! Get in."

"What's got into you?" Adam asked, as everyone else looked on.

"They've dropped the fucking charges; can you believe it, after all this time?"

"That's great news, Mike" Adam shook Mike's hand and then gave him a hug of support. He saw the tears welling up in Mike's eyes and let him go;

"Don't think that this get's you out of a shift though. It's stopped raining, come on let's be having you."

Everyone saw the opportunity to leave the cabin, let the two mates have a moment to themselves. They chatted for a minute or two before Mike picked up his tools and said;

"You'll get a right days work today mate; thanks. I owe you big style."

It didn't need saying, they had been mates for a long time, but it still brought a smile to Adam's face.

FOUR

Penny Hammond looked across at her husband, sat in his favoured old chair, newspaper in hand but with a blank expression on his face that made clear to her that his mind was anywhere but on the pages in front of him.

"Penny for them dear." she asked

"Oh, I don't know, I just can't stop worrying about Jane. She always rings, always lets us know she's ok"

"She's growing up dear; don't you remember all the fuss we put our parents through? She's a sensible girl, she'll ring soon. You never know, she may even visit."

"I do hope so Penny, I do hope so."

It had been three days since the Hammonds had received the last text message from Jane, the one that promised to ring later and despite Penny Hammond saying all the right things to keep her husband calm she too was beginning to worry. She meant every word, Jane was a sensible girl of course but that made it even more worrying in that she had sent a text and then not made contact.

"Maybe we could try ringing her again?" There was a sense of realism in Graham Hammond's voice, one that said I know I've rung twice every day but what else can I do? One that also said I know she won't answer but I have to do something.

"If it helps you then go ahead dear, but surely if she has your earlier messages she will call soon."

"But then why isn't she calling? I wish she'd never sent that damn text."

"Language Graham!"

"Sorry." He was dialling as he spoke. The call went straight to answer phone again so he just hung up without leaving any additional message.

"I'm going to ring Phoebe again Penny, see what she can tell us."

Again his fingers were pressing buttons before he finished talking. This time after just a few rings the phone was answered;

"Hello Mr Hammond" Phoebe had added him to her contacts, so often had he rung over the time Jane had been at university with her, much to Jane's annoyance.

"Hello Phoebe, have you heard from Jane recently, I mean since I last spoke to you?"

"No, I assumed that she must be with you and that was why she hadn't texted me or called."

"I'm worried Phoebe, it's not like her and if she's not with you do you know where she might be?"

"I'm not sure Mr Hammond; I can try her mobile if you want?"

194

"No I've done that it goes straight to voicemail."

"Have you tried emailing her or facebook, if her phones bust she might still have access to the internet with her laptop or iPad?"

"No I haven't, that's a good idea. What about other friends, could she be with them; anyone in particular?"

Phoebe considered that Jane might have gone back to Mikes but didn't want to say anything, she knew very well how prim the Hammonds were and how much they would hate their daughter to be casually sleeping with someone, even at her age.

"I can't think of anyone just off the top of my head but I'll go through my contacts. Do you want me to try facebook?"

"If you would please Phoebe, I'm not very good with it. Please let me know anything won't you, just ask her to call me."

"Sure, will do. Don't worry Mr Hammond, she's probably just not charged her phone up."

"I do worry Phoebe, but thank you." He finished the call and looked even more concerned than before. Phoebe meanwhile had known she was lying when she talked about not charging the phone battery; Jane would never be without her phone, never. She immediately sent a text to Jane's phone, saying simply; "Call me. X" No need for abbreviations or introductions. She then dialled the number and, just as Graham Hammond had found the call went straight to voicemail. "Jane, call me. Now." She hung up again and held the phone in the hope that such a brusque call and message would elicit a prompt response, it didn't. She waited several minutes before using her mobile to send a facebook message and a regular email to Jane's hotmail address; she put on a read receipt request on the latter but didn't really know why. She then sat back and tried to bring to mind her previous conversations with Jane, she recalled how happy she had sounded when she had met Mike, how upset she had been when he didn't attend Sexy Sunday to pick her up. She thought of Darren who had been interested in her but unsuccessful in his endeavours and about Gail who she thought came across as a good friend, at least for the weekend anyway. She then looked again at the last text she had received, three days ago; that was strange, she never really went a day without texting, but then Phoebe thought; well I didn't contact her so maybe that's nothing to worry about?

"Who am I kidding?" it was only a thought but came out as spoken words, to nobody as there was no-one else present but Phoebe had gone over in her mind everything that had happened these last few days and she was now worried. But what could she do, she didn't know where Jane was anymore than her father did. What she did have however was a more realistic picture of the real Jane Hammond.

FIVE

Within ten minutes of the briefing ending Neil Maughan was sat opposite his boss, Sue Collins had been politely asked to make coffees for all three and this had bought Simon Pithers the short time he needed to speak with Neil alone without advertising the fact.

"Not a very good result in Wales Neil?"

"Well it was a bit of a fishing trip sir, we didn't really have much hope but we couldn't progress without asking the questions."

"Well make sure it's all written up in the report; however I notice that there is a change between you and Sue since you got back, is there anything you want to tell me, anything I need to know?"

"Nothing you need to know sir." Neil Maughan placed great emphasis on the word, need, and hoped that was all he needed to say at this time.

"Well I hope you're right Neil as I don't want personalities interfering with the investigation; it's proving hard enough to move forward as it is."

"There are no problems sir; you have my word."

"Good I'll hold you to that. Now let's move on."

"I liked that suggestion from Sally sir, it seems so obvious in a way but I suppose there is a chance that a foreigner could be missing and if, say, she was on a long holiday; touring maybe she might not even have been missed for weeks, then you have the issue of where would she be missing from."

"I thought we had made those enquiries Neil, but I accept your point, she might not be on our radar yet. Make sure we have it covered now please."

A light knock on the door was followed by Sue Collins walking in holding a tray, precariously in one hand whilst using the other to push the door shut again.

"I got biccies too." she proffered as a way of joining the conversation discussion. Was it just her or was there a palpable pause in conversation; she suddenly felt slightly uncomfortable.

"Thanks Sue, ever reliable." Simon Pithers gestured for her to take a seat next to Neil.

"Sorry, I'm not interrupting am I?"

"No; not at all. We were just saying it was a good call from young Sally, good thinking."

"Yes, if only everyone was prepared to speak up instead of just sitting through the briefings and waiting for a task."

"If we have any of those on the team Sue, I want to know. There's no place for inertia on a murder enquiry. Neil, your thoughts?"

"I just think that some are quieter in the presence of a senior officer sir."
"Well they need to grow some balls then Neil or get back into uniform."
"Changing the subject Boss, I've just seen Des Mason in the corridor, he's coming back to work next week, and he's asking if he can come back onto the enquiry?"
"I need good D's on the team, so if he's back and his head's in the right place then yes."
"I thought maybe we could allocate the social network stuff to him then we could manage his time better and he would be visible to us all without it being obvious."
"Good thinking, I don't want any of this half day stuff though Sue, if he's back on the team then he's on it full time."
"I think he knows that Boss, I think we need him back."
"Agreed, I'll leave it with you and Neil. I do want a return to work interview doing though, properly. If he's been off with stress I don't want anyone saying we've dropped him right back in it."
"I'll do that sir," Neil Maughan, jumped in, "I'd like to know where his head's at anyway."
"Right, let's have a proper review of this job then."
Simon Pithers sat back in his chair, looked at his two colleagues and made his own mind up. He had no doubt their relationship had moved onto a more than professional basis and he would have to monitor it over the coming days and weeks, especially if there were to be further trips to other force areas and also that it didn't interfere with their professional judgement. For their part both Sue Collins and Neil Maughan realised that Simon Pithers had been very good with his perception of the situation and now knew that they had to discuss it further at the very least, or even come clean about what happened in Wales. That outcome however would have serious implications for both, especially for Neil.

SIX

It was a cold but beautiful clear sunny day as John Davies drove his son along the A169 towards Sleights, a largish village about 3 miles outside Whitby and above which was a roadside car park which afforded views over to the town, its abbey and the sea beyond; views that had been photographed many thousands of times by tourists over the years and enjoyed by many more.

"Pull over Dad, please."

Without reply, John Davies turned his car to the right and drove into the car park, bringing the car to a stop at the edge of the gravelled area; short of the heather covered moorland itself and facing directly across to the iconic abbey beyond.

"What's up son?"

"I just wanted to look and think before we go back into town. Do you know that I've lived here all my life, played for the football and cricket teams, mended folks homes and worked with half the population, yet they were all happy to turn their backs on me when the chips were down?"

"I think you're being a bit harsh son, there were a lot of people supporting you as well."

"Really? Well they've kept it very quiet."

"Just be yourself Mike, you'll see."

"I won't Dad, cos I'm not staying. I'm gonna get my stuff, see Paul Jeffries and get out of here. I've had enough."

"Come on don't be hasty, let's ring your Mum and tell her to get the kettle on."

John Davies didn't really know what to say, his wife had been upset when Mike had had to leave due to his bail conditions, she would be distraught to think he was moving away permanently.

"You've read the papers Dad; they'd already got me convicted. Mike the murderer."

"You're just being daft now. Reporters are always the same. The charges have been dropped and that's for a reason; you've done nowt wrong."

John was being stronger now, showing his support by taking control of the situation and not letting his son drop into a cavern of self pity. "I'm not listening to any more of this, hold your head up high and show everyone who you really are."

With that he reversed the car back, turned the wheels and drove back out onto Blue Bank and headed towards town.

Stopping off for petrol at Four Lane Ends garage on the edge of town Mike sat in the passenger seat as his Dad stood outside using the pump;

the forecourt, as usual was busy and it wasn't long before John was chatting to another customer. Mike couldn't hear all the conversation but thought he could hear his name being mentioned, winding the window down he heard the end of a sentence;

"...put it behind him now"

Fuck it, he thought and opened the car door;

"I'll pay for this dad." he shouted; as much to draw the attention of the other people on the forecourt as that of his Dad. He watched as a number of the other customers turned their heads in his direction, some immediately turned back hoping not to have been seen looking, others retained their view, watching as Mike made his way across the forecourt to the shop cum kiosk.

Immediately inside the shop was the newspaper rack with the Whitby Gazette taking pride of place at the top.

"WHITBY DEATH CHARGES DROPPED" the headline ran above a front page photograph that had been used throughout the story and an article that Mike saw was pretty much a reworking of past weeks articles amended slightly to throw a different light on the events of that fretful night. Mike picked up a copy as he passed and walked on towards the counter. He saw two women, who he put in their forties, chatting away behind the tills. Mischievously he placed the newspaper on the counter with the photograph uppermost and in full view of the two assistants, almost in a challenge to them to say what he knew they were thinking.

"Just the paper and pump number four please." He said to the woman whom he saw wore the name badge 'Debbie' on her uniform.

Picking the paper up to scan it, Debbie glanced at Mike and then the photograph, before looking again and saying just,

"That's seventy pounds and ninety one pence please."

"Yes it is me," he said, passing his debit card to her, "and I should never have been charged in the first place."

"Sorry, I didn't mean to-" she replied as he tapped his PIN number into the machine.

"It's alright; you won't be the only one. That's until somebody else does something to hit the front page"

He took his card back, picked up the paper and made his way back to the car and his Dad.

"OK?"

"Yeah, fine. Always the same though in nit, talk behind your back but not to your face?"

"It's the same the world over son." putting the car into gear to drive the short distance home.

SEVEN

"It's been five days now, can I please see someone." Graham Hammond was less than pleased at the apparent lack of interest shown by the Police call handler, who seemed hell bent on ending the call by telling him he had nothing to worry about.

"Yes, she's twenty two, I know but she always calls."

"I'll ask the local Neighbourhood Team to send someone down when they're free."

"Thank you." Graham was quite angry now, he felt that he was being patronised, that his call was just wasting their time. Placing the phone back down on its cradle, he stood up and walked back into the living room where his wife was sat in her chair.

"What do the police do these days; everything seems to be too much trouble for them?"

"I'm sure you're wrong dear, you'll see, someone will be here soon."

It was over four hours later when a portly, yet somehow diminutive looking middle aged man in a yellow fluorescent jacket stood at the entrance to Rosinish House, a name chosen to reflect the Scottish background of Penny Hammond's family.

"Good evening, Mr Hammond? I'm PCSO Alan Rodleigh; I've come about your daughter."

"About time someone did, are you on your own?"

"Yes sir, may I come in?"

"Yes, of course, come on through."

Graham Hammond led the way down the hall and into a drawing room, furnished with a range of expensive looking sofas and chairs around an ornate fireplace in which stood a large dried flower arrangement in front of a pale green coloured silk screen. Alan Rodleigh, who despite his years was relatively new to this role having spent years selling breakdown recovery in the shopping malls of Leeds and Sheffield, found himself checking his boots as he walked in on the pale cream deep pile carpet, fearful of leaving marks from his size eights; by the time he reached a leather club chair and accepted the invitation to sit down he was feeling very uncomfortable; this was a world away from his upbringing in the much less regarded area of Bramley.

"Nice place." an uneasy opening line from a fish out of water and not what Graham Hammond needed to assure him that West Yorkshire Police were up to the task of finding Jane.

"Yes, well we work hard and one has to be comfortable."

Seeing the discomfort of the officer Penny Hammond did what most good hostesses do and offered tea and biscuits which were readily accepted by Rodleigh, who had taken his notebook from his jacket pocket and was writing something on the page.

"You say that your daughter, Jane, has been missing from home, how long is it since you've seen her?"

"She sent a text message five days ago; I haven't seen her for weeks."

"So does she live here then?"

"No, she's at Liverpool University but she had told us that she would be visiting us at the start of the week."

"And have you checked with the university or at her digs?"

Graham Hammond did not feel that his urgency was being recognised by this man in front of him, in fact he considered the man to be out of his depth and quite rude."

"Of course I've made what checks I can but she doesn't live at the uni, she lives in digs nearby."

"Have you checked there?"

"What do you think? Do you think I've rung the police before I've checked her home and her friends?"

"I'm sorry Mr Hammond; I have to ask these questions."

"Well what do you intend to do now?"

"Graham," Penny Hammond stepped in to calm her husband down a little, "he's only doing his job."

"That's not good enough Penny, I don't just want someone taking notes and ticking boxes from standard questions, I want the police to do their jobs and find our daughter."

"Mr Hammond, I can assure you that if your daughter is missing-"

"What do you mean if? I'm telling you something's wrong. I know it."

"Mr Hammond, I have to ask you these questions so that I can submit a report when I get back to the station."

"And what station is that? Are there any left open?"

"I'm from Weetwood."

Alan Rodleigh did his best to continue with the questions on his notepad crib sheet but it was a difficult task as he rightly felt that Graham Hammond had no faith in him or his abilities, as a result the answers he elicited were basic, but thankfully at least sufficient to complete a report after leaving. He had spent upwards of an hour in the company of the Hammonds and left feeling that they were paranoid and that at twenty two years old their daughter was probably out enjoying herself at some music festival or other like most other students. He cut a lonely figure as he strolled back down Brownberrie Lane towards The Old Ball pub just off the roundabout.

EIGHT

"Can we talk Neil?" Sue Collins was walking along the corridor with her Inspector after their meeting with Simon Pithers.

"It's not a good time, Sue. Not just now."

"It's your call Neil, but you saw the looks we got in there; he's not stupid."

"I said not now Sue. Will you send Des in to see me please?"

"OK. But we need to talk sometime."

Neil Maughan turned away from her and through the door way into his office, leaving her in the corridor; he needed some space, some time to think. He had not thought that he would be affected this way but after the trip to Wales he was smitten with her; so much so that he was worried that his wife, Helen, had noticed something. So far he had passed off his mood swings as tiredness and frustration at a lack of progress with the investigation but Helen had known him for many years and could read him like the proverbial book. There were also kids to think about; he thought the world of them, he thought a great deal about Helen so was he being stupid? He didn't really have an answer.

"Des, can you go down and see Neil please, I haven't told you, but you're back on the team." Sue Collins had entered the main CID office, still very confident in herself and her own position on the squad; she now wanted to give the good news to her colleague and ease his concerns before he met with the boss. Having given that news she chatted to other team members and updated herself with everyone's allocated tasks to keep abreast of all that she needed to know; she then logged onto her desktop computer, read her emails and got on with her own workload.

"You wanted to see me boss?" Des Mason had knocked on the already open door and let himself in to Neil Maughan's office.

"Yes Des," still sat at his desk, Neil Maughan raised his head to acknowledge his colleague and gestured with his pen for him to take a seat. "How's things? How's Gemma?"

"Much better thanks Boss but it's been a hell of a ride as you know."

Neil Maughan had been keeping in touch throughout Des Mason's sick leave, often just by telephone but with an occasional home visit thrown in and considered the family as friends as well as work mates.

"Yeah, I didn't envy you."

"It's been a great help knowing that I could ring you and the welfare though. Thank you."

"Family should always come first Des and I'm happy to help if I can."

As soon as he said this he considered what he had said. He hadn't thought of family first in Wales had he?

"I know but it's great to be back all the same. I heard in the briefing this morning the comment that we still haven't ID'ed the victim yet?"

"No we haven't, I thought that would be the easiest bit of the investigation as well."

"What do you want me to do then?"

"Sue will brief you properly and then allocate your tasks, it will be working on the social network research but I want to talk about your return to work first Des."

Neil Maughan then went over the issues that had caused his friend and colleague to be absent for several weeks, explained the concerns that Simon Pithers had about part time working even on recuperative duties and received, in return, the assurances that he was looking for, as always seeming to be the case these days making a note of all that was said.

It was only when Des had left his office that he put his head in his hands and said to himself;

"What have I done?" He went over again, in his mind, the foolhardiness of his fling, the impact it would have on Helen and the kids if they found out; and yet he knew that ever since that time he had thought of little else. When was the last time he had felt the way he did that night, was it just lust, excitement? He didn't know; what he did know however was that he couldn't say no if the opportunity arose again.

NINE

He had been home; if that's what you call living with your parents, for several days now. Choosing to stay there to spend some time with his mum who was worried about him, and his dad who had been a brick over the last few weeks; solid in his support and never really questioning him about what did go on but letting him talk when he thought it was right to do so. He hadn't ventured too far away from the Oak Road semi where he had been brought up since the age of four; he and his two older sisters, both now married with families of their own. What had they thought of his arrest and charge on such allegations? No matter how long he thought about it Mike Davies always came up with the same answer, he hadn't done anything wrong.

Mike sat watching sky sports news in the modest comfort of his mothers lounge, a throwback to the nineties with a sturdy and functional, if not currently fashionable, sofa and two matching chairs in a beige and brown floral style, if indeed style was the word to use; blending if not seamlessly, at ease with the magnolia emulsion on all four walls and serviceable Berber carpet of a similar tone, even Holly, the chocolate Labrador seemed to tone in, in fact only the TV, a 43" Panasonic flat screen model mounted on the chimney breast, gave any indication that life in this house had moved into the 21st century. It was home though, a refuge, a place of support and unquestioned love. He was comfortable but was becoming bored, he had agreed to stay here for a while when his father had asked him to, in order to ease his mums concerns. He was feeling that if he didn't leave again before too long it would tend to lead his mum into thinking he was coming back for good, he couldn't do that; he loved them both dearly but you can't go back after you've had a place of your own, and he didn't want to anyway. Adam had said that there would be work for him when he returned to Wales and had understood when Mike advised him of his decision to stay a while, was even supportive of it.

When his mobile rang he was startled out of his tedium and surprised to see that it was Ged Turner,

"Hey up Ged, long time no speak?" He was uncomfortable with the call in as much as Ged had been conspicuous by his absence throughout his recent turmoil and hadn't even attended court even though he had been working for him at the time of the incident, yet he didn't want to sound as pissed off as he really was.

"Yeah, you alright?"

"Well, yeah suppose so, you?"

"Yeah, not so bad, Look do you fancy havin' a chat sometime?"

"What sort of a chat?"

"How you're doing, what plans you got? That sort of thing."

"I'm not planning on stopping Ged if that's what you're thinking."

"You sure, you're jobs still there if you want it?"

As an SIA accredited doorman Mike knew that he could find that sort of work anywhere if he wanted to, what he needed now was some stability in a proper job, not one where he could find himself in this sort of mess again. How long, he thought before he became a target for the local idiots taunting him about the accusations, the charges etc.

"Not a chance. No way." he was brusque but stopped short of cursing.

"Well how about a drink any way?"

"I can't Ged; I've got stuff on this aft." he was lying but thought it better than going out with someone for whom he had lost all respect. If anything this call had made his mind up for him, he would explain everything to his mum and dad and make his way back to Wales, a new start, away from the memories of the last few weeks and months.

TEN

"Can I please see someone in charge?" Graham Hammond had grown sick of his phone calls being ignored and had driven to the closest Police Station that he could find that was open regularly, Weetwood; on the outskirts of Leeds just off the ring road but some distance from Horsforth where the local station, along with many others across the county, had been closed to the public, allegedly to generate efficiency savings.

"Can I ask what it's about sir?" a polite if somewhat untidy Admin Support Officer with a name badge that identified her as Judy stood behind a glass fronted counter, pen in hand.

"It's about my daughter." Graham Hammond snapped, then apologised, "Sorry, I didn't mean to shout, I'm just so very worried about her."

"I understand sir, but unless you tell me about her I can't help you." Despite Judy's obvious acquiescence Graham Hammond couldn't understand her not knowing about Jane. What had the PCSO done with his report?

"Jane Hammond, Rosinish House, Scotland Lane, Horsforth?" He paused, waiting for a response but none was forthcoming, "I reported her missing, here," he said, handing over a card with an incident number written on it by PCSO Alan Rodleigh.

"Thank you." Judy took the card and having viewed it began typing on the desktop computer on the front desk. "Yes, sir, here it is. Have you heard anything from her yet?"

"Obviously I haven't as I wouldn't be here asking to see someone in charge."

"I see that Jane is twenty two years old Mr Hammond?"

"Yes, I told that to the officer that came to my house."

"Well it's unusual for us to pursue the enquiry here sir, when she is actually missing from Liverpool, if at all?"

"I've heard enough of this, what do you mean, if at all? I demand to see whoever is in charge"

"That's Inspector Helliwell sir, Oscar Helliwell, I know he's in a meeting at the moment.-"

Cutting her short he gave a terse, "I'll wait."

Judy nodded and turned away saying, "I'll let him know. Please take a seat Mr Hammond"

Oscar Helliwell wasn't in a meeting but Judy knew that he wouldn't be best pleased to have this dropped on his plate without some background information at least; she returned to the back office, typed in the information again and printed off a copy of the incident report, not that there was much there, it would have been graded as low risk anyway given the circumstances but due to Jane Hammond living elsewhere and because of her age it had been written up merely as a general incident and no local action required; in fact at this point in time, other than Graham Hammond's quite obvious concern, there was nothing to indicate Jane was missing at all and therefore the police had better things to do with their time.

Knocking on the door to the Inspector's office and going straight in Judy delivered the print out to him with the words;

"Oscar, we've got another over protective parent here, won't speak to anyone but you I'm afraid." She then went on to explain what had taken place so far before hearing him say;

"You'd better show him in then."

ELEVEN

"It will fall into place Neil, it always does; we just have to keep doing the simple things well."

Sue Collins was doing her best to reassure her boss that he wasn't failing in his bid to find a breakthrough in the investigation. Sat in her office, but with the door open in order that she could see and hear Des Mason in the office opposite and be there to reassure him if need be; she didn't see it as babysitting but supporting a colleague in need.

"I know and we are doing the simple things well, but not getting anywhere."

"We are though, look at the whiteboards, they are covered in ink; all that is good intelligence, intelligence that will help us get to the bottom of this."

"I know, I know." Frustration was evident and Sue Collins hadn't seen Neil like this before, he was always the one telling everybody else that things would drop into place eventually.

She stood up and walked around her desk to shut the door, brushing past her boss on the way.

"Excuse us for a few minutes, Des." she shouted through, "You ok?"

"Fine Sue, no probs." Des Mason seemed almost puzzled that she should ask.

Closing the door Sue turned back to Neil and placed a hand on his shoulder;

"What's up Neil? Do you need to talk? You sound real tetchy and uptight."

Neil placed his hand on hers and looked into her eyes;

"You don't know?" He was almost pleading with her to show some understanding.

"No Neil, I don't. I'm sorry."

"It didn't mean anything to you then?" it was obvious that he was referring to their night together and he seemed positively aghast that she hadn't picked up on it earlier?

"Neil, I'm sorry, I didn't realise-. I just thought-"

"No it's obvious that you didn't think, didn't think at all."

"Whoa, I'm not having that. As far as I'm concerned it was a one night stand between two consenting adults. I don't recall a great deal of reluctance on your part at the time."

"I know, I'm sorry, it's just that-"

"For fucks sake Neil stop apologising. If you have an issue with it then that's your problem. For my part I've said nothing to anyone and I've moved on."

"As easy as that eh?"

"Yes as easy as that. Neil you have a wife and family and I'm not going to be the scarlet woman for anybody. Deal with it" She wasn't quite shouting but had to rein in her anger and maintain some degree of control if this wasn't going to escalate into a full blown row.

"I've been stupid haven't I?"

"Too right you have if that's what you hoped for; it was never on the cards, never will be."

"I'm sorry."

"Neil, you need to leave now please; before you lose it or I do. We need to be able to work together if we are going to get this case back on track. Do what you do best, find this killer and forget me; us, whatever."

It seemed so wrong talking to her boss like this, almost as if talking to a school child, chastising then tasking him to do better. She didn't feel comfortable with it but knew that one of them had to act in an adult fashion or the whole station would be talking behind their backs; if they weren't already?

She opened the door again and looked at Des, still at his desk across the hall; whether he was in earshot she may never know but he would certainly be curious as to why there had been a closed door and raised voices, he would almost equally be certain to say something to Mark Taylor or one of the other detectives in the office, even if only in passing.

"Shit." she said under her breath but caught by Des and, of course, Neil who in turn was now stood behind her and ready to leave. He walked out of the office and with only a cursory glance in Des' direction he made his way back along the corridor to the incident room. Sue shut the door behind him and raised her fists in frustration.

"Men! For fucks sake why can't they just fucking grow up and take some responsibility?" There was no-one there to hear her and she was grateful for that as she sat at her desk and started typing again; using a little more force on the keyboard than was actually necessary or even wise.

TWELVE

It was shortly after 2.00pm when Mike Davies answered the door bell at his mother's home and was taken aback when he saw the figure of Elli Stanford, note pad in hand stood before him. He had known Elli for some time, both as a friend and professionally when he had given her titbits to bulk out a storyline if he had anything whilst working the doors.

"Hya Mike, I heard you were back in town, but didn't know you were at your dads place. Can we talk?"

"You are joking Elli, or at least I hope you are?"

"No." Elli pointed across the road to a man, who Mike recognised as Dan Elliott an old rugby colleague, stood by a red Vauxhall Corsa, holding a camera with what appeared to Mike to be an oversized lens, "I thought you might want a chance to put your side of the story in the paper?"

"Elli, you have got no chance. There is no story; the charges have all been dropped because there is no case to answer. Has he taken any photos yet, 'cos if he has I'll go fucking ballistic?

"You're wrong Mike there is a story, hell it's as big a story as we've had for ages."

"Well I'm not adding to it Elli, I've done nowt wrong and I don't have to say anything to anyone?"

"What about Fleur Brennan's family, do you want to say anything to them?"

"Who is it dear?" Ann Davies shouted from the kitchen en-route to the front door.

"It's alright Mum, it's for me."

"Well you don't have to stand at the door, you can invite them in you know."

"No it's alright Mum, they'll not be long."

Elli Stanford had heard all this and looked at Mike again,

"Have you got anything you want to say to Fleur Brennan's Mum and Dad Mike? Can you explain why they haven't got Fleur at home right now like your Mum has you?"

"It was an accident and anyway I've been told not to talk to anyone about it."

"That was when there was a trial Mike, not now."

"It was an accident, I didn't push her. She fell."

"Is that what you want me to write?"

"I don't want you to write anything. Just leave me alone."

"Mike I've got to write something, you know that. It won't just go away because you're ignoring it-"

"Ignoring it, you're fucking joking aren't you, I can't get away from it and I never did anything wrong."

Mike looked up and saw that Dan Elliott was taking photos of him talking to Elli.

"Put that camera away or I'll shove it where you really will need a flash you twat."

Dan put his camera onto the front passenger seat of the Corsa and got into the driver's seat, started the engine and drove off before Mike had any chance to carry out his threat. He had taken as many shots as he would need and it looked as though Elli would get enough to put an article together even if she stopped talking now, apart from that, he believed he may just carry out the threat.

"Last chance Mike?" Elli Stanford was looking past him into the hall, trying to see Ann or John Davies; did they have a comment for the press?

"Are you here for a while then?"

"No. Look just leave me alone will you? I need some space; I just want to get on with my life."

"So did Fleur Brennan Mike, so did Fleur Brennan." Elli turned away from him and began the walk along the path to the gate onto Oak Road. She paused at the gate, "I'm sorry Mike, I will be writing my article and I can only use what I have. You can read it on Friday."

Mike slammed the door shut and made his way back into the house. That was it; he just had to get away now, and soon.

"Was that that reporter from the Gazette dear?" Ann asked in all innocence.

"Yes Mum, she's gone now." He bit his tongue, not daring to say what was in his mind.

"Nice girl, I knew her mother at school."

Mike sighed; it confirmed just what he thought, that he was not going to have any peace in this small, inbred town.

211

"Please take a seat Mr Hammond." Oscar Helliwell had met Graham Hammond at the door to his office with a firm handshake and a similarly firm mindset. At five foot eleven inches tall, of slim but muscular build and wearing his immaculately pressed uniform he represented everything one would hope to see in a Police Inspector. A little greying around the temples seemed to add to the look giving an air of experience that was in turn a true reflection of his twenty three years in the job.

"Mr Hammond," he continued, "I've read through the incident report and I'm aware of your obvious concerns about your daughter. I do, however, have to look at what I can do to help you and to how I can use my limited resources in order to obtain the most effective policing for the area." He paused, but only briefly, allowing his words to settle in Graham Hammonds mind but not giving time to respond before adding;

"As I understand it your daughter is currently studying at Liverpool University and has digs over there?"

"Yes, Liverpool John Moores University. She is in her final year."

"Well in these sorts of circumstances we would normally ask for the report to be dealt with by the local police; that is Merseyside Police who would be able to make the local enquiries, visit your daughter's home, check with neighbours and friends; that sort of thing. I'm sure that you will understand that we can't do that in Liverpool?"

"I understand that but I can't seem to get anyone to believe she is missing?"

"Mr Hammond, I understand your obvious concern, but in my experience I have to say that it is not unusual for a young woman of your daughter's age to go off on a short holiday with friends or to a concert without thinking of their parents. ' It's not cool' you might say, to be seen to be beholden to mum and dad."

"You're beginning to sound just like all the others now. My daughter sent me a text saying she would call me, she didn't, she hasn't made any contact since and I can't get in touch with her. I've contacted her friend, Phoebe, who she has just spent a weekend with and she hasn't seen her since either. What do I have to do to make you understand, this just isn't like her?"

Oscar Helliwell listened, as he had to, but sat patiently in his chair still believing that Jane Hammond would more than likely be with her boyfriend or staying with someone her father disapproved of, maybe he didn't approve of the boyfriend?

"Mr Hammond, I will ask an officer to take some further details from you and will then arrange for them to be sent to the local police station in

Liverpool with a request that an officer visits Jane's flat or house whatever and speaks directly with either Jane if she's there or her friends if she's not. I am sure that we will be able to put your mind at rest before too long. I am a father myself and I know the sort of pranks that some of our children get up to when they are away from home."

The look that came over Graham Hammond's face was not the one expected by Oscar Helliwell, instead of being reassured he had clearly found the comments to be objectionable;

"My daughter has been brought up correctly Inspector; she is not the wild child you appear to assume her to be."

"I meant no offence Mr Hammond I was merely trying to suggest that the student years are different now to how they have ever been and there are more activities to become involved in, more reasons not to ring home." He hoped his comments had got him out of jail, reclaimed some lost ground, but his hopes were unfounded.

"I know my daughter very well thank you and if she says she will ring she will do so unless there is something stopping her. Can we please now complete this report and get someone checking, someone actually looking for her?"

Rather than risk saying the wrong thing again Oscar Helliwell picked up his phone and dialled his Sergeant's office number; the call was answered almost immediately by Sergeant Tom Donald,

"Weetwood Police Station, Sergeant Donald speaking, how may I help you?"

More formalities, the corporate handshake as they were told to refer to it, more bollocks and bullshit as most of the officers chose to see it.

"Tom its Oscar, I need someone to take a Misper report for me ASAP? I have the reportee with me now in my office."

"I'll send Ian sir; he's in doing some clerical."

"Thanks Tom."

Replacing the handset he looked across at Graham Hammond and saw for the first time the real look of anguish in his face; gone was the anger at not being listened to, to be replaced by a near tearful expression; one that he recognised as that of a father's genuine concern. He hoped that he was right, that Jane Hammond was indeed just spending the proverbial dirty weekend with her boyfriend and not in any danger.

"An officer will be up in a moment, I will ensure personally that everything is dealt with as quickly as possible and that you are updated as soon as we hear anything." Reaching into the top drawer of his desk, Oscar Helliwell took out a business card and handed it across to Graham Hammond. "I'm on late shift for the rest of this week, five pm to three am after today, my details are on the card and you must feel free to contact me at anytime. If I am not in my office I will return your call as soon as I am able to do so."

"Thank you Inspector."

The knock on the door was followed by PC Ian Hardy entering the room and being introduced to Graham Hammond, together with a potted history and incident number.

"This way Sir," Ian Hardy held the door open and gestured for Graham Hammond to leave the office; Oscar Helliwell stood up and shook his hand;

"I'll be in touch Mr Hammond."

The door was closed behind the two as they left and Oscar Helliwell sat tapping his biro between his teeth, pondering.

FOURTEEN

Neil Maughan had stopped briefly in his own office to collect his thoughts and refocus before walking into the incident room and sitting on the edge of the briefing table, looking up at the whiteboards. He knew them to be whiteboards because he had seen them at the start of the investigation but they were now covered top to bottom, side to side with photographs, maps, names, sketches and comments, they could literally have been any colour.

Down the left hand side of the board was a list of officer's names and collar numbers and in the next column was a brief description of their allocated tasks. The details were all obviously kept on the computer systems but he liked o be able to look at things like this, he felt he could picture things better this way. Des Mason's name had been reintroduced showing him working on the social media checks, Neil Maughan knew of them, he had even opened a twitter account after much nagging from and cajoling from colleagues and family, but never seemed to have either the time or inclination to use it; surely if the victim was a young female she would have a facebook account, didn't everyone under twenty five have one now? Why hadn't anyone missed her then when she had stopped posting her status or adding new photos? It seemed to him that it was possibly even more likely that she would be missed from this virtual community rather than from the real world, with iphones and androids being so common it was inevitable that she would have had regular postings, was it possible to see if Whitby had been a focus for anyone at that time? He stopped his thought process almost as soon as it had started, of course it wasn't, they couldn't narrow down the time frame closely enough and then just how many users would be updating about the town, its villages, events, people, history, the possibilities were endless, and yet; he wondered?

"Where's your thoughts then Neil?" Alison Reed had entered the room and seen him looking up at the boards,

"That the answer is staring me in the face somewhere Ali, and I'm not seeing it."

Ali used a tissue to wipe the tasks against her name clean before adding others;

"You know, we always seem to do this don't we? We either get our man, or woman," she added for effect, "straight away or we go through torture before it jumps out and smacks us in the mouth."

"I'd take the punch right now if it meant we got the breakthrough; what about your team, anything to add?"

"Nothing much, it's all being input right now but no."

215

Ali Reed sat down next to him on the table, despite there being a plentiful supply of chairs at hand. She looked at the boards alongside him and for a while nothing was said; both in deep concentration. After what seemed to be an age, but was in reality only just over a minute, Ali Reed broke the silence;

"How many outstanding Mispers have you got DNA samples for Neil?"

"Not all of them Ali, do you remember the boss asking Geoff Alderson to chase it up at the briefing? He was well pissed off."

"Well we still have unmatched samples from the scene as well as the victim's."-

"I know Ali, but it's a holiday cottage, they could be from anyone."

"They could be the killers?"

"I know. You're right. Are there any with club numbers; CRO's?"

"Yes, including a couple of our locals, but I think they're the builders from the discussions we've had in the office. We found hairs in the 'u' bend under the sink and in the bathroom waste pipes."

"You guys don't miss a trick do you?"

"Crims can spend hours cleaning a crime scene but it's very rare, if at all they even think of waste pipes."

"Well as good as it is we've had the builders in Ali, we got nowhere fast."

"Well we will have to consider partial and familial matching then if we want to make any progress from that line."

"It's an option we're looking at, an expensive one though with no guarantees. We've got to ID the victim, that's where this enquiry is going. Name the victim and find the killer."

There was a noticeable change in Neil Maughan's voice; the lack lustre shell that had been sat down only minutes ago was focusing again, getting his drive, his mojo back.

FIFTEEN

"Bacon, sausage, eggs, beans and a slice of toast for his Lordship" Adam was being sarcastic as he placed the Sunday Brunch on the table in front of Mike, "I didn't expect you back quite so soon mate."
"I didn't expect to be back so soon, believe me."
"So why the big decision, why the change?"
"I was living in a Goldfish bowl, I couldn't move without someone staring at me, asking me stupid questions or pointing at me in the street."
"You wanna talk about it?"
Pausing from pouring the copious serving of HP brown sauce on his plate Mike looked up at his mate; he did want to talk but he didn't really know what to say.
"I just don't know what to do. I feel like I did murder someone when I've done nowt wrong." There were the makings of tears in his eyes, a slight shake in his voice; he had put on the brave show for his parents, for everyone he knew really but the recent events had taken their toll, he was mentally shattered.
"It will pass though, as soon as there's some'rt else to write about in the papers."
"That's just it though, in a place like Whitby nowt else does 'appen."
"What about that bird you were seeing then? Have you heard from her?"
"Jane, no not a word since I got locked up that night. I've rung her, text her and no reply, straight to voicemail."
"Well move on then, she has."
"Yeah, without a fucking word. Bitch."
"Well she maybe thinks you binned her off when you didn't meet up with her?"
"I didn't even get a message on the night, she didn't even ring me, I could have told her what was wrong. Now I can't even speak to her."
"Have you got her address?"
"No, why, what for?"
"Look Mike, I've known you for years and I've not seen you like this before; it might be the arrest but I think this girl's got under your skin. If you know where she is go and see her."
Mike nearly choked on the toast he was eating; "What just turn up, when she's ignoring me. Won't text or answer my calls are you fucking mad or what?"
"You'll find out either way what she thinks if you see her won't you?"
Mike took a drink of his tea and sat back in his chair, holding the mug in his large hands he just looked at Adam, as though in a trance;
"I don't know her address but I know she was at Liverpool Uni."

"Well that's a start, but I doubt that they'll give you much. Data protection and all that shit." Adam's expression indicated just what he thought of that legislation, "Sorry sir, I can't divulge any personal details, Data Protection." Adam mimicked in as feminine a voice as he could muster from his large frame; it brought a smile to Mike's face though, the first of the morning.

They continued their chat as they finished their meal and Mike realised that he felt a lot for Jane but didn't really know that much about her; he had photos on his mobile phone and some text messages that they had shared before his arrest but in truth he knew very little. He thought to himself, "If this were Rebus I'd be able to travel up there with these photos and after showing those to a few people in Liverpool, having a few drinks and a fight I'd find her in no time at all and all would be well with the world."

"Hey, are you still with me?"

"What, yeah, sorry I was just thinking-"

"Well don't think, just do it cos you'll drive me nuts if you don't?"

The decision had been made for him, it's amazing what a good breakfast and a nice cup of tea can achieve. "I'll go in the morning, there ain't gonna be anyone there today."

"Fancy going down to the Dragon then, watch the early kick off?"

"Sounds good to me."

It was two happier mates that set off walking through the town just half an hour later, dirty plates left in the sink, frying pan still on the hob with the remains of the fat from the fry up still visible and a part full jug of micro-waved baked beans keeping them company on the nearby worktop, they could wait until later.

SIXTEEN

Graham Hammond was shown into a small untidy office by PC Ian Hardy; there were numerous forms and papers on the green metal framed desk and more on top of the three filing cabinets under the window. The vertical blinds were damaged and as a result didn't block out the sunlight, which in turn meant he had had to move his chair to one side of the desk in order not be blinded by those rays of light that did get through the gaps. A desk top computer sat in the centre of the desk with the usual array of wires behind it adding to the overall picture of administrative chaos. Things didn't bode well.

"Please take a seat sir." Ian Hardy gestured to the seat opposite him and Graham Hammond sat down on the apparently new chair, possibly the only new item in the room. "Please bear with me just one moment whilst I clear up some of this mess."

The officer was known in the station to be amongst the most organised and particular, with only three years service but already earmarked for greater things Oscar Helliwell was pleased that this job had been given to PC Hardy. It was only two minutes later when the incident had been found on the computer and the actions thus far were being read by the officer, whilst he didn't say so he could immediately see the phrases that had been used were leading to an NFAR. No Further Action Required. The check list had been completed by the PCSO and the incident had been graded as low priority with the full expectation that at twenty two the misper would turn up shortly. The other side of the coin was that the Inspector felt the need to treat this as more important, why, was it instinct or just the persistence of the father who now sat opposite him; either way this now had to be treated with a greater degree of importance.

"Sorry to keep you Mr Hammond, I can see that you have spoken to one of my colleagues previously and obviously to Inspector Helliwell earlier today, I'm going to need to take a statement now and this may take an hour or so, is that ok?"

"At last, someone is listening to me; yes of course it's ok."

Over the next hour or so Graham Hammond covered all the ground he had previously with the different officers he had spoken to and answered the more searching questions put to him by Ian Hardy. In turn the officer made copious notes and wrote out a statement; many officers now typed out statements directly onto the computer but despite his younger age he preferred to write things down long hand. The picture painted by Graham Hammond was that of a 'butter wouldn't melt' girl who wouldn't look amiss if she still had pigtails and freckles. Ian Hardy asked if anyone had searched Jane's room at home and Graham Hammond answered;

"No, why? She is resident in Liverpool at the moment."

"It always forms part of our routine enquiries sir, nothing to worry about."

"If you say so, but I don't see the relevance."

Ian Hardy nodded his acknowledgement and continued writing before asking to see Graham Hammond's mobile phone in order to read the messages received from his daughter. Having made notes of the content of the texts, the time and date sent and replies, he told him not to delete any of them.

Completing the statement he asked Graham Hammond to read it through and sign it, taking the time he did so to update the computer record of the incident.

Ten minutes later Ian Hardy was following Graham Hammond back to his home, noting the slow speed that he was driving in his pristine new black Jaguar XF Sport brake, capable of so much more. Driving through the electric gates onto the yew lined driveway towards the twin garages, Ian Hardy formed the mental picture of Jane as not just having had a sheltered upbringing but being almost hidden from the actuality of the real world, the interior of the house cemented that view, with religious tokens and ornaments displayed throughout. Having introduced his wife to the officer, Graham Hammond gestured to the stairway and said,

"I'll show you to Jane's room. Please follow me."

The deep pile of the carpet throughout the hall, stairs and landing was very noticeable and the tasteful decoration showed that somebody had a real eye for detail and colour. Graham Hammond opened the light oak door to a room on the left of the landing and walked into a large room with an equally large oak sleigh bed and matching furniture. The bed was made immaculately with a Liberty design throw matching the curtains and the white sheepskin rug either side of the bed looking out of place somehow. The room, perfect as it was, was set out for someone of far senior years than Jane; there was not a poster, a picture, music or anything else that would tempt anyone to spend any more time in there than needed. Opening a door to the left of the room Ian Hardy walked into the en-suite, of similar standards to the rest of the house, the slipper bath, separate walk in shower and usual bathroom facilities were impeccable; absolutely nothing out of place. More an upmarket hotel room than a student's bedroom Hardy thought.

"Does Jane have a toothbrush or hairbrush at home Mr Hammond?"

"Yes, in the cupboard above the wash basin." he pointed to the mirror fronted cupboard set with LED lights either side, "Why?"

220

"It's just routine sir, as I said, but we always take something that will provide a DNA sample."

"Why would you need that if you think she'll return soon?"

"I'm sorry Mr Hammond, maybe I didn't explain, but DNA helps us to eliminate people from our enquiries as well as identify them in difficult circumstances. If we have the sample from the outset then we shouldn't need to worry you later."

Ian Hardy took the only toothbrush from a glass tumbler inside the cupboard and placed it into a small plastic exhibits bag before closing the cupboard door again;

"Do you have a recent photograph of Jane?"

"Yes, of course. We have some on a disc as well, I could copy you some of those if you wish?"

"That will be fine, thank you."

Graham Hammond left the room and walked back down the stairs and into a large study that had obviously been fitted with bespoke furniture, a computer and two large monitors dominated the desk that was as clean and clear as the rest of the house.

It was just a matter of a couple of minutes before Ian Hardy took a CD Rom from Graham Hammond and, after a couple more questions about Jane, left the house.

Penny Hammond, who had been watching everything between the two men, felt the tears running down her cheeks; "Where is she Graham, where is our baby?"

SEVENTEEN

The chatter in the room palpably stopped as Sue Collins entered in her usual, almost serene, manner and it didn't take a genius to notice it. Des Mason, Geoff Alderson, Mark Taylor, the visiting DS Andy Goodall and inevitably, Jean Bolton were sat at different desks around the CID office and all were noticeably embarrassed to have been caught out by the subject of their recent conversation.

"Spit it out then." Sue Collins issued the challenge to everyone present, "Come on let's have it, if you've got anything to say let's hear it."

No-one spoke but just exchanged glances, trying to avoid eye contact with their accuser.

"I thought so," Sue Collins continued, "Well if you haven't got the balls to say anything to my face I'd thank you to keep your mouths shut behind my back."

She remained in the doorway, as if challenging them one last time before she left. It was no surprise that the silence continued,

"Jean, I think you had better leave, thank you." she moved aside to let Jean past before continuing; "Geoff, Des, Mark I want updates on your progress on the box within the hour. Andy, we need to speak, now, please." She had said please but in such a way as to leave no room to manoeuvre, if he hadn't held the same rank it would have been seen as an order, and with that she turned on her heels and left the room to cross the corridor into her own office.

It was only seconds later that Andy Goodall followed her into the room, closing the door behind him and taking a seat. Sue Collins had remained standing, staring out of the window across The River Esk towards Whitby Abbey; she turned, leant against the window frame and demanded;

"What the fuck was all that then?"

"As if you don't know?"

"Sorry, what?"

"You must have heard the gossip?"

Andy Goodall left the question hanging for a second or two before adding;

"You and Neil?"

Sue Collins didn't reply, but pulled her chair out from under her desk and sat down, clasping her hands together and audibly sighing.

"And who's spreading the gossip may I ask?"

"You know what it's like in this job Sue, the jungle drums work faster than high speed broadband."

"Yeah but I don't expect it from you. How can I expect my own team to keep their thoughts to themselves when you're part of it and if Jean knows, well then it may as well be posted as a headline in the Gazette?"

"So it's true then?"

"I never said that."

"You didn't have to."

"Shit. Shit shit shit."

"Where's Neil?"

"He's on at two. Late shift."

"Well let's hope he doesn't hear anything before he gets in then."

"In this town, you'll be lucky?"

"It's not me that needs to be lucky if Helen gets a drift of it." Standing up Andy Goodall carried on, "I'll leave it with you Sue, but I suggest that you speak with Simon Pithers before he hears it from the grapevine. Good Luck."

Sue Collins didn't reply, she had moved her thoughts forward and her colleague left the room closing the door behind him. It wasn't yet 10.00 o'clock and her day was falling apart; in truth she wasn't that bothered about Helen Maughan, her problems lay squarely with her husband, though no doubt she would be seen as the home breaker; she was more bothered about her career, she wanted to see this job through to have it on her CV when she came to look for promotion. She picked up the phone and dialled the number from memory; Simon Pithers answered on the second ring'

"Hi Boss, it's Sue Collins, I need to speak with you. It's personal."

"I'm due in a Senior Management Team meeting at ten, Sue, but jump in a car and come to see me after that; should be through by half eleven given a fair wind."

Sue Collins agreed and replaced the handset seconds before a knock on the door stopped her from screaming out loud.

EIGHTEEN

Having set off later than he had initially hoped, Mike decided to stop en-route to Liverpool at Ruthin, having made an earlier stop for petrol he now needed some fuel for himself and saw this charming little town as an opportunity to stretch his legs and have a cuppa and a bite to eat. Parking in a small pay and display car park just off Park Road, he left his car and walked into the town, fastening his coat zip as he walked towards the market square.

As the time passed midday Mike considered that he had covered just over 100 miles of his journey with maybe approaching about half as much again to travel, another good hour on the road would do it, but there was no rush. Not knowing the area, he stopped at the first cafe he saw, Zoe's, which advertised free WI-FI together with 'good wholesome food at affordable prices' on a somewhat gaudy, hand painted burgundy and gold sign in the cafe window.

Taking a seat near the window he perused the menu before asking the diminutive waitress, Zoe herself maybe, he thought; for the steak and ale pie and a large coffee. He watched as Zoe made her way back behind the counter and into the kitchen area, her long brown hair tied up in a pony tail and resting between the shoulder blades of her slim frame and above the knotted apron strings that in turn framed a very pert shapely pair of buttocks. He was brought back from his daydream by a call on his mobile, he saw Adam's name light up on the screen;

"Hey up mate."

"You ok?"

"Yeah, just stopped for a cuppa."

"Just checking', I didn't see you this morning. Are you sure you want to do this, I mean, she might not want to see you?"

"I know, I think she's made that clear, but I want to tell her that I didn't stand her up, I've left it too long already."

"Alright, your decision mate. Good Luck."

"Cheers."

There was nothing more to be said, but Mike knew that Adam was being sincere, asking the questions he had been asking himself, but he had made his mind up now. Placing the phone down on the table in front of him Mike watched the busy market place, people going about their everyday lives, shoppers carrying plastic bags full with the mornings purchases, queues of people at the bus stop opposite chatting, something people in towns tended to do but people in cities, he considered, didn't; the usual mixture of cheap suits with the shiny arses through too much sitting on office chairs, being worn by the local office workers, bankers, estate agents and the like he guessed. He was still watching and wondering about how others might view him in similar circumstances when Zoe reappeared complete with a huge plate of food and a mug of coffee on a tray. Placing the tray on the edge of the table to serve his meal Mike saw that close up she looked a bit older than he first thought, late twenties maybe and though attractive there was something about her that just didn't appeal. Was it the slightly crooked teeth, the forced smile or just an abruptness in her manner that didn't seem to sit well with her purpose of serving a customer, maybe it was a comparison with Jane that he was making and seeing her fall short; whatever, he just thanked her and ate his lunch.

Another forty minutes and he was back in his car for the second leg of his journey, continuing along the A494 and then onto A550 and A41 before paying the toll and entering the tunnel at Birkenhead and continuing under the River Mersey to his destination.

Following roadside sign posts Mike quickly found a multi- storey car park at Mount Pleasant and found a spot that he thought provided the best security from passersby; he was always wary of leaving his vehicle in busy city car parks. Placing his overnight bag and other valuables in the boot he locked the car and set off to walk the short distance to Rodney Street, which from his time spent on Google, he thought would give him the best option of finding someone to help.

Needles and Haystacks came to mind when he reached the university campus; he had printed a couple of photographs of Jane that he had taken on his phone over the couple of nights they had been together and he had thought that these might help him as he realised he knew so little about her, Jane Hammond The Goth was about as far as it went.

NINETEEN

Oscar Helliwell had been as good as his word and having read the statement taken by Ian Hardy he was talking to his counterpart, Inspector Cheryl Burton in Merseyside Police,

"I realise how busy you will be, we all have our priorities but there is something about this one that doesn't sit well with me."

He knew that he would have to lay it on thick to get anyone interested as in Liverpool City centre there were literally hundreds of crimes being committed that would take priority and students not going home wasn't likely to score highly on any matrix form.

"This young woman doesn't appear to be the usual carefree student, my PC tells me that there isn't a speck of dust in her room at home and her parents have never loosened their grip on the apron strings. She really was expected home."

"I hear what you're saying Oscar but, without teaching you to suck eggs, you must realise just how many young people get their first taste of freedom at Uni and go wild, turn into real party animals."

"Well is that maybe a good reason to treat it with more urgency? I don't know, I can only ask but I have a bit of a gut feeling and it's not a pleasant one."

"Send the stuff across, I'll read it through and ask one of the Safer Neighbourhood Team to look at it. We have a dedicated University Officer, Laura Goodman; I'll talk to her and ask her to keep you posted."

"Thanks Cheryl, I'll owe you one."

"If I had a pound for every owed favour I could retire early."

They both laughed, the business element of the call had been concluded and they now chatted briefly about the usual trivia that passed between colleagues to ease the tension of their busy schedules.

Oscar sent the required information across and then updated his computer records after the call, something that always had to be done to show the audit trail of any enquiries made into an incident; the so called paperwork that seemed to tie far too many cops to their desks these days, before sitting back in his seat, hands behind his head, deep in thought, thankful that he was father to two boys not vulnerable girls.

Cheryl Burton checked her emails and found the one from her West Yorkshire colleague and the attached copies of the original incident report, statement and a cover letter in the form of an official email frontispiece, a throwback to the days when Police Force's across the land passed information via fax machines and each had to have a corporate header sheet, ostensibly to prove its authenticity, indicating the opinions of both Ian Hardy and Oscar Helliwell.

Within an hour Laura Goodman was being briefed by Cheryl Burton having been summoned from her beat at the university; universally accepted as a good cop, a career constable who had found her niche in life and had no ambitions towards promotion and the inevitable politics that came with it, she was highly respected for doing what she did very well.

"I hear what you're saying Ma'am but I'm with you on this one; without anything to the contrary it's difficult to justify placing it at the top of my priorities."

"Well, rightly or wrongly I've given my word to West Yorks' that we'll look at it and get back to them. They won't be expecting miracles but their cops seemed to think there was just something out of the ordinary with this one; maybe give the PC, what's his name?" shuffling papers in front of her she looked for the constables name before Laura interrupted;

"Ian Hardy, Ma'am. PC Ian Hardy, he's taken a good statement from the father and he's taken the time to add some good background information as well, it's certainly not just the usual foreign force enquiry; you know the sort, let's get rid of it and let them have the problem; he's put some effort in."

"Yes and maybe we should too then Laura, create an incident on the box and come back to me with something within a couple of days, even if it's a blank."

"Will do Ma'am, but you know that I've got that presentation to give this afternoon so I can't do anything with it until tomorrow."

"No, sorry, what presentation is that?"

"The one telling the intelligent students not to leave their laptops, phones and tablets on display in the windows of their multi-occupancy dwellings, I do it every year at the start of the first semester but after that spate of burglaries the other week, I'm repeating it. That one spree has wrecked this month's figures for the North side team."

"Tomorrows fine then."

Had it been a young child reported missing then obviously other staff would have been directed to respond more quickly, most forces had a priority matrix and graded their response to these sorts of cases by the oft maligned tick box method, the higher the score the greater the urgency placed on the officers responding. Even taking into account the gut feeling of Oscar Helliwell the two Liverpool based officers couldn't score this one too highly.

TWENTY

"Come in." Sue Collins did her level best to keep her emotions in check as she shouted towards the closed door.

"Is it alright to come in Sue?" Des Mason stood one foot inside the office and the other still outside as if wholly unsure that he should even dare to enter at such a time.

"Yes, come in and shut the door behind you Des."

Des did as he was told and took the seat recently vacated by Andy Goodall;

"I'm sorry about just then." he stammered, "I didn't meant to say anything out of order, not after you've helped me so much recently, you know with Gemma and all that."

"Just what did you say Des, and who started the gossip?"

""Sue, you know I don't grass my mates' up-"

"Des, you came here to apologise then you clam up and give me that crap. If you've no more to say then go now."

"Sue, both you and Neil are friends as well as colleagues, it's not for me to say who does or doesn't do whatever they want to do, but in this job you know that even if it's not true; mud sticks."

"Yes I do know that. I also suspect that our good friend Jean couldn't wait to get up here and tell you everything that she's heard during her routine early morning telephone gossip with the Scarborough front office."

"Well you didn't need to hear it from me then did you?"

"Let's move on, I've got to go see the boss soon, what have we got that I can give him as a positive; anything?"

"Nothing concrete; but if I can talk just between the two of us for a minute I might have something?"

"What after what I've just heard?"

"You said we'd moved on from that."

"Just spit it out Des."

"Well you know Gemma is into her social networking and online games; of course you do, that's what caused all the shit recently. Well she was at home yesterday and I asked her about some of the sites she used and how often people use them, what names they use, all that sort of stuff. I didn't say too much but I did tell her it was part of the case I was on."

"Go on" Sue Collin's interest had picked up a little now.

"She said that everyone uses facebook and twitter, but that's mainly done from phones and tablets now; the games though are still usually on laptops though as the screen resolution is usually much better."

"Yes, and?"

228

"Well she said that she used to play on a site called Battle Guile; that is her boyfriend did and so she used to have to as well. She said that up to about eighteen months ago there were a couple of other lasses, from the Liverpool area that used to play as well; she remembers because it's usually lads that play the game. Eighteen months ago they just stopped playing, both of them at once, or almost both at once."

"And how does this help us though Des?"

"I don't know if it does but one of them used the name Scouse Vixen and she was into the Goth scene so I just thought that there might be some Whitby connection with that?

"There just might be, it's certainly worth pursuing. What about the other one?"

"Gemma said she can't remember everything but she didn't think that the other had the same interests but just used the game as a means of adding to her virtual friends, or some'rt like that anyway."

"How would she feel if I spoke to her, how would you feel?"

"I've no problem with it as long as I'm not seen as discussing sensitive stuff at home, that's why I asked about it being between the two of us."

"I'll put it down as an action for me Des, then it's all above board and any way it might just be a break, God knows we need one. Now though I need to be away, I've got to go to HQ to see the boss."

"Good luck with it, and, Sue; I'm sorry about this morning."

"I'm a big girl now Des, don't worry about me. Are you ok though, you know the stress stuff? Everything improving?"

"Yeah, we're a lot closer now, but I wouldn't wish it on anyone else."

Logging off her computer and picking up her bag from the side of the desk Sue Collins stood up and made for the door;

"Thanks Des." She wasn't altogether sure why she had said that but felt that at least she had something positive to give Simon Pithers, it might just ease the pain of the bollocking she knew she was in for.

229

Holding the two printed photographs in his right hand Mike walked hesitantly through the entrance of 2 Rodney Street and made his way to the reception area. He was not nervous by nature, how could he be and do the work he did, had done? He did however feel a bit out of place, not as well educated as the vast majority of people stood around him and quite obviously lost amongst others who all seemed to know exactly where they were going.

"Can I help you?"

Mike was actually pleased to see it was a man who had asked the question, he did not know why he was pleased, maybe he felt that a bloke would see his predicament a little easier, understand his hesitancy?

"Yes, please." He walked the short distance remaining towards the reception desk and, lifting the photos into view of the man, who he saw on an identity pass worn on a lanyard around his neck, was called Dan, "I'm looking for this girl and I believe she was a student here?"

"Are you a relative sir?"

"No, erm, sorry no I'm a friend"

"I'm sorry sir but we can't give out information about our students to anyone other than next of kin or others that have been identified to us as being a close relative or having an interest, by the student themselves. Data Protection."

"I know she's called Jane and we recently spent some time together, look." Mike showed the photographs to Dan, who took a cursory glance before reiterating his position in not being able to divulge any information.

"I only need a message passing to her if you would please."

Dan recognised Mike as being both polite and persistent and wanted to help him, "Do you know anything else about her? I mean what is her surname?"

I'm sorry I don't know."

"You're not that close then?" Dan knew this was a put down but it showed Mike just how little he did know about Jane and just why he would find it hard to make any headway.

"She's a Goth, I know that much. I met her at Whitby recently and just wanted to get in touch again."

Dan picked up the photos again and had another look; he didn't see anyone he recognised and yet he recognised in Mike's expression something that showed genuine concern, not just, he hoped an overnight liaison chasing a lost dream.

"I'm not sure I can help you, but why don't you try the student bars? I can give you a list of some of the bars if that will help, someone might know her."

"I'll try anything."

Dan took a pen and scribbled a short list down on a note pad before tearing that sheet off and handing it to Mike.

"Try these, they're pretty popular due to the prices they charge and the entertainment they put on. Sorry but I just can't do any more. I don't like the phrase, but it actually is more than my job's worth."

"No problem, thanks for your help." Mike took the paper and retrieved his photos from the desk, placing them in his pocket before turning away and walking back out of the door.

He hadn't really expected to achieve anything more than he had and at least he had a list of pubs to try, but first he needed to find somewhere to stay for the night. It shouldn't be difficult, he was surrounded by hotels. Within minutes he had picked up his overnight bag and other belongings from his car and saw The Feathers, a Best Western Hotel; they usually provided decent prices for what you get without being either too dingy or too grand, most importantly it was close to the town centre, the university and, he assumed, the student bars he had on his list. He booked in for the night, bed and breakfast and was shown to his room on the third floor, only then realising that this must be the only hotel in Liverpool without a lift? The staff were friendly and helpful though and the room was very clean and well presented, ideal for what he wanted. Putting his few items of clothing in the wardrobe and his toilet bag in the en-suite shower room he then filled the small kettle to make a cup of coffee and took out his laptop and linked into the WI-FI to do some research on the list of pubs he had been given by Dan, hoping to put together a route that would take him from one pub to the next in some semblance of order.

It was well after 5.00pm when he next looked at the time and understood why he felt hungry. His lunch had been well made and the portion was ample but he was a big man with a big appetite. It was time to look for something to eat, time to look at the first student bar on his list, deliberately chosen for its reviews about good food.

TWENTY TWO

Many officers tried their level best to conduct as many investigations as they could by telephone, this, they would argue, allowed them to conduct more enquiries in a shorter time than would otherwise be the case. The reality was often that it meant they were closer to the kettle and the warmth of a sheltered office away from that old enemy, the general public with their inevitable problems, grumbles and seemingly endless inane questions, "Have you got the time? Are there any toilets nearby? How do I get to anywhere street?" Laura Goodman was not that sort of cop and that is why she was always welcome onto the university campus.

"Back again Laura? You got time for a cuppa?" Dave Preston was a security officer on the site and was always pleased to see Laura with whom he shared a good working relationship and an equally profitable exchange of information.

"Always got time for a cuppa Dave, put the kettle on and I'll be there in a mo." Laura had a desk within the campus reception area where people knew they would be able to find her at certain times of the day; she always made a point of advising the reception staff that she had arrived even if she had to see people elsewhere; even if it was only a cuppa with Dave.

Only three minutes later she returned to Dave Preston's small office near the main entrance, office was actually a very grand word for what could equally be classed as a large broom cupboard, but it had two seats, a small Formica topped table, a couple of lockers and a small TV set and a tiny worktop, sufficient to prepare tea or coffee but little else.

"Weak with two sugars, just as you like it." Dave Preston handed a cup of tea to Laura and she sat down in one of the two seats before taking a sip and leaning back into the chair.

"That's great Dave, thanks. You ok?"

"Yeah, no point moaning is there?"

"Any gossip?"

"Always got some gossip, but none that you'd want to hear today."

"Try me."

"No, really, I'd tell you if there was anything worth knowing. You know that."

"Well what about a missing person then?"

"Who's missing?"

"I'm not sure if that's the right term to use in this case but I'm going to ask at reception about a girl called Jane Hammond, a straight laced, God fearing type we're told."

232

"The name doesn't ring any bells, you got a picture?"

"I have but I've left it at my desk, I'll drop you a copy in later."

There followed a conversation that covered as much of the background as Laura felt she could disclose without betraying professional confidence; Laura knew that she would now have another person dedicated to the enquiry as Dave couldn't resist playing the detective and as long as she kept him on a tight rein he provided very good support.

"Thanks for the tea Dave, keep in touch."

"I will; you're welcome."

Laura made her way across to her desk and spoke with the reception staff again, covering the same ground as she had just done with Dave, this time though there was a more positive response, if that was the right perspective to put on the answer.

"Jane Hammond, not been present at any of her lectures or study groups since the October break." Yvonne Milton, an administration Team Leader that Laura knew well, stated as she read from the monitor in front of her, "Her course tutor is the lovely Alan Gregson." said with sufficient sarcasm to register with Laura but not enough to cause offence should she know him.

"Has anyone tried to make contact with her then?"

"I can only assume so but I don't have access to that sort of information, Alan will have and so will the pastoral care unit."

"Would you be able to make some enquiries for me or can you point me towards them?"

"Sure, leave it with me and I'll get back to you as soon as I find anything out."

"Thanks Yvonne, I knew I could rely on you."

Leaving Yvonne to it she made her way to her own desk and re-read the supporting information added to the missing person report by Ian Hardy, she had listened to what Cheryl Burton had said and knew that she wasn't someone to be conned into upgrading a wild goose chase, yet on the surface it appeared to be no more than that. Ian Hardy had indicated that he had serious misgivings but it wasn't too unusual for a PC to add some gilding to their work if they wanted to promote it as a good job well done, and yet there had to be something to get not just past his own boss but hers too. The more she read the more she tried to imagine this house on Scotland Lane, in some place called, Horsforth; the best she could come up within her own mind was to imagine a large house with the ambience of a museum or place of worship; a house full of good intentions but little actual understanding and yet the parents were quite obviously worried sick and genuinely cared very deeply

233

about their daughter, they appeared to have love, warmth of heart and care but archaic principles and even older social boundaries. The photographs in the file were said to have been taken recently and yet they showed a woman she knew to be over twenty years old dressed so conservatively that she could be mistaken for Mary Ellen in the nineteen seventies TV series of The Walton's, a teenage God fearing waif dominated by the will of her parents and limited by the location of their home.

She picked up the phone and dialled the direct line number for Weetwood Police Station hoping to be able to speak with Ian Hardy; as usual she found that he was on a different shift that day, nights in fact and then onto rest days. She told the call taker, another PC by the name of Brian Morton that she would email Ian Hardy, but then asked if Oscar Helliwell was in his office?

"He is; I'm sure he'll be really pleased to play second fiddle to PC Hardy." Brian taunted Laura, "I'll try to put you through"

"Weetwood Police Station, Inspector Helliwell, how can I help you?"

The same old corporate handshake thought Laura before asking,

"Good afternoon Sir, my name is Laura Goodman, PC Laura Goodman from Merseyside Police, I wondered if you could spare a couple of minutes to talk about Jane Hammond?"

"Of course, yes Laura, go ahead, shoot."

Laura explained her position, the fact that she had read thoroughly all the paperwork she had been given and had initiated enquiries at the university but that she was having difficulty marrying the facts with the modern girl at university scenario. She explained that she wished to speak with Ian Hardy to obtain as full a picture as she could before making any decisions and asked, "Can you give me anything else at all, any additional comments you could make about the father, mother, domestic arrangements, over and above what has been included in the report?"

"I discussed a lot of this with Inspector Burton Laura but I suppose you're wondering why I am so concerned about this one when all appears straight forward?"

"Well something like that sir, yes."

"We might just have to call it instinct, a gut feeling if you like but I spoke at length with Graham Hammond and I had the chance to look into his eyes. They were the eyes of a father on the brink of tears and quite obviously genuinely concerned about the whereabouts of his child."

"Child, sir?"

"We are always our parent's children Laura; you will be too in the eyes of your father."

234

If only Oscar Helliwell knew that Laura's father had left her mother as soon as he had realised she was pregnant he may have thought otherwise, but she knew what he meant;

"Can you tell me a bit about Horsforth sir, I know I can Google it but what sort of place is it?"

"I can tell you that Scotland Lane is a highly respectable area in a very desirable small town location just outside Leeds and that Rosinish House is very much at the better end of that nice little trio. Imagine downsizing from Downton Abbey and you won't be too far away; but from what PC Hardy tells me it is very much a house rather than a home to be comfortable in and maybe therein lays the problem?"

"But you did say that there was genuine concern, real love from the father?"

"Yes, and I am sure about that, absolutely certain, but there are many ways to show affection and some people maybe just don't find it easy, I don't really know."

The two discussed Horsforth and the surrounding area, the type of people resident there; even if stereotyping was frowned upon these days it sometimes helped to paint a picture, before Oscar Helliwell had to end the call to meet an appointment. He thanked Laura Goodman for her contact and realised even from the brief discussion that the job would be handled well; he then updated the West Yorkshire record of events on the computer whilst it remained fresh in his mind.

Laura meanwhile tidied her desk and put on her jacket for a walk to Russell Street, L3 5LJ.

TWENTY THREE

The drive across to Newby Wiske had given her time to think and Sue Collins was an optimist by nature anyway, whilst she expected the formality of a dressing down for unprofessional behaviour she was the junior rank in the liaison and she knew how these things tended to work; Neil Maughan would be the one facing the true wrath of hell; at home and at work.

Driving into the grounds surrounding Police Headquarters didn't ever seem to change, the open gates hung on stone pillars that once led to the grand hall, a grade II* listed building, which was constructed in the 17th century by Northumbrian landowner William Reveley and after many different incarnations eventually became the administrative centre of North Yorkshire Police in 1976.

She parked her car in the visitor's car park and walked up the steps from there to be faced by the two ornamental lions that stood either side of the huge front door, ostensibly guarding the entrance. Opening the door she felt she was walking quite literally into the lion's den.

She knocked gently on the closed door to Simon Pithers office and was somewhat surprised to have it opened by the Assistant Chief Constable Toni Magennis, a woman shorter than herself, but then most were; with a brunette bob cut, surrounding a smiling face with dark brown eyes she was maybe slightly heavier than she would ideally prefer to be but she was immaculately presented in full uniform and exuded a natural air of authority;

"DS Collins, come in."

Sue had been prepared for most things but not this and was still a little taken aback as she entered the room; Simon Pithers stood up and gestured Sue to sit down at the table in the corner of the room.

"Right Simon, I'll leave it with you, but I need some answers before I see the chief at five"

"Will do Ma'Am." he replied even as he watched her leave the room and close the door behind her. Sue Collins had taken her jacket off and sat at the table as she had been bid to do.

"I hope I haven't dropped you in it sir?"

"What? No. She was here on something totally unconnected, or at least I hope it is as we have someone being a little less than careful on the computer."

"No, I'm clear on that one"

"But? And I feel there is a 'but' to be added to this sentence?"

"Yes, if you haven't heard already that is?"

Simon Pithers didn't answer, he had heard the rumours as they were currently still to be regarded but he was not one to pass on gossip or believe rumours until he had evidence one way or another.

"I need to talk sir, about Neil Maughan and me?"

"And a trip to Wales?"

"Yes."

"Well thanks for coming to me now, but you may recall that I asked you about this not long after you returned?"

"I know sir and I apologise."

"How fucking stupid are you two? You are heading up a murder enquiry, he is married, you are ambitious and yet you both put yourselves up for gossip, ridicule and potentially disciplinary measures. I gave you both more credit than that."

He stopped short of ranting but his anger was evident and had not been helped by the visit of the ACC adding to his workload and who would no doubt ask about the sergeant's visit when they met again at 5.00pm

Sue Collins for her part considered that the best form of defence in this case may be to get onto the front foot, if stopping short of going on the attack;

"These things can happen sir; we are after all two consenting adults who have still done a good job so far."

"I'll be the judge of that thank you I don't exactly see any remarkable progress being made; in fact we still don't even have a name for our victim let alone a suspect? So tell me how this represents a good job?"

"That's unfair sir. You know that we have followed up every lead we have had and we have come to nothing, but that doesn't mean that we haven't tried. We just need a break from somewhere."

"Yes I'm sorry that was a bit of a cheap shot. Let's talk about you and Neil first then we'll talk about our nameless girl"

Sue Collins talked for the next few minutes, explaining that the night spent with her immediate boss was just that, to her at least, a night and nothing more. She accepted the stupidity of it in hindsight she had to accept that there were already rumblings across the force area and that something would have to be seen to be done in order to quell the rumour machine before it got into top gear, but confirmed that she had moved on and was not going to let it interfere with her ability to do her job.

"That might not be your decision to make Sue," Simon Pithers looked his watch and saw that it was approaching 2.00pm, "Neil will be in the afternoon briefing now, there will be officers and staff sat around that table nudging each other and passing knowing smirks to their colleagues. This sort of thing can undermine authority and that's when it matters most, when people are focused on gossip and not on the job in hand."

"I caught everyone in the office this morning sir, talking, that is whispering. I made my views very clear."

"That won't stop them talking as soon as your back is turned will it? You have been stupid, you are a good looking woman Sue, and you don't need to be shagging a married colleague." He knew he shouldn't have phrased his comment that way but he was frustrated at being put in this position by two people he had so much faith in. Sue Collins let it pass, deciding not to put herself further into the firing line by making the obvious challenge about who she should and shouldn't be sleeping with.

"I'll have to accept that on the chin sir, but I do think I can offer something positive on the case," she paused for a second, "If you're happy to move on that is?"

"It's not over Sue, I will need to speak to Neil and then we will take it from there, but let's have something positive then shall we?"

Sue related the conversation she had had with Des Mason and, as tenuous as it was it was at least another thread to pursue. He noted the conversation gave instruction that it was to be acted upon directly and updated as soon as possible. He confirmed that he would attend the briefing the following day and expected Des to be in a position to speak about progress.

She had barely been at HQ for much over an hour and yet she felt knackered as she left the office and strode back across the forecourt area back to the car park; throwing her bag onto the front passenger seat she got in and just exhaled loudly to release the tension she felt. Her mobile automatically connected to the car's blue tooth device and she called Des Mason's personal mobile.

"Des, can you talk?"

Again the question that only cops it seemed asked when they made calls to friends or colleagues, are you free to talk could equally mean are you driving or more usually is there anyone listening that shouldn't be or will it put you at risk if I continue talking?

"Stand by."

Des got up from his seat and walked out into the corridor before continuing;

"Go ahead now."

"Two things; will Gemma be free this afternoon to see me for that statement and what has Neil said?"

"In answer to the first, I can call her, but yes I think she should be ok; in answer to the second, nothing; and we weren't going to ask him. He

238

knows where you are though, obviously so will no doubt be saying something to you or the Super."

"Well that's one reason to stay away then, will you ring Gemma and get back to me, I can drive straight there from here, be there in about an hour or so if that's ok?"

"Will do." He paused, "Are you ok?"

"I'm fine, but thanks for asking. The boss wants an update at the briefing tomorrow though on Scouse Vixen so get to it Des, get me something for him, anything."

"I'll do my best."

The call ended with their personal friendship and working relationship seemingly still intact, each with an opportunity to help the other out of a difficult situation.

Sue Collins started her BMW, put on her seatbelt and set off back out of Newby Wiske, the drive would do her some good she hoped.

TWENTY FOUR

The Pilgrim, at the top of his as 'recommended by Dan' list was on a street of the same name and certainly from the outside looked just as a proper pub should. The walk from The Feathers, although it had only taken him a few minutes, had increased Mike's appetite and he hoped that the reviews he had found during his Google search were well founded. Walking in through the green wooden doors he saw what he considered to be a real pub, surprisingly old fashioned in the sense that it quite obviously didn't rely on an overzealous use of music but yet had an obvious atmosphere, allowing people to talk; laughter emanated from a group of six or seven young people in a huddle around a table under the window, other smaller groups were already gathering, some eating meals, others seemingly happy with crisps or pork scratchings eaten from a bag to accompany their pints, as that's what just about everyone was drinking.

Mike got a drink from the bar and picked up a menu before taking a seat near to the big screen television which didn't have any sound on but was showing a re-run of the weekends premier league match between Everton and Norwich City at Carrow Road. Mike had seen the game previously but wasn't really interested in watching anyway. With what he thought to be a degree of irony he ordered Fish, chips and mushy peas, noting that the blurb in the menu placed emphasis on the fish being prime Whitby Cod. He then returned to his seat and sat watching as other customers came in and the place started to fill up; he took the photographs of Jane from his pocket and placed them on the table in front of him, in stark contrast to the pictures on the walls, which were mainly black and white photographs of The Beatles in their early days, Jane was smiling under her bright purple hair, matching lipstick and beautiful white teeth. Did Jane ever use this place he wondered, would she be here tonight, would anyone else recognise her otherwise? All questions that ran through his mind as he waited for his food to be brought to him. Norwich City scored through a Coleman shot from just inside the penalty area and this brought a mixture of groans and delight but mostly apathy from the student crowd whose allegiances must lay elsewhere; then his dinner arrived, a fish that almost hung over the ends of the plate at each end, a very portion of home cooked chips and mushy peas on the side, two slices of bread and butter completed the meal and Mike thanked the waiter, before pointing to the photographs on the table;

"Hi I don't know if you've worked here for long but have you seen this girl recently, does she come in here?"

240

It was obvious that the waiter didn't have too much time but in fairness to Mike he stopped, picked up each photo and appeared to study them before saying;

"Can't say I recognise her, broken your heart has she?"

"Something like that."

"I've only been here a couple of months but you do get to know the regulars, but it's a busy place."

"Thanks anyway."

The size of Mike's task became apparent, had he really thought that he could just turn up in a place the size of Liverpool and hope to find one person who may not even want him to find her?

He left the photos on the table and ate his meal, wiping the plate with his bread to finish off the peas; he then polished off his drink and sat pondering for a minute or two. The pub was over half full now at least and the noise was beginning to rise but it seemed that everyone was in good spirits. Standing up he picked up the photos and walked to the nearest table, where he interrupted the frivolous chat between a crowd of mainly female drinkers;

"Sorry to interrupt you-" he started, "but I wonder if any of you know this girl?"

The chat stalled as the individuals in the group all looked towards Mike,

"Are you a cop or some'rt?" one asked,

"Who's asking?" Another asked.

"I'm sorry," Mike continued, "I'm concerned that I can't find her, we, erm, we were close once."

"She booted you out has she?" A third voice asked

"No, it's not like that, I just wondered if anyone knew her or if they had seen her in here?"

A hand reached through from near the back of the group; "Let's have a proper look then."

Mike handed one photo to the group, via the hand that he now saw belonged to a young fair haired woman in a rather large and loose woollen sweater and jeans; she held on to the picture for a while and didn't initially speak, leaving Mike to wonder if he had found someone who knew Jane at the first attempt?

After a couple of minutes however the photograph was returned to Mike without anyone claiming to know Jane, Baggy Sweater took the time to say;

"I thought it might be someone I knew but it ain't, sorry."

"Her name is Jane if that helps?" Mike looked along at the faces but most were turning away now back to their earlier conversations. Undeterred he moved on to the next table and repeated the process with similar results and after the fourth table he was approached by the door staff. Two equally large men in black T-shirts with the word STAFF written on the back and an SIA badge on their arms, each with a shaven head and numerous tattoos visible on their arms and necks stood close to him; Mike recognised them for what they were, after all they were only doing what he had been paid to do until only recently.

"We're getting complaints." The taller of the two men spoke first, "You're upsetting some of the customers." he continued.

Mike knew not to argue and he had no grudge with the men who were only doing the job they were paid to do.

"I'm sorry." he said, "I don't mean to cause any trouble or upset. Maybe you can help me?"

"What are you doing?" asked the second man, shorter in stature than the first but only marginally and still probably six foot tall.

"I'm trying to find this girl." Mike handed the photos to the second doorman whilst adding; "She's a student here." Looking at the men he quickly added, "I'm in your line of work myself but on the East Coast, Whitby, do you know it?"

"Whitby?" scoffed the first man, "Isn't it full of woolly backs, weirdoes and poets? It'll be quiet there in nit?"

"Compared to here, no doubt, but it has its moments." Mike could have added, for bravado that he had just spent some time on bail accused of manslaughter but thought better of it. "I just thought you might be able to help?"

"I don't recognise her but we get hundreds of students as well as our locals in here mate," he passed the photos on to his colleague; "You got a name for her?"

"Yes, Jane, that's all I know."

"Tell you what, leave me one of the photos and I'll ask around for you, as a fellow doorman. How long you here for?"

"I don't know, today, tomorrow, I can leave you my number if you like?" Mike introduced himself properly and exchanged mobile numbers with the two men who he now found out to be Dale and Chris. They in turn looked at his list of pubs and agreed it was a list of the most likely student haunts but that his task was equal to the proverbial needle in the haystack search. It was Chris who suggested that if Mike had a photo on his mobile that he could send it on to colleagues at the other pubs and ask the question rather than have Mike going through the same trouble in each place. It was certainly worth a try so he sent the image via MMS to Chris' phone and bought himself another drink, putting one behind the bar for each of his new friends at the same time.

He waited another half hour before making his excuses and leaving, shaking the hands of Dale and Chris as he did so and hoping that they would be in touch later if they got anything back from other doorman as the night progressed.

TWENTY FIVE

Russell Street comprised about 40 houses and flats, many given over to student lets and investment properties, Scholars House, set three quarters of the way along was amongst the smallest of the houses but benefited from still having two reception rooms when many had lost one to have it replaced as a ground floor bedroom with the hope of drawing a greater rental payment.

Laura Goodman had walked the relatively short distance from the university to the address having tried and failed to make contact with Jane Hammond via mobile; her very presence, in full uniform walking down this street caused some curtains to be twitched as both young and old watched to see where she was going. For her part, Laura was still disappointed to see so many ground floor windows open and laptops and tablets clearly visible from the street as she passed.

As she approached Scholars House she was pleased however to see that there were lights on, both upstairs and down, maybe she would solve the problem in one visit, maybe Jane Hammond would be at home and not even be aware of all the fuss she has caused? Knocking on the door, in Laura's experience many doorbells failed to work or needed batteries replacing, she took a step back and waited, looking in through the front window as best she could without it being obvious. There was no reply so she knocked again; this time very loudly as she heard music coming from somewhere inside, she again stood back but this time without any subtlety at all; in fact hoping to be seen. She looked through the window again and saw, quite surprisingly, a tidy room with two, two seater sofas arranged either side of a gas fire, a quite large plasma screen TV on a stand and an Xbox wired into it. A large beige squared rug covered the laminate flooring and all in all this looked like the home of sensible mature people, not wild students, but then wasn't that exactly what Jane Hammond had been described as being?

She was still looking through the window when the front door opened and a young female asked, "Hello, can I help you?"

"Yes I'm looking for Jane Hammond."

"She's not in." It was Phoebe at her worst; she wasn't curt by nature and couldn't tell lies very well as she had already demonstrated when scraping through conversations with Graham Hammond.

"And you are?"

"Phoebe, Phoebe James, I live here, well I do during term times anyway."

"Can we talk inside then Phoebe?"

Laura hadn't so much asked a question as made a statement of intent and she moved past Phoebe into the room she had just viewed. "Do you share with Jane Hammond?"

"Yes." Phoebe was very nervous and it was obvious to Laura that her visit wasn't a total surprise.

"And where is she at the moment?"

"Has she done something wrong?"

"Phoebe, I'm here to check that Jane is ok, that she is fit and well and to ask her to contact her parents who are worried sick that she hasn't been in touch." She was going to continue by asking Phoebe to tell her where Jane was but she saw the reaction on Phoebe's face and knew that wouldn't be necessary, the colour could be seen draining away from her face and her hands clasped together;

"I thought she would have rung them by now."

"Maybe we should sit down and talk this through."

Laura Goodman helped Phoebe into one of the sofas and took a seat next to her to offer support; she could see that the young woman was in shock.

"Phoebe, I have a statement from Jane's father saying he hasn't seen her since the holiday started, that he hasn't heard from her in days and that she promised to call him. Do you know where she may be?"

Phoebe's eyes filled with tears and she began to whimper;

"I'm sorry, I'm so sorry. She asked me not to say anything to Mr Hammond."

"Go on."

Phoebe related the lifestyle that Jane now lived at university and how she had gone to Whitby for the Goth weekend, how she had met someone there and that she had not seen her since.

"Has she been in touch recently?"

"Her last text to me was ages ago, let me get my phone and I'll show, I've kept them all-" she tailed off as she got up from the sofa and made her way to a nearby table on which her Samsung mobile sat. Picking it up her fingers and thumbs pressed and scrolled in unison and in no time she had the most recent message from Jane on her screen;

"Hi Babes, its bn gr8 @WGW but OMW BCNU soon. LU XX"

Phoebe handed the phone across and sat down again, tears filling here eyes but not yet falling down her cheeks, as they were surely set to do.

Laura, despite her not being in the same age group as Phoebe had had to come to terms with modern text speak in order to carry out her role as well as she did, most of the students that contacted her at the university would use the abbreviations she saw on the phone but Phoebe spoke anyway just to clarify;

245

"WGW is Whitby Goth Weekend; Jane was really into the Goth scene."
"Was?" Laura was really surprised to hear that word; of course there was always an outside possibility that she was right but Laura didn't believe she had suggested anything that bad, not yet anyway?
"I'm sorry, I didn't mean, I mean; where is she?"
"I rather hoped you might be able to tell me Phoebe, can you show me her room please?"
"Yes; it's upstairs."
She stood up, wiping her eyes with the end of her sleeve in the absence of a tissue, and walked through to the small entrance hall and then up the stairs. At the top of the stairs was a small landing with three white painted doors, two open and one shut. Laura could see that one was the bathroom and she looked past Phoebe into that room to see a very clean and well presented space with the usual three piece bathroom suite with a shower over the bath and a small mirror fronted cupboard over the wash basin; apart from two towels thrown over the radiator nothing looked out of place. Casting her eyes around to the second open door she saw books open on the bed, a light was on and music was playing, though she didn't recognise it or like it.
"That's my room; you can go in if you like? That's Jane's room there, I always keep the door closed, and then if anyone's here they don't go in; you know if they're looking for the loo or anything?"
Laura didn't take her up on the offer to look in her room, anyone that so easily offered you the opportunity to look didn't have anything to hide in her experience; she did however open the door to Jane's room, pushing it back and standing to look before entering. She was a little surprised but not shocked, she had half expected to find everything kept immaculately after reading Ian Hardy's comments but then Phoebe had painted a different picture of Jane; what she found lay between the two. The bed was made, the room was generally in good order but there were clothes laid on the bed and the wardrobe doors were open showing the usual array of clothing you would expect from a university student, if a little tidier. There was no sign of any phone, laptop or iPad but then she would have taken them with her, wouldn't she?
Laura spent a few minutes looking around the room without moving any items that she may decide to look at again later if the need arose for forensics; you never get a second chance to preserve evidence, she thought, already thinking that something was wrong, but what?
"Phoebe, has anyone at all been in here since Jane left?"
"No, at least I don't think so. No not that I know of anyway." she was nervous now and it showed in her answer, was she a suspect and for what, where was Jane, what had happened?

"Laura ushered Phoebe out of the room and closed the door behind her; "Can I ask you to keep the door closed please, at least until I let you know different."

"Sure, but why, what's wrong?"

"I don't know, but if Jane hasn't contacted her parents and you haven't seen her since she sent this text, then I'd like to know where she is now?" Laura looked at the message again and copied it into her note book, noting the time and date it was sent; "Wednesday 2nd November, I know this may sound stupid but when does The Goth Weekend actually finish?"

"It finishes on Monday but some stay until Tuesday; I expected Jane back that day."

"We need to talk."

Laura explained to Phoebe again about Graham Hammond receiving a text the same day as she had and that she was expected to call later that day; she would now need to take a full statement and submit a report from Phoebe as well.

In return Phoebe opened up and explained that Graham Hammond knew little of his daughter's lifestyle now she was a student that she had rebelled against the strict upbringing and had become not only somewhat rebellious but also quite promiscuous.

"That's why she wouldn't tell her parents where she was going; they would have done all they could to stop her."

"So, to clarify, Mr and Mrs Hammond didn't even know she had gone to this weekend event?"

"No way; they thought she was with me all the time."

"And where do you think she might be now?"

"I don't know, really I don't. When I got that text message I thought she was coming back here, to tell me all about it."

Laura made copious notes in her book before commencing a detailed statement, in truth one she hadn't expected to have to take but one which she now knew would have to be thorough and detailed.

TWENTY SIX

Sue Collins took a slightly different route back from Headquarters, travelling up towards Northallerton and across to the A19 before coming off at The Cleveland Tontine and picking up the A172 to Stokesley where she parked up for a short while in order to pick up a sandwich. She had contacted Gemma Mason and agreed to meet up with her but as Gemma wasn't immediately available Sue had a little time on her hands and didn't want to go back to the office where she would no doubt get embroiled in all sorts and end up being late. Stokesley Police Station couldn't be more central to the town itself and Sue had parked in one of the spaces reserved for Police vehicles only directly outside. A brisk walk across the road to the bakers and back again she went to the rear of the building and keyed in the numbered code for the door and walked in to an almost eerie quiet. She knew that this was one of the smaller, quiet stations around the force effectively seen as a satellite station from Northallerton, nearby. She walked through to the appositely named report writing room, where if anyone was present she would expect them to be. Sure enough, there was Liz Coghlan, a uniformed PC known to Sue and who was said by many not to have done a days' work in the last ten years, claiming one disability after the other and flitting between sick leave, recuperation and restricted duties seamlessly and causing much frustration to many supervising officers who had tried to bring her to book; most chose just to accept the situation as being too difficult to deal with and thus treated her as an administrator, tasking her with menial jobs and preparation of reports for others whose time was better spent elsewhere.

"Hi Liz, just to let you know I'm here; I'm going to use the Sergeants office to update some work on the box; if anyone rings I'm not here, understood?"

"Understood; fancy a cuppa?"

"Coffee please, black, no sugar."

"Coming right up."

Sue carried on to the Sergeants office, such as it was, but it did have a desk, phone and computer or box as everyone in North Yorkshire referred to it. Making herself as comfortable as she could in the old chair she unwrapped her sandwich, turned off her mobile, logged onto her computer account and set to work. Liz was as good as her word and brought in a coffee, placing it on the desk and leaving her to her work; Sue thanked her without looking up from the screen.

She had been over half an hour answering emails, updating incidents and checking crime reports before she knew she must set off again, what a change; in that half hour she had probably managed as much work as she would normally get through in three times that amount of time in her own office where she would be constantly interrupted by telephone calls and visitors of one sort or another at her office door.

Thanking Liz for the coffee again as she left she set off again along the A172 and onto the A171 at Guisborough before cutting across down Grinkle Lane on the Cleveland border to the small and oft photographed, coastal village of Staithes. Turning left off onto Staithes Lane she passed the old Police Station on the corner, now a detached house in its own right and drove the short distance to a large Victorian terraced house on the right. Thankful to find a parking space nearby, but knowing that it was highly unlikely that any Traffic Warden would attend anyway she pulled up near to Des Mason's very des res.

Shutting the black wrought iron gate behind her and walking up the neatly laid footpath to the door she saw Gemma in the living room window, obviously waiting for her. Gemma got to the door before Sue and opened it up to let her straight in;

"Hi Gemma, thanks for seeing me, are you ok?"

"Yeah fine, a bit embarrassed really but-"

"Don't be embarrassed Gemma, we all have issues and your dad tells me you're getting on ok now anyway?"

"Yeah, s'pose so." dressed in tight fitting jeans and a loose tee shirt Gemma led the way barefoot through to the well presented sitting room and gestured to one of the two matching leather sofas opposite the original cast fire place. Sue noticed the attention to detail given to decorating the room, period features restored and replica pieces added to complement them; very well done, especially on a PC's salary she thought.

"What do you wanna know then, Dad says it's some'rt about my gaming?"

Sue liked the direct approach Gemma invited; it saved a lot of time beating about the bush,

"Yeah, he tells me that you were well into a game and made friends with some girls from Liverpool?"

"Well' as he tells me now, they were virtual friends and could have been from anywhere, but they did say they were from Liverpool."

Sue just nodded as a prompt for Gemma to keep talking;

"Well, you do get to know people you know; it's not all about grooming."

"I know Gemma, I'm not here to take sides or give you any lectures, I promise. All I want to do is hear anything that may help me in this case. Has your dad told you much about it?"

"Not much, he says you've asked him to look into some social network stuff and he just asked me about some games and the links from those; he's better than most dads at his age but he's still a dinosaur really."

Sue laughed as Des was considered to be a bit of a whiz kid in the office so to hear of him referred to in such derogatory terms was something of a reality check.

"Well, when I was erm; well when I had my problems shall we say, I chatted to two girls, one called herself Scouse Vixen and the other was just Pheebs so presumably she's called Phoebe and doesn't have too much imagination? They were both right into chatting right up to Goth week and then nothing after that, it was as if they just decided bollocks to it all and yet they were keen right up to then to put everything online."

"Is that Whitby Goth Week?"

"Yeah, but not this year, it was the October one, you know they have two every year now?"

"Yes I know, so was that October 2012 or 2011?"

"2011"

"Did you have any other contact with these girls then, on facebook or twitter or any other site I might not know about, me being another dinosaur?"

"No." Gemma was smiling now, reacting well to Sue Collins' easy going approach, "they're for losers; oh sorry, I didn't mean-"

"It's ok; I don't use it much anyway."

Gemma went on to explain how the game worked, how you could make contact with other players and effectively build up a relationship built on a shared interest in the tactics, cheats, strategy and so on related to it and then she spoke about how it drew her in to spending everything she had to remain online and involved; how she spent almost every waking hour to the detriment of her studies and her health.

"I became a right bitch." she ended

"Gemma there are pitfalls in lots of things and we sometimes fall into them, think of how many people get addicted to gambling, smoking, alcohol, etcetera. Nobody sets out with a view to getting addicted but it does happen, it's how you cope with it now that matters and your dad says you're a different person now." Sue stopped short of disagreeing with her comment as from what Des had said she had indeed become a bitch.

"I still get scared though, you know of going back to it."

"Well stick at it and don't forget you have a great family who can help you. Now shall we get some of this down on paper?"

"I can't believe you people still use paper," Gemma quipped, "we live in an age of technology and you still write statements long hand."

250

"We do, sorry, so let's get started or we'll be here all night"

TWENTY SEVEN

It was nearing 10.30pm when Mike arrived at the last pub on his list, Lago; he had become accustomed to having door staff at the entrance now, something that in Whitby only happened at certain venues and not always every night; he introduced himself to the male and female, black clad staff as he reached the door and asked if they had received a text from Dale and Chris; they had, as had every other doorman he had spoken to that night; they had been as good as their word. The bad news was, that like every other person he had asked, they couldn't help him but didn't mind him asking questions inside as long as he didn't make a nuisance of himself.

Sadly as he entered he felt very much out of place, the place seemed to be full of very young people and the music was loud electric and not at all what he would choose, but then it might just be what Jane would opt for. He bought himself a drink and wandered around the bar looking for Jane initially and then repeating the process of showing her photograph to those customers who appeared responsive to him; although none were dressed in Gothic attire he did think that some were dressed in clothing that Jane might like to wear, slightly provocative and with piercings and tattoos there was a tendency towards an anarchic atmosphere without the violence.

Despite his initial misgivings he did speak to many but was not surprised at the continual negative response, after all he had come up here on a whim and he didn't even know which pubs Jane used let alone if she used any so regularly as to be recognised by other transient customers. He finished his drink and left Lago to walk back to his hotel with an air of defeatism and a dawning realisation that he would have to accept that she had chosen to move on without him; without giving him the opportunity to explain himself he thought with a ting of bitterness.

Back at The Feathers he bought himself another pint as he couldn't bear returning to his room just yet; knowing that he would just sit and brood, at least down here he had some company, if it was only other customers, residents and staff.

He watched the television again, Sky sports news was playing, repeating over again everything it had shown at least twice that night already, with each new pundit trying to put a different spin on the same story; but he wasn't listening really it was just there as a background noise. He had been sat for about fifteen minutes when his phone sounded and he picked it up to see a message from Chris from The Pilgrim; his heart lifted slightly with the hope of something positive as he selected the message icon and opened the text.

"Sorry mate, nothing 2nite will try thro week for ya. Good Luck, Cheers, Chris"

It was no more than he could realistically have hoped for but seeing it in black and white made it certain and took away that last element of hope that he had held on to. He finished his drink and promptly bought another with a whisky chaser. He drank those rather more quickly and headed off up the three flights of stairs to his room beginning to feel the effects of his night's intake. He took off his boots and threw them into a corner before lying on top of the duvet and channel hopping through the TV stations available. Settling on another showing of the film Transporter 2, a film which he had seen at least twice before he half heartedly watched as Jason Statham drove his customised Audi at crazy speeds across Europe, stopping only long enough to fight against all the odds using martial arts skills that left him without so much as a scratch in defeating endless armed opponents. Still, you didn't need to be alert to keep up with the plot and Mike just let it play as he pondered whether to stay any longer?

In reality it was a no brainer, why would he stay in Liverpool, he had no plan B and other than trawling around further pubs more hope than expectation, no it was time to go home.

"Did you enjoy your stay Mr Davies?" the polite and efficient receptionist, Tara, asked

"Fine, thanks." Mike was nursing a little bit of a hangover that three cups of strong coffee and a full English breakfast had done nothing to shift and as such was not as communicative as he would normally be, coupled with the feeling of loss he had he was not going to be good company for anyone today but there was no need to be rude to anyone he thought.

"If you could just enter your PIN number and press enter please." Tara continued without looking up from her computer screen.

Mike did as he was asked and watched the machine as it told him the transaction had been completed and he could remove his card. He picked up his bag and made a point of thanking Tara as he left onto Hunter Street to begin the short walk back to his car and then the much longer drive back to Wales.

He was not sure of the road layout and his SATNAV seemed to cause him more frustration than it did answers and he was becoming fractious as the morning went on, stop start driving in the morning queues as he headed for the Mersey tunnel he thought he would be pleased to see the back of Liverpool, he was still of this opinion and not concentrating on the road when he felt a sudden thud and his car came to an abrupt stop;

"Fuck!"

He had run into the back of the car in front of him and he was now in a line of traffic with people behind him waving their arms in frustration and gesticulating towards him in none too pleasant terms. By the time he opened his car door the woman driver of the car in front, a Red Ford Fiesta which now sported a damaged bumper and a smashed light cluster, had made her way to the back of the car and was stood surveying the damage and shaking her head in obvious dismay.

"You idiot." she screamed in the general direction of Mike

"I'm sorry." he replied as he struggled out of the car into the traffic in the opposite direction, "I obviously didn't fucking mean it." Looking at his own car he saw a headlight had broken and paintwork cracked above the number plate, not a lot of damage in truth but sufficient to add to his feelings of woe.

"I've got to get to work." she pointed in the general direction of the ferry terminal

"I'm not stopping you missus." Mike spat back

"You're gonna have to pay for this." she pointed to the rear of her car

"Look, I'll give you my details, it's an insurance job." he made a move to open his car door for a pen and paper just as those other drivers behind him started to sound their horns and start waving their arms around, gesturing for them to get out of the way and which seemed to fire the female driver up again.

"Where you going?" she hadn't read his actions correctly and thought he was just getting in the car again

"Don't get on your high horse, I'm not running off. I'm tryin' to get a fucking pen."

It wasn't long before the commotion had come to the attention of others and someone must have called the police as a marked car, blue lights flashing, filtered between the lanes and parked up just beyond the two damaged vehicles. The officers quickly established that no-one was injured and got the cars moved to the side of the road sufficient to allow the other traffic to flow freely again, taking much of the tension out of what was only a minor bump anyway.

That part of the job done the younger of the two cops took out a notebook from her pocket and spoke to Mike;

"Are you the driver of this car?" she pointed to his damaged Fiat

"Yes, I was just trying to write my name and address down for that woman," he pointed to the still angry female, "but she's just gone off on one."

"Excuse me sir, but have you been drinking?" The young cop, still under supervision as a student officer was very much polite and correct but had a hint of nerves in her voice as she thought she had picked the faint smell of stale alcohol.

"Don't be daft; I'm on my way home." Mike hadn't give a thought to what he had drunk last night, nor to the fact that he may still be over the limit this morning.

Looking across to her colleague, the young officer indicated for a breathalyser kit to be brought over. "I'm going to have to ask you to provide a specimen of breath for a roadside breath test."

"For fucks sake, give me a break." Mike interrupted

"I must warn you that failure to provide a specimen of breath for this test will leave you liable to arrest, do you understand?" The young officer continued robotically, ignoring his comment.

"Yeah, Yeah. Just fucking finish me off this will" Mike lost all his anger at the accident as he realised the position he may have put himself in. He could only hope now, as the other officer approached with a device in his hand that he had sobered up enough.

TWENTY EIGHT

"I'm really concerned Sarge; no-one's heard from her or seen her for over a week now." Laura was updating her immediate supervisor before she made a report back to Inspector Cheryl Burton; "The last we know is that she sent a text message on Wednesday 2nd November promising to contact her mate and her parents."

"And this friend, what's she called?" Sergeant Kevin Dixon said flicking through the paperwork, "Phoebe, she lied to the Misper's parents about where she had gone?"

"Yeah, she accepts it was stupid and I don't think she's malicious, just trying to do a friend a favour."

"Have we got details of the mobile phone?"

"Yeah, it's all in there but is it our job or West Yorkshire's?"

"I could argue it either way Laura, at the moment it's theirs as she's been reported as missing from Leeds, but I personally think we should be doing some digging as well in case things go tits up."

"Shall I see what the boss wants to do; I think she's made some sort of promise to West Yorkshire."

"Let me just add my comments before she sees it otherwise it'll not be allowed on the computer and one of us, me, will get it in the ear."

Ten minutes of writing time later Kevin Dixons comments had been added and the report was signed off before Laura took it up to Cheryl Burton's office.

"I agree with Kevin Laura, don't put it at the top of your list just yet but make some enquiries where you can. Send all the originals over to Leeds but keep a copy of everything here in case we need it later and keep me in the loop please. I'll contact Oscar Helliwell and tell him what we think and we'll take it from there. Good work."

"Thanks boss, I'll get it done today."

Laura took the file back and returned to the main office to top and tail everything ready to forward it on to her West Yorkshire colleagues whilst for her part Cheryl Burton rang Oscar Helliwell with the details fresh in her mind.

Having listened again to what she thought was the robotically inane greeting given by her counterpart, Cheryl, knowing why he did it still commented, "Hi Oscar, it's Cheryl Burton, don't you ever get fed up of repeating that line over and over again?"

With a knowing smile but a competing sense of loyalty he replied, "You know I can't comment on that, if I can't set an example then how can I get on to the troops about using it?"

She recognised his view point and sympathised with it whilst thinking about how long it would be before the phrase became a parody of its own politeness, like MacDonald's Have a nice day had become;
"Oh I know, sorry. Anyway I've got an update of sorts for you."
"That's great, go ahead."
"You might not think it's great when I tell you. You've spoken to Laura I believe, PC Goodman that is; well she's put a report together which will be sent over to you today, email with hard copies in the post. She has some genuine concerns that our Jane Hammond is a real Misper."
Cheryl went on to give the reasons behind her shared viewpoint and indicated that her thoughts would be to raise the priority grading in West Yorkshire and that she would keep the incident log open in Merseyside should a follow up be required.
"I agree, but without wishing to question PC Goodman's judgement can I just confirm what you are telling me about Jane? You want me to believe that she has a dual life; a twee little Daddy's girl, butter wouldn't melt home bird and a rampant, Goth loving sex chick?"
"That's about the long and short of it Oscar, at least from what we know so far."
"Jeez, this going to be some update for the father to take in."
"It's not one I envy you."
Cheryl Burton knew the anguish this would unleash, the challenges that lay ahead for both the parents and the investigation, as it had now become. Somebody's world was about to implode and Oscar Helliwell would feel the full force of the resultant fall out.

TWENTY NINE

Neil Maughan and Sue Collins had to meet at some time and it was an early 8.00am on the morning of Wednesday 27th March; both had been spoken to by Simon Pithers separately and he now wanted to see them together. Neil Maughan had come off by far the worst so far, his wife Helen had moved out to stay with her mother, taking their children with them; it was the Easter school holidays so she had taken the opportunity to get out of the marital home and down to Cambridge where she would find comfort and support whilst she decided where to go, what to do. Neil himself had been told clearly that he had been stupid and that he had left his integrity in question. Both he and Sue Collins now wondered what this morning held in store. They sat in wait, avoiding eye contact like two school children waiting for the headmaster to walk into the room; they didn't have to wait long before the massive frame of their superior officer walked in, shutting the door firmly behind him and taking his seat behind the desk. The two had barely had a chance to stand up before he told them to sit down.

"I will keep this brief, so listen carefully. You have both been lucky to escape formal disciplinary proceedings, not so much for what you both chose to do, after all I am led to believe that you are both adults though at times I could question that; no, what concerns me most is that you did not take the chance to come clean with me when I asked you directly about the rumours. If I cannot trust my staff then they are of no value to me and they bring the credibility of everybody into question."

He took a second to look directly at each officer in front of him and gauge their individual reactions; for their part each had the humility to look back at him and accept what he was saying, they both knew however that this was not the time to speak whether to offer further explanation or just to say sorry.

"It is only your previous good work and reputations that has allowed me to make this decision and I have had to explain to my bosses why I have done so. You will both be clever enough then to understand that if I risk my own reputation to protect yours then I will not tolerate any future lapse. When we leave this room we have a briefing to lead and I will expect you to deliver and to deliver in spades; this investigation needs a kick up the arse and you two are going to provide it or I will and you don't want that to happen today I can assure you."

He paused again to let his words settle on their recipients minds and to take a drink from a glass of water on his desk.

"Now I hope I have made myself abundantly clear."

"Yes sir." spoken in unison by the two.

"Right, then let's hear no more of it, there will soon be other things to fill the minds of the gossips, there always is. Sue, can you leave Neil and I for a few minutes and we'll see you in the briefing shortly."

She needed no second bidding, she was happy to take any opportunity to get out of the room in one piece. Closing the door behind her as she left she gave a huge sigh as she walked away from the office towards her own.

"Neil, I want you to head up this briefing as I said, then I want you to update your own actions on the box and take some time off. It's Easter weekend coming up, I am working as duty cover so we shan't need you on that score and I hear that Helen is at her mums?"

"Yes, word soon gets round doesn't it?"

"Well get down there then and get things sorted one way or the other. I don't want to see you again before Tuesday at least. You're due some leave anyway so it's not up for debate. You've been bloody silly and you know it, don't risk losing that family of yours. Now go and get ready for the briefing."

Neil Maughan didn't reply, he couldn't really argue and he would welcome the time to try to patch things up at home even if he was unsure that Helen would be receptive, but first he had a briefing to give.

"Good morning everyone, Wednesday 27th March 2013, 9.00am and the seventy seventh day briefing of Operation Caedmon. You have all had a chance to read up on the latest intelligence and this morning DS Collins will update you with a new lead that has potential to take us forward but first I want to thank you all for your efforts so far and to ask you to give me your best as we move into the next stage of this investigation. I am still convinced that the identity of the victim will lead us to the identity of the killer and with that in mind I will hand you over to DS Collins."

"Thanks boss, good morning everyone." She paused whilst the gathered troops each mumbled a reply of sorts, some may have mumbled a comment about their respective Inspector and Sergeant but would not dare to be heard by either let alone Simon Pithers. "Let me first echo what Neil has just said and thank you all for your dedication so far but, as always, just being dedicated doesn't always bring results so we need to carry on redouble our efforts and keep our noses to the grindstone. Some of you may know that I have recently met with Des Mason's daughter, Gemma; Gemma has been an avid gamer and may just have given us an alternative line of enquiry. At the end of October or early November 2011 Gemma was involved in a form of social networking with two girls from the Liverpool area before, without any warning they just stopped using the site they were on. Neither has returned and neither has responded to her messages, now this may not be anything to do with our case but as yet we have had nothing from our other lines of enquiry and the timing suits our autopsy timeframe."

She paused again to look around the room at her colleagues and to gauge their reactions to what was when all was said and done nothing more than another hopeful punt.

"Des, I want you to continue with the social networking enquiries as before but Geoff I want you to look into the gaming side of it and these players in particular. Anything at all I want on the board and in the system pronto. I don't need to tell you I'm sure that I want Merseyside contacted as a first port of call after the techies have looked at the username info and ISP addresses."

"I'm on it Sarge." whether it was the presence of Simon Pithers or just a willingness to get on, his response was immediate and pleasing for Sue Collins to see.

"Thanks Geoff, the rest of you make sure you pick up your tasks before you leave and let's make it happen." She stood down and Neil Maughan took her place to wrap up the briefing;

"You will all have seen that Superintendent Pithers is here this morning and he will be on call over the weekend as I am away until Tuesday, I don't need to remind you that he expects total commitment from us all and I am sure you won't disappoint. Thank you ladies and gents, get to work."

Those present left their seats and dispersed from the office, some to ask why Neil had suddenly taken some leave, others to answer that same question with either what they knew or what they assumed they knew. For Sue Collins she was pleased that she had got through this far into the day without having to discuss things again with Neil and wasn't disappointed that she would now have the weekend free of that same challenge.

THIRTY

Mike Davies never thought he would see the inside of a Police custody suite again, let alone see one so soon, but here he was going through the booking in process again, name, date of birth, place of birth, home address and empty your pockets please. The roadside breath test had shown a figure of 45 on the small screen and the student officer, PC Clare Roberts, had explained to him that that exceeded the permissible level and she was therefore arresting him. He had been compliant and was placed in the back seat of the car rather than a van being called but his already low mood sank even further as he stood before the custody sergeant answering the basic questions that would no doubt show him to have been arrested previously.

After completing the initial procedures Mike was shown through, not to a cell this time but to a smaller room adjacent to the custody reception, where another officer asked him to take a seat in front of a large grey metal covered machine, an evidential breath testing device, it was explained. The following procedure, all recorded by the latest officer in a paper booklet and containing printed records similar in appearance to a till receipt, took another fifteen minutes or so and had Mike wondering just what was happening?

"So what does that mean then?"

"I'll explain everything in just a moment Mr Davies." The officer, a well presented man, clean shaven, short hair combed neatly across from the left, in a short sleeved white shirt, black trousers and highly polished boots, picked up the booklet from the desk and showed it first to the arresting officer; turning away from Mike Davies and just out of earshot he spoke to her.

"Can you see the figure here?" pointing to the till receipt he had stapled into the booklet, "This means that he's over the limit, but because he's only just over the limit we have to give him another chance to have a blood or urine sample tested."

"He'd be a fool not to, wouldn't he?" it seemed an obvious choice to her, but one that not everyone chose to take.

"He's a bloody fool drink driving in the first place though."

Turning back to Mike the officer looked him in the eye,

"The alcohol limit is 35 microgrammes per 100 millilitres of breath," he paused to let the details sink in before carrying on, "your reading is 42."

"Shit. That's all I fucking needed."

"Mr Davies, because your reading falls within the range of 41 to 45 I have to give you the opportunity to have a further test." The officer went on to read directly from the booklet in his hand explaining the process and that he would choose the blood option unless there was a reason that couldn't be so.

Mike looked for guidance from the officer, the upset clear in his face, "What would you do?"

The officer, recognising Mike's distress, but having seen it all before responded;

"I can't advise you mate, but what have you to lose. If you don't opt for the blood test you'll be charged now and back at court in a few days time."

"How long does it take?"

"Not long, the docs on call and as soon as he's here we'll get on with it."

"And if I don't I'll be banned any way."

"Yep, at least a year, a fine and a load of grief if you need a car for work. You will probably still get all that if the bloods come back positive though"

"Let's go for it then."

The officer updated his booklet recording Mikes decision to opt for blood analysis before the necessary process was set in motion. Almost another hour had passed before Mike left the Police Station, having had two samples of blood taken by the on call doctor, carrying yet another bail sheet telling him to come back in three weeks time, his own blood sample and a small booklet advising him of what he could do to have it tested himself; he wouldn't bother. In the meantime his car had been towed away to clear the road and he had been given details of where it was being kept; more delays, in fact it was well into the afternoon before he was able to continue his journey back to Wales, a journey he hoped that would have been all but over by this time and after all that he was still no wiser as to where Jane was or if she even knew or cared that he was looking.

THIRTY ONE

It never seems to be that Police attend your home to deliver good news and when Penny Hammond answered the door to Oscar Helliwell and Ian Hardy she immediately thought the worst;

"Oh my lord, is it Jane, have you found her? Is she erm, is she-"

"Can we come in Mrs Hammond?" Oscar Helliwell wouldn't normally have become involved in this part of the job but he felt somehow that he owed it to the Hammonds, in some sort of recompense for the poor handling of the initial report.

"Yes, sorry, do." she stood back allowed the officers to pass her into the hallway and on towards the well fitted country house style kitchen. "Have you found her?"

"No Mrs Hammond we haven't but we do want to talk to you about Jane, is your husband at home?"

"Yes, he's not been home long, he's just getting changed. I'll call him down." she left the two policemen stood in the kitchen, forgetting even to offer them seats such was her consternation.

"I hate this part of the job boss; they're going to fall apart when we tell them."

"Sshhhh, Ian, I'll give the message, but I don't want them to overhear us chatting."

Less than a minute later Graham Hammond led his wife back into the kitchen;

"Inspector Helliwell, Constable Hardy, please take a seat." he gestured with his free arm to the table and chairs in the centre of the room, keeping hold of his wife's arm with the other.

"Thank you." Oscar Helliwell replied, "We do have an update, of sorts but I can't tell you that we are any nearer to knowing the whereabouts of your daughter."

"Oh, what do you mean?" there was a quite obvious look of uncertainty on his face as he asked the question.

"Maybe you should sit down too Mr Hammond, Mrs Hammond." Oscar waited for them to take a seat before he continued, "I have spoken to my colleagues in Liverpool and they have now made some further enquiries on our behalf; visited the house where your daughter stays and spoken to her friends. It appears that Jane has not been home, that is at her digs for a few days now and she has not made contact with even her closest friend."

"That'll be Phoebe." Penny Hammond interrupted,

"Yes, that's right Mrs Hammond. A Police Officer has spoken to Phoebe however and I am afraid I have some rather awkward things to tell you

263

and some equally difficult questions to ask you as a result of that conversation."

"I'm intrigued Inspector." Graham Hammond wasn't really sure how to respond to the comments, but he remained sat down, holding onto the hand of his wife, who in turn was now physically shaking.

"Your daughter, Jane, has developed as a person whilst she has been at university and I am not sure that you would approve of everything she has become or of what she has developed into."

"I beg your pardon Inspector." Graham Hammonds uncertainty exploded into a confrontational stance, protective of his daughter and his family, without yet even knowing what he was about to be told.

"Mr Hammond, I promised you that I would update you with any news that I received; I am trying to do just that, if I could please just ask you to bear with me for a short while?"

"Yes, sorry, it's just that-"

"I understand; it is never easy in these circumstances. The information I have is that your daughter has developed an interest in the Gothic ways of life whilst she has been at Liverpool and has taken to wearing that particular style of clothing and following certain music types linked to that way of life." Oscar Helliwell wanted to ease into the promiscuity by giving what he hoped would be easier to digest news first; "she, it would appear, has maybe kept this from you for fear of causing you any upset."

"Why would she think that? What are you suggesting?"

"I'm not suggesting anything Mr Hammond; I am just trying my best to explain what I know and what I have been told." In order to establish some degree of control he decided to ask a question at this stage, "Did you know that Jane now has a tattoo?"

"Certainly not, and I do not for one minute think we are talking about the same person here."

"Mr Hammond, it is exactly for that reason that I asked the question. Officers in Liverpool have spoken to Phoebe James, whom you have already agreed is possibly Jane's closest friend and they tell me that Jane has indeed got a tattoo and has recently spent time in Whitby, North Yorkshire attending a Goth festival. It disappoints me to say that Miss James lied to you about Jane staying with her but she had been asked to do so by your daughter who feared you may not approve of her going." Thinking he had said enough for the time being he stopped and looked across at the disbelieving parents, who in turn appeared to be dumbstruck with shock.

"I'm really sorry to have to be the bearer of this news but the positive side of things is that we now know that she spent time in Whitby and sent texts to both you and to Phoebe James whilst returning from there.

264

That itself is a step forward in finding her current whereabouts. We now need to go through some other details with you and see where we are after that."

"Thank you Mr Helliwell." It was Penny Hammond who answered first, squeezing her husband's hand as she saw just how crestfallen he was, but wanting to pick up on the positive side of Oscar Helliwell's revelations "Maybe we could have a moment or two before we carry on?"

"Certainly, Mrs Hammond, we have no desire to make this visit any more difficult for you and will be ready to carry on when you are."

Penny and Graham Hammond excused themselves from the kitchen and moved into the sitting room across the hall where they exchanged guarded looks before holding each other closely, tears in their eyes. For their part the two policemen sat quietly in the kitchen knowing that the hardest part of their job today was over now, but that an uncomfortable hour or so lay ahead as they explained how Jane had become less of the person her parents knew, and still believed her to be, and more the stuff of their personal nightmares.

THIRTY TWO

Neil Maughan had left almost immediately after the briefing and was not present when Geoff Alderson began his search for information about Battle Guile; he had heard of it, even played it at a mates but hadn't taken to it in the same way as literally hundreds of thousands of others had, preferring to stick with his FIFA games and attempting to win trophies on a virtual football field that he never ever could have in reality.

It wasn't going to be easy however, the American base of the game creators and the Far Eastern home of the manufacturers and distributors ensured that, but at least they had a starting point and an encouraging one at that. Sue Collins, had, as would be expected, taken an excellent statement and added comments made by Gemma to her report that pointed to Scouse Vixen being of a similar age to Gemma and being a student of zoology.

Where to start, Google always came near to the top of the list and Geoff typed in the words 'Battle Guile' and obtained a list of thousands of sites that his computer indicated had been found in 0.37 seconds; it would take a damn sight longer to find the right one. Scrolling down only a few lines Geoff actually found what he was looking for in double quick time and started interrogating the site for information and contact details, it was going to be a long day.

Because of the type of enquiries he had to make he had to seek permission from the Force Professional Standards Department to access social forums and gaming sites, both of which would normally be against Force Policy on internet usage, frustrating as it was, taking over an hour for authorisation to be considered, he turned to Simon Pithers, walking the short distance back to the incident room to speak with him he asked for some strings to be pulled.

"Just do it Geoff, leave them to me."

"Thanks Boss, but you know what it's like?"

"I do, but unfortunately without the policies in place there will always be some clown that abuses the system and messes it up for everyone else."

"It may mean working late as well boss, I take it that's no problem, you know with the overtime issues?"

"Do whatever it takes Geoff, we need this. Big time."

Des Mason brought coffees into the office for everyone and took his seat at his desk;

"How's it going Geoff?"

"OK, just jumping through all the hoops about confidentiality and data protection shite"

"As usual, anything I can do?"

"Yeah, your Gemma said that this so called Scouse Vixen used another chat site, WGW or Whitby Goth Weekend; that's obviously got to be on our radar, can you do some checks on that, see what records they have?"

"Sure, send me the details."

Seconds later Des received an email with the details he needed to contact the organisers of one of Whitby Town's biggest annual events and he set to work.

The two officers did not speak for what seemed to be hours after that as they both tended to their respective tasks, ignoring phone calls, knowing they would be picked up by others elsewhere in the building or that messages would be left if it was important enough, their sole focus was on ensuring a positive result.

They had worked past their normal finish time without even seeing the clock when Des shouted;

"Got her!"

Looking up from his monitor Geoff saw Des punching the air as though he had just scored a Wembley cup final winner.

He left his own seat and walked around to Des' desk, looking over his shoulder at the screen in front of him he saw a chat thread with the name Scouse Vixen clearly shown as a participant. Another window open, showed details of the email conversation Des had been involved in with the site owners and there, on the bottom were details of one Jane Hammond, Scholars House, Liverpool.

Des replied to the email, thanking the organisers and explaining to them that he would need to meet up with them in due course to record everything in statement form, but that could wait for now.

Geoff was chuffed for his mate, he'd had a rough time of it lately but this was a real boon for him even though he had hoped to be the one with the breakthrough. Des hit the print key and waited for the machine to kick itself into gear before lifting off what he hoped would be the golden ticket to solving this crime.

Des Mason and Geoff Alderson burst into the incident room mid afternoon with smiles on their respective faces and a sheet of A4 paper held firmly in Geoff's right hand.

"We've found her, we've fucking found her."

The audience they were expecting however wasn't the one they found; the duty Sergeant Tom Stead, sat by his computer and a couple of administrative staff acting as in-putters to the computer system were chatting calmly at their own desks, in fact the only Detective present was Simon Pithers who was sat examining the white boards in much the same manner as Neil Maughan had been apt to do, sat perched on the end of a table and stroking his chin with his own right hand.

"Well spit it out then lads." he prompted, "let's all hear it." he made a sarcastic gesture of looking around the room, devoid of over half the current team who had gone home, were on their breaks, catching up on missed annual leave or sent back to their respective divisions to resume core duties.

"Jane Hammond Boss, Jane Hammond. Missing from Leeds for over eighteen months, a positive, exact match."

"You little beauties. You little fucking beauties."

"It was Des's daughter that put us on to it boss, you know she said about that lass called Scouse Vixen, well it's her."

Geoff Alderson explained what he and Des had done and that having got the details they had asked for the DNA to be analysed against what had been taken as part of the 'missing from home' enquiry by West Yorkshire Police and once the name had been put forward it was just a matter of checking the details to confirm the identity of their victim.

"It's the girl they keep showing on TV Boss, you know went missing, car found at Manchester airport but no sign of her passport being used to travel from there, seemed to just vanish into thin air," pausing mid sentence to reflect on just how much he knew and how much of his own thoughts was prudent to pass on at this moment before continuing; "the parents wouldn't accept that their daughter had a promiscuous lifestyle and kept saying that the police were trying to sully her reputation."

"I remember it very well Geoff, in fact it's supposed to be high priority in West Yorkshire and Merseyside; what's she doing over here?"

"I don't know yet sir, but I'm working on it, it's got to Goth related though; just from the sites she visited online."

"Excellent. Now the real work can start." Simon Pithers said, directing his comments towards the duty Sergeant, "Let's get some info on that box and some new tasks out there; this is what we've been working towards. Jane Hammond"

Those words set the tone for the few in the office and Geoff Alderson remained in the incident room to update the Superintendent and Sergeant with exact details while Des Mason went off in search of Sue Collins.

"It's all a bit strange though boss; I still need to get the full details from Leeds, I've only just got the results so they don't know yet but the info on the box says she was reported missing by her father in November 2011, our Goth weeks are in April and October."

"Do the necessary then Geoff, update them with all we have and make sure it's recorded on our systems who we spoke to and when, if this doesn't prove the value of taking DNA samples in missing person enquiries I don't know what will."

"Are you going to tell Neil sir, sorry I mean DI Maughan sir?"

"No Geoff; I know what you're thinking but I think Neil needs some time to tend to his own affairs at the moment, and there is certainly no pun intended there."

"You're right sir, but he has always said that if we can I/D the victim we'd find the killer."

"And for what it's worth I agree with him, but there is a long way still to go."

Geoff Alderson left the room and returned back to his own office where he set about updating the computer before making the call to Weetwood Police Station.

Simon Pithers turned his attention back to the whiteboards and using a cloth picked up from the table at his side wiped clean the question mark over the victim's picture before adding the name of Jane Hammond in its place. He then stood back and asked himself the question,

"Now who in Whitby would want you dead my girl?"

Using the same pen he drew another arrow across the board and created three further headings under which he wanted the investigation to progress; Scouse Vixen, Liverpool and Leeds; underlining each he turned to the duty Sergeant and said, "Big day tomorrow Tom, don't be late."

and with that he left the room, walking with something of a swagger down the corridor confident that this was the breakthrough they had been waiting for.

THIRTY THREE

"What's happened to you then? Adam had seen the damage to Mike's Fiat as he walked up the drive and on entering the house saw a glum looking Mike sat in a chair, feet up with a can of lager in his hand.
"Don't ask mate, don't ask."
"It didn't go well then?"
"You could say that," Mike took a sheet of paper from his pocket and handed it across to Adam
Taking the paper, Adam looked at it and read that it was a bail sheet from Merseyside Police requiring Mike to return there in three weeks time;
"Jeez mate, what you done this time?"
"I've been fucking stupid, that's what. Drink driving."
"Shit, you're not joking either are you?"
"You've got the bail sheet; you can see I'm not joking."
"I don't know what to say, what happened?"
Mike explained what had happened in Liverpool, the unsuccessful search for Jane, the accident and the breath test procedure, not to mention a bill for a hundred and twenty quid to get his car back from the pound after it had been recovered from the roadside.
"A great trip all round then?" Adam's sarcasm was not lost on Mike but not that well received either.
"A total waste of time mate, the only good thing from it all was that at least I didn't spend a night in the cells this time."
"Well be grateful for small mercies then, but you're gonna be stuck without a car aren't you?"
"Absolutely, absofucking-lutely"
Adam got himself a beer from the fridge and another for Mike and sat in another of the chairs to watch Bradley Walsh taking the piss out of another contestant on The Chase on the TV. Mike would really struggle without his car but he didn't have a lot of sympathy in truth because that is one thing that can be controlled, everyone, he thought, had the choice to make; drink or drive, not both.
They sat in silence for a while, the only sounds coming from the television, before Adam could stand it no longer;
"It's pointless just moping around, what's done is done and you don't even know what the blood result is yet, look what happened with the other stuff."
"I know but I'm just pissed off generally, I still don't know any more about Jane than I did before I went either."
"You knew before you went that was likely to be the case though."

"I know, I know, doesn't stop you trying though does it?"

"No, s'pose not. I'm off for a shower anyway, some of us have still been working you know, not off getting pissed and crashing our cars." Said in jest and taken as such Adam was trying to lift Mike in a way a mate would, by showing little sympathy and by taking the piss.

Mike threw his empty can at his mate as he went out of the door and grinned; it was that or grimace and he knew now that there was no point in that or in just aimlessly wasting his time sulking in a chair, he had to move on now and forget Jane; after all it seemed that she had chosen to forget him. Decision made, Mike would try to put everything behind him and repay Adams faith in him by being himself again.

THIRTY FOUR

Left to their own devices after the two officers had finished passing the information they had acquired, including the fact that she was believed to have shared a room with others at the Goth weekend, that she had met a man with whom she had appeared to be besotted and with whom she was considering staying over a little longer, the Hammonds were stunned;

"It must be right darling; the police wouldn't waste their time or ours if they hadn't have thought it through." Penny Hammond, whilst still in a state of some shock and disbelief herself, was trying to help her husband come to terms with the news that had been delivered so unexpectedly.

"A Goth; tattoos, I don't believe it for a minute dear, I mean we would have seen it wouldn't we; and what about Phoebe, she wouldn't tell the lies that the police say she did? No they have either made a serious mistake in identification or they are just exaggerating everything again."

"They wouldn't do that dear and they must have spoken to Phoebe, how else would they know who she was?"

"Well I don't believe it Penny, I won't believe it anyway. We brought her up properly, not to be some waster like most of the young today."

The two continued to talk; in reality they must have known that what they had been told must be right but Graham Hammond simply would not accept the obvious; looking around his beautiful home he allowed his thoughts to drift back over the years as he recollected his beloved daughter running from room to room as a child, pigtails flowing behind her, grin as big as the proverbial Cheshire cat; this surely was not a child who would turn into a woman with such low moral standards?

"I'm going to ring Phoebe, ask her directly what is going on."

"Is that wise dear, I mean she may not want to speak to us if the police have been to see her?"

"I don't really give a damn whether she wants to speak or not, the police have told us that she has spent days, if not more telling us a pack of lies. I want to know the truth."

Graham Hammond could not make it any clearer that he intended to speak with Phoebe come what may and he walked across to the telephone on the large polished walnut cabinet on the wall opposite the door. As he picked it up he had tears in his eyes, he knew that he had to make the call but did not in reality know what he wanted to hear. He dialled the number from memory, pressing each button carefully, deliberately, allowing himself time to focus, to think about just what he was going to say?

The phone rang and rang until the answer phone facility activated, asking the caller to leave their message; Graham Hammond seemed to be caught unaware, he was angry but still wanted to believe that Phoebe could put some better perspective on things, give him some hope and as such he didn't want to vent his anger to a machine;

"Hello Phoebe, it's Graham Hammond, Jane's father, I wonder if you could possibly give me a call back when you get this message. The sooner the better please. Thank you. Bye"

For her part Phoebe had seen the caller display on her phone and chosen not to answer, she didn't feel able to answer Graham Hammond's questions just now; she was still reeling from her grilling from the police, telling them how she had covered Jane's tracks by telling the Hammonds anything but the truth to keep them happy. She wasn't happy with herself; in fact she was feeling very disappointed almost tearful at the deceit and yet very concerned for Jane, it wasn't like her not to make any contact at all.

Back at Horsforth Graham Hammond sat on the edge of the sofa cushion, head in hands, tears running down his cheeks and falling onto his shirt front. Penny crossed the room, sat next to him and rested her head on his shoulder, the two of them lost for words.

They didn't know it at this time but this was to be the beginning of a terrible period in their lives, one which would cause them to question everything they had always taken for granted, and the belief that their perfect life, their perfect daughter and their beautiful home in its semi rural idyllic setting was the basis for endless contentment; all had been turned upside down in one day of turmoil, a day that was to set in motion month after month of anguish and despair.

273

Having confirmed with colleagues that the message of their daughters discovery and DNA identification had been passed to the Hammonds, Simon Pithers set in motion the next phase of Operation Caedmon. "Ladies and Gentlemen thank you all for coming here this morning; I will keep this brief as I know you will have questions afterwards." Simon Pithers sat alongside Sue Collins addressing the gathered press contingent at Spring Hill Police Station, "I can today put a name to the body found on the East Cliff on Saturday 12th January 2013," he paused to allow all those present time to collect themselves, ready their notebooks and pens before continuing; "that name is Jane Hammond." A collective sigh echoed around the room as the magnitude of the revelation of what he had said sank in; voices began to be heard as journalists repeated the name to each other or just spoke it aloud to confirm to themselves that they had heard correctly.

"If I may have your attention please." he continued, "you will all obviously realise that this discovery brings to a conclusion the search for a missing person that has occupied so much of your attention over the past eighteen months or so but it also represents a significant stage in our murder enquiry. We will continue to work alongside our colleagues from Merseyside and West Yorkshire to determine the final movements of our victim, Jane, before her untimely demise and I would ask again for anyone with any information whatsoever to contact us via the incident room helpline."

Simon Pithers took a break in the delivery of his address again, but in doing so he allowed the journalists to shout their questions out to him.

"Was she killed here?"

"Is there any comment from the family Superintendent?"

"Do we know yet how she died?"

"What's the link to Whitby?"

Shouted from each corner of the room the questions were quite valid as far as journalists were concerned but of little consequence to Simon Pithers who would not digress far from his prepared script.

"The discovery of our victim's identity will allow us to focus our efforts to better effect and as such this represents a key factor in our investigation. My team of dedicated detectives will now redouble their efforts in order to bring the perpetrator of this crime to justice."

"Mr Pithers," Elli Stanford stood up as she spoke, "throughout the investigation into the disappearance of Jane Hammond there was thought to be a link to The Goth community, is that still an ongoing line of your enquiries?"

"We never close any line of enquiry until we can absolutely confirm that all questions have been asked and all answers have been obtained, evaluated and considered. We will continue to have an open mind as to the cause of death, the identity of her killer and the background of all those concerned. I would however appeal to The Goth community to come forward if anyone knew Jane, met her at one of our Whitby Goth events or had any other connection with her at all. We do know that Jane did have a keen interest in the ways of the Goths and we would therefore be foolish not to be open to that line of enquiry."

"Should the Goths be concerned then about someone out there with a grudge against them?"

"No, absolutely not. There is nothing yet to suggest that Jane Hammond was killed because she was a Goth or had an interest in that lifestyle and it would be foolish of anyone to draw that conclusion from what I have said." He stood surveying the room as he spoke, looking for any sign of dissent from those present; "we have literally thousands of Goths attending Whitby on a regular basis and I am pleased to be able to say that they enjoy their visits here enough to return so frequently, bringing their own diverse sense of theatre and enjoyment to the town and very seldom do we encounter any problems with them as they do so."

Despite this being a press conference about a murder investigation there was always someone who would notice any comment that would distance the police from the public or the commercial sector of the town, he was therefore very cautious in the choice of his words as a result.

"The body was uncovered in the garden of a house Superintendent; do we now assume that the house owners are suspects?" A tall, slim man in a checked shirt and pale chino's holding a small notepad and pencil in his left hand asked the question.

"I'm sorry but I don't recognise you," Sue Collins took the question in place of Simon Pithers, but didn't know the individual making the enquiry, "We are not prepared to make any assumptions and nor should you really expect us to. Our enquiries have been under way for some time and will continue to be made until we conclude the investigation by bringing the offender to justice."

The reporter continued however, "Can I assume that the house is a second home for the owner then?"

"I am sorry but I do not deal in assumptions and I would suggest that it is wrong for you to do so either."

Simon Pithers, not wanting the session to proceed much longer as he wanted to get stuck into what he considered to be the real police work, stood up and spoke again;

"Ladies and Gentlemen, that is all for now, I trust that I can rely on your ongoing support and I assure you that as soon as we have something of value to share with you then I will bring you all back here to do so."
One or two reporters tried to ask further questions but Simon Pithers remained standing and gestured for Sue Collins to make a move also; leaving two uniformed PCSO's to empty the room on their behalf.
The two detectives walked down to the CID office still discussing the case and how they would lead the next briefing.
"I will need you to open the briefing Sue, I have some urgent calls to make but I'll follow you down there as soon as I can."
Taken a little by surprise as she would normally have liked to update herself completely before taking on such a role, she replied;
"OK Sir, anything you particularly want to cover?"
"Sue you know the score, arguably better than I do, being involved at the sharp end. I want all the new evidence looking into and I mean properly looking into with clear tasks set and reports submitted back as soon as. I'm relying on you at the moment and you owe me this as Neil will be away for a few days yet, believe me."
"Understood Boss." she hadn't known that Neil Maughan was going to be off as long as the superintendent seemed to be suggesting and she knew that she would be held, at least in part, responsible for his loss from the team. She decided there and then that she would show she was up to the task; after all she had led no end of briefings before but never a full blown murder enquiry.

THIRTY SIX

It was difficult for Mike to come to terms with just how lucky he had been, yes it was unfortunate in each case that he had been arrested and had to undergo two different types of investigation but for each one to come back with the same decision; not to prosecute, was more than he could reasonably have expected. The legal limit for a blood \ alcohol test was apparently 80 milligrammes of alcohol per 100millilitres of blood and according to the letter he had received from Merseyside Police he had scraped under that with a reading of 77 milligrammes meaning that there was no reason to attend to answer his bail in Liverpool and that once again he had been released without charge.

"You're just a jammy bastard." Adam had remained a constant in Mike's life and a key support prop over the last few weeks as Mike fretted over how he could possibly cope without access to his car.

"Don't knock it mate, I feel like a bloody cop magnet at the minute, every time I go out I'm looking over my shoulder for the next one."

"I know; I don't normally employ crims."

"Well that's it I promise you, never again."

"Never say never Mike, I hope you're right but I never thought you'd be arrested once never mind twice."

"I said never and I mean it."

Both men looked at each other, gave a knowing smile which subsequently broke into laughter, in Mike's case the first for at least three weeks; he felt good again.

"Are we celebrating tonight then?" with the weight of all his problems lifted Mike felt he could let go again and enjoy himself.

"Not if you're driving we're not." Adam responded, resulting in a pen being thrown across the room at him, striking him an almost imperceptible blow on the arm and lifting the mood even higher as Adam laughed at the child like reaction of his friend. Adam was genuinely pleased to see that his mate had returned to being the man he knew him to be and continued, "I'm sure Kate will be pleased to see you though if we go down to The Crown."

"Eh?"

"Don't give me that shit, she's been coming on to you since you got here; if you hadn't been such a miserable git all the time you'd have been well in already."

"Kate?"

"Yes Kate Bevan, the cracking brunette with all the right curves in all the right places."

"Yeah, bit stuck up though i'nt she?"

"She likes to think so but I've known her a long time and she certainly has no cause to be."

"What do you mean?"

"She's no different to the rest of us, same school, same town, just got lucky."

"It's like pulling teeth Adam, what the fuck does she do that makes her think she's a bit upper crust then?"

"Interior design they call it. Her dad is a builder and she started out telling him about colours and stuff when he was decorating a house then one of his mates saw what he had done and asked Kate to look at his place, the rest they say is history. Got her own business now, web site, the lot."

"And what the fuck does she see in me then?"

"God only knows, but if you're fishing for compliments you're in the wrong pond mate cos there ain't any here."

Mike set off with Adam for that days' work with a real spring in his step, things could really be on the up for a change and if Kate was available and half what Adam had gone on to explain she was then he would be a very happy man in the days and weeks to come.

THIRTY SEVEN

"Right folks,, let's crack on," Sue Collins stood alone at the head of the table in the incident room, "Detective Inspector Maughan sends his apologies, but he is unable to attend for a few days and that means I will step up over that time with the support of Detective Superintendent Pithers, who will be here shortly."

The opening address was intended to paper over the cracks that had begun to show in the professional relationship between Sue Collins and Neil Maughan. Maughan, in turn, had made arrangements to take some further time off in an attempt to save his marriage.

Using the whiteboards as a reference Sue Collins continued,

"The investigation has reached a critical stage and you will all note the victims details have been added with a stream of enquiries resulting from that. For those of you still unaware of the background the victim has been a high profile missing person that has somehow slipped through the net in a cross border enquiry. West Yorkshire Police and Merseyside Police are in the process of damage limitation in the media after the victim's parents have accused each of failing them in the search; let me make it very clear that Mr Pithers does not want us to become involved in any media frenzy and will come down hard on anyone failing in what is now a very public enquiry." Having been briefed over the phone by Simon Pithers Sue Collins made it very clear that she was passing on a message that she expected everyone present to note and adhere to.

"Since the I.D. we have been able to confirm that Jane Hammond visited Whitby over the Goth weekend in October 2011 where she met and stayed with other Goths. She also got very close to one of our previous suspects, Mike Davies, who was one of the builders working for Willie Raynor on the Esk View cottage-"

"I thought he had an alibi Sarge?" Mark Taylor interrupted

"No Mark, he gave us an account that covered what we knew at the time; we certainly didn't know he'd been shagging the victim." It was quite a terse comment, but Sue Collins was for the first time leading a briefing on a murder enquiry and needed everyone to be absolutely clear that she intended it to be full of clarity and with no room for any ambiguity.

"Do we know where she stayed when she was here?" Des Mason piped up; recognising that his boss was a little edgy, and thinking that an easy question would help her settle into a more relaxed mood.

"Yes Des we do, thank you," she recognised the question for what it was and knew that Des already had the answer to it, "The Harbour View Guest House, I now want some enquiries made there, the guest diary, statements from the owners and any other staff and I want every guest that stayed there over that period tracing and questioning, did they see Jane did they meet her, what was she like whilst she was here, did she spend time with anyone else but this Mike Davies, what sort of girl was she in reality?" Pausing for breath and to compose herself, she carried on, "Between these four walls the girl's parents are still very much going through a grieving process and despite being devout church goers are looking for someone to blame, I therefore am asking for and expecting total discretion from all of you. No smart arse comments, no judgemental remarks and certainly no responses to questions from the media outside of the party line."

Looking around the room she saw in the expressions around the table that the message had been received and acknowledged.

"I also want the builders visited again to go over their accounts and I want all the local doormen speaking to. Mike Davies worked as a bouncer and you will all remember the furore over the death at The Resolution during that same Goth weekend, is anything connected? Geoff can you take that line of enquiry on please?"

"Will do Sarge, I remember Colombo being involved at the time, I'll speak to him first."

"Good, make sure you update the box as soon as you know anything. I am going visit this Phoebe James to get a clear picture of what she can tell us about Jane Hammond, I have arranged to meet with a local officer in Merseyside and will travel after today's end of day de-brief. We are at a pivotal moment in this investigation and I want this new evidence to be a springboard for the operation. I want to see some real progress from here on in."

She finished the sentence just as the doors to the incident room opened and Simon Pithers walked in; "Morning all," he opened, "thanks for that Sue, I heard the last remark and I just want to endorse it; we've all worked bloody hard on this operation and so far haven't had much to show for it, I know the effort that's gone in and want to thank you all for your endeavours but now is the time to kick on and really make it count." He placed his bag on the table as he spoke, looked at the whiteboards that he had become so au fait with recently and noted the actions that were now listed. A nod of approval indicated that he was satisfied with what he had seen and heard and he dismissed the gathered troops, "If there are no further questions, make sure you have your tasks and keep up the good work."

The room took only a minute or so to empty as the detectives, with newly gathered enthusiasm set about their respective enquiries, leaving the Sergeant and Superintendent in discussion.

"You ok Sue; sorry to drop that on you like that but Neil needs the time and I'm sure you of all people will understand that?"

"Not a problem sir, I think it went well any way but a bit more notice might have helped." she grinned as she said it before adding, "But then again we're paid to think on our feet aren't we?"

"You know you can do it Sue, I know you can do it and the results better show you can do it. Now let's go and get that kettle on and you can update me with who's doing what?"

They walked casually down the corridor back towards Sue's office, chatting en-route.

THIRTY EIGHT

Sat in his own office the following morning with an array of newspapers opened on his desk Simon Pithers saw the headlines that he feared after the press conference were just those that had subsequently appeared in the local and regional media. The Whitby Gazette ran the provocative lead;

'GOTH VICTIM OF WHITBY MURDER'

Whilst Jane Hammond was said to have been involved with the Goth weekend there was absolutely nothing to suggest that the reason she died was linked to that at all and yet he knew that the wording would create a flurry of interest both locally and in the wider Gothic field and, of course, help to sell more papers . The article continued with derogatory comments suggesting that Police inadequacies were a contributory factor. There was nothing to clarify that the so called inadequacies were those alleged against the other two forces in the missing person enquiry and not anything at all to do with North Yorkshire Police.

Radio news programmes and phone in chat shows highlighted both the same strands and as usual were subject to take over bids by callers with an axe to grind and, often, without any chance to rebut outrageous allegations made, that Jane Hammond was attacked because of the way she looked or the people she mixed with; that the police did little to properly investigate as they did not recognise Goths as a recognised group as they did with others like race, religion, sexual orientation and the like. He was pleased that he had taken the time to speak with the press office in his own area and asked that they make specific calls to their counterparts in West Yorkshire and Merseyside. The feedback he had received was that those forces were already preparing responses to allegations made by the Hammonds and that the usual protocols were being followed as there were still outstanding lines of enquiry and that the Independent Police Complaints Commission were involved.

The regional papers, as may be expected, were a little less focused on the Goth angle but stayed very much focused on the alleged police failings, in particular asking questions about the length of time Jane had been missing and why the investigation did not lead them to Whitby so much earlier? The Yorkshire Evening Post ran the following article under the headline,

'BODY FOUND ON CLIFF IS JANE'

282

'The body found following the land slip on Whitby's famous East Cliff has been confirmed as that of Leeds girl Jane Hammond, (22 years), police have confirmed. Detective Superintendent Simon Pithers revealed in a press conference at Whitby Police Station that DNA evidence had been used to identify the body as that of Jane who had been reported as missing by her parents Graham and Penelope Hammond of Horsforth. D/Supt. Pithers remarked that his dedicated team of detectives were now in the process of following up new lines of enquiry and reiterated his earlier appeal for anyone who believes they have any information that may assist with the investigation to come forward now; he assures that all witnesses will be afforded absolute discretion.

The revelation brings to an end the torturous process of investigation that has, at times, appeared to have been beset by problems. Our reporter has been unable to obtain a comment from either parent for this article but a spokesman for the family has asked that they be given time now to come to terms with the dreadful news and they thank everyone who has supported them over the months that have passed since her disappearance.

The Hammonds have previously been widely reported as having a difficult time with the police since the November 2011 when they allege that Merseyside Police began a slur campaign against their daughter to cover the inadequacies of their own enquiries into her disappearance. A spokesperson for Merseyside Police responded by saying that, "The investigation into Jane's disappearance has been thorough and has been made more difficult by witnesses initially providing incorrect information and by Jane, unbeknown to her parents apparently leading something of a dual life. We are now working with North Yorkshire Police to share whatever information and intelligence we have to help to bring what is now a murder enquiry to an early conclusion with the perpetrator being brought to justice."

Not the best start to the day he considered but in truth nothing that couldn't reasonably have been foreseen. He had known that Sue Collins had travelled to Liverpool the previous night and thought he should give her a call to ensure that she was aware of what was out there, so picked up his phone and dialled her number.

"Morning Boss." she answered his call, seemingly bright and cheerful

"Morning Sue, have you seen the papers?"

"Not yet, but I have seen the local tele' news in my room and they are all over it."

"Well keep your nose clean then and don't add to the problem."

"I don't think I will sir, the issues are all about the local cops over here, I might even be seen as the good guy for once?"

283

"You appear to have it all in control Sue, let me know how you get on. I'm going over to the incident room this afternoon so call me there eh?"

"Will do."

No more needed to be said and they hung up to go about their respective work or so they thought; he had no sooner ended that call than another came through from the press office.

"Simon, it's Griff from Media Relations, have you got a moment?"

"That's about all I do have Griff but go ahead."

"I'm just wondering if you're planning to put something together as a response to today's media or do you want me to arrange the usual straight bat stuff?"

"I'd be grateful if you would Griff, stress the fact that we are a step further forward and that we will be liaising with other forces to ensure that we take everything into consideration and for God's sake please play down the Goth thing."

"Yeah no problem, I've drafted something out along those lines and I'll send you a copy across shortly. You need to be aware though that Elli Stanford has been on the phone and she is looking to build up the Goth link, linking it to the Sophie Lancaster incident."

"You know the ropes Griff, let her get on with it but keep us at as big a distance as you can, we'll keep an open mind, blah blah blah and treat all information with appropriate consideration."

"Yeah I get the picture Boss, give me another ten minutes or so and send you a brief, I've also emailed Jean to advise her that all requests come through to me with Neil and Sue being away."

"Thanks Griff, I'll get back to you at the end of the day, cheers."

THIRTY NINE

Sue Collins met with PC Laura Goodman at her desk on the university campus believing it would help her to get the feel of the place and also it would enable her to park her car safely within walking distance of where she needed to be. Laura Goodman had dressed in casual clothing instead of her usual high visibility uniform, the reasoning being that she could take Sue wherever they needed to go without drawing too much attention to the casual onlooker.

Initial introductions made and coffee taken Sue quizzed Laura about her feelings in respect of their intended meeting with Phoebe James later that morning.

"She's agreed to meet us at the house as you requested but she is very nervous."

"She should be; if she'd been honest at the outset she's have saved you and West Yorkshire hundreds of man hours and loads of grief from the press."

"I know and she knows that now as well but I think she's suffered enough in a way, you know she flunked her finals because she couldn't cope with the stress, now she's taking her final year again and this happens."

"Is she on her own?"

"I'm not sure to be honest but I think so."

"Come on then let's do it, she'll be sat waiting and the longer we leave it the worse she'll be."

"It's a pity she's not still at Scholars House, you know where she stayed with Jane Hammond at the time but she couldn't cope with it, she's not too far away though."

They left the university and followed the same route Laura had taken many times over the last few months to Freedom Close where Phoebe now lived. The town was relatively quiet for the time of day and Sue Collins took in the surroundings as they made their way; she had been a student herself but remembered her digs being much less salubrious, in fact she had thought of them as being more of a squat than a home.

As they walked towards number 81 Sue Collins saw a figure stood in the ground floor window and had her first sight of Phoebe James; by the time they reached the front door it was being opened by a sullen looking female in faded tee shirt, ill fitting hoodie and jeans.

"Hello, Phoebe? I'm Detective Sergeant Collins from North Yorkshire Police; I believe you know PC Goodman already?"

"Yes, come in." She stood aside and let the two officers pass her directing them towards the living room.

Sue Collins saw that some effort had been made at cleaning up, the carpet still showed visible marks from the recently used vacuum cleaner and there was no washing up to be seen in the kitchen sink as she cast her eyes around to take in as much as she could, a far cry from the usual student approach she thought.

"Sit down if you want," Phoebe pointed to the sofas whilst remaining standing herself.

"Thank you," it was Laura that spoke this time, "Phoebe, try not to be so nervous, we all know what happened with you covering for Jane, it's what a friend would do; it's just that now is the time to come clean with absolutely everything."

"I told you everything when you came before."

"I know but we didn't know then that Jane wasn't coming back, DS Collins is here to ask you again if you can remember anything else?"

"I don't think so, I just feel so awful for Jane's Mum and Dad, they're lovely people and I've told them lies when Jane was lying dead in a back garden."

Sue Collins felt it was time to talk now;

"Phoebe, it is very important that we now have the truth about everything. I want you tell me everything you know about Jane from the day you first met; what was she like then, how has she changed, who did she get along with and who did she not? I'll only prompt you if I need to or if I feel we are straying from course. Is that OK?"

"Yeah but it'll take ages."

"Don't worry there's no rush and if you need a break we'll take one, are you happy to do it here?"

"Yeah, I don't want to go down to the nick, what do you call it, helping you with your enquiries?"

"Something like that." Sue Collins saw that the mood had lifted if only slightly but took Phoebe's earlier statement from her bag together with a notebook and pen.

"I'll make us all a drink if that's ok Phoebe?" Laura felt comfortable making the offer; she had visited so often, it was almost a natural action of a friend.

"Yeah, please it's all in that top cupboard." she pointed through to the kitchen

"I'll find it don't worry."

Sue Collins then prompted for Phoebe to commence her account;

"We got to know each other as fresher's, we both enrolled at the same time and then met when we were both looking for someone to share a house with, it sounds snobby but we're both from fairly wealthy backgrounds and thought it would be better to find a house instead of just a room in a house. I'm sorry that sounds real bad doesn't it?"

"I'm not here to judge you Phoebe, you're doing fine."

With a little prompting where necessary from Sue Collins, she continued talking, providing a great amount of detail about their times together indicating a growing friendship and closeness and pleasing the officers with the amount of fresh intelligence on her victim and also corroborating what they already knew.

After over an hour Sue Collins realised that Phoebe was struggling, emotionally at least, as they chronologically reached the time to talk about Jane's increasing promiscuity; and so suggested they take a break for a while.

"We're going to need you to continue shortly Phoebe, are you ok or do you want some fresh air or something to eat or drink?"

"I'm ok I think" the reply was spoken quickly but the expression behind the words indicated to Sue Collins that Phoebe needed time to compose herself again.

"Well I need a short comfort break; can I just take a minute or two and use your bathroom please?"

Whether there was a need to use the bathroom was immaterial she wanted to get a quick look around the upstairs, if only to get a bit of a personal view of Phoebe. Following directions Sue left the two of them downstairs, relying on her colleague to ensure that Phoebe remained onside and focused but giving her time to relax a little.

Making her way upstairs she looked around the well decorated spaces and thought that she knew some well paid cops that didn't live in as nice a property as this one, it was small and probably not worth an awful lot in the grand scheme of things but it represented a very good starter home and was well kept, though when she thought about it she knew that it was parental income that was providing this. She saw the bathroom door open but decided she didn't need to enter just yet, opening another door she saw a very tidy room with a double bed, wardrobes and a small desk under the window. It must surely be the spare room, that or the cleanest student in living memory she thought. Closing the door again she opened the only other door and saw what must obviously be Phoebe's bedroom. A laptop was open on the bed, obviously having been used earlier that day with the cable running to a socket at the side of the bed behind one of the two matching bedside tables, books were laid out on the desk that matched the one in the other room and a pair of jeans and a sweater laid over a chair arm in the corner of the room, nothing too startling but an apparently well adjusted individual she thought to herself. Realising she had taken enough time

Sue Collins went into the bathroom, flushed the toilet and ran the taps for a few seconds before making her way back downstairs to continue.

"You ready to carry on?" she asked Phoebe

"Yeah, suppose so."

"So you've told us that Jane became, what did you say, a bit wild? What do you mean by that?"

"I don't know if wild is the right word but it's just as if someone took her shackles off; she kept saying that she hadn't been allowed to do this or that and that whilst she was at Uni she was going to try everything."

"What like?"

"Drinking, drugs, music, sex, everything."

"Can you tell me more? What did she actually get involved in, she wasn't an addict was she?" Sue's background checks with both Merseyside and West Yorkshire had shown nothing in respect of any arrests or suspicions of using drugs and if she had been addict there would most certainly be something.

"No I never said she was an addict but she tried dope, E, MDMA you know the usual low level stuff, it's easy to get hold of. Sorry I shouldn't say that should I?"

"Don't worry Phoebe, we know." it was the first time Laura Goodman had spoken for a while and she knew better than most just how easy it was to access the so called recreational drugs, she also knew that the attempts to interrupt the supply were way above anything Phoebe was likely to have seen in her somewhat sheltered life.

"She liked to drink but you could still see that she got drunk very quickly so only really drank when she went out clubbing but she lost her virginity here when she was drunk, I mean in Liverpool, not here you know what I mean?"

It was seemingly becoming a little more difficult for Phoebe to talk about her friend now; the sense of betrayal seemed to confront her as she talked.

"Take your time Phoebe; are you saying she didn't want to lose her virginity?"

"No quite the opposite, she did want to, but she was drunk and it didn't seem right; this bloke had been plying her with drinks all night and she wouldn't listen to me and you know, one thing led to another."

"How long ago was this?"

"After about 3 months here I suppose, before we left for Christmas anyway, trouble is once she crossed that line she was a different person; if anything that's what she became addicted to and she got quite a bad reputation if you know what I mean?"

288

"Yes I know what you mean; how was her relationship with you then? I mean did it cause any problems if she was going off the rails a bit?"

"No, she was always great with me." At this Phoebe couldn't control the emotions anymore and began crying, softly but enough to stop talking for a while.

Sue Collins excused herself again to give Phoebe some more time to compose herself; they had reached the point where she knew that real and valuable intelligence about the victim was imminent and wouldn't want to break off once that started, better to have a break now.

FORTY

"Sir, I've got that list of bouncers, sorry Doormen. The company as you know is called GT Security Consultants a rather grand name for a group of local doormen run by Gerald or Ged Turner, based in Bracken Close on the Barratt Estate." Geoff Alderson was talking to Simon Pithers who in truth didn't have the time to be taking such a hands on approach, but knowing that he had allowed Neil Maughan the time off had to make sure it didn't affect the continuity of the investigation.

"No surprises there then Geoff, have we spoken to Mr Turner yet then?"

"Not yet, he's apparently unavailable until later today having worked last night. We did speak to him and all the others though during the Fleur Brennan case"

"Well ain't life a bitch eh? Make sure you see him today and all the others ASAP and do full background checks on all his staff again, they should all be CRB clear if they're badge holders but-"

"It's in hand sir," Geoff cut in, "but I wanted to let you know that we've uncovered a photograph of Jane Hammond and another girl taken during the Goth weekend."

Simon Pithers attention was stirred somewhat more by this announcement and he looked at Geoff Alderson and saw the outstretched arm holding a picture obviously taken by a professional photographer. Taking the photograph and looking at two very good looking girls dressed up to the nines in Goth garb he considered the waste of life any unlawful killing created and sat silent for a moment. After watching his boss for just a short while Geoff Alderson explained that the photographer had seen the paper and knew he had taken a number of photos over that weekend so trawled through his records and found the picture in question. He had given a statement in which he had included the name of the second girl and was happy to provide any further copies of the photo or any other information as required.

"Excellent. Where does this other girl live then?"

"Thankfully just across the border boss in Cleveland."

"Mark has contacted her and is heading across there now; it ties up with the names we have from Harbour View Guest House nicely."

"Get the info on the box then Geoff and pass on my thanks to Mr erm-"

"Preston sir, John Preston from Sandgate Studio."

"Just one other thing sir, if I can?"

"What's that Geoff I am in a bit of a rush?"

"its Neil sir, I mean-"

"I know who you mean Geoff."

"Well we were all wondering when he might be back?"

"We'll have to wait and see Geoff, it may be some time but I'm sure you'll understand that I can't divulge any more than that."

"No, I appreciate that sir, and we haven't contacted him but wondered if you might pass on our best wishes when you next speak, let him know he has the support of us all."

"I'll do that and I'm sure he'll appreciate it Geoff but he needs time away from work just now, there are some things that are still more important than work; even our work."

"Ok boss thanks." Geoff turned on his heels and left the room, he hadn't really needed to pass on the information about the photographer as Simon Pithers would have noticed it later anyway but he had wanted to pass on the good wishes of the team and as he had something new it fell to him to do so.

The team were missing the drive of their Inspector, the daily impetus he always seemed to provide; yes they were professionals and would always do their best but Neil Maughan seemed to possess an almost encyclopaedic knowledge of policy and best practise as well as which corners could be cut and when. He was also a friend.

FORTY ONE

Sue Collins and Laura Goodman had planned to be with Phoebe for about two hours; they were now in the fourth and were still eliciting more information.

Phoebe had been quite embarrassed at first when she spoke about Jane's sexual appetite after what she referred to as the drunken awakening; she had had many different partners and was not averse to having more than one partner at a time and several in tow, something which Phoebe found difficult to comprehend. She didn't understand the fascination with tattoos either and spoke of how astonished she was when she turned up with the snake on her leg;

"I was totally gobsmacked. It looked awful when she first came home and she said it hurt like hell. She said that about the piercing too. I take it you knew about that?"

"Yes we knew." Sue Collins tried to reconcile her own acceptance of the tattoos and piercing with Phoebe's shock; after all Phoebe had never been exposed to the same visions as Sue had in her professional career. "It's sort of sick; it's the only thing we ever fell out about really."

"And how much of this have you told Mr and Mrs Hammond?"

"Well certainly not all of it, I spoke to them when she was reported as missing, Graham, Jane's dad; he rang me a few times and was asking questions; he must have thought I knew where she was but I didn't." she reached into her pocket and pulled out her mobile phone, "I've even kept some of the text messages, even now. I showed you them didn't I Laura?"

"Yes you did. There all detailed in the report Sue."

"Yes thanks Laura I saw that. As I recall there were text messages to both you and the Hammonds on the Tuesday after Goth week?"

"Yeah, she said she was on her way home."

"If it was her?"

"What do you mean? I've saved the messages you can look if you like."

"No I meant was it Jane that sent the texts."

"I'm sorry I don't understand."

"We know the messages came from Jane's phone but we can't be absolutely certain that it was she who sent them. What if somebody else had access to her phone?"

Sue was wary now of saying too much, but Phoebe wasn't a streetwise kid, she was a young woman from a protective background and as such somewhat naive in the ways of the real world. Getting back to the present and the job in hand Sue continued;

"Have you met the Hammonds since Jane went missing?"

292

"No, I wanted to but it never seemed right, they are still very upset at me for hiding the truth but I didn't kill her, I thought she was having a great time and was on her way back to tell me all about it."

"Is there anyone here, in Liverpool or anywhere else that maybe had a crush on Jane and you think would travel across to Whitby for the Goth weekend?"

"No, I know she went alone and she met with a few people there, stayed with a few others."

"Yes we're looking into that."

"I remember how upset she was when this Mike let her down on that Sunday, she was really crying and upset the next day."

"What do you mean let her down?"

"They were meant to meet up at the end of the night, he was working; he was a barman or a doorman or something like that and she was going to meet him after he finished work but he didn't turn up." Phoebe went on to explain how she thought Jane had been absolutely besotted by Mike Davies and how distraught she appeared to be on the Monday morning." They clarified the dates and Sue made a note to check everything later, not that she needed to make notes, it was crucial information and Mike Davies certainly hadn't been forthcoming with this when she had last spoken to him, even though she considered, she hadn't really had all this information to challenge him with. What did he know?

It was late afternoon by the time the three stopped talking; Phoebe had learnt a lot about herself in a way she hadn't expected to, that she could talk openly if someone would listen and she felt that maybe that she could now face speaking to the Hammonds. For the police enquiry it had been a very worthwhile afternoon and Sue Collins now had a decision to make, did she travel back that day or stay over and try to learn some more from other potential witnesses. In the end it was an easy decision, with Neil Maughan away she would be expected back; non negotiable was the phrase Simon Pithers would use if asked.

She tried to phone her boss but found that he was in yet another meeting; when do you stop being a copper and start being a politician she thought, if it wasn't for all the meetings maybe a lot more could be achieved at ground level? She may have thought but she knew the true reality of it, that meetings were a sad but necessary part of all cops lives these days.

FORTY TWO

Bracken Close was a small cul-de-sac on the East side of Whitby consisting of about three dozen small houses and bungalows in mock stone and formed part of what was known locally as The Barratt Estate, reflecting on its original builders name some forty years earlier. Ged Turner lived in a semi-detached bungalow at the end of the cul-de-sac up a slight incline and overlooking most of his neighbours' homes and gardens, a collection of mostly well kept lawned front gardens and neat borders. Geoff Alderson and Des Mason had parked on Eskdale Close, an approach road and gone around there on foot without any formal arrangement in the hope of speaking with him about his business and employees.

There were no signs of movement as they walked up the block paved drive to the white uPVC door but Des, looking over the high wooden gate saw a light on in a room to the side of the property and steam from the central heating boiler vent. Geoff rang the doorbell and stood back from the door, as he saw through the opaque glass a shadowy figure approaching.

"Hello?" A puzzled Ged Turner recognised CID before any introductions had been made; very few people in Whitby wore suits and called at his house.

"Mr Turner?"

"Yes."

The two detectives showed their warrant cards and identified themselves before Geoff Alderson added,

"We'd like to talk to you about your business employees Mr Turner, may we come in?"

"What about them? I run a respectable business and pay my taxes."

"We don't doubt that Mr Turner but if you could spare us just a few minutes of your time we'd appreciate it."

"Do I have a choice?"

Neither of the detectives answered the question as of course he did have a choice but they would prefer him to think otherwise. Ged Turner stood back into the small hallway and beckoned the officers in. In the absence of any other direction Des Mason walked into the sitting room which was dominated by a huge television screen hung on the wall which at one time would have been a chimney breast but now merely provided a mount for the entertainment. A large black leather sofa and two matching chairs arranged around a beige coloured rug almost filled the room which altogether felt quite claustrophobic as the two men stood waiting for the invite to be seated. It never came.

"Well gents what do you want, I have places to go, things to do?"

"We can come back if you wish Mr Turner but we'd sooner talk to you now." Des Mason was not the most patient man and was taking a bit of a dislike to what he saw to be the arrogance of Turner, "We need to talk to you about some of your staff, particularly those that have been working for you since 2011 and also any others that may have worked for you but have since left."

"What's it about then, I can't just give you personal details like that, its data protection you know." Turner was fishing for information in case any of his employees were working cash in hand and not declaring their income or worse, if any had committed an offence he wasn't aware of; he didn't want to be the one that grassed them up.

Des Mason rose to the challenge as he saw it;

"Mr Turner we are investigating a murder and have come here to further our enquiries. We can return with a warrant if you wish us to, in which case we will take as long as it takes to glean any information we can and to seize anything we think might be helpful in that cause, that is unless you wish to be a little more amenable and answer a few simple questions?"

"No need for that, is it that girl in the papers?"

"We don't have too many murders in Whitby Mr Turner so that's a fair assumption, now do you have a complete list?"

"Yeah, give me two minutes. I did give you this when you locked Mike Davies up though, haven't you still got that?"

"The list please, Mr Turner." Des Mason was not prepared to be questioned and had no fear of Turner despite his reputation of being a mean hard man of few morals or principles.

Turner took a laptop from the top of a small table in the adjoining room and typed in his password before searching through some stored documents and finding the file he was looking for. Hitting the print key he heard the printer whirring into motion and a few seconds later he handed the copied document to Mason

"The names in red are no longer employees, those in black are regulars and those in blue fill the gaps, on an as and when basis."

Quickly scanning the two sheets of A4 paper Des Mason noted that Mike Davies' name was in red and he was pleased to see that there were contact details against each name.

"That wasn't too difficult was it?" he taunted Turner before adding, "there are more names on here than I remember from the previous list.

"Yeah, well Mike never came back from Wales did he after you lot shafted him for some'rt he never did and a couple of others left for different reasons so I've had to add some new staff."

295

"Are you still in touch with Mike Davies then?

"No. I offered him his job back cos he's good at it but he wouldn't come back cos of you lot, he thinks you're setting him up."

"So have you spoken to him recently, since this body was found?"

"No why should I? It's nowt to do with me and nowt to do with him as far as I'm aware?"

"Just curious Mr Turner, just curious. Now can you tell me who would have been working where over the Goth weekend in October 2011?

No not without going back through my books."

"And would that take long?"

"Yes it would, well longer than I've got just now anyway. I thought I'd given you all this the last time."

"No you told us who was working at The Res last time, I need to know who was working anywhere in Whitby this time."

"You'll have to come back then."

"Maybe you could drop it in for me or email me the details." Des Mason handed Turner a business card with his details on, "I must emphasise the urgency of the enquiry though Mr Turner if I can ask you to look into it with all haste." Des stopped just short of what he considered to be condescending; he had not met him previously but did not like Turner. Returning to their car, the two officers had slightly differing views of how that had gone;

"I thought you were a bit sharp with him there Des."

"I thought he was a twat, sorry but I just couldn't take to him and he was never going to pass the attitude test for me."

"Yeah but he's not going to be too amicable now is he and he could help us in the future."

"That's help I probably don't need Geoff, not at the cost of being in his debt anyway."

They had pretty much got what they set out to get though and completed the short journey back to the nick in quick time.

FORTY THREE

Simon Pithers had just been updated by Sue Collins following her return to Whitby and after a behind closed doors meeting with her, called the CID team together in their office;

"Good morning everyone, I wanted to talk to you all outside of the incident room for a while, firstly to thank you all for your continued efforts on Op Caedmon and also to explain that Neil won't be coming back to Whitby."

There were intakes of breath all around the room and looks between individuals as well as those straight at Sue Collins who some still saw as the root cause of the problem.

"DS Collins will take the role of Acting Detective Inspector and I will put an Acting DS in place shortly after liaising with her." He glanced around the room, noting the different reactions and trying to gauge dissent or otherwise from any source.

"I am sure you will continue to give Sue your full support and co-operation and I will expect and accept nothing less. The decision has been made following a request from D.I. Maughan who is to be seconded to work at HQ on the Operational Review team for the foreseeable future." satisfied that he had delivered the difficult news he moved on;

"I also wanted to have a bit of a brainstorm session with you guys outside of the formal briefing and give everyone here a chance to speak without any inhibitions about where we are at now. Despite the news that I have just relayed I see this last week as having been possibly our most productive yet and I want to capitalise on that so I want everyone's views and opinions please."

Sue Collins who had only been told the news a few minutes earlier decided that her best option was to remain on the fringes at this point and not be seen as Pithers lapdog or favourite.

"This Mike Davies has to be our number one suspect now sir, surely?" Mark Taylor opened the discussion.

"Go on Mark."

"Well he's the one that we know has been shagging the victim and the reason why she was thinking of staying beyond the end of the Goth weekend."

"I agree but we need to harden up some Intel first Mark; you will recall that he actually spent the Sunday night in our cells on suspicion of causing another death."

"Hardly a commendable trait sir."

"No but it means that he does at least have a solid alibi for that night though we believe that the victim was still alive on the Tuesday following as we have text messages sent from her phone so we need to know where he was after that."

"What about the other bouncers then sir, if they knew he was in the cells they would have an opportunity." a young and recently added aide to the team, Callum Jones suggested. Callum was a recent transferee from Selby; another market town that some in the force thought should be in South Yorkshire such was its location within the county.

"Maybe Callum but there's a lot of a gap between having time to commit a murder and having a motive and means to do so."

Even though the Superintendent had said there were to be no inhibitions Callum immediately felt as though in his rush to impress he had spoken before engaging his brain fully and nervously withdrew into his shell, he had not been at the station too long and even though he had confidence in himself and liked to be considered the joker in the pack, he was not yet accepted by everyone within the team in that same capacity.

"Mark please follow up on Davies' whereabouts over the week after his release, we'll formalise it all in the briefing proper but I want a full breakdown on where he was, who with and why. You know the score."

"No problem boss."

"What about the rest of the staff at the building firms' boss, Davies was meant to be working on that cottage when he was locked up, who finished the job and what checks have we done on that?" Geoff Alderson asked.

"Sounds like you've talked yourself into a task as well Geoff, follow it up." Geoff didn't reply but wrote something on his pad.

"What about Davies' friends?" Sue Collins couldn't stay in the sidelines and spoke out, "If he had friends that knew he was away, in our cells or wherever, then did they bear a grudge or something?"

"Good point Sue. What do we have on file? Look into it please."

"Sir, I take it that we've traced and checked the victims mobile and tablet or laptop? I mean that would obviously tell us who she was in contact with just before her death?" Callum Jones was hoping to salvage his pride as well as promoting a line of enquiry with which he was more than comfortable having worked for one of the network providers before becoming a cop.

"There was no phone found with the body, or any other personal effects other than her clothing and we must therefore work on the principle of the perpetrator removing those items and disposing of them somewhere else. Checks made with the network indicate that the phone was last used on the Tuesday after the Goth weekend which we now know she attended but I'll go over that in more detail in the briefing after this then everyone will hear it."

It was obvious that they were now moving into an area that had to be done on a formal basis and would therefore need to be in the briefing and recorded in the actions book. Thanking everyone present for their input Simon Pithers asked to be left for a moment. "Sue open up the briefing will you, I won't be long."

Searching through the information on the computer, the box, to everyone in North Yorkshire Police he checked to see what they knew about the car Jane Hammond had used for her journey to Whitby, where was that, did it still have the laptop computer in the boot and did that hold the key to identifying the killer?

Taking those thoughts with him to the briefing he took a seat at the back of the room as he listened to Sue Collins formally delivering the updates and allocating the tasks they had just discussed in the CID office before asking;

"Guys where is the Clio? What happened to Jane Hammond's car and why haven't we found it yet?"

"It was registered to The Russell Street address in Liverpool sir, it has a trace marker on PNC and is flagged on ANPR but we've had no sightings of it since that same Tuesday after Goth weekend. It was seen on the A64 and M62 that day and we thought it was on its way back to Liverpool."

DS Andy Goodall was reading from his notes rather than offering his own opinion but this didn't save him from a sharp retort.

"Well if it was it wasn't Jane Hammond driving it so who was? Come on guys this car has been missing for 18 months now why?"

No-one chose to reply as no-one had the answer; it was certainly unusual for a stolen car to be missing for so long, even the burnt out ones were identified at some point and insurance paid out.

"Allocate it as an urgent task and get onto West Yorkshire and Merseyside again, emphasise that this isn't just a stolen motor enquiry it's a high priority murder investigation."

FORTY FOUR

"Thank you for seeing me Mr Hammond," Sue Collins had made the journey to Horsforth and sat with Graham Hammond and the Family Liaison Officer allocated by West Yorkshire Police to keep the Hammonds updated with the enquiry and provide assistance where possible, Penny Hammond was unable to be present, "We want to reassure you that the investigation into Jane's death is our single most important case at the moment and that we are doing everything we can to identify the perpetrator and bring him or her to justice."

"That won't bring her back though will it? Why didn't you take it seriously when we reported her missing?"

"I can't answer that question in a way that you will be comfortable with Mr Hammond as I wasn't involved at that time, though I am sure that everything was done in accordance with best practice." Sue Collins knew the start of this conversation would be difficult as Graham Hammond didn't differentiate between the separate constabularies and, she considered, why should he, wasn't it possible these days to properly communicate between two or even three disparate forces?

"Best practice didn't include listening to us Detective, when we knew that something was wrong."

"I understand Mr Hammond but if I can ask you to help us now, to help us find out who did this to Jane then I promise you that I will do all I can to work with you. We need to find Jane's car, the Clio"

"It was registered to Jane and we used the college address in case there ever was an issue and someone needed to contact Jane and not me-" Graham Hammond held back tears as he spoke the words, "sorry, I meant for parking tickets and the like, not this."

"The car could lead us to the killer Mr Hammond, but we've no sightings of it being used since it travelled back to Liverpool."

"I do have some paperwork for it, in fact I haven't even opened it, it will be insurance renewals and tax disc renewals and the like; obviously I haven't any interest in them and if I'm honest I hadn't even considered the car recently."

"Can I see the paperwork please?"

"Yes, I'll go and get it, would you like a drink or anything whilst I'm up?"

"That would be nice, a tea please, white no sugar." Sue Collins knew that this simple exchange had changed the dynamics of the meeting and that Graham Hammond was now looking forward and not backward. She looked at PC Martin Oakes the Family Liaison Officer after Graham Hammond had left the room and asked, "What's happened with the complaint he made about the enquiry?"

"It's caused all sorts of problems to be honest, everyone knows why it was low priority at the time but no-one dare say that to him and those upstairs seem to be looking for a scapegoat as usual."

"Oh dear, sorry for asking."

"Don't worry, I just do my bit now and try to stay clear of the politics. What he can't accept though is his precious little daughter was actually quite a bit of a slapper, putting it about everywhere by all accounts."

"Well we can't let that detract from our investigation can we?"

"No but-"

Graham Hammond walked back into the room with a tray of drinks and a few envelopes on the side, immediately causing the conversation to halt. Placing the tray on the small coffee table near to Martin Oakes he took his drink and pointed to the unopened correspondence saying;

"Feel free; I've nothing to hide and no desire to open them myself."

Sue Collins reached forward and took the mail from the tray, eyeing each envelope as she did. As had been suggested some were quite obviously from DVLA and one clearly indicated the logo of a well known insurance brand, others had no external markings and she decided to open these first.

It was obvious that Jane had booked to attend other events as two contained tickets to different concerts that had now passed, each indicated however a propensity to music of a genre that Graham Hammond would not approve of, that is if he even recognised it.

After several minutes Sue Collins saw a windowed envelope with a Manchester postmark stamped on it; the location caught her eye as she had no reason thus far to link Jane with Manchester. Opening it her eyes lit up and she let out a stifled triumphant gesture, "Bingo!" before opening the letter to read it out fully.

The two other occupants of the room looked at Sue, each wondering what she could have found in a letter that was so obviously significant.

FORTY FIVE

Mark Taylor had arranged to meet with a colleague in Cardigan before once again speaking with Mike Davies. He had rung the previous day after the request from Simon Pithers and arranged to meet with Mike Davies at his new home, one he now shared with the curvaceous Kate having become besotted with her after Adam's no too formal introduction in The Crown one night.

It hadn't taken too long before they became recognised as an item and Mike had begun to spend more time at Kate's than he did at Adams so was invited to stay. Mike had reluctantly explained his recent past to Kate and she seemed to accept that he was a victim of circumstance and appeared also to believe that they could put it all behind them and create something new together.

The fact that the police had agreed to meet with him at his home suggested that he wasn't going to be arrested again but he was still anxious as he had been told that DC Taylor wanted to take yet another further statement to confirm his whereabouts at the time of Jane's death. Though uncomfortable Mike had asked Kate to stay home with him in order that there were no secrets and, in his mind at least, for moral and emotional support. He still felt scarred about the news of Jane being found in the way she was and that he had been, in fact maybe still was, a suspect?

After initial introductions had been made Mark Taylor opened the conversation with; "Mike, I'm sorry to have to go over all this yet again but I hope you will understand that we have to be one hundred per cent sure that we don't miss anything. We know that you spent some time with Jane whilst she was in Whitby, when did you last see her?"

Sighing at the seemingly repetitive nature of the questioning he had faced over several months now Mike answered, "Sunday, the night you lot locked me up in that Fleur Brennan nonsense"

"Mike, I said I'm sorry and I'm not trying to open old wounds, we did explain why we took the actions we did and we would very likely do the same again in the same circumstances so please can we stay on track with Jane?"

"Yeah, but I thought I'd already done this at least twice before?"

"I know but we now have some additional evidence and want to investigate that further."

"Have you ever been in her car?"

"No, not that I can remember any way."

"Do you know where her car was kept whilst she was at Whitby?"

"At the B & B I suppose, I can't say I knew."

302

"Who else did you meet in terms of Jane's friends?"

"Not many, she didn't really have friends there, just those that she met at The Goth Nights; Gail was one, then a couple, a bit younger than Gail, Geoff and Linda I think it was. There were probably others but I don't recall anyone in particular, she spent most of her time with me when I wasn't working I suppose."

"Where did you go when you first got bail from the Magistrates court?"

"I came here; well to Adams that is, I wasn't allowed to stay at home as you know."

"So how did you get here?"

"My dad brought me in the car, I was gonna get the train but he came and brought me here."

"And did you remain here for long?"

"I'm still here, no intention of going back thank you very much." Mike took hold of Kate's hand and gave it a gentle squeeze as she sat beside him. "Well, having said that I said I'd take Kate up to meet them at some time, it's my mum's birthday soon so we might go then, if that's ok." he had let himself get carried away and had never broached the subject with her. She just smiled at him and squeezed his hand in acknowledgement.

"I'm sorry I meant did you go back for your things, when did you get your belongings, clothes and tools etcetera?"

"My dad brought some clothing with him then I asked some mates to take my stuff around to his house and he brought them later."

"Which mates would that be?"

"I dunno; it would have been Ged or Sandy I would think. It's been a long time now, eighteen months I can't be certain."

"Be as certain as you can Mike, it's very important."

"Well yes it would have been one or both of those two, I'm sure."

"And you never met Jane again after that weekend?"

"No. I tried calling her, texting, yer know. I even went to Liverpool to look for her but got into more shit there and gave up. I then met Kate and am very happy here now." Kate squeezed Mike's hand now, she had heard a bit more than she had expected, realised that Mike's feelings for Jane must have been a bit deeper than he had portrayed but she felt sure that he was being honest now, she could feel a tremble in his arms as she held his hand.

"That'd be when you were arrested for drink driving then?"

"Yeah and I wasn't over the limit then either, you lot have got it in for me."

"You were over the limit Mike but not by enough to charge you, be careful, and no, we haven't got it in for you but you seem to find ways to keep us interested don't you?" Not wanting to get bogged down Mark moved on;

"When did you find out it was Jane's body that had been found Mike?"

"Only last week, I still read some of The Gazette stuff online if I've got time and my dad keeps me up to speed if he rings, he knows I still look out for the rugby scores and stuff like that, you know local gossip I suppose."

"And have you spoken to Ged or Sandy since then?"

"No, why?"

"Just asking Mike, no reason." Mark Taylor didn't want to confirm what should really have been obvious, that both would now move up the suspects list.

"Will Adam be able to confirm that you have been down here since that court date then?"

"You'll have to ask him but I don't see why not, I've got his number if you want to ring him, he knows you're here cos I've had to take some time off to talk to you."

Mark Taylor made a note of Adams phone number on his own mobile and said he would call him later, for now he needed to get this morning's discussion down on paper, after all if they had wanted to concoct a story for an alibi they would have had eighteen months to have done it.

FORTY SIX

"Am I OK going up to Bandit Country Des, to see this Gail Matthews; you know the one who stayed with our victim at the guest house?" Callum Jones had taken details of guests staying at The Harbour View and was keen to make an impression on the investigation so had arranged to attend the home of Gail in a less than salubrious estate just outside Middlesbrough Town centre.

"No problem Callum; take Fi with you if she's free but be careful where you leave the car, they can sniff out cops at over a hundred yards on that estate and; well I needn't tell you the rest." Des Mason was settling into the role of Acting Detective Sergeant in place of Sue Collins but was not a natural born leader and was a little unsure just how much advice to offer. He decided less was more on this occasion.

"OK see you later then." Callum paused a little, then even though new on the team added, "if my luck holds." and threw up a quick salute in jest. The lump of rolled blue tack flew just past his ear as he made a dash for the door with the words of his new supervisor close behind, "I hope they nick your fucking wheels."

Feeling better for the light hearted approach of Des, Callum approached Fi Prentice, who took little persuading to get out of the office and minutes later they made their way up the A171 road across The North Yorkshire Moors, via Guisborough to the post industrial town of Middlesbrough. The approach was not one anyone would normally choose, given an option, with the sight of houses having doors and windows boarded over and security mesh and grills over shop windows effectively hiding any attempt that may have been made to dress them. Overgrown hedgerows and cars parked across grassed areas with missing wheels and broken windows completed the picture. Fi knew the area reasonably well as she had driven the route many times in her short time whilst still in uniform at Whitby, often in a marked car in pursuit of cross border criminals; those that travelled down from Cleveland into the apparently more affluent and rural North Yorkshire to ply their trade. A stereotypical view some had said, but many of the local cops knew that without the restraints of the new politically correct culture that pervaded, most would agree.

In amongst the run down council housing, or housing association accommodation as it was now known were a few houses that had quite obviously become owner occupied and which had upgraded uPVC doors and windows, alarms clearly visible on the gable ends and neatly trimmed lawns and hedges. Callum felt for the occupants, as try as they might to improve themselves and their homes, they would never rid themselves of a post code that spelt increased insurance costs and lower house prices unless they sold up and moved on. It was one such house that Callum had to visit that day though and parking on the street not too far away, he and Fi made sure that nothing was left in the car that would obviously identify it as being a police vehicle before making their way up the short footpath alongside the flagged garden area that now provided off street parking for the occupant.

Gail had seen them approaching and opened the front door before Callum had time to ring the bell, anyone in a suit, even under a Berghaus coat, was either a cop or a disillusioned harbinger of a religious persuasion she had no interest in, when two showed up together the same principle applied. The detectives were allowed straight in with Gail remaining briefly at the door to see if anyone had seen them arrive; the last thing she wanted was for someone to think she was a Grass. In truth she would have preferred to meet somewhere else but had difficulties with child minding arrangements for her young daughter Chelsey.

After brief introductions and the making of tea Gail sat down on a comfy looking sofa in the small but very clean and tidy sitting room. The wall mounted TV was playing but the sound had been muted, as indicated by a small banner in the bottom left of the screen and Chelsey was sat at a small plastic table seemingly engaged in playing some doll type game; all in all this represented a great change to the norm where officers often had to shout to be heard over the noise from televisions or radios and kids were running around screaming.

"I read about Jane" Gail opened the conversation before either of the cops had even asked a question; "I could never understand why she just dropped me; I mean she never replied to texts or messages on Facebook, I actually thought she must be a stuck up cow that didn't want to know me after Whitby."

"So you were close at the time then?" Callum took the lead,

"Well not really close, we'd only met that weekend but we had a great time."

"And when did you last see her?"

"Monday dinner time, she was still at the bed and breakfast but I had to catch the train."

"Can you remember the time?"

"No, but I don't think the timetables changed much, it'd be about two-ish I guess."

"Do you recall if she intended staying or leaving?"

"She intended seeing that bloke again, she was really taken with him."

"That bloke?"

"Mike I think, Mike Davies. He was a looker mind, if you know what I mean?" Gail cast a glance at Fi Prentice who smiled, knowing full well what she meant.

"So you think she was going to stay a bit longer?"

"Yeah, she planned to go and see him that day if I remember right; it was a long time ago."

"I appreciate that Gail but your information will really help the investigation so please try to remember as much as you can."

The three of them remained in discussion for over an hour with Gail doing her best to explain the strangeness of sharing the room with others that she had not met previously, but the cost savings and friendliness of such an approach; the pub crawls the evening events and the different themes within the Goth culture and as best she could, the people they had met and spent time with.

The visit was very worthwhile but had generated more tasks and enquiries, each of which would now have to be followed up. The two officers thanked Gail for her time and closed the door behind them as they left the house for the short walk back to the car which was now subject to a lot of attention from a group of youngsters on mountain bikes.

The officers were not at all fazed by the presence of the group but hoped in turn that they hadn't been seen leaving Gail's. Some hope, these kids wouldn't have missed a trick. Checking that the car hadn't been damaged before they left the cops wondered if Gail would suffer when darkness fell or whether the kids would even be bothered, often the appearance of such a group was worse than the actuality, either way it was not really their concern.

FORTY SEVEN

"I'm on my way over there now." Sue Collins was back in her BMW on the M62 heading westbound and explaining her actions via her Bluetooth connection over the phone to Simon Pithers.

"I'll get someone local to meet you there, but surely they won't still have it now?"

"Not sure, the idiot I spoke to on the phone either couldn't or wouldn't tell me anything at all."

The letter Sue Collins had opened was from a recovery company that had been used to collect the Renault Clio form the airport car park and Sue had immediately made contact with the company to check its current whereabouts. Explaining her actions to Graham Hammond she had left Martin Oakes to tie up loose ends in Horsforth and made the decision to drive to Manchester as she was about half way there anyway from Whitby.

"How long has he had that letter then?"

"It's one of loads that were addressed to Jane at the Liverpool address, he made arrangements to have them all sent on to him but this one he's had about six or seven months now."

"And what did he plan to do with them?"

"I don't think he'd thought about it at all, he's still grieving boss; not sorting out the practicalities and didn't even care about the car, has no use for it and doesn't need the cash."

"Can you do some background checks on the recovery company boss or at least get Des to sort it please, usual stuff?"

"Yes leave it with me, I'll get him to ring you back directly, I'll speak to GMP CID and get a D out to meet you before you go in."

"Thanks Boss, I think we're really starting to get somewhere you know, I have a good feeling about this."

"Well keep those thoughts, chat later." With that Simon Pithers hung up from that call and dialled Des Mason with an update and order to sort out the background checks.

It never seems to be a simple drive on the M62, there appear to be almost permanent road works and average speed checks to limit progress and today was no different; a journey of not much over forty miles had taken well over an hour and a half and Sue Collins struggled to hide her frustration when she met with DC Safi Khan at Sharston Industrial Estate in the Wythenshawe area of Manchester.

Dressed in jeans, sweatshirt and trainers Safi Khan looked the least likely detective Sue Collins had seen for a very long time. Explaining that he had earlier in the day been part of a team involved in a drugs search the lean, athletic looking cop felt obliged to comment on his appearance next to the immaculately dressed ADI Collins.

"You sure you want to go to a breakers yard dressed like that?" he added

"It wasn't exactly planned." She replied with a smile, "and besides I keep my trainers for the gym."

"If you can rough it for a few minutes there's a greasy spoon just round the corner, we can have a chat over a cuppa, see what it is that you're after."

"Sounds fine to me but I had hoped that you'd know what we're looking for."

"Yeah we've been given some bare bones but you can never have too much information can you? We'll go in my car; yours will stand out like a sore thumb round here."

Sue Collins locked her car and got in an unwashed Vauxhall Vectra that she wouldn't have minded leaving in a breakers yard and Safi drove the short distance to the small cafe that obviously served as the estate's no frills eatery. The odd looking couple were the source of many raised eyebrows as they queued for their drinks, Sue Collins adding a bacon sandwich, Snickers bar and bag of crisps to her order as she suddenly realised she hadn't eaten since breakfast and was unlikely to get a decent meal until late. The chocolate and crisps she placed in her bag after paying whilst she took her drink and the cloakroom ticket that acted as a receipt for when the sandwich was delivered to a table near the window, as far away from other customers as she could.

"So what can you tell me about this recovery firm then Safi?"

"Not an awful lot really, but then that's a good thing as I would be able to tell you all sorts if they were on our radar. I did some checks before I set off to meet you and they're on a rota for airport recoveries and do some Green Flag work as well. We've even used them ourselves for motorway stuff when we've had big pile ups and our regulars are busy."

Sue Collins explained that she was looking for the Renault Clio and showed the letter she had taken from Graham Hammond with all the details on to her new colleague. She went on to give details of how long it was thought the vehicle must have been missing and that she hoped it was going to be a breakthrough of sorts if they could locate it.

"And this is the victim's car then?"

"Yes, if they still have it that is?"

"Well finish off your butty then and we'll go and see shall we?"

Sue Collins did just that, swilling it down with her tea as Safi did the same and they returned to the Vectra for the journey a couple of roads away on the same estate.

Safi was very relaxed and Sue considered that if she didn't know he was a cop she wouldn't guess either, at least not from what she'd seen so far; hopefully he would be just as good at gleaning information from a witness as he was at hiding his identity.

Driving through the large metal gates, that were topped with razor wire, and into the heart of the yard Sue Collins saw that the expected Portakabin style temporary offices were situated on her left with plainly obvious CCTV cameras sited on the roof as well as on a large central telegraph style post deeper into the yard. Large floodlights were positioned at regular intervals near to the perimeter fence which was again topped with razor wire and warning notices about the use of guard dogs and security patrols. All a bit of a cliché so far she thought as the car stopped near to the offices, only for the stereotype to be broken when a reasonably well dressed woman, smart trousers, well fitting top and well styled hair, probably in her early fifties stepped outside the office and watched as the cops got out of the car.

"You gotta be the cops then?" the language didn't quite match the well worked image she had engineered but she didn't care about that she had nothing to hide and no-one to play up to.

Sue Collins saw the smile on the woman's face and realised that this was actually a switched on business woman who would have worked out that after a call from nowhere about a car they had had for months then she should expect a visit from the cops.

"Yes, I'm ADI Sue Collins and this is my colleague DC Safi Khan, can we talk to you?"

"You already are doing but it would be much comfier inside, come on in." The two detectives followed the woman into the office and were surprised to see that it was actually quite clean and presentable, there were two desks facing each other, each with a computer monitor on, the towers visible below the desk top. A bank of three separate CCTV monitors each with four images showing appeared to cover the entire yard with clear colour recordings of all that was taking place. A younger, equally well dressed, girl, probably in her very early twenties sat at the other desk and raised her head to acknowledge them before continuing typing on her keyboard.

"I'm Linda, I own this place for my sins and this is Tanya who makes the place work; we'd be stuck without her wouldn't we Tan?"

Tanya raised her head again and replied, "If you say so Mrs Carter, shall I put the kettle on?"

"Yeah, usual for me please love." Linda Carter responded before looking at her guests.

"Not for me thanks," Safi said, "I'll be crossing my legs if I have much more."

"Coffee for me please, white, no sugar." Thank you

Sue Collins took the letter out again and showed it to Linda Carter who read it through before acknowledging, "Yeah, definitely one of ours, my signature even so can't walk away from this one."

"I know it's a long shot Linda but do you still have the car now?"

"Sort of; I mean yes it's still here but it's subject to an insurance claim now for our costs and storage and from what you tell me for being stolen as well."

"I didn't say it had been stolen Linda, but I did say we now have an interest in it. Where is it please?"

"At the back, when we didn't get any reply from the owners we moved it into the long term storage and started the court proceedings, you know the bailiffs and such, what a carry on, hardly worth it sometimes but it's a nearly new motor."

"Yes but the owner is now dead, that's our investigation, the murder of this cars owner. Is it under cover?" Sue asked, more in hope than expectation,

"Sorry love it's not, we only do that when we're specifically asked, takes up too much room and time moving them about you see."

Tanya returned with a small tray and two cups, placing it on the desk in front of the two women.

"Tanya love, will you see what the current state of play is with this one please?" she handed over the letter to her and watched as she typed away.

"No further on really Mrs Carter, the owner can't be contacted and the bailiffs have made several visits. The last insurance company have said that the cover ran out before we recovered it so they aren't interested."

"Thanks love."

"You realise that we will have to seize it now Linda?" Sue Collins looked at her as she spoke

"I expected as much." She replied, "Out of pocket again."

"We'll need to have it fully examined, inside and out, can this be done here?"

"Inside, under cover I expect?"

"Yes please."

"And who's paying for that?"

Sue Collins again saw a hint of a smile and realised that she was asking in jest, the reality was that she was a mother as well as a business woman and as such she was willing to do anything she could to help the police catch the person responsible for taking this girls life.

311

The group chatted for a short while whilst they finished their drinks, before they all walked down the yard to the car in question; Linda Carter arranging for the car to be moved under cover with a call to one of the yards men, Safi making arrangements on his mobile for GMP CSI to visit the following day.

The Renault Clio, covered in dust from its long stand in the yard looked very much out of place in amongst the damaged repairable cars either side of it but was a tangible item of evidence towards finding Jane's killer.

FORTY EIGHT

"Good morning everyone, Monday 22nd April 2013 and we have reached one hundred days in this investigation." Simon Pithers sat at the head of the briefing table and faced those in front of him, fewer in number than when the investigation was launched as other priorities had taken staff from him but still sufficient to drive forward now with the impetus gained in the last few days. Loosening his tie a little he continued;
"We're starting to see some results for all the hard work you're putting in and I'd like to start today by bringing everything up to date."
Standing up and turning to the whiteboards he started by pointing to the name at the top of the board;
"Victim, Jane Hammond, 22 years old, we now know that this young lady led the life of a party animal student with an interest in the Goth scene when not at home with her parents. This had caused quite a few problems with the early investigation as she had a friend providing local police with false information in the misguided belief that she was helping her. To her parents, Jane Hammond was a little angel; typical butter wouldn't melt type of kid. We must concentrate on the reality and rely on the truth to lead us to our perpetrator." He took another short pause as he paced up and down the room, the eyes of all following him as he did so;
"We have now taken statements from those friends she stayed with whilst in Whitby, that is from Gail Matthews, Geoffrey Reynolds and his wife Linda. As is always the case these have created additions to place on our tasking list. Des, I want you to allocate someone to identifying everyone in the photographs we have taken from the witnesses and arrange for statements from them as soon as."
"Yes sir." Des knew that Simon Pithers was being clear about his role as a supervisor now and not just another team member
"I also want contact made with any official photographer from that weekend and names of anyone he or she has photographed with the victim, if any? We do know that the victim was alive on Monday morning and up to about 1300 hours that day and we know her phone was used the following day, was it she who used it or did our killer do so? Where is that phone now?"
Continuing with his account he went on;
"The Renault Clio was found parked at Manchester airport and it has not been possible to determine when it arrived there as the CCTV has been recorded over and ANPR was not alerted at that time so can provide nothing of value. The assumption has to be that our killer drove the car there deliberately and left it, so do we have a Manchester connection or

another reason for that choice and where did he or she go after that? Des, I'd like all the flight lists for that date checking please and as far as possible any vehicle hire from the airport or train bookings."

"No problem sir." Des didn't actually think that these enquiries would be beneficial but at the same time knew they had to be done.

"Sue, I'm going to ask you for an update about the car now please."

"Yes sir," she rose from her seat as he took his;

"The Renault, as Mr Pithers said earlier, was recovered from the airport and taken to a nearby secure yard where I arranged for our friends from GMP to examine it for us. The good news is that after recovery no-one has had access to it, the bad; we don't know for certain just how long it was in the car park before it was noticed nor who may have used it in that time, had it been taken straight from Whitby there, had it been used for any length of time? A suitcase with our victims clothing was found in the rear boot but there was no phone, tablet or laptop so again we have to make an assumption that they have been disposed of by the perp. That, if correct would tend to corroborate the theory of the phone being used by the perp possibly on the journey across to Manchester? If we stick with that theory then what has happened to the laptop I know the victim used?" She took a short breath to let people have some thinking time before continuing;

"Moving from theory to fact we have fibres and prints from the car but we are still running matches on the prints and the fibres will be secured for analysis as necessary, it may be that they are all from the recovery crew we'll know soon. GMP are also obtaining statements from everyone at the breakers yard for us and we'll have them by the end of the day. The car did not contain any purse, credit cards or anything of that nature either and as far as I can ascertain there have been none found nor used since that Monday of The Goth week. That's about it for the car for now."

"Thank you Sue." Simon Pithers took over again; "Callum, I believe you and Fi met with Gail Matthews, who for those of you who don't know is the last person we know to have seen Jane Hammond alive. What can she tell us?" He prompted for Callum Jones to stand up in order to address his colleagues, not always requested or expected, but in the opinion of Simon Pithers the best way to ensure the message is both delivered and heard.

It was a nervous Callum Jones who stood up and walked to the front of the room with his note pad held tightly in his hand, "Gail Matthews last saw our victim at about 1.00 o'clock on Monday 31st October 2011." He stopped, gathering his thoughts, it would have been easy if it were just his office colleagues he was addressing but as Simon Pithers was present he felt somehow under greater pressure; "At that time she believed her to be returning to the Harbour View Guest House to pack her belongings and thought it was her intention to visit Mike Davies." He again let his nerves show and Simon Pithers for all his authority recognised this and wanted to ease the pressure a bit;

"She was looking to get shagged again Callum?"

All in the room fell about laughing, which was just what Simon Pithers had hoped for but he also knew that it was a formal briefing so had to be able to draw the reins back in when needed.

"Yes Boss you might say that."

"Well come on then tell us what else you've got."

"Those are very similar words to those used by Gail Matthews's sir and she suggested that she was smitten by him but for all that I got the impression that she was uncertain where Mike Davies lived."

It was more of a conversational tone, less stressed but the information coming out very clearly.

"I also got a few other names from her and one in particular, Darren, no surname but we did get some photographs from her phone. Apparently this Darren made a play for Jane on the Sunday night but didn't get much past first base if you know what I mean? I included a description in the statement but to be honest it could be any white male between the ages of 18 and 30 and between 5 foot 10 and 6 foot tall, we need to concentrate on the photos so I've uploaded them onto the system. Gail did say that Jane intended driving to see Mike Davies so it might be worthwhile putting out a request for sightings in one of our press releases sir?"

"Thanks Callum, I'll look into that after the briefing. Thanks Fi as well I know you were involved and we managed to get the car back in one piece too. Des, please task out work on identifying this Darren and any others on that list"

He waited just a brief moment to allow Des to make his notes before adding;

"For my best guess folks, I would be betting on someone with legitimate access to Esk Cottage. I emphasise that this is only a gut feeling but I want our list of suspects looking into carefully with a view to placing them in groups of friends of Jane's, acquaintances, those who were employed at the crime scene, those employed by Willie Raynor and those who worked for Ged Turner on the doors or otherwise. I want each one cross checked with alibi evidence and each individuals prints checking again against the scene and against anything from GMP from the Renault. We have made some real inroads over these past few days and I thank you all once more for your efforts, now let's finish the job and find the bastard."

It was maybe not his most prophetic speech but it was certainly effective and everyone in the room was enthused and motivated.

FORTY NINE

'NEW LEAD IN MURDER ENQUIRY'

The headline in the Whitby Gazette, one of the few newspapers still to show any interest in what was now an old story rather than a breaking news article was, as are all such headlines, designed to generate interest and boost sales. In this case Simon Pithers and Sue Collins didn't mind though, they had discussed the press release in depth and the feeling was that divulging this information was a good move and may unearth other witnesses or create anxiety in the killer if he or she were to think it more of a lead than was actually the case. They had made specific reference to the finding of the car and that it was now undergoing top to toe forensic analysis; it would be a confident criminal to ignore such information and they did not believe they were dealing with a hardened villain, the victim wasn't high profile enough to warrant that; no this was, they felt, something that had gone wrong and been covered up, if not perfectly then pretty well.

The article went on to give details of Jane Hammond and portrayed her as a much loved, studious young woman who was making her first trip to Whitby Goth weekend and would be greatly missed by friends and family.

"The usual stuff really" Sue Collins, sat comfortably behind her desk and looking very relaxed, didn't want to appear blasé but she was of the opinion that the media always liked to define a victim as being a 'whiter than white' even when the evidence clearly suggested otherwise.

"Little Miss Innocent eh? To be fair it's just what I agreed with Griff I thought it might just work in our favour this time Sue; if the victim is such a darling then the public may just wrack their brains and remember something important."

"Yeah, have you read the comments at the end though, from an interview with Graham Hammond? He's quite damning of the police."

"The man is still grieving Sue and is looking for a channel to vent his anger at his loss. As always we are an easy target; and let's not forget the comments are really not directed at us but at the Liverpool and Leeds cops."

"Mud sticks though."

"Don't lose any sleep over it, I won't and anyway I've got an interview with our friend Elli Stanford later today, a chance to put our case forward."

"And I trust you will in your own inimitable way." Sue Collins was flirting slightly, massaging an ego and adding a smile.

The two chatted on as they completed their respective reading of the article before Simon Pithers made his excuses and left the room. He had a good hour to kill before the press interview but he had numerous cases elsewhere in the force area to oversee and calls to make as a result.

Elli Stanford had been busy also, making contact with colleagues in the West Yorkshire and Merseyside areas to see if she could use their background work in her own articles; in truth the information was already in the public domain but for the sake of a couple of calls she hoped she would be able to glean additional unused material to bulk out her own work.

Bang on 11.00 o'clock Elli Stanford was shown into Simon Pithers office by Jean, no offers of tea this time as the detective wanted to ensure he could end the process at any time and not have to wait for the slurping the dregs from the bottom of the cup. She placed the digital voice recorder in clear view on the desk between them and in a belt and braces fashion took out a notepad and pen too.

"What did you think of this morning's article Superintendent?"

"It should sell you some copy Elli, attention grabbing headline. Yours or the editors?"

"I'd like to think we agreed on it together."

"And now we need to add some flesh to the bones Elli. Fire away."

"Thank you. You've said that you have recovered the victims car, can you say where from?"

"I can't I'm sorry, but I can confirm, as it said in your piece this morning that it is now undergoing intensive forensic examination and I am hopeful of further interesting developments as a result."

"Can you say if the victim was killed in the vehicle or transported after her death?"

"Until the results of the examination I wouldn't want to second guess, let's wait and work with fact rather than assumptions or guesswork."

"And does the finding of the car open other lines of enquiry that could identify the killer?"

"As you know Elli, we always keep an open mind but obviously this is an important find for us and I am sure that the investigation will benefit as a result."

"It's now nearly four months since the body was found Superintendent. Do you still have a team of officers dedicated to this enquiry or have you scaled back the numbers?"

"Elli, I am surprised you have even asked that question given what I have just told you. This investigation does indeed have a dedicated team of trained detectives and other experts working on it and we are determined to bring the investigation to a successful conclusion with the arrest and prosecution of the offender."

"I ask the question Mr Pithers because the victim's father, Mr Graham Hammond has been critical of your colleagues in other forces for their perceived ineptitude and lack of attention when he says he reported Jane as being missing?"

"I cannot and will not comment on what other forces may or may not have done, I am certain however that North Yorkshire Police have acted in a professional and diligent manner and will continue to do so. We have made considerable inroads towards our goal and we continue to work conscientiously, as a team to that end."

"Very eloquent Superintendent but do you actually have any suspects?"

"We have evidence available to us that we continue to evaluate and which will, and I have no doubt about this, lead us to our perpetrator."

"Do you think it is someone local?"

"We do not rule that out, we have now narrowed down the timescale for the time of death and that has opened up other lines of enquiry which are currently being followed up. I would like to say we will have the offender arrested today but I am a realist and whilst I do not doubt we will make that breakthrough I know that it will not happen immediately. We are though much closer and the offender will be looking over their shoulder and will know we are closing in."

"How would you describe the victim Superintendent?"

"I did not know the victim before her death and I believe that your question is undeserving of any more of an answer than that Elli. I am not going to become embroiled in any catfight between other forces and the media. I will be briefing my team shortly and I feel very positive about where this investigation is going."

"Are the streets of Whitby safe Mr Pithers, what can I tell our readers?"

"You can tell your readers, as I have repeated many times over, that Whitby is one of the safest places in the country to live, work and visit. Such an incident as this one is thankfully very rare and we are thankful of such. We have wonderful countryside and seaside around us and a wonderful caring community. We strive to keep it that way and if any reader has anything they feel will help us to bring this particular investigation to an earlier conclusion then please don't hesitate to contact the incident room on the number we have provided."

Simon Pithers reached across his desk and turned the recorder off before continuing,

"Elli we have made some real progress this last week or so and we are genuinely hopeful of significant progress. You know I can't put a time on making an arrest but I would ask that your article emphasises the positives because that's where I believe we are."

"I'll do my best, but I was hoping for a comment about the good girl gone bad."

"It's not going to happen Elli; the Hammonds have enough to be coping without me adding to their woes."

FIFTY

It had been several months since he had even given thoughts to the deed that had resulted in the demise of Jane Hammond in fact such was his arrogance he had been close to committing it to history, a memory that only he held and to which no one else had come close to even considering. He had been surprised when, in the early days after the body was unearthed, that he hadn't been questioned further; what was it he had said to that cocky young cop;

"Yes I know Mike Davies, but I haven't spoken to him since he left town. I didn't want to be associated with him after what happened at The Resolution. No, I haven't done any work at Esk Cottage, I only do door work now, and I earn enough for my keep that way."

The daft lad had taken it all in and even written it all up in his notebook, how very 'Heartbeat' of him, but this was real life and he had covered his tracks eighteen or more months ago, there was no chance of forensics now and anyway he had wiped all the surfaces of the car clean when he left it. Why then did he feel a sense of anxiety, nervousness about the confidence in Superintendent Pithers' comments to the press?

Sat in The Granby for his usual lunch time pint he was reading The Whitby Gazette whilst sat at the bar;

"Penny for 'em" the barman and current landlord Ian Storr, asked;

"Sorry, Ian I was miles away."

"You looked it. What's up, you look like you've seen a ghost?"

"Nah, don't be daft. I was just reading about this lass they found on East Cliff. It says here that they've found a car now and they're checking forensics or some'rt. I didn't think they could do that after all this time?"

"It's amazing what they can do now. Don't you ever watch them CSI programmes on the tele?"

"No you gotta be joking; it's all bollocks anyway. American shite."

"Ah, it's not bad, they show you how they find all sorts that you wouldn't think about but some of the crims must just be fucking stupid; they don't even wear gloves half the time." Ian waved his hands in the air mocking those he referred to and bringing a smile to his customer's face.

"It's all guns and gangs anyway over there. Our cops'd be scared shitless, they'd be so busy doing health and safety checks first they'd get to the scene and they'd forget why they'd gone in the first place."

It was Ian's turn to smile now, it was part of his job to keep customers happy and he was a natural at making small talk;

"That programme might be American shite but what they do today, well it's not policing really is it, it's scientists that do all the work and then they just tell the plod who to lock up. Another pint?"

"Aye go on then."

Ian set about pulling another pint of bitter and placed on the bar before taking payment and placing it in the till. Turning to give some change he said, "Why the sudden interest anyway?"

"Eh? No interest really, just been reading that's all." the answer was a bit snappy considering the last few minutes had been a light hearted exchange.

"OK no need to bite my head off I was only making conversation."

"Aye sorry, I didn't mean owt."

Within seconds the mood had turned back to one of apprehension and Ian looked on puzzled, he handed over the coins and moved along the bar to another customer putting on his ready smile once again for what he hoped would be a more deserving recipient.

The pint was drunk with a certain degree of haste and without further conversation and as Ian watched him leave he was perplexed at the mood swings as he saw it from a person he always considered was in control and even tempered.

He picked up the discarded newspaper and replaced it at the end of the bar for other customers and set off to collect some glasses back in, not that there were many on a quiet midweek afternoon.

Another regular; that is Joe, a local fisherman who spent very little time at sea these days, choosing instead to spend a lot of time but very little money, making each drink last rather too long to be profitable for Ian's liking; looked up from the racing post, pen in hand pointing at the door and said, "Miserable git, he's obviously not getting any is he?"

Ian muttered some bland reply, not really wanting to get involved. Joe didn't say much and when he did it didn't really amount to a great deal anyway.

FIFTY ONE

"Darren James Suddaby, born 16.12. 1990 at Salford, Daz to his mates, now lives in Huddersfield but has an alibi for just about every minute of his time from about 4.00am on the Monday morning for the next week. Apparently our Victim blew him out before she went back to her digs and he went back to his mates and then on to their own digs. He had made the mistake of taking some selfies though on his phone and when his girlfriend saw Jane there was one hell of an argument and they ended up going home as soon as they were sober. She hasn't let him out of her sight since." Fi Prentice was updating Des Mason and Sue Collins in the incident room and watching as her boss put a line through Suddaby's name on a suspect list that she had drawn up adjacent to the official one, this was another brainstorming session but just between the three colleagues who knew each other very well and could bounce off each other without fear of any comeback.

"Who else can we rule out then?" Sue Collins was hopeful that the list could narrow down considerably.

"Willie Raynor. Cast Iron alibi. Corroborated." Des Mason read from notes in his hand.

"John Sigston, Out of the country at the time, three weeks in Egypt. Flights in and out checked. Andrew Ward, Offshore for just short of three months. Checked with employer, in order." Des stopped for a second before saying; "This is all assuming we are looking at that Monday and two weeks afterwards as we discussed?"

"That's the intelligence and the evidence we are working on Des and we have to narrow it down as best we can to have half a chance."

"Ok then, carrying on; Paul Coles, another on our builders list. He was in Whitby at the time but as far as we can tell did not have direct access to Esk Cottage and we can't find any motive or link to the victim."

"Can't find doesn't mean wasn't there Des, let's keep that one on the board."

"OK. Mike Davies, he's been our number one suspect from the start but you know about him more than any of us and he certainly wasn't here at the time, but he more than anyone seems to have a motive, if not the opportunity."

"Could he have been involved with someone else, you know paid to have her killed or maybe even just to have the death covered up? I know this sounds ridiculous but I'm just throwing it in as an option." Fi wasn't sure that Mike Davies should be scrubbed off the board yet.

"I hear what you're saying Fi, but we can say with certainty that he was in our cells on the Sunday and Monday, at least before court and we have checked his whereabouts since then no end of times. I don't like the man but I don't think that makes him a killer."

"So do we keep him in or scrub him out then?"

"I hate sitting on the fence so I'm going to say scrub him out, though I don't know what the boss will make of it, he even went looking for her in Liverpool, it could have been an elaborate cover up but why draw attention to yourself. No he's out, for me at least."

"He can go back on if we find something else Sue, but I agree with you, I think if we lose him now we can focus on whoever we have left." Des had been hoping Sue would call this decision as he believed that Mike Davies was merely a bloke beset by bad luck, bad luck brought on by his own actions at times but bad luck all the same, he didn't see him as a bad man. The three cops went through the remainder of their lists and ruled out as many as they could, noting their reasons as they did so. It was over two hours later, much longer than they had first anticipated but worthwhile in the view of all.

"Who does that leave us with then?" Sue Collins looking and feeling tired, looked at her colleagues hoping to see a much shorter list.

"Ged Turner, Alexander Sanderson, Robert Downes and Beverley Anderson." Des equally tired looking after the intense nature of their time together went on to say, "I wouldn't trust Ged Turner as far as I could throw him and I'd like to throw him a long way, he's a nasty piece of work with the opportunity and background to be our man. Pre-cons for assault and very anti establishment, he was very defensive when we spoke to him. Sandy Sanderson, not as nasty a git as Turner but still capable of doing harm to someone, one of the doormen that worked with Mike Davies, in fact he was working the night Davies was locked up. Bob Downes another doorman and from what we know of him a bit jealous of Davies, especially of his success with the ladies. Apparently they were usually kept apart when working as Davies didn't trust Downes to back him up if things got out of hand. We don't have a motive apart from jealousy but he can't tell us where he was during the period we are interested in, says he doesn't keep a diary, clever shit. Beverley; well she just can't give us an alibi, can't or won't anyway. Obviously she's the only female we have on our list, big lass, capable of committing the crime in that she is also a doorman, sorry woman, but I can't think why she would want to? I mean why should she?"

"Was she jealous, did she have a crush on Davies?" Fi responded with her thoughts.

"I doubt it she is very much batting for the other team." Des added and struggled to stifle a smile that might have broken the serious debate that was ongoing.

"She could have been jealous of Davies then, did she fancy her chances with our Jane?" Fi replied.

"Good point Fi, what do we know about her; she's not even been on our radar so far has she?"

"Hardly, she's been there but low priority."

"Well she isn't now; I want a cradle to grave history on her please, and soon."

"That'll be difficult Sue, she hasn't been buried yet." Des Mason needed a break and hoped this bit of levity would prompt his boss into seeing that, what he didn't see was the potential for a slap on the back of the head that was duly delivered by a smiling Sue Collins.

"Coffee I think." she said, "That's a good afternoon's work folks, Fi will you do the honours please and we'll regroup in here in ten minutes."

"Sounds good to me." Des added, "I need a piss first however."

"Subtle Des, Subtle, comfort break is the accepted parlance if you want to get on." Sue Collins administered a second slap to the back of the head which was equally as unexpected as the first but just as accurate.

FIFTY TWO

"6.00 o'clock tonight at The White House then." PC Tom Parsons was confirming with his shift mates the starting location for a celebratory drink to mark his twenty first birthday. He was a bit of a light weight in the drinking stakes but had had no hesitation in agreeing to a pub crawl with his shift. Any excuse for a bender some may say but every now and again most cops would succumb to a night on the tiles as a way of relaxation and so didn't really need the excuse. John MacFarlane had arranged with other shifts in the station to contribute to a gift for Tom and the idea was to start at the pub furthest from the town and work their way from there into the centre and, for those still capable, to finish at a night club.

Tom had digs on Hudson Street, a fairly short, but mostly uphill, walk from Spring Hill Police station, high on the West Cliff in the middle of a row of large terraced houses, many of which were given to providing short term Bed and Breakfast for the tourist trade but which he found ideal having negotiated a rolling twelve month contract now he had been confirmed in post. He was unsure about what he considered an early start to the forthcoming evening, especially having just completed another set of nights, but at least his body clock was telling him that he wanted to sleep now, at 7.00am on a cold but dry morning so he should be fit for it.

It was to be a short sleep for Tom as he woke to the sound of his mobile ringtone, with his parents ringing him just before lunch, not taking into account his shift pattern; to wish him a happy birthday and go through the parental routine of checking on the welfare of their offspring regardless of numerous hints to let him go back to sleep. He found that he just couldn't return to his slumber and so decided to go out for a jog to properly wake up, he loved running and found that Whitby provided a great choice of beach, footpath or cross country circuits each of which he used. His circuit today took about an hour after which he showered and then decided he would go for a pub meal, something more substantial than he would normally have as he knew he would be drinking more than he was used to later that night.

Calling in the local newsagents on the corner of Havelock Place he bought himself both The Whitby Gazette and a National red top and walked the few extra yards to the nearest pub, The Granby; not noted for its cuisine but still capable of providing a decent filling meal it was just what Tom needed. Ordering his meal and a coffee rather than anything alcoholic he took a seat at the back of the pub and started on his newspaper, paying scant attention to anything else going on around him.

He had only been sat for ten minutes or so when Ian, the landlord brought his meal across and placed it on the table in front of him and next to the unopened Gazette.

Seeing the headline on the Gazette again and recognising Tom as a policeman, having seen him walking past and even calling in his pub on duty; but not knowing him personally Ian pointed to the paper and spoke in what he saw as a jocular manner;

"Hey you lot put the wind up one of my customers with that."

"Sorry." Tom was hesitant as he hadn't really heard what Ian had said and hadn't yet seen the local paper.

"New lead in murder enquiry." Ian pointed again at the headline, "Anyone'd have thought he was involved."

"Really?" Tom was a little taken aback by the comment and was a little uncertain as just how to react.

"Well from the way he commented but you know what it's like, he thinks he knows everything about everything and he just got a bit snotty when I said you lot can work wonders these days."

"Oh, right. It's not really us but the CSI crews and the science bods; well they really can work wonders."

"Yeah he started chatting about CSI programmes on the tele then he just upped and off."

"Maybe something to hide eh?"

"Hey I hope not, he's one of my regulars." Ian made the comment and then quickly turned away and walked back to his kitchen leaving Tom to enjoy his food.

Tom, for his part, started to read the gazette article instead of the back pages about another betting scandal engulfing football, players he thought already earned too much anyway; as he did he began thinking of what Ian had said and wondered if whoever it was he was talking about knew something that would help in the case. He told himself not to be daft; it was just a punter in a bar who watched too much TV and had too high an opinion of himself, but he couldn't let the thought go. He must be having one of those hunches that the best cops always referred to, a gut feeling that there was something even though it seemed stupid to everyone else; or he could just be stupid and reading too much into something that wasn't there?

Not being certain of himself either way he didn't know what to do now so put the thoughts to the back of his mind and carried on eating his meal; after all this was his birthday and he was looking forward to a knees up with his mates and colleagues later.

Lunch over he took his papers and left the pub, walking around the town centre on what was turning into a nice day, the sun just about warm enough to enjoy without being uncomfortable and not too many tourists clogging up the roads and footpaths. Since moving to Whitby he had never really come to terms with why everyone appeared to think it was acceptable to walk on the roads in town, regardless of the traffic; he certainly couldn't recall anywhere else with the same problem.

Tom returned to his flat shortly before 4.00pm after spending a leisurely afternoon doing not a great deal and feeling good about it; he took a relaxing bath, got dressed and with an energy drink in hand set off out again to The White House.

FIFTY THREE

Ged Turner had been arrested, by appointment; not a practise that was supported by Simon Pithers, but a decision Sue Collins had made to make life easier for her team on the ground and hopefully go some way to placating Turner and thus making the interview process a more comfortable experience for all. Collins had known that she could have just turned up at his door, arrested him and taken him back into custody but she also knew that he would then be angry, that he would ask for his solicitor to attend and that that may take hours; hours that in turn would come off his detention clock which allowed a maximum of only 24 hours before she would have to charge him, bail him or seek an extension which she couldn't be certain would be granted. The downside to this approach, of course was that he would be well prepared with any answers he may wish to give; she reasoned that if he had been involved in the killing of Jane Hammond then he would have had almost two years now to make those preparations. Time would tell.

After the formal introductions had taken place and the recording equipment set in motion, Sue Collins, with Fi Prentice at her side, started what she hoped would be a case changing interview;

"Mr Turner, we believe that you may be able to help with our enquiries into the death of Jane Hammond, I want to give you the opportunity to speak now if you have anything you wish to volunteer before I ask you any further questions."

A bold opening that went against the normal practise of interviewing techniques but one which she favoured every now again as her gut instinct prompted.

"I have nothing to volunteer as I do not know how you believe I can help you."

To be expected she supposed, why would he show his hand if indeed he had anything to show.

"I understand that you knew the victim?"

Turner looked at his lawyer, who gave a deft shake of the head.

"No comment."

"I understand that you are a friend and work colleague of Michael, Mike Davies?"

"No Comment."

"Can you tell me where you were on Monday 31st October 2011 and the following two days?"

"Not off the top of my head I can't, could you?"

Harry Arundel gave Turner a look of disapproval; he didn't want him becoming embroiled in any battle of wills as he was sure he would lose.

"I would like to know Mr Turner as I believe that this is the time frame in which Jane Hammond was murdered."

Having witnessed the look given by his solicitor, Turner reverted to the plan;

"No comment."

"I shall be seeking an alibi that can be both verified and corroborated Mr Turner so I will again ask you to be careful in your answers."

In answer, Turner did not even speak but looked straight through his inquisitor with unblinking eyes.

"Mr Turner I understand that you run a security company that supplies door staff to many of the local hostelries in the town, is that correct?"

"No comment."

"Let me put it this way then, we know that you run such a company and indeed we have spoken quite recently to you about this, do you recall that?"

"No comment."

"You may recall that one of your staff was arrested on Sunday 30th October 2011, can you confirm that you made appropriate records of that arrest and the circumstances surrounding it?"

Turner knew, of course, that she was talking about Mike Davies but didn't know where this line of questioning was taking him, he looked to his side for guidance but other than another shake of the head he got nothing. It hadn't helped that he didn't think to tell his solicitor that the police had already spoken to him about the case and as such had already asked some of these questions, albeit in a different manner.

"Can you please confirm that Alexander Sanderson, Robert Downes and Beverley McFarlane are on your payroll?"

"No comment."

"Did you help Mike Davies in any way after his arrest and subsequent bail Mr Turner?"

"No comment."

"Would I be correct in saying that you helped him gather his belongings together whilst he stayed in Wales?"

"No comment."

"That, of course would have given you a reason to attend Esk Cottage wouldn't it?"

"No comment."

"Did you see anyone whilst you were there Mr Turner; Ged?"

"I don't know what you're talking about, where's Esk Cottage?"

"Did you help Mr Davies collect his things, clothing and work tools?"

There was a pause now as Turner felt unsure about whether to answer or not, he had been told to say nothing but he had already messed up twice and given unrehearsed answers.

"Mr Turner did you visit Esk Cottage on Monday 31st October 2011 or at any time in the following week?"

"No comment."

"Did you go on your own or did one of your friends or work staff go with you?"

Ged Turner was becoming increasingly frustrated, unused to this sort of situation, certainly in recent years anyway he was uncomfortable and thought he should maybe just answer the questions instead of trying to stick to a script.

"Am I correct in thinking that you once worked in the building trade? What were you, a brickie, plasterer, joiner?"

"No comment."

"Capable of laying a patio or flagged yard?"

"No comment."

"Did you at any time socialise with Mike Davies over the Goth weekend in October 2011?"

"No comment."

"You will be aware, of course that we will be speaking to others and asking similar questions Mr Turner, I am sure that there will be those that are happy to confirm that was the case."

"No comment."

Sue Collins continued with questions for the next quarter of an hour or so, with Ged Turner managing to remain on track with his no comment replies but looking increasingly hot under the collar before wrapping up the interview process for now;

""I will be expecting you to provide me details of your movements over the aforementioned period of time and I can assure you that we will be continuing with our own enquiries into exactly that. Just one final question before you go though, Did you kill Jane Hammond?"

"No!" the answer was shouted back with a venom, "And you fucking know I didn't or you wouldn't be asking daft questions about other people."

Sue Collins calmly placed her paperwork back into some semblance of order and looking at her colleague, said

"Wrap it up will you please Fi."

She then left the room closing the door quietly behind her. She knew it had been a bit of a fishing trip but it had still been useful, very useful in fact as far as she was concerned. She had a smile on her face as she walked down the corridor and up the stairs to her office, where she sat in her chair and visibly relaxed. For the first time in this investigation she felt that she was moving in the right direction at the critical time.

FIFTY FOUR

The White House Hotel sat proudly at the edge of Whitby Golf Clubs links course with views down the fairways to the club house and the seascape beyond, Tom Parsons had arrived in good time but still found that he was not the first, in fact three of the late shift were sat at the bar with different soft drinks, waiting for him before going on at 7.00pm and John MacFarlane and Howard Small were already there too but they each held a pint of bitter in their hands and raised them as they saw Tom walk through the doors.

"What are y'having Tommy Boy?" Howard shouted across the almost empty room.

"A party" I hope replied Tom, "But I'll start with a pint if you're in the chair Howie, cheers."

"A pint it is then, anyone else?" Howie, not known for his spending was making a show of offering to buy drinks when no-one wanted or needed one but was then disappointed when he saw another group of colleagues walk in together, the first of whom, Chris Aston, had heard his kind offer.

"That's another four pints here Howie and CID are on their way whilst you're buying. Cheers."

Howie's face sank as he realised his mistake but he couldn't see a way out without losing face. The remainder of those present saw how this had worked out and simultaneously burst out in laughter. The night was off to a good start and the group moved across to a large seating area in a bay window, effectively laying claim to it. It was only a matter of a couple of minutes or so before Des Mason walked in with Mark Taylor, Fi Prentice, Geoff Alderson and the new boy Callum Jones, Sue Collins had sent word that she would join them later when she had written up the day's events on the ongoing log. John MacFarlane was very quick to point out that Howard was buying and invited Des and his team to join them whilst Howie settled the bill.

Drinks flowed and everyone seemed in very good spirits as the evening unfolded; they made their way into town, calling in at The Granby first followed by The Resolution and then into The Little Angel, working their way downhill towards the town centre. Tom was already feeling quite merry as the group commandeered a corner in the main lounge of The Little A as it was known. Sue Collins had made the decision not to attend as she had heard Neil Maughan may turn up and didn't want to create any atmosphere that would taint the evening, but one thing that always cropped up when cops got together was talking shop and recent events meant that the Jane Hammond case was to the fore. Tom listened to what was being said, albeit in whispered tones due to the location, and chipped in with;

"I might have a suspect." It wasn't the most positive or eloquent statement he had made, especially as it delivered with a slight slur but it caught everyone's attention.

"Well I don't know if he's a suspect or a witness really."

John MacFarlane picked up on Tom's hesitancy and didn't want him spoiling the night for himself so tried to divert things with a throwaway line;

"Only twenty one but he's solved his first murder already, get the lad a drink."

Howie saw what his mate was trying to do and added;

"Not bad going for a probie eh?"

"Hey, I heard that; I'm not a probie now, I am officially one of Whitby's finest." He paused mid sentence to gather himself again, "At least that's what the boss told me."

The place erupted with laughter as Tom made himself look foolish by attempting just the opposite. John MacFarlane, who was taking on the role of guardian almost looked relieved but still filed away Tom's earlier comment and would return to it when he thought Tom was more able to explain himself; that certainly wouldn't be tonight. More drinks appeared, seemingly out of nowhere and all were instantly grabbed from the table as the colleagues let their hair down. Next stop would be the local curry house where a table had been booked by John and then, for those still able and not required to be in for work the next day, on to Raw, the only night club currently open in the town and often the location of their late night calls. As he looked across the table John wondered already if his ward would last the pace; he had severe doubts. As it was he needn't have worried, Tom seemed to find a second wind from somewhere; the food had certainly helped and had slowed everyone down in the drinking stakes yet the high spirits remained and as they made their way across Newquay Road to the club they could have easily been mistaken for any group of revellers on any other night of the week, much to the amusement of the CCTV operators who knew the group were going out and were making a tape of any sightings they had which would be used to cause maximum embarrassment at a later date.

FIFTY FIVE

Ged Turner hadn't given them much at all but Sue Collins still felt that the arrest and interview had been worthwhile as well being necessary; Robert Downes and Beverley Anderson had since been brought in and had equally given very little away, if in fact they had anything to give; Sue had her doubts but Beverley had been very edgy and had mentioned something about her male colleagues being jealous of Mike Davies, whom they all saw as being just a bit too smug.

"They all see him as God's gift." she had said, "And he was a better brickie than the others as well so often got paid extra, that really pissed some of them off."

Beverley had confirmed that she had no interest in Mike, nor in any other man for that matter and that unlike her male colleagues she had said that she felt Mike was a gentleman and knew how to talk properly to people and was trustworthy. She had gone on to say that Ged Turner and Sandy Sanderson were the polar opposite of Mike and treated everyone with total disdain and contempt; this she explained made it difficult for her at times as she was often the butt of their jokes because of her sexuality. She had twice asked for confirmation that what she was saying would be treated in confidence as she was fearful of losing her job and work was difficult to come by in Whitby.

All had been bailed to return to Whitby Police Station in the coming weeks and now it was time for Sandy Sanderson to be brought in. Sue Collins made the decision to ask uniformed cops to bring him in and to make it as high profile as they could;

"Take the transit and park directly outside his place, double park if you have to it will cause more curtains to be twitching that way; I want him to be uncomfortable. I hate bullies and I want everyone to know that he was brought in, handcuffed and impotent." The Detective Inspector was addressing two very burly constables known not to suffer fools gladly and each of whom relished an opportunity to put their strength to the test, she almost hoped that Sanderson would struggle.

As it happened the cops found no one in when they first called at Sanderson's home address and therefore made some calls at neighbouring households more to let it be known that they were looking for him than in any expectation of finding him, they didn't believe him to be the sort to pop round to his neighbour for a cuppa. Having tried the home address they visited some of the local pubs with the same result; no Sanderson but everyone knowing that he was being sought.

It was another hour or so later that the cops radioed in with their result; negative. Sue Collins thanked them and instructed that they should try again later before their shift ended.

One outcome of the quest for Sanderson however was that Elli Stanford had been alerted on the grapevine and was on the phone in double quick time asking for the DI. Sue Collins decided to take the call and began the conversation before the reporter had a chance to speak;

"Hello Elli, have your snouts been reporting in?"

"You could say that Inspector, what conclusions can I draw from what I've heard? Are you looking for someone in connection with the Hammond case?"

"I'm always looking for someone Elli, but as far as you are concerned you may say that we have made arrests in connection with the investigation and we are hopeful of making further arrests shortly. Whilst we continue to keep an open mind there have been developments that are being followed up and we remain confident that this team will bring the investigation to a satisfactory conclusion"

"Can I say who you are looking to arrest?"

"That wouldn't be appropriate Elli, although I am sure that your question was somewhat rhetorical in its nature?"

"You may say that but you would have been disappointed in me if I hadn't asked." Sue Collins didn't respond to that and Elli continued;

"Can I say, off the record of course, that the man you are looking for is local and that you've visited his address already today?"

"I don't have too much faith in the phrase off the record Elli as I know others that have had their fingers burnt."

"Can I ask if the man you're looking for is the person you believe to be responsible for the murder?"

"Elli, the whole world loves a Trier so you can take it from me that you must be well loved, but no I cannot confirm or deny that, however I will say that the person we are seeking at the moment is a very important piece in the jigsaw."

"Well I assume he'll still be working the doors this evening then if I go to The Resolution."

"I couldn't possibly comment Elli."

Each party knew that the other was now just playing games and that there was little to be gained by continuing the sparring. Elli Stanford knew that she had the name of the man the police were looking for just as Sue Collins knew that she knew. For her part Sue Collins knew that the reporter would continue her own hunt for the same man and that she would find out in no time if he turned up, if there was something in the paper as well then that would be a bonus in terms of applying pressure to the small group of people she was now interested in. Having ended the call Sue Collins walked the short distance to the incident room and sat looking up at the white boards again, fewer names now headed the boards but a greater number of lines linked them all together; there were genuine signs of real progress.

"I'll get you, you bastard" she thought as looked, "And soon."

She was still sat there when there was a tap on her shoulder;

"Excuse me Ma'am." A young uniformed cop had been sent up from the custody suite to deliver the news that Alexander Sanderson had been arrested and was sat in a cell downstairs."

FIFTY SIX

Tom woke very late and with a very sore head, as he had expected to do, yet still wondering why he had allowed himself to get so drunk that he had to be escorted back to his digs by the appropriately named blue light taxis, that is on duty cops in marked cars helping colleagues in need. Through blood shot eyes he saw that his phone had a number of missed calls and voicemails on but made a quick yet hazy decision to leave it until he had managed at least his first mug of coffee before attempting a conversation with anyone.

In matter of fact it was a couple of hours before Tom felt able to get back to his phone, he had tried coffee but after a quick dash to the bathroom realised he wasn't ready for anything and lay back on his bed, falling into another deep slumber to be woken by the shrill ringtone of the mobile again;

"Hello." it was as much a question as a greeting

"Tom, it's John, I'm at your front door, I've been ringing the bell for ages. Let me in."

"Uh, sorry, wait a minute." he rolled out of bed for the second time that day and made an unsteady trek to the door, opening it to see a very refreshed looking John MacFarlane stood in the doorway. He didn't so much invite him in as just turn away leaving the door ajar. John stifled a laugh, he had been there himself many times before but not for a long time, age, family and responsibilities eventually change most people and he had stopped drinking at the nightclub, choosing to keep an eye on his colleagues and ensure no-one did anything too stupid.

 "Opening the blinds to let in what bit of sunshine there was John continued to poke fun at his mate, "Happy Birthday then Tom, I see you really enjoyed the night, ready for a fry up now?"

"You are joking aren't you?"

"No, come on lets go round to the pub and get something to eat, trust me it will help."

Not taking anything but a yes for the answer John began jostling Tom along and it was less than an hour when the two walked around to The Granby. In all honesty John would have to admit that after his conversation with Tom the previous night he also had an ulterior motive. The place, as usual for an early afternoon, was not very busy and they chose a table away from the cool draught caused by the door and John went to the bar and ordered two all day breakfasts and bought a couple of pints;

"Here you are; hair of the dog. It'll do you good."

"No it won't it will get me pissed again."

"Trust your favourite tutor constable Tom and get it down ya."
Tom took the drink and took a tentative sip from it before taking a second larger drink as his food arrived.

The breakfast looked fantastic, if not a little large with a full platter of fried sausage, bacon, eggs, mushrooms, beans, toast and hash browns but Tom appeared very cautious even so.
"Come on, get it down." John had already made a start and gestured to Tom with his fork; "I wanna talk about this so called suspect or witness you started babbling on about as well while we're here."
Tom seemed to perk up a little at the mention of this, but could not remember just how much he had said last night and hoped he hadn't spoken out of turn or been overheard; he was very much aware that whatever he said about the case should be confidential, for police ears only.
"What did I say last night?"
"Not much, I stepped in before you did, but you were saying some'rt about a suspect?"
"I'm not sure; it was from here actually, I was in yesterday lunchtime as well-"
"Proper little plonker are we?"
"No I came in to line my stomach with something, not that it's done me any good mind. Anyway I was chatting to the landlord for a couple of minutes and he said one of his regulars had been a bit shaken up when he read the Gazette, you know that piece The Super put in about the car and stuff."
"Did he say who?"
"No but I didn't ask him either, I didn't want to step on anyone's toes."
"Don't worry lad, you're not gonna get in bother trying to do your job and nowt's lost any way we can ask today if the landlords in."
Tom looked across towards the bar and saw Ian, the man he recognised as having spoken to the previous day and said,
"That's him, there." and pointed with his knife still in hand.
"Let's get this finished and we can have a chat after then."
They both tucked in to their meals, Tom even began to enjoy it much to his surprise and when they finished and pushed the plates to one side Ian walked over to collect them.
"Everything alright lads?"
"Lovely thanks, a proper breakfast," John replied
"They can't be that bad if you keep coming back, Ian looked at Tom as he spoke, "You were in yesterday weren't you?"

"Yeah, I wondered if I could have a word about that, if you've got a minute."

Looking and feeling a bit puzzled, Ian said, "Yeah, not exactly run off my feet am I?" They looked around the pub; most of those who had been in only minutes earlier had now left leaving just a couple of old lags sat near the jackpot fruit machine counting their losses even though they would never admit to being out of pocket.

"Shall I bring a couple more drinks over then?" Ian wouldn't miss the opportunity to make another sale

"Same again please," it was John that answered, but knowing it was Tom's shout he added, "And one for yourself if you're joining us."

Two minutes later the three sat around the table, each with a fresh drink in front of them, Ian taking a soft drink in lieu of a pint at this time of day.

"How can I help you then?"

"Do you remember what you said to me yesterday about one of your regulars?"

"erm, yes, you mean about the Gazette?"

"Yeah, do you remember you said one guy got quite wound up about it?"

"Well, he's usually a very calm bloke, you know, takes everything in his stride. In fact you fellas will know him if you're both on the beat, he works on the doors most nights."

"It's a growing business now Ian, the licensing people ask for it with just about every new application. Which one anyway, which doorman?"

"Sandy Sanderson they call him, been in the job a long time. Hard man."

"Yeah I know him," It was a non-committal comment from John; he did know him and didn't very much like his attitude but couldn't let it show.

"A bit old fashioned in his ways sometimes but very effective." Ian said this with a mischievous smile on his face as he knew that whilst Sandy was a regular he didn't need a doorman in any paid capacity and could denounce any responsibility if things got out of hand.

"Has he been in today?"

"No, a bit surprised really he usually says when he's not gonna be in, but hey I'm not his keeper."

"So what did he say that made you notice?"

"Like I said to Tom here, it wasn't anything too particular he just seemed to get quite het up when he read that article, it was as though he'd had a bit of a shock like." Looking at the two cops on the other side of the table he continued; "Hey you don't think he had owt to do with it do you, surely?"

Tom and John each knew the value of a hunch and John in particular had that feeling that they needed to speak to this Sandy Sanderson.

"Funnily enough there were a couple of your lads in here earlier looking for him but I didn't think it was owt to do with this, maybe that's why he's not in, you lot might be feeding him today."

John picked up his pint and finished it before prompting Tom to do the same, "C'mon lad we need to go and see a man about his dog."

Tom, not knowing the phrase looked a bit bewildered and decided he couldn't finish his drink anyway. They thanked Ian for his time and the meal again and left the pub to head for the station.

FIFTY SEVEN

"Sue, what's the score, I see you've been busy making arrests and getting up peoples noses, how are you doing?" Simon Pithers was at his desk at HQ and calling Sue Collins for an update having read the incident logs and briefing himself as best he could from the computer.

"You'll have seen that we had a bit of a brainstorm boss and I've got another suspect in now; I wanted to send out a message to the public that were actively seeking our man and making good progress. I'm not actually sure if we do have our man yet but the town is shaking and twitching a bit and if something falls out of a tree as a result then all to the good in my books."

"Mixed metaphors I think there Sue, but I get the picture, who have you got in now and whose doing the interview?"

"Sandy Sanderson and Des and Fi are talking to him now, not that he's saying much."

"Have we searched his gaff?"

"Not yet boss."

"Well get on with it Sue, I'm surprised your talking to him without a search result."

""I'm waiting for a POLSA team to get here boss, I want a proper job doing."

"OK point taken, anything from the car yet?"

"Yes boss, GMP have done us a great job, they've got some fibres from both the driver's seat and passenger seat and they also recovered a load of gear from the boot, must be Jane's clothing, in suitcases but nothing with name and address on so we can't blame the scrappers for not getting in touch sooner."

"No prints or DNA swabs then?"

"No the car had obviously been wiped as there were dried smear marks on the dash and steering wheel but the fibres are worth a bit more work on, a dark blue cotton material or similar on the driver's seat and black I think from the front passenger seat; I've asked for a full analysis and that's why I want POLSA involved in any searches, this might be our chance."

"I can see that you've got it all in hand Sue, I will be across there later but it will be much later, I've got to see the bloody PCC again today and let her know why there has been a rise in cycle crime this last month. Such Fun."

"Can't the local Inspector do that sir; I mean I don't want to be rude but-"

"Don't even go there Sue, he's already fully explained it but there seems to be a reluctance to listen on this occasion."

"I'm happy staying well clear of that one then. See you later."

"I look forward to some good news Sue, see you."

Sue Collins placed her phone back in her pocket and walked across into the main CID office hoping that there would be an update for her on how the interview was going.

"They're still in I'm afraid Ma'am." Callum Jones sat alone in the office and could add no more.

"OK Callum, thanks, please ask them to come and see me as soon as they get back."

"Will do Ma'am."

"And stop this Ma'am nonsense. it's either Sue, boss or Guv, I don't mind but I do not like Ma'am sounds like jam."

"Sorry Ma'am, I mean Guv."

Sue walked back past her own office, down the steps and into the main office on the ground floor where Jean was working, if that was the right word. She was busy replenishing the chocolate display that she ran for the benefit of the troops; anyone could come in and buy a chocolate bar and chilled drink, usually cheaper than at any shop and the profits went into a social club fund to benefit all the staff at the station. It was particularly welcomed by night shift workers who were devoid of any all night shopping and could supplement their packed meals.

Jean didn't wait to be asked she went and put the kettle on to make Sue a coffee and minutes later returned with a cup for her and one for herself.

"Thanks Jean. Ever reliable"

"Well you're too busy to be messing on making drinks and we've hardly had anyone through the doors today."

"Lucky you."

"No the days seem to drag if no-one comes in, I'd rather be busy."

"You're welcome to have some of my shit Jean; I'm just giving my head a rest from the mountain of paperwork upstairs."

"Oh I've plenty of paperwork, I'd swap you but I'd make a right arse of yours though."

Jean always seemed to be able to bring a smile to Sue's face even though, at least on the face of it they had very little in common.

Sue took a call on her mobile and said to Jean, "Sorry, but I've gotta go." taking the coffee with her she left for the CID office again where Des and Fi had just returned.

"Just finished Sue." Des said as an opener, "We've not challenged him yet, just got what little bit of an account he would give us. He started with a no comment interview then forgot where he was I think and started rabbitting on without really saying much. He did say he couldn't remember where he was for the few days after Goth weekend though."

"He did say he worked for the Thursday, Friday and Saturday though." Fi added without invitation.

"Well we know he was working on the Sunday cos he was part of the Brennan enquiry."

"I'm just telling you what he said Guv."

"I know Fi, but if he doesn't remember working Sunday then where was he on Monday and Tuesday or is he playing for time?"

"I'm not sure he's that bright to do that Sue, but I'll wait until we challenge him later before making that judgement."

"Any forensics back yet?"

Sue explained about the fibres and hoped that the house search would produce something blue to match it, but nearly two years on it was a long shot.

"Go and get a brew then guys and I'll get onto Graham, see how long it'll be before we get some results from the house search."

As it was Graham told Sue they would need about four hours and probably more and then time to book anything in that might have been seized. Sue gave the forensic results from the car again and asked for special attention to be given for anything that might be a potential match. She then updated the custody officer with the status of the enquiry and explained that Sanderson would need to be kept for further questioning and would need an Inspectors review. The Police and Criminal Evidence act or PACE required any detainee's detention to be periodically reviewed by someone not directly involved with the investigation, either way Sanderson was not pleased and made his views known.

"What the fuck do you mean you're keeping me in, you can't do that you've got nowt on me." He shouted

"We've heard it all before Mr Sanderson." the custody sergeant replied; "We can keep you, subject to review and we will. I'll call the inspector now and he'll explain all." the sergeant was apparently almost bored with Sanderson's shouting, he had indeed heard every possible retort from prisoners in this situation over the years and they simply just didn't register with him anymore.

"You bastards, you're all in it together. I've done nowt. Get my fucking solicitor now." Sanderson was apoplectic, red in the face, fists banging on the cell door, "I fucking know where you live, you bastard."

The custody sergeant turned his back on Sanderson and walked back to his desk before calling the inspector down for the review.

"He's rather upset boss." the laconic tone in which the message was passed was at odds with the prisoners rage and the smile that accompanied it was clearly there to show that this was just yet another detainee shouting the odds but making no headway against the well practiced systems that were in place.

The duty Inspector, managing to look smart even in a uniform that now consisted of, to all intents and purposes, a black tee shirt and black trousers asked a few questions of the custody officer before delivering his decision to Sanderson in his cell.

"Mr Sanderson, I am authorising your further detention in order to secure and preserve evidence and to do so by questioning. The rights you were given when your detention was first authorised continue, including the right to free legal advice. You will be aware that officers are currently conducting a search of your home and that further questions may arise as a result of that. Have you anything you wish to say?"

"You're all bastards trying to fit me up. Get me my solicitor now; he'll get me outta here"

"I will ask the custody officer to contact your solicitor again and he will advise him of your current position and the reasons behind it. Anything else?"

"Yeah, you haven't fed me and I want a drink."

"I will arrange a drink for you and I will check that you have the opportunity for a meal at the appropriate time."

With that the Inspector closed the door on Sanderson, who in return remained sat on the blue plastic covered mattress, seemingly accepting his fate.

"Get him a maxpac Gerry, whilst I write up the review."

"No problem Guv."

"Just another day at the office, get on to his brief again as well please, though I'm sure it won't be unexpected. Anyone else due whilst I'm down here?"

"No boss, all in hand for at least a couple of hours yet."

The two officers went about their routine tasks with an air of purpose if little enthusiasm.

FIFTY EIGHT

"Hey up you two, can't you keep away?" Jean was working in reception when she saw John MacFarlane and Tom Parsons coming in.

"We just wanna see the DI if she's in Jean, have you seen her?"

"Yeah, she's in alright, upstairs; they've got someone else in on the Hammond job."

"Oh, right. Is she on her own then?"

"How do I know, go and see her. She won't bite, not you anyway she doesn't like bad meat and looking at him," Jean pointed to Tom, "I don't think she likes pickles either."

"Very funny." Tom replied, "I thought I looked ok now anyway."

"Well you know what thought did don't you?"

The cops ignored the last comment and made their way up the stairs to the DI's office, seeing the door open John knocked and poked his head around to see if anyone was in.

"Come in." Sue Collins shouted, then looking up she saw John and Tom, "What's this, overtime lads?"

"No Guv, but have you got a few minutes?"

"I've always got a few minutes if it's worthwhile John, come in, sit down." she gestured to the chairs on the opposite side of her desk before continuing, "What's up?"

"Nowt's up Sue but Tom here may have something useful for you, at least it's a possibility anyway and I didn't want to not tell you if you know what I mean?"

"I think so John, I think so but I wouldn't have put it that way. What is it Tom?"

Tom Parsons went on to describe his visit to The Granby on his birthday and then again that day and related the information that Ian had shared with them, in great detail."

"And you say this bloke was Sandy Sanderson?"

"That's what he said."

"Well surprise surprise; guess who's enjoying our hospitality today?"

"Really, the landlord said the lads had been in looking for him."

"We're searching his gaff now and then we'll be talking to him again when they've finished. Will you write up what you've told me and I'll make sure Des gets hold of it before he resumes the interview."

"No problem Guv."

"Great and Tom, sorry I didn't make it to your birthday bash but I gather it went well and looking at you now I think it must have done."

"You should have seen him a couple of hours ago boss."

"I'll give that a miss if that's ok boys."

346

The trio shared another minute or so of idle chat before the two junior officers went off to the report writing room to complete their task.

"I didn't expect to be doing this on my day off John."

"You didn't? I'm supposed to be picking the kids up from school, I'll have to ring Susan and let her know where I am, I think she half expected me to be bringing you back round for some tea and a bit of mothering."

"I'm happy to have the tea, Susan's a great cook."

"Let's get this done first then eh?"

They spent another hour or so writing up a statement each that could be used by their colleagues later in the day before deciding that they had done their bit for Queen and country and, with Tom now completely sober, headed across town to John's for the promise of tea.

FIFTY NINE

"Would you pull in here please Kate?" Mike was sat in the passenger seat of Kate's Audi A5 Sportback; she had wanted the special black edition cabriolet but couldn't justify spending the extra thousands; as they approached Whitby on the A169 above Sleights and pointed across the road to the car park that provided a view across to the town and the sea beyond. Having become every inch the so called item, Mike had arranged with his parents for them to stay in Whitby for a few days, a holiday if you could call it that, staying with parents.

"Sure. Are you OK?" She indicated and pulled across the road and into the car park, taking up a place that took best advantage of the view.

"Yeah, fine, it's just-" he let out a little sigh before continuing, "Well it's just the last time I came back here, with my dad; we did this. We pulled in just like this and talked, we talked for ages before we went back and I just wanted to do the same with you."

The weather was being kind to them with the sun over the sea and behind the abbey making a picture post card type scene, Whitby at its finest."

"It's beautiful Mike."

"I know; you tend to take it for granted if you live here but when I drive over and see that." he pointed to the seascape that filled the whole of the windscreen, "Then I remember how lucky I've been."

"Hey, if you hadn't moved you wouldn't have met me, how lucky can you get?"

Kate sensed Mike's tension, there was something preying on his mind and it was obvious to her that it was memories of Jane and his recent past that were coming back to him; she was concerned for the first time about their relationship, was it strong enough yet to cope with this trip?

"No, you're right." he reached across and took hold of her hand; he seemed to be ever more reliant on Kate's support these days.

Kate placed her other hand on top of his and patted it gently, saying nothing but just being there for him. They sat in silence for a couple of minutes before Mike settled his nerves and said,

"Come on then Kate, let's do it." It being the first introduction to his parents. Kate had even dressed to impress with a smart suit with skirt in autumnal colours, a matching fitted jacket and a bright orange coloured top that emphasised and complemented her curves, her strappy sandals made Mike wonder how anyone could ever drive in such footwear. She looked stunning, even if, in his eyes she had gone a little over the top, too dressy.

"You told me your folks were a bit old fashioned." she had said when he first commented, "So I wanted them to see me in a good light, not in scruffy jeans and tee shirt." He in turn had just shrugged and true to form worn his comfortable boot cut jeans and Ben Sherman checked shirt. The two were very much a contrast in style but when they smiled as they were doing now they looked every inch the item they now were. The smiles were still evident when Mike knocked on the door of his parent's home but opened it before it was answered and walked straight in with Kate still holding his hand. John and Rose Davies for their part had seen the couple walking up the drive and were already stood up as they entered the newly dusted and polished sitting room, everything in its rightful place and a vase of newly bought fresh cut flowers sat on a place mat on the coffee table, their colour providing a bright focal point that lifted the mood of the room from its otherwise dour beige.

"Hi Mum, Dad, this is Kate." stating the obvious he turned to introduce Kate and saw that her hand was already stretched out in front of her and greeting his Mum with a gentle if slightly formal handshake and air kiss, John Davies leant across and did likewise before Rose did what she always did and went into the kitchen and put the kettle on.

"Please sit down Kate," John said, "you'll wait forever if you're waiting for Mike to offer you a seat." The ice was broken and Kate felt that she had passed her test of making a good first impression. Now for the third degree she thought as she took a place on the recently fluffed up cushions on the small sofa. Mike followed his mother into the kitchen and John Davies sat opposite Kate, ready to make small talk, yet regretting that he hadn't got the offer in first to make the tea and left his wife to do the entertaining.

His unease was short lived however as Mike and Rose returned moments later with tea and biscuits for all together with a smile for Kate. The group settled themselves in for the evening, it had been a long drive and the young couple didn't want to go out on their first night back.

SIXTY

"It's 6.26pm by my watch on Thursday 2nd May 2013 and the same people are present for the interview as were present for the first; they are-" Des had started the recording equipment again and stopped talking to allow everyone else present to identify themselves as the second interview of Sandy Sanderson got under way. He then continued;
"For the benefit of the records I can say that Mr Sanderson via his solicitor has expressed a view that he does not wish to make any further comment and as such will not reply to any questions put to him. In order that everyone is clearly of the same understanding, my colleague and I will continue to ask questions and allow Mr Sanderson to make a decision as to whether he wishes to remain silent or otherwise." he looked across the table and saw Sanderson in turn looking at his solicitor, Dan Aldridge; a young man starting to make his way in a local partnership who sported a shaven head and an oft broken nose gained playing his beloved rugby union. "Mr Aldridge, have you anything you wish to add before we start?"
"Not at this time, other than to say I remain of the mind that you have not yet provided any evidence that implicates my client in any way in your investigation and that as such I feel that this is no more than another fishing trip by yourselves." His voice was soft spoken and at odds with his battered features.
"Mr Sanderson, you have heard what I said, I must remind you that you are still under caution and that you do not have to say anything, but it may harm your defence if you do not mention when questioned something which you later rely on in court. Anything you do say may be given in evidence. Do you understand this?"
"Yes."
Des allowed himself a little smile, Sanderson wasn't a hardened criminal and he was certain that he would answer some questions at least during the interview. Someone who genuinely had no intention to speak would not even have answered for the caution; some would not even make eye contact but would stare elsewhere and just not engage at all.
"Sandy, may I call you Sandy?" Des continued in a soft tone,
"If you want."
"Good, Sandy, can you tell me if you have a regular pub that you frequent?"
"No comment."
"Do you use a particular pub quite often?"
"No comment."

"DS Mason that is just the same question phrased in a different manner, my client gave his answer."

"Sandy, do you drink at The Granby public House on Skinner Street, Whitby?"

"No comment." the answer was the same but Sandy's expression was one of confusion, he could not think why anyone would need to know that.

"How would you describe yourself Sandy, in terms of a number of friends? Are you a loner or do you have a lot of friends?"

"No comment."

"My suggestion would be that you are something of a loner, someone not readily missed by anyone if you were away for a day or two say?"

"No comment."

"Have you taken any holidays this last year or two Sandy, a holiday or any short breaks, a city break maybe?"

Sandy was genuinely puzzled at the line of questioning but continued with his game plan;

"No comment."

"Maybe holidays aren't your thing then, why would you go away on your own, might as well stay at home eh, stay where you're known and where you're comfortable?"

"This time Sandy didn't even respond at all, he wasn't sure even that he'd been asked a question or if the cop was just making a statement.

"Do you have a girlfriend Sandy or a wife or partner?"

"Eh, what ya getting at?"

A swift glance from Dan Aldridge at his client indicated his displeasure at any answer being given.

"A simple question, Sandy, do you have a wife or partner of some sort?"

"No comment." Sandy had seen the look from his solicitor and was now back on track.

"My information is that you are not married and that you do not have a girlfriend either is that correct?"

"No comment."

"Do you have a male partner then?"

"Fuck off, I'm no poof. Do I look like a fucking poof?" Sanderson slammed his fists onto the table causing Fi Prentice to slide her chair backwards a little as Des Mason remained almost motionless but smiling; he knew he would touch a nerve whichever way Sanderson answered.

Aldridge chipped in, "DS Mason I see no reasons whatsoever to question neither my clients' marital status nor his sexuality, and it can have no possible bearing on your enquiry."

"My sexuality, I've just said, I'm no fucking pooftah." This comment was addressed towards his solicitor rather than the two officers

"Please calm down Sandy, it was simply a question amongst others and from your answer I take it that you are in no long term relationship. Is that correct?"

"Yes it is." he answered, adding under his breath, "Do I look like a fucking queer?"

"Please allow me to continue with my questions then Sandy. When did you last have a partner, a girlfriend?"

"DS Mason," Aldridge jumped in, "I have made it very clear that I do not believe this line of questioning is appropriate nor is it necessary, my client has made it more than clear that he is uncomfortable with any insinuation you may be making and for whatever reason, that he is homosexual." He was livid and it came across in his terse manner.

"Very well," Des continued, "let me put it another way, were you jealous of Mike Davies and his obvious success with the ladies?"

"What?"

"Simple question Sandy, were you jealous of Mike Davies; you know how he always seemed to get the girl?"

"No."

"Did you see Mike Davies with his succession of pretty girlfriends then?"

"He couldn't keep them though could he?"

"I don't know Sandy, why do you say that?"

After another withering look from his brief he returned to, "No comment."

"What about Jane Hammond, did you know her?"

"No comment."

"She was one of Mike's girls wasn't she?"

"No comment."

"Did you like her?"

"No comment."

"She was a bit of looker by all accounts."

"No comment."

"Were you jealous that he was getting it on with her and you weren't getting any Sandy?"

"No comment."

"That would give you a motive wouldn't it Sandy?"

"No comment."

"Did you meet up with her whilst Mike was in Wales?"

"No comment."

"Are you sure Sandy, are you certain that you didn't meet Jane Hammond? Did she turn you down?"

"No comment."

"That would be hard to take Sandy wouldn't it; being turned down by the girl who jumped straight into bed with Mike Davies, your mate, your work colleague. Did he rib you about it? Did he take the piss out of you with his successes?"

"No comment." Sanderson was really pumped up now; he felt that it was Des Mason trying to take the piss not Mike Davies.

"Were you at work on Monday 31st October 2011?"

"I don't know, I've told you already."

"Who would know Sandy because it's very important?"

"Ged Turner, he's the boss, he'll know when everyone was working or should do."

"We believe that that may be when Jane Hammond met her death Sandy, so you see why it's important that we know where you were that day and the next few days after that."

"I've told you I don't know."

Dan Aldridge had just about given up hope of keeping him from answering questions by this stage.

"Can I ask you straight out Sandy, did you kill Jane? Did she turn you down and did you lose your temper and kill her?"

"No! No."

Sandy looked genuinely frightened for a big man, he was completely out of his comfort zone here and Des Mason knew that he had something he wanted to say, he just had to find a way of getting it out of him.

"Tell me Sandy, how long have you worked for Ged Turner?" Fi Prentice had waited for Des to pause, she recognised that he had reached a point where he wanted time to think so had stepped in with a different, but linked, line of questioning.

"Years, I dunno really." the plan of a no comment interview seemed to be a thing of the past now, Dan Aldridge had tired of prompting a client who wasn't, or didn't know how to, take advice and just let things roll on; much as Des Mason had expected at the outset.

"Do you enjoy your work?"

"Yeah, s'pose so. Not much else round here is there?"

"So how many hours do you work?"

"Five nights a week, usually, depends if there's owt special on."

"Like Goth weekend?"

"Yeah, that sort of thing."

"Well did you work any extra nights for that weekend?"

"I dunno, cos I normally work weekends anyway, that's when it's busiest."

The interview carried on for another half hour or so under the guidance of Fi Prentice without any obvious further gain before Sanderson was returned to his cell and the detectives gathered their thoughts and updated Sue Collins.

"We're gonna have to bail him boss." Des suggested, "He knows something and I actually think he wants to say something to us but he's just not there yet."

"Is he our man? Is that what you're saying cos I don't want to bail him if you think he is?"

"I don't know and I can't say yet, but I reckon that he does know something. We need something tangible though, he has a possible motive, he has no alibi for the time frame which we're working in and he certainly has the means."

"Do we need to keep him then, do we need any more time now?"

"I think we'd be better to let him go and stew for a bit, maybe watch him a bit more carefully and then bring him in again. Give him a fortnight, it's not as though he's going anywhere is it?"

"OK Des, it's your call but I'll go with it. We certainly haven't enough to charge him."

"I'll sort it with the custody officer then Sue; I'll just check my diary for a date."

SIXTY ONE

"Hello Love, did you sleep well?" Rose Davies, as always seemed to be the case, was in the kitchen pouring herself a second cup of tea of the morning.

"Yeah fine thanks Mum, is there another one in the pot?" I'll make you a fresh one, is Kate coming down or do you want to take her a cup upstairs?"

"Get off wi' ya Mum, I'm not starting that game, I'll be expected to do it every morning if I do that."

"Well she is a guest Mike; take her a cup and some toast, just for me then, she's lovely, you want to keep a tight hold of her."

"OK Mum, you always get your own way." he leant forward and kissed her cheek, then added, "but do mine first eh?"

Rose smiled and did just that, placing a mug on the table next to the teapot and then passing her son some newly made toast; "Are you going out today?"

"I thought we might just pop into town, you know do the touristy bit for Kate, East side shops, Abbey Steps, that sort of thing; see what she says when she comes down."

"That'll be nice and it's fine out today so she should enjoy it."

"She will Mum, she seems very happy."

"And so do you son, its ages since I saw you smile so much."

"Yeah well-" he was cut short as his Dad walked in the room, reached across the table and stole a piece of Mike's toast;

"What are you two whispering about then, as if I didn't know? She not up yet then?"

"No Dad, she isn't." Mike placed a lot of emphasis on the word 'she' as he looked at his Dad, "And she has a name remember."

"Yeah sorry, I didn't mean owt." He took his place at the table and the three of them continued with their breakfast, chatting and catching up with each other's news before Mike took the hint from his mum to take Kate a cup of tea and some toast. She prepared a tray for him with the best china cup, saucer and plate and even put a serviette on for her; Mike gave her a puzzled look at first but closely followed it with a smile knowing that she wouldn't have made any effort had she not approved of her.

"Thanks Mum." was all that he said but it meant so much more and she knew it and took delight in seeing her son smiling again

Returning to the table she looked at her husband, who by this time had taken to his daily routine of reading his Yorkshire Post as he ate his breakfast; "You used to bring me breakfast in bed when we were younger."

"Aye, I used to do lots of things when we were younger." he turned his paper down a touch, smiled at his wife and then carried on reading, Rose, as was her way just got on with her chores, tidying up after everyone else.

It was another hour or so before Kate came down with Mike, thanked her hosts for the breakfast and sat with them for a couple of minutes as Mike found his phone and wallet.

"Right Mum, Dad, we're off into town, don't know when we'll be back but I'll give you a ring later when I know what we're doing."

John Davies lifted his head up from the sports pages and replied, "OK son, see you later, Bye for now Kate, I hope you enjoy the bright lights of Whitby Town."

"I will I'm sure, I've got the perfect guide to show me."

"Come on now you'll have me blushing between you."

The two of them left the house and walked along Oak Road and via Byland and Chubb Hill Roads before entering the gardens of Pannett Park, taking in the time shown clearly on the huge floral clock in one of the garden beds. They sat for a while on one of the many park benches and to all and sundry passers-by they looked to be any loving couple of visitors taking in the joys Whitby has to offer.

"It's beautiful Mike," Kate leant into her man and placed her head on his shoulder, she was enjoying herself and didn't want the moment to pass.

"I know but I wanted to show you the town, come on let's walk a bit further."

Walking onto Bagdale and entering the town centre past the bus station Kate saw for the first time Whitby's famous harbour; there were few boats moored up but enough to give an impression of what once was a thriving fishing port and all overlooked by the majesty of the abbey high above.

"Wow" Kate was genuinely thrilled by the view, the sun shone and the river water shimmered as it lapped the sides of the boats, the blue sky and white clouds gave the whole scene a sense of the perfect photo opportunity and one not to be missed as far as she was concerned, taking out her mobile phone she took a couple of shots of the scene, a couple of Mike and then as has become so popular, a selfie with the abbey in the background, not perfect but good with the sense of fun shining through. She really did see herself as a full blown tourist now and wanted to cross the swing bridge, over the River Esk and onto the East side, tugging Mike's sleeve she led him on along the river's edge to the bridge, stopping half way across to look down the river to its mouth and the North Sea, beyond the two piers on which Lowry type figures were visible walking along.

Mike pointed to The Dolphin pub and explained that it was once his local and that they may call in later in the day if they were still in town.

"I'd love to" Kate smiled at him, "I'd get to see some of your mates then, maybe get to know a bit more about your previous life?" It was said with an air of fun but had Mike a little concerned as he had a colourful history, especially of late.

"Maybe not a good idea then." he joked back and received a playful elbow in the ribs for his troubles. Enough of a dig for him to jostle her further on to the road and onto Sandgate with its individual shops, many stocked with touristy trinkets for the thousands of visitors that walked the same route they were taking now.

Window shopping as they went Kate stopped outside the photographer's studio and pointed at some of the pictures displayed in the window;

"He's good isn't he?"

"Yeah but pricey, aimed at catching the tourists."

"Well what am I if not a tourist?"

It was only then that Mike looked at the photographs on display and saw a face he instantly recognised. He shuddered a little, not, he had thought, outwardly, but sufficient for Kate to notice.

"What is it Mike? What's the matter?"

There was no reply and so she looked directly into his eyes and saw a look she hadn't seen before, a sort of stare, somewhere between fear and haunting.

"Mike what is it? Talk to me."

"That picture there." he pointed to the bottom left corner of the display window, "its Jane and Gail"

"Jane? You mean the girl who-?"

"Yes." he interrupted, "The girl who was killed, who they blamed me for killing. What's her picture doing in the shop window?"

"I meant; I was going to say-" Kate was now having some difficulty getting her words out in any semblance of reason.

"I know what you were going to say, yes my Jane, the one who I lost, who I went looking for. There I've said it, are you satisfied?"

Kate was taken aback now; she had meant exactly that but was looking to say it without hurting his feelings not throwing it in his face.

"I'm sorry, I didn't mean to-"

Once again Mike cut her short, "No I'm sorry Kate, and I didn't mean to say that, I don't want her to come between us, what we have. I just didn't expect to see that picture there."

"Oh Mike, don't worry, you've told me about her, it's not as if I didn't know."

"I wanted this day to be special Kate, for us."

"It is Mike, it is special, come on lets walk on a bit further."

Taking his arm Kate tugged him gently and then set off walking again even though she did not know where she was headed, Mike walked quietly at her side, his thoughts drifting from the present to the past and back again in just moments. Kate hadn't seen this side of him before and was uncertain how best to manage the situation, deciding patience was probably the better option she saw a cafe on The Market Square and headed towards that.

"I could do with a coffee Mike, you?"

"Yeah, if you like." it was not a considered response but merely a reaction to the question and it probably came out exactly that way. They went in to the cafe however and found a table at the back of the tiled, ground floor space, Kate ordered the drinks and they waited, almost silently, for the waitress to deliver them.

"Come on, we might as well go home if we're going to be like this all day."

Mike looked at Kate and saw the smile and look of genuine concern she had for him; "I'm sorry, give me a minute and I'll get myself together. I know I'm being stupid, I mean I only knew her for a weekend after all, I suppose it's because of how we parted and all that followed it; you know the arrests and all that?"

"Mike, we've talked about it before, I know that you thought a lot about her but it was two years ago nearly; we've been together a long time now, surely that means something to you?"

"Of course it does. I love you Kate." He hadn't expected to say that, it was the next step he supposed, but it seemed so natural to say it aloud.

"Really?" Kate was equally surprised as Mike was not a man of outward expressions or public displays of affection.

"Yes really, I suppose that's why I wanted you to meet my folks, not for their approval, though they do approve; but for me to show you off. I want to be with you Kate; I've never felt like this before."

How quickly things had changed she thought, only seconds earlier she feared that his past may drive a wedge between them and now he was expressing his love for her, and publicly at that.

SIXTY TWO

Sue Collins and Des Mason sat at the table in the large conference room at Newby Wiske Hall, summoned by Simon Pithers, together with Alison Reed and Graham Dawson on behalf of the Assistant Chief Constable, Toni Magennis. "There's nothing to worry about." He had said when he spoke to her but Sue Collins was no fool and knew, as did everyone else at the table, that the ACC didn't ask for a meeting without good cause. Sue poured herself a glass of water from one of the bottles provided; "they never seemed to be provided for the meetings that ACPO didn't attend," she thought to herself, "but hey, it's only water."

They were kept waiting for about ten minutes after the expected start time of the meeting and were reaching the point of wondering how else they could usefully be spending their time when Simon Pithers and his boss Toni Magennis walked in. Everyone present stood up as a mark of respect, but it was a gesture that Sue Collins had never really liked, respect had to be earned she considered, not given with a badge.

"Sit Down, sit down please." Toni Magennis had a soft voice but one with a powerful undertone that afforded her some degree of presence; she took a seat at the head of the table and gestured for Simon Pithers to sit next to her. Placing a small file of papers on the table she addressed the meeting;

"I apologise for the short notice given to you all and the lack of any agenda, however I beg your indulgence for a minute or two and I believe the reason will become apparent."

She paused and looked around the table to gauge how her opening comments had been received before continuing,

"Quite obviously I wish to speak about Operation Caedmon, the investigation into the murder of Jane Hammond. I have spent some time with Detective Superintendent Pithers and covered the ground up to and including the recent arrests of Turner, Sanderson, Downes and Anderson so I want to start at that juncture; however before we begin I wish to bring you up to date with the state of play in respect of complaints made by the Hammond family about the original missing person investigation." Pausing again and pouring herself a drink of water she continued, "The IPCC are due to make an announcement tomorrow morning at a press conference that will create another media frenzy, that is why I wished to speak to you all today. The announcement will be that certain officers from both West Yorkshire Police and also Merseyside Police are to be disciplined for failing to conduct the enquiries with due diligence and for not giving adequate attention to detail in their reports thereby resulting in evidence going missing and forces not being able to communicate sufficient detail in correspondence. In short, Neglect of Duty folks. This in itself is not going to cause me to lose too much sleep, however I am led to believe that Mr Hammond is now looking to sue those forces and that everyone is where I do start to worry. I need to know that we have done absolutely everything we could have done to complete any enquiries in our force area and that all our actions have been properly recorded as such. I also need to be absolutely certain that we have left no stone unturned in our subsequent investigation into Jane Hammond's death. It is likely to be a long afternoon everyone so make yourselves comfortable. Simon, will you start us off please?"

"Thank you Ma'am," it was not often that Simon Pithers had to use that expression, he spoke to her frequently on first name terms but never in a formal environment; "As you know I have now conducted a full review of the Missing Person enquiry and from a North Yorkshire perspective I can say that our input was all that was asked for at the time. Having said that, that is all it was, we did only what was asked of us and no more. With the huge benefit of hindsight I can suggest other lines of enquiry that were not asked for nor suggested by us. I am however certain that we can answer any questions asked of us by the media and indeed I have drafted something for the press office which I will discuss with you before it is given over to them."

"Thank you Simon, it concerns me that we appear only to have done the bare minimum?"

"I can only repeat that we did do all that was asked of us and in defence of those involved, at that time we had no reason to believe it was anything more than a routine enquiry."

"I don't like that expression Superintendent and I believe it sends out the wrong message when we refer to routine; every missing person is important to someone and we should always do everything we believe we can."

Simon Pithers was disappointed as; after all, he had been the one who had overseen the recent review of Missing person enquiries and felt he had made good progress in introducing new protocols which, had they been in place at the time may have been of great benefit. He acknowledged however his senior officer's comments and continued with his debrief for a further twenty minutes or so before he paused and Toni Magennis took the opportunity to move the debate forwards;

"And the murder investigation?"

"As you have already said we have now made a further four arrests this week of which all the detainees have been bailed 47/3 back to Scarborough within the next few days. I think maybe Acting DI Collins may be best placed to continue from here Ma'am."

"If you will then please Sue."

Sue Collins accepted the baton and gave a clear and concise précis of the work undertaken by her team over recent days, including the arrests, the search by Graham Dawson's team and the items seized as a result before asking Alison Reed to add her update from the forensic perspective.

Alison in turn gave a professional summation of her team's involvement and included the awaited results from analysis of some clothing seized from Sanderson's address to match against the fibres found in the Renault Clio.

"And if those results are negative what else do we have?" Toni Magennis had listened to two very professional updates but was not one to be swayed by delivery over content.

Sue Collins and Alison Reed exchanged glances across the table before Sue took the initiative; "Very little substantive evidence Ma'am, but still the four main suspects under arrest and bailed."

"Yes we've said all that Sue, what I want to know is what are we going to do with them when they answer bail, because at this point in time if I were to make a decision we would be releasing them all without charge."

Simon Pithers saw the look from his Acting DI, the one that said, "I need some help here please boss." and interjected, "We haven't yet searched Turners home properly have we? As I understand it we seized his computers and are still waiting for the Techs to get back to us on that but when we did search his place we didn't have the car. I suggest that we get another warrant and get onto that ASAP before he twigs that is what we are looking for, hopefully he will be thinking we can't search again, Sue get onto it please after this meeting."

"Des, will you do it now please, we can get a team around first thing in the morning."

Seizing the opportunity to get out of the meeting Des Mason replied, "Straight away Guv." before leaving his seat and walking out of the room, but not before Toni Magennis gave him a wry smile that suggested she knew just what he had done.

"Graham, can your team drop whatever it had planned for the morning and help out with this one please?"

"If you square it with Western Sir, we had a job arranged for them first thing."

There followed a short discussion about the job for Western area after which Toni Magennis made the decision to call out another team for Western as Graham's team was already deeply involved in Operation Caedmon.

"Right sorted then, what time do you want us Sue?"

"On site for six then please Graham."

"Ladies and Gents, this is becoming an operational discussion now, I don't need to be involved in this at this stage but I want an update by the end of tomorrow and I want something positive for the media as well Simon." With that Toni Magennis got up and left the room, leaving the remaining few to consider further arrangements for the next stages of the investigation.

As she opened the door she caught sight of Des Mason walking aimlessly in the corridor outside, feeling a sense of mischief she approached him and said,

"It's alright to go back in now Sergeant, the enemy has just left."

Des immediately coloured up and nodded at the senior officer, who, herself, couldn't resist a smirk and a smile as she continued along the corridor to her own office remembering times when she had been in very similar situations.

SIXTY THREE

'NET CLOSES ON WHITBY KILLER'

A bold headline in The Whitby Gazette, one which Elli Stanford had pressed her editor to run with despite his reservations;
"I'm telling you boss that's what she said, the net is closing."
"It's a broad statement." he had replied, "We can go with it if the article doesn't name names or make promises"
The article that followed was all that the editor had requested, it made a clear suggestion that the police had made significant progress and that since the last report four further arrests had been made;
Acting Detective Inspector Suzanne Collins, currently head of Whitby CID, refused to give the names of those arrested but sources close to the investigation have indicated that all four are local to the Whitby area and all are currently on Police Bail. It is now over six months since the body of Jane Hammond, 22 yrs, was found following a landslip on Whitby's famous East Cliff leading to one of the longest manhunts seen in this area in living memory.
Miss Hammond, originally from the Leeds area and an under graduate of Liverpool university is believed to have links with The Goth scene and it is thought that this may have brought her to the town as far back as 2011. ADI Collins however wished to make it clear that the police have never considered this to be a hate crime and there is no reason to connect her death and the Gothic weekends that are an important part of Whitby's events calendar.
There followed a detailed description of what was known about Jane and her background, mention of the IPCC enquiry and the failed search whilst she was reported as a missing person together with the usual 'watch this space' type of comment to keep the readers interested in the newspaper in general.
Mike saw the headline as he sat back down in his parent's living room; he had spent another hour or so with Kate in the cafe before they had decided to move on, returning home across the swing bridge and walking hand in hand along Pier Road and up to the Captain Cook monument where they rested a short while and sat looking out to sea and across to the abbey;
"I'll take you there tomorrow if you want."
"You can take me any way you want to just now, I'm so happy."
Mike smiled and held her closer to him; she had not stopped smiling since he had expressed his true feelings in the cafe, not something he had planned to do but something which felt so right; but there seemed to be

something about the day that kept bringing Jane back into his thoughts, first the picture, now this article; he wished he could just put the paper down again and let it go but he knew it was folly and so read on; Kate watching from his side as he did so.

"You know, if that's right and there have been four people arrested, I bet you'll know at least one if not all of them. You might even know the killer" Kate knew she wouldn't be able to keep his mind from it and thought therefore that maybe the best option would be to show her support in a positive way by taking an interest.

"You forget love, they arrested me that night for a crime I didn't commit; no-one did, it was an accident, so just because they make arrests it doesn't actually mean much."

"They also make arrests for the right reasons too. Mike it might help you if they do find the killer; it might help you to forget and let us get on with our lives. I don't want to fear coming here if every time we do I have to watch you and wonder where you are in your head."

"It's everywhere I look today though isn't It." he folded the paper up and threw it down into the magazine rack at the side of the sofa.

"Mike, we were both very happy just minutes ago when we came in, now look at us. I can't be looking over my shoulder all the time just in case Jane and the Whitby murder thing crop up. I know its cut deep but we need to be solid on this"

"I know I don't choose to be like this, I didn't choose to put the photo on display or write the headline."

"No but look how you're reacting." She leant across him and gave him a kiss on the lips, holding him tight. He returned both the kiss and the caress, he felt the stress leaving him as he did so; this woman seemed able to do what no other ever had, to ease his pain, calm his thoughts and yet excite him at the same time.

It was to be a short embrace however as they heard the kitchen door open as John and Rose Davies arrived home from their own afternoon trip. Mike and Kate shuffled like two young teenagers caught in the act but each had a smile for the other and by the time John entered the room all was again a picture of peace and tranquillity.

Rose followed moments later and true to form the first thing on her mind was to ask everyone if they had drinks and to begin the seemingly endless process of tidying up and cleaning non-existent dust from surfaces that were quite clean already. Kate smiled as she saw this and knew that it was probably for her benefit, to make that all important good impression. She stood up and said," I'll put the kettle on Rose, you sit down. Mike do you want to show me where everything is?" It was as much an instruction as a question and one which Mike recognised. He too stood up and they made their way back into the kitchen to complete the task in hand.

Returning to the sitting room a short while later, Mike carrying a tray with teapot, milk jug, sugar bowl and four cups and saucers they sat together and chatted; Mike would never normally do this, in fact he had had to think where the cups and saucers were as he had always been happy with a mug of tea or coffee, but he recognised that circumstances dictated otherwise on this occasion.

"Been anywhere interesting then Dad?"

Looking at his son with a wry smile John Davies responded, "As if; Bloody Scarborough again, shopping."

"Oh is it nice there?" Kate asked.

"No, not really." Mike jumped in, "It's just that Mum likes the retail therapy thing and Scarborough is closer than anywhere else so it's dad's first option; that is if he's given the choice."

"Mike, that's not fair, how can I get things if I don't go out and I didn't expect you two back this early, I thought you'd be out 'til tonight."

"It's a long story Mum but we'll be going out later," Mike looked across at Kate, "Won't we?"

Kate nodded in reply and took a drink from her cup.

"Met a friend of yours while we were there though."

"Yeah, who was that?"

"Bev Anderson."

"Another girlfriend Mike?" Kate asked but with an obvious air of frivolity and humour

"No, you wouldn't say that if you knew Bev, anyway you're more her type than I am."

"Oh I see."

"What did she have to say for herself then?" Mike continued.

"You'll never believe it, but she said that she's one of them who's been arrested for that murder enquiry."

"What?" Mike couldn't believe his ears, nor could Kate for that matter but for different reasons, would she never be free from Jane Hammond, she seemed to be there at every turn.

"Yeah, she seemed calm enough about it though, said, why shouldn't she be as she's done nowt wrong?"

"I can't believe anyone would think she would have?"

"Yeah, she said they questioned her for ages, but she sends you her best anyway, asked how you were and seemed really chuffed when I said you were here with Kate."

"I'll give her a call some time Dad; that's crazy though locking her up. You couldn't meet a quieter person; I can't even come to terms with her doing the job she does."

Turning to look at Kate, John added, "That's Whitby for you Kate love, everyone knows everyone else and you can't get away even if you go somewhere else for the day."

"I'm beginning to realise that John."

"Where you off to tonight then?" Rose butted in trying to change tack a little

"Dunno, not thought about it really."

"What about taking Kate to that nice little place on the Marine Parade, you know the one, or The White Horse and Griffin, that has nice food I'm told."

"I'll think about it, see what takes our fancy."

In truth Mike was not thinking about venues to eat so much as Bev Anderson and why the cops had thought she was involved in Jane's murder. If they thought Bev was involved who were the other three? Did he know them, and why if he did would anyone he knew want to harm Jane?

SIXTY FOUR

"Is it right then, they locked you up for that murder as well?"

"Yeah, like I told you."

"What the fuck did they ask you then?" An impatient Ged Turner was talking to Sandy Sanderson in a quiet corner of the vault, a basement area of The Resolution Pub. He had heard on the grapevine that Sanderson had been arrested and wanted to know more.

"That bitch, you know that new woman Inspector, well I reckon she's trying to set me up for it."

"What sort of an answer is that, what did they ask you?"

"Did I kill Jane Hammond? Where was I on that night? All that sort of stuff, what did you expect them to ask me? They think it's me I'm telling ya"

"So what did you tell 'em?"

"I told 'em to fuck off, what do you think?" Sandy Sanderson was genuinely edgy now and he felt as though Ged Turner's questions were in the same vein as those that the police had been asking.

"I dunno; do you know they locked up Bob and Bev an 'all?"

"Yeah, they're just groping around in the dark; they dunno who done it."

"That's not what it says in the papers."

"Course it i'nt, but they've gotta pin it on someone."

"You watch too much tele' they can't just do that."

"It's all bollocks anyway, if you read it they're more bothered about telling the tourists how fucking safe it is to 'live work and visit'" He was mocking what he considered to be the political statement that's always peddled in the media from police staff.

"They must know some'rt cos they wouldn't be allowed to write it."

"Don't be fucking stupid, they write anything to sell papers and if they get it wrong they just say sorry next week."

"Well what did they ask you, the same?"

"Just about yeah, just fishing"

"I reckon they know some'rt though."

It was a strange conversation as one of its participants knew all there was to know about the murder of Jane Hammond and was taking some solace from the fact that the cops appeared to be no nearer in real terms to putting all the pieces together. The other felt he should know more and was a bit pissed off about the affect all this was having on him.

"Come on any way, we've a job to do, should be a quiet night though."

"You reckon?

"Gotta look on the bright side mate and don't forget I'm putting a shift in tonight."

"There's a first time for everything I suppose." Sandy was trying to show some levity but he was in truth still on edge after the conversation.

"Fuck off; do you want Flowergate entrance or Skinner Street?"

"Skinner if I've got the choice but I'm not bothered."

"Go on then, I'll brief the others when they come in and sort out a relief for you later."

"Cheers, here's hoping you're right for a change and it's quiet."

The two men ended their brief meeting, neither convinced in their trust of the other and set off up the few stairs to their respective doors. Ged Turner didn't work the doors very often but wanted to pick the brains of his staff, those he knew or believed to have been arrested and any others who had a comment to make; Sandy had been so blatant about it when he was released that it had taken no time to identify him, not to mention all the fuss the cops had made at the time, Bob had rung him to ask if it would affect his job, as he thought he may lose his SIA accreditation so he would speak to him next but who else?

Also present in The Resolution pub that night were two cops from outside the Whitby area, brought in by Sue Collins to keep some eyes and ears open for any fallout from the arrests; dressed casually in jeans and informal shirts they would drop comments into conversations where they were able and listen to replies, look for corroboration of anything they had heard where possible and just seek to add further intelligence to that already known by the investigation team. For them it may have been better if the pub had actually been a bit busier but what they could say was that Ged Turner was looking increasingly ill at ease as the night progressed, but that might just have been because he was actually having to work for a change. Robert Downes, in contrast, seemed quite comfortable, even amiable as he just got on with his job in time honoured fashion and Bev Anderson was conspicuous by her absence until much later in the evening. Nothing much then but the night was still relatively young and they would repeat the exercise a few more times over the coming days and nights and report back before each of the suspects answered their bail, but for now it was another pint each.

SIXTY FIVE

Despite the many other options available Kate made it clear that if they could get a reservation she would like to eat at the famous Magpie cafe that she had heard so much about and so that's where they went, well, Mike considered, he had some ground to make up, or so he felt.

Placed halfway along Pier Road, The Magpie Cafe was famous for its Fish and Chips but more recently also as a Seafood Restaurant; the distinctive black and white building overlooking the harbour and had views across to The Abbey and St. Mary's Church. It had been built as far back as 1750 as a Merchants house and had once belonged to a member of the Scoresby whaling family, famous in these parts, before undergoing a number of changes and being opened as a cafe in 1939.

They managed to get a table and it was only when they took their seats that Kate began to have second thoughts; not because of the food, which was very much to her liking, but because of the views; they were beautiful and serene in the semi darkness but they once again drew the attention to the East Side, to the site of Jane's temporary grave. Sensing what could become a mistake she was determined not to let it turn out to be so and engaged Mike in constant chatter about themselves, about their time together, playing footsie with him under the table and ordering a second bottle of Muscadet Sur Lie—Clos de Chapelle the first of which had gone down very well, if not a little too quickly. The respective moods of the two converged on the happy side by the time desserts were offered, but declined by each and they sat, holding hands across the table as they finished the wine and awaited the bill.

It was close to 9.00pm when they left The Magpie and walked arm in arm back along Pier Road towards the town;

"Can we have a drink at The Dolphin Mike? I'd love to see your old local."

"It's not so much a local as a meeting place, it'll be a lot different to where we've just been that's for certain."

Already feeling a little tipsy Kate wasn't for taking no for an answer and so they ventured across the swing bridge again and straight into the dolphin, immediately overlooking the river from whence they came.

"Bloody Hell, look what the cats dragged in." A large booming voice came from the bar as one or two of Mikes old mates sat and stared, more at Kate than Mike in all honesty; but there was no doubting who the comments were aimed at.

"Hey up, you tossers." Mike shouted back, initially surprising Kate, but when she saw the smile on his face she realised he was among friends. He had let go her arm but was quick to introduce Kate to his old pals, and proud to do so as she looked stunning that night; despite being dressed casually, she wore clothing that emphasised her figure beautifully, with tight fitting black jeans and a red top with a low cut front, only covered by her long cardigan cum shawl, her red lipstick matched the top almost perfectly and sent out just the message she had hoped for; she was a catch and wanted Mike's mates to know it.

Mike was the recipient of handshakes and man hugs for the next few minutes and continued to be so as new customers arrived in the pub, seeing him for the first time in many a month and welcoming him back to the town, they moved across to a table in the front of the lounge and Kate listened to tales of old as the mates reminisced, no doubt gilding the lily with their tales and embroidering each with a degree of bravado for her benefit. Kate didn't actually remember being asked if she wanted another drink and she certainly never got up to buy one but every time she looked at the table there appeared to be another round placed in front of them. She was quite capable of holding her drink but was beginning to regret the second bottle of wine earlier as her eyes began to glaze over a little.

It was close on 11.00pm when Mike suggested they get a taxi back, but was met with an unexpected response;

"No, let's walk; I don't want to get back home without having a chance to get my senses back in order."

"Don't be daft, you're fine." Mike challenged,

"I am but I'll feel better for the walk, and anyway I want to be with you."

Feeling he was onto a loser Mike soon caved in and agreed to walk home, so standing up and holding Kate's shawl for her as she weaved her arms back in to the sleeves, and offering his jacket as well; he said his good-byes and led her from the pub, leaving his mates, no doubt, to chat about his new girl and share their views and opinions whether asked for or not.

The weather had held, with no rain to spoil the walk but a cold breeze, just enough to make it a less than pleasant walk as the couple set off up Golden Lion Bank and onto Flowergate, a steep incline not to Kate's liking in her high heeled shoes. Mike, more used to the hills of his home town took pity on her and slowed down to her pace and helped her along.

He hadn't given it any thought really and was surprised therefore when he heard his name being shouted from higher up the street. He recognised the voice but didn't really want to talk, to Ged Turner. He feigned deafness by just ignoring the shout, but this merely invited a second shout;

"Oy, you gone deaf then Davies?" Turner shouted from the lower door of The Resolution,

Mike couldn't ignore the shout a second time and was sure that Kate would have responded if he didn't;

"Bloody hell, times must be bad if you're having to put a shift in."

"Now now Michael, you know I'm always willing to help my lads."

Turner reeked of insincerity and continued with; "And who is this lovely lady?"

Mike introduced Kate and she smiled at Turner whilst keeping hold of Mikes arm for fear of losing balance on the sloping footpath.

"You coming in for one?"

"No thanks, we're on our way home?"

"Oh, not good enough for you now eh? Did he tell you love that he used to work here? Was one of us?"

"Fuck off Ged, there's no need."

Mikes retort was ignored as Turner, who was still puzzled about the arrests of him and his other staff, continued;

"We were good enough when you brought that Goth tart in. Have you gone up in the world now then?"

Mike was becoming ever more angry and turned to walk away but knocked in to Kate as he did so restricting his movement away from his accuser;

"Keeping this one to yourself then?"

"I've told you Ged, just fuck off will you."

Kate sensed Mikes arm tighten as he pulled away from her, tipping her slightly off balance for the second time in a matter of moments; he turned back to her and grabbed her arm again to prevent her fall before turning his gaze back to Turner'

"I'm glad I'm well out of it."

He had no sooner spoken than they were joined by Sandy Sanderson who had heard shouting and walked around from his door to see if help was needed.

"Fucking Hell, if it ain't the prodigal son returning."

"Thank fuck you've come Sandy, get this idiot out of my hair will you?"

Sandy felt awkward, Mike was a mate, for sure, but Ged was his boss;

"What's up won't he let you in?" He had hoped a bit of levity might ease the situation; it often did in his experience.

"Just take him away Sandy, he's out of his depth on the doors, put him back behind his desk will you?"

"Listen at the big man eh?" Ged Turner was not a patient man and had a very high opinion of his abilities to hold his own against any other man, but was letting his mouth get ahead of his thought processes now; "Has this little beauty got a nice tattoo as well Mikey boy?"

It was too much for Mike in his drink affected state and he threw a punch at Turner but was stopped by Sandy Sanderson, who was in professional mode and could see it coming; he moved between the two combatants and tried the passive talking approach to both as he held Mike at bay.

"How the fuck? What-" Mike couldn't remember that he had unwittingly shared a photo after his first night with Jane, in his daft moments of bravado around that table, Craig, he recalled, had snatched the phone but he didn't remember Turner being there?

"Nice little church girl turned bad eh? Did you break her in then Mikey?" Turner was in full on taunting mode now, obviously feeling safe with his colleague holding Mike back.

"You bastard." Mike began struggling with Sandy and he in turn called out for assistance which was not long in arriving in the form of Robert Downes together with the CCTV operators turning the cameras to that door. There were three doormen now and Mike knew it would be foolish to remain involved; he hadn't wanted to speak to Turner in the first place. He looked at Kate who was now crying and shouting for him to leave.

"Sorry Babe, I keep fucking up. Sorry."

"Come on, let's just go." It was as much an order as a request and Kate started to walk away, Mike set off after her.

Turner couldn't resist a final taunt, "Go on run to your new slut, has she got a nice little ruby too?"

Mike turned back and set off towards Ged Turner who raised his arms and beckoned him back in a taunting fashion as two Police vans arrived on the street, blue lights flashing. Mike stopped in his tracks, he couldn't go down that route again and so far he hadn't actually hit anyone, if he walked away now he might just get away with it and more importantly, Kate might just forgive him.

SIXTY SIX

It was a long walk home for Mike and Kate; he had thought about calling for a taxi but decided against it, thinking he needed all the time he could get to claim back any semblance of respect he might still have from her after his latest brush with Jane Hammond induced troubles.

Sorry wasn't going to cut it this time and he needed some inspiration from somewhere, but where? To his huge surprise his answer came from Kate, they had reached the top of St Hilda's Terrace and she sat down on the bench seat outside the park; "Just how much of your life do you share with your mates?"

Sitting alongside her Mike looked at her with a confused expression, "Sorry, what do you mean?"

"Well I hope you don't talk about me the way you must have talked about her."

"I still don't know what you mean?"

"Don't be so fucking stupid Mike, photo's tattoos, gem's what's that all about? What else do you discuss?"

"Gem's" he repeated, "That's it, how did he know about that?"

"Excuse me?" It was Kate's turn to be puzzled now

"When Jane sent me a picture one night before work, one of the lads nicked my phone and showed it around, but there was never a picture with her gem showing."

"What fucking gem?"

Mike did his best to explain about the ruby without feeling either too embarrassed or otherwise uncomfortable, but found it difficult, he was angry upset and very self-conscious; he was also getting cold now, Kate had his jacket around her shoulders, over her shawl and the night was getting seemingly colder by the minute.

"So how did this Turner man know about it then?"

"That's exactly what I'm saying Kate; how did he know?"

The question hung between them and gave them a brief pause from their own issues, they seemingly sobered up in seconds and common sense kicked in as they set off walking home again. Mike put his jacket back on but placed his arm around Kate's shoulders and held her tight; they talked as they walked and by the time they arrived back at Oak Road much of the anger had disappeared, Kate had listened to what Mike had said and realised that the argument he had just had had been very much provoked by Ged Turner and that whilst he should have been big enough to walk away he had only reacted to provocation and hadn't Turner referred to her as a slut? She had seen worse before and may well do again the future she thought, for now she was still feeling a longing to hold her man in her arms.

Rose and John Davies had retired to bed and so the two sat together on the sofa and continued talking, mainly about what to do now, where to go from here?

"I should call the cops straight away."

"CID won't be working nights Mike, well not if there anything like the area around us anyway."

"It doesn't need to be CID does it, and any way if I tell 'em what it's about there'll be someone to talk to."

Unknown to them two detectives were en-route to speak with them at that very moment; having seen the fracas outside The Resolution the two officers had put together what they had seen and heard with a few observations from other witnesses and also the CCTV evidence; having taken advice on the telephone from Sue Collins they were driving on Byland Road when Mike made his phone call.

In less than five minutes the two casually dressed cops were identifying themselves at the door in Oak Road and within another five the two lovers were joining them on the return route to Whitby Police Station. It was something of a change for Mike to be allowed to walk upstairs from the rear door instead of being taken to the cells or custody area but he was taken to a small office at the front of the building by one of the officers with Kate being shown into an adjoining room by his colleague. Closing the blinds for reasons of privacy the officer identified himself again as DC Nick Horsfall and offered Mike a well received cup of coffee and explained that the ADI was on her way to see him personally.

"What about Kate?"

"She's just next door; she's fine, we're just taking a statement from her whilst things are clear in her mind."

Accepting his fate Mike relaxed, other than fearing a relapse in Kate's confidence in him he actually felt that he was able to contribute something positive and he drank his coffee in a state of calm relaxation as he waited for Sue Collins to arrive.

It was in fact the best part of an hour before she did arrive, she had been briefed by DC Horsfall and based on what he had said she had taken the decision to bring forward the arrest of Turner who was presently en-route, in the back of a van, to Scarborough Police Station some twenty miles away, his home was being sealed off by uniformed officers ready for the search already arranged for the following day and other officers were being despatched to obtain further statements from all present at The Resolution that night. She was ready for a long night and day to follow, she knew now that she had her man and that it was now only a matter of time before he was presented with evidence that only someone on the team or with access to the victims phone could possibly have known.

EPILOGUE

It was Elli Stanford who broke the news two days later on the front page of the Whitby Gazette that a man had been charged with the murder of Jane Hammond and would appear Scarborough Magistrates court the day after that.

The search had provided a number of items of blue clothing including a rugby shirt that would in time be shown to match the fibre that had already been analysed by the forensic team. Turner could not or would not say how he knew about the ruby and ultimately there was no way he could have done.

Sue Collins had worked through the night to obtain a flawless statement from Mike Davies and who with Des Mason the following day had interviewed Turner for over six hours despite him saying very little, she challenged everything about which Turner had been vague previously and showed his thinly veiled alibi to be what it was, a mixture of fiction and bluster.

Graham Hammond still struggled to come to terms with the fact that his beloved daughter could have led what in his view was such a vile life and his mental health struggled as he blamed himself for not being there when it mattered. His wife Penny retreated ever more into herself and became almost hermit like in her existence.

The Goths, who only ever seem to bring glamour and costume to the town held a minutes silence on the Sunday of the next Whitby Goth Weekend and then got on with their diverse lifestyle in the manner only they seem able to do.

A successful prosecution several months later and a commendation from the presiding judge put the seal on Suzanne Collins promotion to substantive Detective Inspector and a transfer to Headquarters Special Operations team allowing her predecessor, Neil Maughan a return to his beloved coastline.

About the author

Steve Pearse is a former Police Officer who has worked extensively in the coastal areas of North Yorkshire and in particular the historic town of Whitby with its iconic abbey and links with the Gothic community.

Using his extensive knowledge of the area and its people, traditions and events he has created an exciting and contemporary combination of the oft missed 'Heartbeat' style policing and modern day crime detecting methods to bring together the first compelling story of murder and intrigue involving Detective Sergeant Suzanne Collins.

After leaving the police service early, Steve now spends much of his time in his beloved rural Yorkshire and is developing a new career that makes use of his skills and expertise. His first novel, Finding Jane, brings together the diverse culture that is 'Goth' and contrasts it with the day to day life of everyday people across Northern England. When the savage weather of 2011 caused a landslip below the historic Whitby Abbey and destroyed a whole street of holiday cottages he used the scene to develop a sometimes complex and always interesting, detective story commencing with the unearthing of a body below one of the cottages and thereby introduces the myriad characters that are involved in a present day murder enquiry.

Steve still resides in North Yorkshire and is optimistic of creating a series of novels based on the characters introduced in 'Finding Jane' and in the different locations he has lived and worked. Using contacts he retains to keep abreast of new techniques and changes to policing tactics and procedures and bringing a more modern look to the writing about the policing of rural North of England he is confident of cementing a reputation as a crime writer of the future.

Lightning Source UK Ltd.
Milton Keynes UK
UKOW04f1857220515

252154UK00001B/69/P